THE RETURN MAN

The dead thing had been hugging the blind spot along the base of the wall, hidden from Marco's lookout above – yes, he should have checked there, he always did, but this goddamn time he hadn't, because he was distracted, and sick, and exhausted, and heartbroken – so that when Marco leaned out, the thing hissed and leaped upward. Its rough hand seized Marco's wrist, jerked him a foot over the edge, and he yelled in surprise. He felt his jeans rip, his knee grind against concrete chunks. His free hand slapped at the wall, seeking the Glock. Couldn't find it. Couldn't turn to look.

He shouted, cursed, his face burning with frustration.

The corpse tightened its grip on his wrist. And pulled.

THE RETURN MAN

CIVILISATION'S GONE.
HE'S STAYED TO
BURY THE DEAD.

V. M. ZITO

www.orbitbooks.net

Orbit
Hachette Book Group
237 Park Avenue
New York, NY 10017
Visit our Web site at www.orbitbooks.net

Orbit is an imprint of Hachette Book Group. The Orbit name and logo are trademarks of Little, Brown Book Group Limited.

Printed in the United States of America

First edition: April 2012

10 9 8 7 6 5 4 3 2

For Krissy and Maggie.
You brought me back to life.

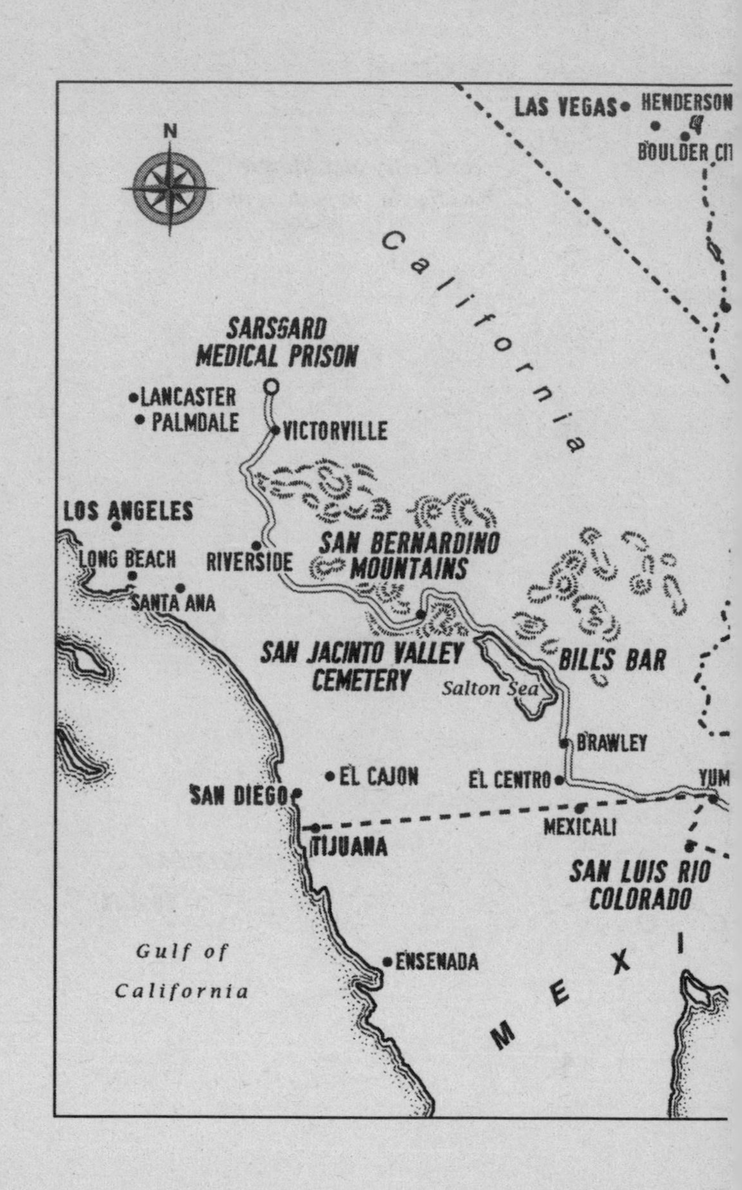

N
LAS VEGAS
HENDERSON
California
SARSGARD MEDICAL PRISON
LANCASTER
PALMDALE
VICTORVILLE
LOS ANGELES
LONG BEACH
RIVERSIDE
SANTA ANA
SAN BERNARDINO MOUNTAINS
SAN JACINTO VALLEY CEMETERY
Salton Sea
BILL'S BAR
BRAWLEY
EL CAJON
EL CENTRO
SAN DIEGO
MEXICALI
TIJUANA
SAN LUIS RIO COLORADO
Gulf of California
ENSENADA
M E X I

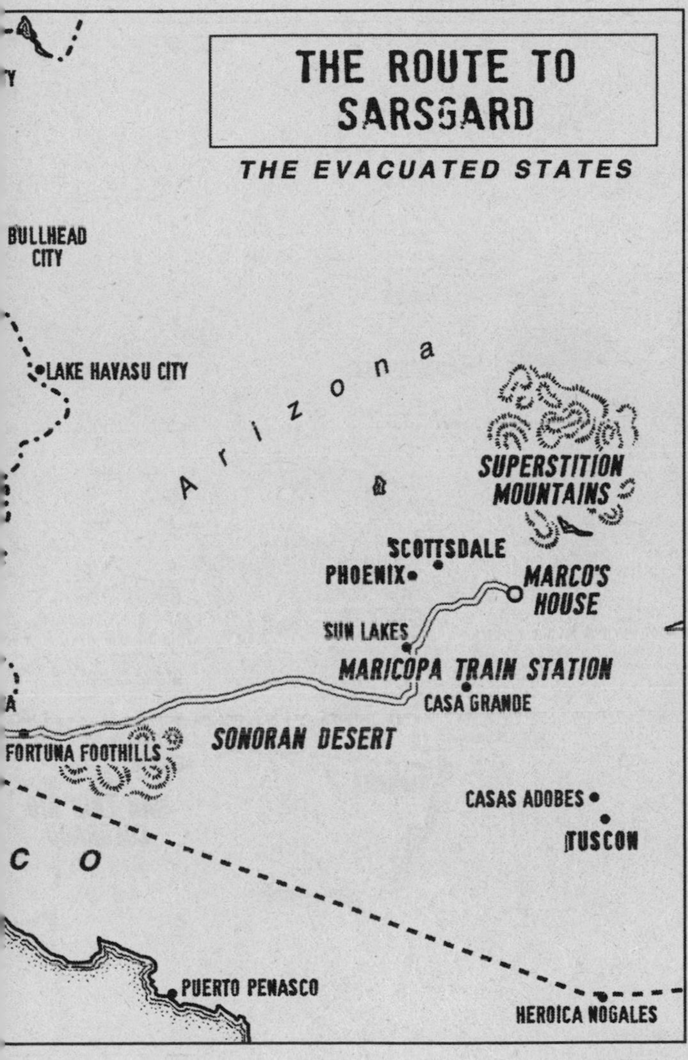

THE ROUTE TO SARSGARD

THE EVACUATED STATES

BULLHEAD CITY

LAKE HAVASU CITY

Arizona

SUPERSTITION MOUNTAINS

SCOTTSDALE

PHOENIX

MARCO'S HOUSE

SUN LAKES

MARICOPA TRAIN STATION

CASA GRANDE

SONORAN DESERT

FORTUNA FOOTHILLS

CASAS ADOBES

TUSCON

PUERTO PENASCO

HEROICA NOGALES

THE ROARK CONTRACT

1.1

The corpse crouched in the shallow mud-water along the lake, shirtless and saggy chested, grabbing at minnows that darted between the green rocks. Marco studied it through his binoculars. Sometimes the dead surprised him – so quick with their hands, but so uncoordinated. Like toddlers. He watched the corpse strike and come up empty, then again, gawking at its palm while its reptilian brain groped to understand the failure. Failing at that, too, it splashed after the next silver flash of fish.

Marco squinted.

There. On the dead man's left hand.

A wedding ring.

He zoomed in on the ring. Jewellery was a godsend for making the ID. Skin fell off, hair fell out; fat men rotted themselves thin, and thin men ballooned with gas and bacteria. But if you were lucky enough to find the corpse with original jewellery, some identifiable piece that hadn't been torn or bitten off, then you had your proof. Bring the jewellery back, and nobody disputed you'd done the job.

Down below, the corpse shoved its hand again beneath the water, stirring up the mud.

'Come on,' Marco muttered. 'Come on, show me.'

The corpse splayed its fingers out for inspection, as if it had heard.

Which, of course, it couldn't have. The tree blind where Marco had camped for three days now was a cautious two hundred yards up the mountain – tucked high into a young lodgepole pine, plenty of coverage, long green needles to disguise the canvas assembly. The platform was only five feet wide, five feet long; with all his gear there wasn't enough space to stretch his legs while sleeping, but cramped muscles in the morning were a fair trade for the safety of altitude. The perch was accessible only by the iron spikes he'd driven into the trunk at intervals – impossible for a corpse to climb.

He'd learned to build the blind from a hunting magazine scrounged out of a dark Barnes & Noble a few months back, with parts from a ransacked Sports Authority. His Cornell education was officially useless; hunting magazines and topographical maps were the new required reading. Back before civilisation tanked, he hadn't known an ounce of shit about outdoor survival. Now he went nowhere without a yellow, dog-eared copy of *Camping for Dummies* in his backpack.

A sharp, tiny pain speared his neck. He slapped a biting gnat, crushed it into his skin.

Christ. He felt dirty and ripe. He'd been tracking this same corpse for almost a month. And the hike to the lake had been especially draining. He'd had to ditch the Jeep twenty miles south, where the mountain road had been blocked by the wreck of a thirty-foot Ryder truck. The trailer had wedged sideways between the trees – years ago, judging by the corrosion along the torn bed. Mildewed furniture, smashed electronics, scraps of orange-rusted metal strewn everywhere. In the cab sat the driver, skeletonised, arms eaten. Some idiot taking all his toys with him during the Evacuation. Flying hell's bells down the twisty road, losing what control he had left.

The wreckage was impossible to clear, and the forest too dense for off-roading. On the map, Marco had measured an alternate drive to the lake – three hours of circumnavigation that would burn a dangerous amount of gas, which was already in short supply. And so he'd decided to risk the remaining distance on foot, backpacking for a day with his gun drawn.

Compared to that, the tree here was a safe haven. From a height he enjoyed a clear view down over the forest, to the water, to the shore – past the man-made beach, the docks, the rustic vacation cabins clustered at the western inlet of sparkling Lake Onahoe. All calm.

Still, he now felt a twitch of unease, as if something weren't right. He exhaled and studied the ring on the corpse.

Grimy, but the thick gold band was visible enough. Twelve millimetre or so. Square diamonds in a milled linear pattern, a fit for the description Joan Roark had given. Wives were good like that, he'd found. Men struggled for details – funny how they always remembered the price – but the women? They'd draw a ring from memory if you gave them pen and paper.

With his thumb, Marco idly played with the platinum band on his own left hand. It wobbled on his underweight finger. Only a matter of time, he knew, before it slipped past his knuckle in the middle of some craziness and plunked to the ground, unnoticed, gone. He had to start eating more, stop wasting away. Until then he should just take the ring off, store it back at base when he was on a job – or maybe get a chain, wear it around his neck like a dog tag.

Perfect, right? A reminder why he fought this war.

Danielle—

He didn't allow the thought to finish. He tucked the binoculars into the mesh side pocket of his pack and refocused his mind.

The corpse.

Yes, there was a good chance Marco had found Andrew Roark.

He glanced at the printout tacked to the canvas beside him, a colour photo Joan had scanned and sent from her home in the East, in the Safe States. Roark when he was alive.

The photo was a headshot – *headshot*, Marco thought wryly, *always aim for the head, the only way to kill a corpse for good* – taken from the annual report of Roark's company, Tylex, some big Fortune 500 number. Andrew J. Roark, CFO, an executive in his fifties. Sharp suit, double chin, a chubby neck squeezed into a starched white collar.

Roark's cheeks were tinged red, his nose big with a round bridge that made him look like a large goofy bird. But friendly, Marco had decided, a guy who laughed a lot. A good-sounding, unguarded laugh – a guy who didn't feel comfortable being boss, a guy who wore a baseball cap at the company picnic and wanted the lunchroom people to call him Andy. His eyes were a bright, insightful blue; his short hair glistened silver on the sides and dark across the top.

The corpse below Marco had blind white sacs for eyes, a few strands of hair on a rotten scalp. *But the rest is right*, Marco thought. If you used your imagination. If you ignored the toll of two postmortem years, the skin mottled like bad cheese now, the ears shrivelled, the tip of the nose missing where something had gnawed the cartilage. Ignore all that, and what do you see?

Marco nodded. He was almost certain the thing down there was Roark. And yet . . .

He couldn't know for a fact.

Not until he saw that ring up close.

1.2

Moving slowly to minimise noise, Marco reached down next to himself in the blind and retrieved his rifle – a sleek Ruger 1-A he'd been lucky to find last year beside the mutilated body of a hunter in Utah. A good weapon. Long-barrelled but not too heavy, built for mountain killing, accurate at three hundred yards. Serious punch.

He trained the scope on the corpse. Miraculously, it had caught something. A frog hiding in the mud. One flipper, crooked and green, popped from the corpse's fist, kicking at the air. The dead man flattened its hand against its mouth, shoving mud and frog inside, and bit down with a vicious jerk of the head. Brown sludge oozed from its teeth.

Marco shuddered. Bad luck for Kermit there. That was the problem with hiding places – down in the mud, up in a tree.

You think you're safe, until you're not.

The joints in Marco's neck cracked as he scanned the forest below him and to the sides, searching for irregular shadows between the straight charcoal trunks. He listened for the crackle of feet dragging through dead leaves. But everything sounded right, looked right. Even the air smelled like the drizzly rain that morning, like clean pine. No trace of the giveaway stink that permeated an area when corpses gathered together.

But it worried him that the dead were good hiders, too. Sometimes they seemed to come from nowhere. And from experience he knew that one rifle shot could draw a crowd.

As remote as the forest seemed, the town of Wilson was just over the mountain, five miles down Route 78. Wilson, population five thousand – *former* population five thousand – an oasis in the Montana wild, catering to the summer lake vacationers who once flocked here.

The four-aisle grocery store, the lone movie theatre, the video store still packed with titles on VHS. Marco had resisted the temptation to pass through town for a supply boost on his hike. Instead he'd cut a wide path around. Places like Wilson were trouble. God forbid he stir up five thousand corpses. Christ, as far as he knew, they were out here already, enjoying a nice walk in the woods. Any careless sound could attract a pack, clamouring like dogs around the bottom of his tree, and he'd have to waste bullets – or worse, they might keep coming, outnumbering his ammo. He'd be stuck where he was, while Wilson held a goddamn town meeting below him.

Damn it. He hated taking a shot unless he knew.

He concentrated his memory on the photo album Joan Roark had shown him. The trajectory of a man's life. Andrew Roark, younger, thinner – even his nose looked smaller – in a white tux on his wedding day, black hair combed tight to his scalp, cigarette tucked in his grin. Roark through the years, turning older, heavier, better dressed, in a better house. Birthdays, Christmases, trick-or-treating in a scarecrow costume with the kids. Roark again in his fifties, at a banquet table, beaming, arm around Joan, champagne flutes before them on a white tablecloth. His hand held up three fingers for the camera. 'Our thirtieth anniversary,' Joan had said.

And their last.

But it was the vacation snapshots Marco remembered most. Decades of them. Andrew and Joan at the lake. The first photos were just the two of them, newlyweds. In a canoe, on the beach, cuddling in a hammock on a cabin porch. Then joined by an infant, then another. The kids aged, and then it was grandkids on rafts, rolling on the lawn, fishing on the dock with Roark. In one of the last pictures, Joan and Andrew in the canoe again, waving back at the camera.

Lake Onahoe was their place. Every July for thirty

summers. 'He loved it so much,' Joan had said. 'Couldn't wait to get through June, just to get up to the lake again.'

Which was the reason Marco had made the trip to Montana. He'd already wasted three weeks on two failed stakeouts. First Roark's home town, then his office in Seattle.

But this place seemed like the jackpot.

Roark's corpse had migrated three hundred miles, just to rot here.

All the dead did it. Picked their own place to haunt. No thought behind the decision; the corpses couldn't think but were herded instead by an impulse they couldn't understand. Not that Marco understood, either. But as a neurologist – *ex-neurologist,* he reminded himself, *you're nothing now* – he could guess. Their brains had gone dark, whittled down to the stems. Functional operations took place in the primitive reptilian complex, ruled by rage, fear, survival, hunger. Yet up in the neural pathways, something else remained, the weakest electricity from the amygdala into the prefrontal cortex. A drip of emotional memory from the higher brain.

He doubted the dead drew comfort from it. They didn't seem to care. It simply acted like a gravitational pull, drawing their cold bodies to wherever the warmth of their lives still lingered.

For Roark, this lake was where it would end.

Marco swept his Ruger up and down the shore, checking one last time through the scope for signs of trouble before he took the shot. Through the crosshairs the lakefront seemed quiet. Nothing new, nothing he'd missed. No sign of any hiders.

Focus, he thought. Caution was good – but too much and the corpse might wander back into the trees, and he'd lose the easy shot. And no damn way did Marco want to track the dead man through thick forest and mountainous terrain. Swinging the rifle back, he fitted his outside arm into the leather sling to stabilise the shot from his seated position.

He fixed his sights. Two hundred yards, into the black hole of the corpse's shrivelled ear. The walnut stock pressed cold against Marco's cheek.

He could see the mandibular muscles on the side of Roark's head flexing, the jaws still working the chewy cartilage of the frog. The corpse gazed across the lake, emotionless.

Marco waited for its head to still.

There. The crosshairs met in the middle of its ear.

Lingered.

Marco fired.

1.3

The crack of the Ruger tore through the trees, the pine needles quaking a million ways around him. He glimpsed a fragment of skull explode from the corpse and spin sideways into the water, like a rock skipping, twice. The echoes of the shot rocketed back towards Marco from the mountains on the other side of the lake, and he watched, his head ringing, as the corpse flopped face-first into the shallow water, staining it with that obscene fluid the things bled – not blood, but black and liquid like diarrhoea. It lay there without a twitch.

Whatever remained of Andrew Roark in that reanimated flesh – gone now.

All parts equally dead.

Marco watched the corpse bob a few feet from shore. The lake and forest sat in utter silence, stunned by the rifle-shot. He imagined the insects, the birds, the animals holding their breath, hearts jackhammering in their chests.

He ejected the spent shell and set the rifle on the platform. Then he closed his eyes and listened, his head tilted back.

He inhaled the scent of pine, let it tingle through his body before breathing out through his mouth. He waited. Minutes passed. The quiet overwhelmed him.

Lately, after the kill, he'd felt this odd emotion – like a sadness that he'd lost someone he knew, someone important to him. It shouldn't feel personal, Marco knew. And yet it *was* personal. It had to be. For the past two months, Roark had been a companion of sorts, in all Marco's thoughts and incessant planning. Pathetic, but true. And now it was over.

Roark had been returned.

And so Marco sat, waiting for the sadness, the silence, to lift.

Gradually the hum of wildlife resumed. Squirrels chirped. Chickadees and dark-eyed juncos resettled in their trees and conversed shrilly. Cicadas started again like motors. Marco allowed another ten minutes to pass, just to be careful, sifting through the forest noise – no sound of trouble. He fetched his binoculars again and checked on the corpse.

Roark's splayed body bobbed a few feet beyond where Marco had dropped it, bumping against rocks in the shallows. The cloudy lake water rippled underneath the corpse, discreet waves caused by winds coming off the mountain and crossing the lake. *Shit*, thought Marco. The body was buoyant, bloated with gas and decay. If the rolling water nudged it from the rocks, just a bit to the right, the carcass could float out to the deep.

It wouldn't sink – but Marco was in no mood for a swim to retrieve it.

Enough meditation. Move your ass.

In confident motions he removed two handguns – a police-issue Glock .40 and a Kimber he'd found in an abandoned Phoenix SWAT truck – from the side compartment of his backpack and holstered them to his chest. From another bag he pulled his hunting knife and slung the sheath from his belt, then slipped another three ammo clips into his vest. He grabbed a coil of nylon rope in case he had to lasso the corpse back to land, and then, moving to the rear of the blind, he turned himself around and stepped onto the first spike down . . .

. . . when he heard it.

That noise that always made his eyes water, his spine contract.

The cry. Strangled, wet, gurgling . . . not a low moan, but a high, sickening squall that seemed to churn unnaturally in the throat, choked off for ever from dark dead lungs.

Somewhere to the east. Still distant, thank Jesus, a long wail rising from the trees, and Marco saw nothing but forest. He swung back atop the platform, his breath quick. Moments later a second cry echoed the first. More than one corpse. Then a third cry, then a fourth. And then too many to count.

Marco shuddered. God, he hated that sound.

He hated it, because *this* was when they seemed their most human. The miserable noise was the touch-point between his existence and theirs, the awful joke played on them all. They suffered. He suffered. Listening to them now, he heard the pain. The frustration, the dread that beat in his own chest every night as he tried to sleep, suffocating in his room at base, wanting to scream but afraid to make a sound. Too careful to release his anguish out loud.

In that small way he envied them.

He scanned the eastern horizon. A small cluster of black specks bustled above the treeline, about two miles away, swooping in and out of each other. Turkey vultures. The birds were a great early warning system, Marco had discovered, like canaries in a mine. The stench of death attracted them, and once they'd locked onto a corpse, they might follow for days, launching attacks on the walking carrion, swinging down to tear at a leg or a neck. Two or three birds could devour a corpse alive. It was justice of sorts, if justice still existed.

With larger crowds of the dead, the birds tended to keep high in the sky, on the lookout for stragglers. Their presence had tipped Marco off in the past, saved his ass more than once, and he'd come to think of them as allies. *Says a lot,* he thought sourly sometimes. *My only friends are vultures.* Back at base in the mornings, he had a habit of peering out through his bedroom window the moment he awoke, scanning the sky for vultures like people used to check for rain. Seeing what kind of day it would be. A lot of vultures meant a bad day.

Now the ghastly wailing continued, louder. Marco judged it would take the horde – from the chorus he guessed there might be as many as fifty – maybe half an hour to cover the ground, figuring the terrain was uneven and choked with roots and rocks. And, besides, they might not even be heading in his direction. With luck, they'd wander away.

He frowned. There was no real reason for the shiver in his stomach. He himself had a short walk to the lake, a quick errand: check the body, get the ring, return to the blind. Fifteen minutes, tops. Up here with the canvas drawn tight, he'd never be detected. Not the perfect situation, but workable. Better than letting the corpse float to the middle of the lake.

Deliberating, he absently pinched his left earlobe between his thumb and index finger – a habit of his while thinking, ever since childhood. His knuckle pressed into a small triangular notch in his lobe, a missing piece of cartilage the size of a tooth. Dog bite when he was seven. The injury had occurred on a summer morning, thirty-five years ago, as Marco crawled between the hedges in his yard to dislodge a rubber ball. Without warning, Frankie, the yellow-eyed mongrel next door, had crashed through the branches, teeth snapping. The utter terror of that one single moment remained vivid to Marco even now. The roar of animal anger, the black head exploding from the leaves, the hot, reeking weight of fur crushing him into the garden mulch.

I'm getting eaten, he'd thought, dazed, as claws tore his shirt, raked his back.

His first lesson that monsters weren't pretend. Things could get you in real life.

To this day, dogs scared the shit out of him.

'Oh hell,' he decided. 'Let's go already.'

Feeling the press of time, he lowered himself again onto the top spike, then dipped his right foot until he felt the spike below. In swift increments he descended the tree, keeping close to the trunk, listening to his holster knock a hurried rhythm against the evergreen wood.

At the bottom, he surveyed the immediate area. The tall ferns carpeting the forest floor were green, bright with life. Globules of dew glistened in spider webs between the fronds, and sunlight pierced the treetops like white javelins. The only sign of disturbance was a corridor of partly crushed stalks heading south – a trail he'd made himself yesterday on his hike to the lake. He drew the Glock, just to be prudent, and started off down the path.

Stretching his legs felt good, to uncramp and get moving again.

The air grew noticeably warmer a hundred feet lower and, when he looked back, he saw a light mist above him. He'd been sitting in a mountain cloud without realising it. The mist obscured the bent vegetation. *Could be an advantage,* he thought.

Or not. He doubted the corpses were smart enough to track him. Instead he realised he'd better pay attention to his surroundings, take note of landmarks. Like a giant grey flat-sided boulder, and a half-toppled tree growing sideways from a mound of intricate roots. Marco added them to his mental map. He couldn't afford to get lost on the way back to the blind.

Especially if monsters were after him.

Closer to the lake, as the trees thinned and the air began to smell like a damp basement, he came across a mash-up of footprints – some barefoot, others not – in the soft earth.

The area had recently been hot.

He wasn't too concerned. He'd seen these tracks already, inspected them a few days ago on his first morning at the lake. He'd ventured down to the cabins to check if he was alone out here. The row of eight identical houses had greeted him – impressive structures chiselled from ruddy brown logs, two storeys high, flanked by stone chimneys, windows ominously dark.

The doors were all locked, which he found reassuring. The former residents had likely left on their own, still alive and ahead of the violence, probably back when the evacuation orders first came down from the state. He doubted he'd find any squatters, but of course he had to check. In each front door he shattered the glass pane, using his bedroll to muffle the sound, then crept through the shadowy hallways with his gun pointed ahead of him. His heart knocked heavily, his pulse flared every time a squirrel ran along the roof outside.

Empty, all of them. Safe. Cleaned out, too, the pantries and closets bare. On the dinner table in Cabin Seven – next door to the Roarks' – he'd found a handwritten note:

Jay, hope you didn't come here, but if you did, we had to go to Kim and Robert's in Connecticut. Please call. Sorry. We didn't know where you were, and the army won't let us stay longer. We're okay and went with the escort. Hope you are, too. Dad said to leave you the Remington in case you came. It's in the hall closet.

Marco had checked the closet. Nothing but a few wire coat hangers and sawdust on a plywood shelf. He'd slipped the note into his vest. A phone number was scribbled there, too, and he thought maybe he'd try ringing Connecticut when he returned to base. See if Jay had ever shown.

At any rate, these footprints were fainter now, the mud resculpted by the morning drizzle. Except in one spot – a fresh, sharp set of prints, pressed into the rust-coloured pine needles.

His hand tightened on the Glock. He eyed the new prints, following them with a studied gaze in both directions. To the north they moved out of sight, away from his own path, back into the woods; southward they angled through the last remaining trees and down into the sandy pit of the shoreline. Exactly where Marco himself was heading.

Roark, he thought, relaxing. This was where Marco had first spotted the corpse, shambling out of the treeline towards the water.

Bolstered, Marco hiked along the tracks the last fifty yards to the beach. Emerging from the forest, the prints disappeared where the sand loosened. No problem. He cut straight to the water, then followed the lake shore towards the dock and cabins at the far end of the beach. Half a minute later he recognised the rocks, slimy with algae, where he'd dropped the corpse.

'Shit,' he declared.

The body wasn't there.

1.4

'Shit,' Marco said again, angrier this time.

He scanned the lake surface, out towards the deeper water. Floating there was the corpse, just as he'd worried, thirty feet into the lake – the sopping dark green of Roark's pants, limbs splayed, the blasted-out side of its head turned up, carrying water like a cup. Streamers of brain and broken skull trailed alongside the body as it drifted farther away by the second.

Immediately Marco knew the rope he'd brought wouldn't do any good. His little cowboy fantasy of lassoing the corpse seemed far-fetched now as he squinted at the diminishing target.

He rubbed his forehead. He supposed there were two options. Swim out there – which meant leaving the guns ashore and stripping down to avoid waterlogged clothes all night, since he couldn't risk a fire with so many corpses in the area – or just turn around, return to the blind, and chalk this one up to a bad day. Joan Roark would have to take his word, without physical evidence to prove he'd done the job. Unfortunate, but permitted by the contract.

Neither option appealed to him.

He glanced hopefully towards the dock. In the sand next to a piling lay a faded red canoe, belly up. But even from here he could see a hole in the bottom where the wood had simply imploded from winters of neglect. Not seaworthy.

Aware that his indecision was costing him time, he glanced back over his shoulder. The mountain blocked the sky to the east, and he was unable to see how far the vultures had advanced, but the clock in his head told him that he'd better choose fast.

Cursing, he bent and unlaced his boots, kicked them off, then tugged down his pants.

He removed the pants along with his vest and ClimaCool long shirt, but the holster with the Kimber he shortened to a small loop and placed around his neck, unwilling to disarm completely. With some overdue luck, he might be able to wade the whole way out. He placed the Glock atop his folded clothing, then pulled his knife to take along, too.

The water was colder then he expected in September, even for Montana. Clenching his teeth, he splashed deeper as fast as possible, ignoring the shock in his balls as they went under. The lake bottom alternated between rocks and squishy mud. As a kid, he'd hated the sensation of mud squeezing through his toes; he'd been scared of bloodsucking leeches hiding in the ooze. Now he couldn't resist a smirk. He'd been a timid boy, afraid of everything.

And yet look at me now. If leeches are all that eat me today, I'll be happy.

Two dozen steps later, the water had climbed to the middle of his chest but then levelled, and he went twice as far without getting any wetter. From down here in the water, it was harder to see the corpse; he wasted some effort moving towards what he soon realised was a floating tree branch before noticing a greasy trail like an oil spill on the water surface.

Discharge from the head wound. Guided by it, Marco spotted Roark moments later, floating just a few yards ahead.

He pushed his way over to the body. Roark's bare back rose like a hump from the water, the skin purple and white, marbled with countless bruises and lesions – almost beautiful, like the markings on butterfly wings. Marco reached his free hand towards the body, eager to grab hold before it drifted farther, then thought better. With his knife, he jabbed the corpse's back, springing a fresh rivulet of black fluid that trickled between two emaciated ribs and dripped into the lake. Marco watched.

The corpse didn't even twitch.

Satisfied, Marco grabbed hold of its shoulders and spun it. Roark's dead face goggled at the sun, mouth open, two rows of worn brown teeth exposed. God, the thing stank.

Marco studied the pale eyes, the jaw frozen wide. Seeing a kill up close was often an anticlimax. A let-down. He sometimes wished they'd look peaceful, or relieved, or maybe even grateful. He'd read a story by Poe once – 'The Facts in the Case of M. Valdemar' – where an old man had been kept alive unnaturally by hypnosis, only to crumble to dust as the trance broke. Now *that* would be satisfying. A puff of smoke, a hissing noise. A bright flash. Something significant. Instead, this: a poor dead bastard who never knew what hit him.

Normally Marco snapped a picture or two, but he'd left his digital Nikon at base. Joan Roark had emphatically refused photos, which was fine with Marco; the prize souvenir was the ring, anyway. He pulled Roark's left arm from underwater, the skin tough like rawhide as Marco took a firm hold of the wrist. The ring glittered gold, polished by the lake.

Just then the hair follicles on Marco's neck shot up straight.

He'd had this feeling before. A subconscious awareness of background noise. Sometimes, joking, he called it his 'zombie sense'. He wheeled and faced the nearby shore.

And there they were. Twenty corpses, maybe more.

His veins chilled, as if the cold lake pumped through him.

They were a dishevelled group on the sand. Grey-skinned males and females, eyes vacant, decked in tattered, worm-eaten clothes like some grim portrait from the Great Depression. Hair thick and knotted, matted with blood and god knows what else.

They stood facing him, arms limp, bodies swaying in place – that eerie slow dance they did at times while waiting for another instinct to kick in. He stood frozen himself, afraid to trigger the attack, but he knew it was inevitable. They were hungry. Their dead eyes locked on him with emotionless interest, their necks craned forward. Evenly he drew the Kimber.

Nice and slow, he thought. *And then the fun begins.*

This couldn't be the pack he'd heard earlier, the one from the east – no way could they be so fast. His forehead burned, angry at himself; he'd been so damn obsessed with one threat, he'd ignored a dozen other dangers. Probably these things had been waiting nearby, dormant in the woods behind the cabins, emerging as soon as they'd heard him splash into the lake.

Any second now, they'd charge. He ignored the voice in his head whispering, *You're fucked.* Roark's body bumped against his hip. He steadied himself and raised the Kimber towards a corpse at the water line, a narrow-bodied male with no shirt, only a bolero tie circling its torn-out neck. Marco aimed carefully. This shot was the only one he wouldn't need to rush.

So make it count.

The scene in front of him was silent; he heard a horsefly buzz past his ear.

The gun exploded.

And all hell broke loose.

1.5

The thin corpse's cranium slammed backwards as the bullet hammered it, dumping wet white brains down its spine; the dead man's eyes crossed and it sat down hard on its ass before toppling over. The other corpses roared – a furious, unified sound, like a cry to battle, and Marco's heart shrank as the dead pack charged, crashing and swarming into the lake.

Go. He took fast aim and fired off three more shots in a five-second blur, sweeping bullets from left to right across the front line of attackers. *You. You. And you.*

He scored just a single headshot, dropping a blubbery-breasted male corpse with a long wet beard, and saw one of his other shots blast through the bony shoulder of a wild-eyed old female with no ears. His shot at a teenage girl in a pink Hello Kitty T-shirt disappeared into nowhere. Incensed, wailing, the things continued to splash in from shore, lurching towards him.

They weren't fast – the footing underwater was even more treacherous for them than it had been for Marco – but they were spread dangerously, so that he couldn't direct his gunshots in any single direction. Then again, he'd never intended to keep shooting. Knocking a few corpses out from a pack was smart, to thin their numbers and improve your odds of escape. But a full-out killing spree? That was just stupid asshole bravado. He'd seen too many soldiers go down, guns blazing during the Evacuation, realising too late that the enemy had advanced from unworkable angles. Men and their useless weapons swallowed beneath a ravenous mass of corpses.

Retreat. Always the best option. *Remember – you can't kill 'em all.*

The corpses crashed closer, arms wild and flailing.

Too many to dash between, especially in water. He'd be grabbed, tackled, torn apart.

Thinking furiously, he calculated his best route. Deeper into the lake? The dead couldn't swim . . . but they didn't need to breathe, either. They'd pick their way along the bottom, out of sight, reach up, pull him under by the ankles. Shit, there could be corpses down there already, sloshing towards him; he'd seen men pulled from rowboats, ambushed by underwater attacks . . .

Something else. They'd closed to within twenty feet.

He had to choose. *Now.*

The shore by the cabins – fifty yards to his left, away from the onrush. Perfect. He'd race there, slip between the houses, lose them in the confusion. He blasted another round at the nearest corpse, a young male in army fatigues; the bullet punched through the soldier's drippy right eye. Satisfied, Marco splashed a full two steps towards the cabins before he remembered.

Roark. The ring.

Shit. He spun and splashed in reverse, back to the floating body, seconds ahead of the attack. Already he knew this was a mistake, turning around, but now the stubborn son-of-a-bitch in him had to see it through. His head buzzed, eyes pinned to the horde almost on him as he grabbed for Roark's hand, felt their fingers entwine. *Find it, fucking find it.*

There. Cold hard metal. He yanked in a panic, and with a pop and a squish the ring slid off, pulling Roark's ripe flesh with it, like meat from a greasy turkey bone. Marco jammed the ring onto his thumb – even dead, Roark had beefier fingers than his own – then stumbled backwards to avoid a pasty-white black male lunging at him from across Roark's body. Three more corpses charged from the left, snarling. Time was up.

Off balance, still back-pedalling, Marco raised his gun.

And tripped.

His foot caught on something hidden, a chunk of rock or wood buried in the silt, and he yelled out as the lake closed over his head. Darkness cut him off. The silence underwater was terrifying. He kicked, trying to right himself, felt his leg make contact with another leg – *they're on top of me,* his mind screamed, expecting to feel cold hands clamp down all over his body – and then he pushed away and broke surface a few feet from where he'd gone down, desperate for air to breathe and light to see.

The dead were everywhere now, the lake slick with black feculent blood lapping at his bare chest. The Resurrection couldn't be absorbed through the skin, thank god; he'd been doused in enough corpse slime over the years to be sure of that. Brazenly he broke towards the cabins, slipping between two corpses in quilted hunting vests, and as he ran he wiped a stinging gob of mud from his eye. It was then he realised with shock that his right hand was— *empty.*

The Kimber was gone.

Stupid fucking asshole. He'd dropped it underwater. Gone for good.

'Fuck!' he screamed, and it actually felt good to be as loud as he wanted for once. Discretion didn't matter now.

He tightened his grip on his knife and pressed on towards the cabins. Picking up speed as the lake grew shallow and his knees cleared the water, he reached the shore with a good lead on the corpses still struggling in the deep. They'd been baited away from the beach, and now all he had to do was circle back to retrieve his clothes, the Glock and . . .

. . . and there came the fuckers from the east.

Pouring out of the woods all along the lake, from the cabins to his escape route through the trees. More than the fifty he'd predicted. A hundred, maybe more. Maybe *way* the fuck more.

Suddenly the attack had opened from another side, and as he stumbled to a stop, the army of corpses sensed him – swivelled to face him all at once, so perfectly synchronised that he wondered if the fucking things were able to communicate in a way he'd never detected.

We have you surrounded.

There was no way to reach the forest.

Give yourself up.

As a boy, he'd always been the kid who panicked during games of tag, who froze in the middle of pursuit and let himself be grabbed, simply because the resolution of being caught felt better than the terror of the chase. That same sensation returned to him now. His legs buckled, and for a moment he actually considered sitting down in the wet sand. Sitting there cross-legged like some kind of Buddhist monk, blissful and transcendent, merging his mind with the serene blue sky, the cool water and happy green trees on the opposite shore; taking one last look, closing his eyes and waiting, and the end wouldn't even hurt.

Except that he knew it would hurt.

Bad.

So instead he forced his legs straight, opened his eyes wider, looked for options. *Options, goddamn it*, he repeated, like an affirmation of life. To his left, the cabins had been sealed off behind a wall of corpses, collapsing on him fast; to the far right sat the old dock. Lopsided, falling apart, it led back out into the lake, a pointless dead end. But the beaten canoe next to it . . .

For the second time that day he seized on the thought of the canoe.

And this time he had an idea.

Gasping, he dashed back across the beach, racing along the precarious seam between the two packs of undead, those staggering from the woods and those pursuing him from the water.

The opportunity would be gone in seconds – the corpses were converging fast. He focused on the canoe ahead, but in his peripheral vision the dead faces were impossible to ignore. Dark and savage, teeth snapping at the air as he ran past.

He covered the final yards to the dock in a sprint, awestruck by the gamble he was taking.

His mind reeled.

Am I crazy? Will this work?

1.6

The canoe had long ago been flipped and laid lengthwise on the shore beside the dock, like a long wooden bowl turned upside down. It leaned slightly in the sand, inviting

Marco beneath; at full speed, he launched himself towards it and belly-flopped hard to the shore. The impact knocked him airless; with a grunt he wriggled below the overturned boat, as if he were entering a tight and narrow cave, his elbows scraped raw by pebbles and his navel full of wet grit.

Here in this dusky, hollow shelter, the air was rank with mildew and an oily smell of fish, and invisible cobwebs stuck to his face and arms. Sunlight punched through the gaping hole in the canoe hull overhead. He felt like a small animal cowering in its den. He lowered his cheek to the sand and peered back out at the beach through the crevice he'd entered. Dozens of grotesque feet, naked and swollen purple, shuffled towards the canoe.

So far, so good.

Sweating, he jammed his knife into the wooden hull, inches from his face, all the way to the hilt so it wouldn't fall out. Now both hands were free. *Hurry*, he thought; if the corpses outside piled their weight onto the boat, he was lunchmeat. He contorted himself into a crouch and shoved his shoulders up into the hull, ready to lift the canoe onto his back . . .

. . . except the goddamn boat didn't budge.

Bitch! The canoe was heavier than he'd guessed. It sat atop him, immovable as he strained, and the blood in his head felt primed to squirt from his eyes. But although Marco was thin, what he did have was muscle – a body whittled to its core by endless angry workouts in his basement gym, two or three hours on days he really hated the world. Now, enraged, he screamed . . . and felt the canoe shift. It lifted off the ground, dripping sand, the yoke digging at his neck.

And away we go!

He stumbled to his feet, half bent, the upside-down canoe

cupped over his spine like the shell of some ridiculous turtle. The bow pointed straight and long ahead of him, ready to launch, but he hadn't yet taken a step before a loud boom sounded on the exterior, next to his ear; the entire boat quaked, and aftershocks rumbled down into his vertebrae.

The canoe's weight shifted sharply as the first corpses dove against it, and he fought to keep it balanced overhead. The physics were simple: *If it tips, I'm dead.*

The pounding on the boat doubled, merged with the pounding pulse in his ears. His legs shook, and then more corpses arrived from the left, counterbalancing the attack from the right, so that he had an easier time keeping himself upright. He couldn't see in any direction but down to his bare white toes, and a bit to the left and right. Outside the canoe, a hundred corpses crowded the rims from both sides; he saw only their crooked legs and rotten feet.

Seconds later the corpses mobbed the hull, an all-out attack.

Blows rained onto the canoe, the crack of the wood terrifyingly loud, and he prayed the boat wouldn't simply fall apart around him. Angry cries joined the violence; the corpses were confused by his improvised defence, but the confusion wouldn't last.

Sure enough, the canoe began to pull upwards as they tried to tear it off him. Alarmed, he held it down with all his strength. *Time to go.* He drove hard with his legs, relieved as the boat slipped easily through their grasp – he heard them scrabbling for grip, but the wood was worn smooth – and stumbled forwards along the sand, wearing his canoe armour.

The point of the bow parted the crowd, dealing hard punches to those in its path. He gained momentum, whooping aloud as if each hollow clunk, each speared skull off the metal bow-ball, were another block of coal thrown into his internal boiler.

Pop. Pop. Pop.

He surged ahead like a locomotive knocking cows from the rails, barely checked by the impacts. A white-eyed male corpse fell, rolled under the canoe. It hissed and grabbed at his ankles, but he high-stepped over it, resisting the urge to kick its forehead.

If only he'd had his boots on.

The canoe grew heavier by the moment, but Marco's legs kept churning despite the pain. He had no idea where he was going. Looking down, he followed the foamy dark sand along the shore, concentrating on the wet impressions of his feet, confident he was at least headed back to his starting point, where Roark's body had first hit the water.

As he cleared the initial mob, a jolt from the side nearly sent him sprawling. He recovered in time to see a pair of obese legs, enormous and pickled and veiny, below the left rim of the canoe. A fat corpse had broadsided him and now hung on, pressing against the boat with all its weight, driving Marco sideways a step into the lake, then two steps, three. The water rose to his shins.

Any deeper and he was fucked.

Desperate, he threw his shoulders up into the boat, freeing one hand to grab the knife still embedded in the hull; he retrieved it with a furious yank and in the same motion drove the blade into the bulbous rotted belly outside the canoe. He jerked hard . . .

. . . disembowelling the dead man; the knife cut up into the ribcage and popped from Marco's grip, gone. The corpse bellowed as its guts cascaded onto the shore. Surprised, it released the boat and flopped forward, chasing its own entrails. Marco splashed back to the sand.

The sounds of awful wailing fell farther behind as he

maintained a quick-footed trot, grimacing but afraid to slow down. A hundred yards later he was rewarded for his work. His folded stack of clothing and the Glock appeared at his feet.

'I'm back,' he announced, his voice raw.

Panting, he tilted his body and managed to dump the canoe without collapsing. The boat crashed into the shallows, startling the same minnows he'd watched Roark hunt an hour before.

He glanced around in haste. As he'd guessed, the corpses were a good distance back, still labouring towards him, but their slow, singular advance wasn't half the threat of being surrounded. He'd survived. He would continue to survive. Trembling, he grabbed his Glock and clothes, jammed his sore feet into his boots, then turned and bolted north to the trees.

He found his earlier path without trouble. At the edge of the forest he paused and turned.

The beach crawled with dead men and women, arms and legs jerking like ugly puppet limbs as they staggered up the shore. *Men and women*, Marco repeated to himself. Easy to forget sometimes. He wondered how many had wives, kids, lovers in the Safe States, mourning for them, sick with grief and wondering where they were now.

Christ, how fucked up the world had turned. How it made the dead so alive and the living feel so dead. He doubted there was any fixing it, any way to turn it back.

But, shit, he could at least help make things better.

Grim-faced, he jogged up the mountain, past the tree that grew crooked and the flat-sided boulder, into the mist and the walkway of broken fern. Up in the blind, he shut the canvas curtain and sat undetected, unafraid, listening to the groans of the dead pass through the forest and fade as the mob lost his trail. And as he waited for them to leave, to wander off to wherever their tortured minds beckoned them, he held Roark's ring – yes, he was certain now, he *had* found Roark – and read again the words etched inside the band.

Together we make a circle, one life without end. Always, Joan.

SETTING THE MEAT TRAP

2.1

'One more thing,' Joan Roark said. Her grainy image transmitted from the Safe States, materialising on the computer screen atop Marco's desk. He sat in his study, in the dark, an hour before dawn. At midnight he'd arrived back at base – the house he'd owned with Danielle for a year before the Resurrection – his legs and arms heavy with a fever he'd picked up on the trip. Months of undereating and poor sleep had left his immune system for shit.

The flu, that's all. He didn't dare wonder if the Resurrection had gotten to him somehow.

He'd unchained the iron gate and rolled the Jeep up his long cobblestone driveway, while in the hills the keening of coyotes welcomed him back to Arizona; inside he'd squirmed in bed for a few hours with stomach cramps and a sore throat before getting up to contact Joan. He'd left the lights off in the study. But on Joan's end of the transmission, the room was bright; the sun was up in Baltimore. The Safe States were all east of the Mississippi River – a natural, easily defended border behind which America still functioned. The government had pulled back as the Resurrection spawned and spiralled out of control in the West. Now the Safe States were in lockdown – nobody in, nobody out. The Evacuated States had been surrendered to the dead.

Here in Marco's study, the image of Joan's face was a

luminous window in the darkness, seeming supernatural. He'd been about to power the computer down. Instead he nodded at her on the screen. It was his sly way of avoiding eye contact; the webcam mounted on his desk captured him in partial profile, denying her an easy read of his face, his thoughts. He was glad he never had to debrief in person. God, how he'd hated those awkward moments during his residency at Cedars-Sinai – explaining EEG results to the patients and distraught families. Often he'd catch himself tapping the page erratically with his pen, as if he had a neurological problem of his own.

He watched Joan shift in her seat. Her gaze sank low. Perhaps she sensed her husband's wedding ring sitting on his desk. Marco pocketed it discreetly. No need to show her again.

'I'm sorry,' she said, her voice shaking. 'I don't mean to be . . . it's just . . . it's just that I want to ask you. I mean, you've done so many of these. You must know.'

She looked awful. He hadn't seen her in weeks, and the difference in her appearance alarmed him. She wasn't wearing make-up as she always had before, and he felt a sting of guilt for even noticing this. Her eyes were veined red, the lower lids grey and puffy. A meniscus of clear snot bulged from her right nostril; she sniffled it up, but it re-emerged at once. Her shoulders slumped forward, arms straight down, her hands pinned between her knees. She was dressed in a dull green sweatshirt with an obvious bleach spot on the shoulder – the first time he'd seen her in anything but ritzy designer labels – and he had a hunch she'd slept in it. The sweatshirt was snug around her breasts, the nice figure she still had in her fifties, but her face looked older than that, coarse, as if widowhood had dragged her through a few phantom years.

He waited. 'Know?'

'Yes,' she said. She looked at him, determined. 'Did I do the right thing?'

He sucked in his breath.

She continued, stumbling again. 'Please, I just want the truth – honestly, Mr Marco, like you would tell a friend. You can tell me now. I've already paid, and you've made the sale, either way. So, please.' Her bottom lip quavered. She bent towards the camera, her face expanding on his screen.

'Did I?' she asked.

He deliberated for a moment, which surprised him – not that she asked, but that he actually gave thought to his answer. He'd heard the question before. Sometimes before the job, sometimes after. His clients were like children, inexperienced and uncertain; the whole world had started over on them, trashing what they knew, handing out new rules to learn.

Horrible new rules.

Nobody knew what to do, how to feel, how to adapt to life after the Resurrection. The Evacuated States were a silent wasteland; the Safe States, meanwhile, raged and roiled – overcrowded by fifty million refugees from the West, the economy shot to shit, not enough jobs or food to go around. The loss of contaminated farmland across the Midwest and California had been devastating. Half the populace was on welfare, either Food Relief or Property Reimbursement or Survival Assistance; in the months after the border shut, the Garrett administration had authorised multi-billion-dollar relief packages. But Garrett was ousted now; the New Republicans had been voted into power, and relief programmes were being scaled back.

It was overwhelming . . . and belittling. And often Marco's clients looked to him for advice, as if he must have some secret insight into the Resurrection – why it had done this, what it wanted from them – just because he was the guy out here, out where it first began, face to face with it on his own. And, at the end of the miserable day, he was supposed to tuck these poor people into bed, kiss them on the head and tell them that everything would be all right.

Me, a father figure. Now there's a big fuck-you from the universe.

'Did I do the right thing?' Joan Roark had asked.

He sighed and then almost told her the truth – that he wasn't sure whether any of it really mattered or did a damn bit of good. But he liked Joan. So he settled instead on what she needed to hear, and then he nodded slowly. Slow meant serious. Like he would never lie.

'I believe you did,' he said. 'Yes.'

At that she began to cry again, covering her mouth with one hand, cheeks puffing. A carat of diamond glittered from her ring finger.

'You didn't do the easy thing,' he admitted. 'But you gave your husband peace. If it were me – I mean, if I were the one out *there* – I would've wanted you to do the same.'

She shook her head. He wasn't sure whether she disagreed with what he'd just said, or perhaps was just horrified at how easily she accepted it.

'Joan,' he said in a softer voice. 'Listen to me.'

She stopped and regarded him, and he wondered what he looked like on her screen in the Safe States – if he were anything more than a shadow projected from his dark office. Could she see the fever on his face, the lumps of cold sweat? 'You saved his soul,' he said. 'He's returned now, wherever we're *supposed* to go in the end. When it was done, he looked . . . peaceful.'

Maybe she believed him. Maybe it didn't matter if she did, just that she heard somebody say those words. She laughed, and the snot from her nose dripped down to her lip.

'Okay,' she said, nodding back at him.

'I mean it.' His tongue stuck to his teeth as he spoke. *I did mean some of it.*

'Okay,' she said again. 'Thank you.' She pulled a tissue from off screen and dried her nose. 'I'm sorry. I cry at every movie, too, even bad ones. Even comedies. It used to drive Andy crazy.' She shrugged. 'Anyway. What's done is done.'

He swallowed, the spit like acid in his sore throat. The few seconds of silence seemed to satisfy them both as a goodbye. 'Good luck,' was all he added.

She managed a weak smile. 'Good luck to you, Mr Marco.'

He waited another moment. His instincts told him it was important for Joan Roark to take the final action, that she should reach across and shut off her computer, then stand up from her chair in Baltimore and start over. A second later the screen went black. For Joan, life could now begin again in the Safe States. For her, this was done. She'd said it herself.

What's done is done.

'Not for me,' he commented, his eyes adjusting to the pure darkness. Silently he added, *Is it wrong that I'm jealous?*

An unpleasant grin pulled at his lips.

See, Joan? he thought. *Everybody's got their doubts.*

2.2

Marco shut down the computer and plodded along the hall to the bathroom. His head throbbed, and each lungful of air antagonised the dry passages in his nose. In the cabinet he dug out a bottle of Sudafed gelcaps. *Expires Oct 2016*, the label read. Two years ago.

He swallowed three caps anyway, just in case there was still any life to them. He'd stop by the Walgreens in Apache Junction on his next trip for supplies, but most likely all the pharmaceuticals there had expired, too. Everything was going bad in the drugstores and the supermarkets, even the dried goods. He was outstaying his welcome.

He felt exhausted, but the idea of returning to bed and sleeping the next twenty-four hours wasn't smart. He'd come home in half a coma last night and hadn't checked the property for break-ins. Neglecting it again would be reckless. The barricade he'd erected was nearly corpse-proof, but not a hundred per cent. Plus he had to check the trap.

To his annoyance, his hopes rose, a pathetic optimism that today might be the day. The end of his hunt. Maybe . . .

Stop it, he thought crossly and returned to his office.

He'd wait for a lighter sky. Another thirty minutes. He pulled an afghan blanket from the leather couch and slid open the glass door to the balcony. The morning still held the chill of the desert night, sharp on his skin. He clutched the blanket around him and leaned his forearms on the balcony rail, surveying the land. At the base of the eastern sky, a light blue band divided the earth from the deeper universe, while, somewhere below, a dawn of pink and orange waited to emerge. The Superstition Mountains towered on the horizon, gnawing the stars like monolithic black molars in a jawbone of dry earth. Beneath them lay the bajadas, a mile of gentle hills and dried scrub, scattered with saguaro and creosote bush, populated by spiny lizards and owls.

Before the Resurrection, he'd often found peace out here in the evenings, after hard shifts at the hospital. A glass of red wine and Danielle's hands massaging his neck, the tension leaving him like heat escaping the desert dirt. Everything cooling. Now he could never relax – not with a hundred wild cactuses staring back at him from the bajadas, man-sized silhouettes that could easily mask a corpse advancing towards the property.

Shivering despite the blanket, he thought about Joan Roark. She'd asked a difficult question, and he'd answered. He tried to recall his exact words. He couldn't remember precisely, but one word had lodged in his mind like a briar. *Soul.*

Had he really told her that? *You saved his soul.* His ears warmed with guilt. He felt like some sleazy televangelist, peddling bullshit, whatever it took to make himself rich. But no – that wasn't fair. He didn't say it because of the pay cheque. He just wanted her to be okay.

He hadn't believed in souls since high school, when he was a good Catholic kid. But medical school had erased that notion with a rag of empirical common sense.

'There's only one life force,' he'd remarked once to Danielle, on their way home from a dinner with her California friends in which the talk had centred earnestly on *chakras* and *energy healing* – notions so absurd he might have laughed out loud if it wouldn't have hurt her feelings. Danielle's spiritual beliefs were part of her charm, one of many reasons he loved her. And she'd always seemed to find him just as charming – just as out of touch with reality – whenever he articulated his own beliefs. 'The electrophysiological current of a hundred billion neurons,' he'd said. '*That*'s the voodoo of human life.'

'Yes, Doctor,' she'd patronised him from the passenger seat, leaning across to tease his ear with her finger. She knew how to both love and annoy him with a single gesture. 'But that's your problem, babe. You need to know how everything works. Can't anything be magic?'

He'd answered her with a sardonic smile. 'Sorry. All the magic courses at Cornell were full. I had to take pre-med instead.'

'You're a jerk,' she'd laughed, and playfully bitten his hand.

But while Marco didn't buy into souls, he did believe in

identity. The sum of individual experience, everything you ever did or thought – memories stored magnetically in brain cells. Identity remained even when life did not, locked away like a closed wing of a library, where the books smelled yellow and musty. Identity was physical, anatomical. Not a spirit.

Andrew Roark had died. And yet he was still Andrew Roark, always would be, until he crumbled to zero on a cellular level. His identity had simply been buried inside his corpse.

So what *was* the right thing to do? Marco remembered a woman in Florida, years before the Resurrection – a car-crash victim, comatose for years in her hospital bed, and yet her eyes were open and she sometimes moved. The courts had exploded into an uproar over living wills; loud debates raged about whether her damaged brain was still aware or wasn't. In the end her life support had been discontinued. Watching CNN that morning, Marco had sipped his coffee, feeling only relief that the mess hadn't happened at Cedars-Sinai. Danielle sat across the breakfast table, carving out a melon slice, watching an interview with the woman's distraught husband.

'I hope that's never you,' Danielle had said, her eyes glistening. For a moment he'd wondered who she meant – the husband or the wife. But Danielle had finished her melon and left for an audition, and he'd never asked.

At least he knew now which tragic figure he'd turned out to be. And only now that it was *his* decision – pull the plug, or no? – did he realise what he really believed.

Sometimes euthanasia was the correct choice.

Joan Roark came to mind again. Her face, chalky without make-up, skin flaking at the top of her nose between her eyebrows. He hoped she'd be all right. He hoped she had enough money to set herself up properly; too many people's finances were held hostage out West, stagnating in dark local banks and credit unions. Proxy banks had been created in the Safe States to transfer funds, but the process was slow and rife with bureaucracy. Hopefully Joan had gotten hers.

Goddamn it. Why was he *still* thinking about Joan Roark? Usually when he powered down the computer, after the job was done and closed, the client's life disappeared from his with the same abruptness as the screen image. Case closed, and he could think only of the next contract, the next life he would share. The next corpse to return.

Perhaps his problem now was that the next scheduled job was an entire three months away. Before setting out to Montana, he'd told Benjamin that he'd needed a good long break. Benjamin was his business partner in the Safe States, and his former brother-in-law.

No more for a while, Marco had said. *I'm worn out, Ben.*

Although Benjamin had grumbled at first – Marco never pried, but he did wonder occasionally what financial obligations Ben had in the Safe States – in the end he'd agreed. No new contracts. Shop closed, October, November, December, open again for business in January. Ben had booked the next contract for a corpse named Thomas Flynn, a twenty-six-year-old logger last seen somewhere in a million muddy square miles of Oregon forest.

Fun, Marco had said to Ben. *Should be eight feet of snow by then. Are you punishing me?*

You know it, Ben answered. *Besides, you'll be nice and rested after your vacation.*

The truth was, Ben could gripe all he wanted about the loss of business, but really, what choice did he have? Marco was the whole operation – the one out here risking his ass in a corpse wasteland. If he wanted a break, goddamn it, then he was getting one.

The talent. That's what Danielle would have called him. *Keep the talent happy.*

He winced. Sometimes he caught himself writing lines for her like a playwright, and then her voice was really there, performing in his head. Sly, sensual alto, and with it the suggestion of her mouth, that funny half-smile she sported when she teased, and her breath on his cheek, and that hurt him, too, the invocation of her physical presence.

He'd been remembering her too much lately. He did better when she remained an abstraction, a formless fog with a name.

He coughed, and she was gone again. From the roof, a brown bat zigzagged low over the balcony, scooping up a final bug on its way home to roost in the mountains. Dawn had arrived without fanfare, not the candy colours he'd hoped for, instead a gradual lifting of the light to reveal a cloudless sky to the east. The details of his balcony sharpened, and he saw the leftovers of his last dinner here, the night before he'd ventured to Montana to find Roark.

He'd been in a grim mood that night, like a soldier shipping out the next day. A wine bottle lay tossed in the ashes of the adobe fire pit; on the bench was his wine glass, tipped over in a dried stain of red. He'd left it full. Some squirrel must have helped itself to a good buzz.

The congestion in his ears made clicking sounds as he stretched his jaw. He leaned out over the balcony rail. With one finger he pressed against his nose and blew a missile of snot to the patio below, then repeated with the other nostril, a habit he'd developed while trail-running the Arizona mountains. Uncouth, but nowadays he had only himself to offend.

Jesus, he hadn't even showered in weeks. How long before he stopped wiping his ass?

Disturbed by his own joke, he went back inside, intent on completing the security check on the grounds. He closed the balcony door and had nearly crossed the room when he remembered the wedding ring in his pocket. He fished it out and returned to his desk. From the side drawer he pulled out a manila folder labelled 'ROARK' – thick with contents wrapped in a red rubber band, everything from scans of photos and bank receipts to transcripts of his interviews with Joan – and a box of Ziploc sandwich bags. He placed Roark's ring in a bag and tucked it into the folder, then returned the folder to the desk and closed the drawer. Someday he'd bring it back to Joan. Someday he'd bring back all the other rings he kept stored in there, too, trinkets from past jobs. Bring them back to the mourning families of the dead.

If the Quarantine ever lifted, and if he was ever allowed back in the Safe States.

If the living could forgive him.

2.3

On his way downstairs, Marco stopped by the gun room, formerly a large linen closet off the master bedroom, and equipped himself with the fully loaded Glock.

The wistful idea of rejoining the Safe States still played in his mind. *Fat chance,* he thought, sobering. Not with Hoff in the White House, not with the New Republicans keeping everything in lockdown, guarded against the slightest sign of trouble.

New Republicans. Power-hungry bastards, a bunch of zealots morphed from the old right wing. After the Resurrection, their ideals had spread like a fresh infection, exploiting the weak tissues of wounded America. The Safe States were afraid, everyone's breath held waiting for another outbreak, wondering when the Resurrection would come back to finish them off. Hospitals remained on alert; posters on trains advised *What to Look For,* with colourful illustrations of alpha-stage Resurrection patients – sallow white cheeks, parched lips, pink weepy eyes – peering constantly over the shoulders of nervous morning commuters.

The New Republicans had promised to cure the fear, but at the same time they strived to preserve it. Hoff's campaign in 2016 emphasised the danger still lurking: President Garrett had been neglectful and weak, Hoff criticised; not proactive enough to stop a virus – a terrorist attack, perhaps? – from annihilating the West. *The next time Garrett fails, we'll all be dead*, warned the ads on television, on billboards, on radios. Hoff won in a landslide.

Marco had observed from his laptop in Arizona, disappointed, an expatriate without a vote. *Crap*, he'd thought. *These guys know the formula for power.* Stoke the fear, encourage alarm. Frightened citizens were willing to trade freedom for safety.

And sure enough, stricter laws passed; the Patriot Act sharpened its teeth, bit down harder on private life. Mandatory blood tests. Court-ordered hospital visits. Gasoline rations, based on mileage applications approved by the Resource Office. Army trucks patrolled low-income neighbourhoods. The controversial Survivor Tax – *forced charity*, critics cried – squeezed money from every man and woman to fund the ongoing recovery.

The laws kept coming. Capitol Hill was a mess; votes from the 'Ghost Congress' – senators and representatives from the now-empty states – were ruled unconstitutional and then voided. Within a year President Hoff had more power over twenty-eight Safe States than he *ever* would have held over all fifty. The New Republicans controlled the floor.

The Quarantine wasn't going to be lifted, not anytime soon.

The Quarantine kept people afraid.

Standing in his hallway, Marco shook his head. *You think*

they'd let you back? he asked himself. *Sure, just walk up to the border, wave your arms and say, 'Hey guys! I've been out here four years with the corpses! But I promise I don't have the Resurrection cooties on me!'*

Yeah, right. You'd be shot dead before you opened your stupid mouth.

He shrugged. Screw it. No use worrying about that right now.

Right now he had to check the trap.

From the back of the closet, he grabbed an aluminium softball bat with duct tape wound in strips around the handle. Bringing the bat always made him feel silly, but there was no sense in wasting bullets when a good Willie Mays swing could bring down a single corpse.

He descended the back staircase into the kitchen. The room had once been bright and airy, with its breakfast nook built especially for a stunning view of the Superstitions, but since then he'd drilled thick sheets of pool siding across all the ground-floor windows. Now the only light was a rectangular shaft beaming through a skylight on the angled ceiling, spotlighting an island countertop of red and orange-brown mosaic tile. The kitchen was the only room in the house where Danielle had insisted on a desert decor. Ironic, considering she didn't like southwestern cuisine. But coloured kitchen tiles? She'd loved those like candy.

He poured himself a glass of orange juice from the fridge – not real oranges, of course, just the same powdered Tang he'd been mixing himself for years, but at least it had 100 per cent of daily Vitamin C to battle the flu. He hadn't noticed any improvement from the expired Sudafed. The drink burned his hurting throat.

He wiped his mouth with the back of his hand and picked up the bat, feeling like a parody of a kid going out to play ball on a Saturday. All that was missing was Mom, telling him to be home for lunch. He exited the kitchen into the garage stairwell; even through his congestion the garage smelled like oil and grease. The Jeep was in its stall, over-worked, resting from the long drive home, its tank almost empty. He'd fill it from the reserves out back later.

Unlocking the side door, he emerged onto the yard.

On the ground the shadow was a crisp rendering of the gabled roof behind him. The house was Spanish revival, a contemporary mix of varying rooflines and pilasters carved from white plaster, curving around a wide slated courtyard. A 'drug lord house', he'd teased Danielle once, just to embarrass her in front of the realtor, when secretly he couldn't help admiring it.

For several tense seconds he stood and listened, assuring himself that all was quiet, then walked outwards from cover. At this early hour, the sun already felt like a stinging insect on his neck as he crossed the desert property to the barricade on the western end.

The barricade. His masterpiece. The first year after the Evacuation he'd slaved out here, obsessed with the waist-high wall of brick that ran the property line, the need to build it higher with huge sheets of plywood and corrugated aluminium he'd looted from Home Depot. And then he'd piled whatever else he could find in the neighbourhood along the inside for support – stones, cinder blocks, lumber, wheel-barrows, barbecue grills, patio tables, umbrellas, watering cans, anything at all to add strength and weight – until the structure measured from the left of the driveway gate, all the way around the house, and back to the right.

For weeks that summer he worked in a sadistic heat, afraid to stop despite the sunburn, the blisters, the salty nicks on his arms as he hoisted tons of clutter and spooled a mile of barbed wire along the top; at any moment he expected to turn and see the dead pouring from a weak point he hadn't yet addressed. At night he suffocated himself to sleep in the house's hot attic, insane with sweat, certain the property was not secure.

And then, gradually, things had gotten better. Stepping outside in the mornings, he began to notice a feeling of satisfaction. Calm. Control – the first hint of it in a long, long time.

The barricade stood higher than his head, too tall for the things to climb but low enough so that he could see over the top when he stood on the house porch. Every inch of it allowed survey of the desert and the abandoned houses in the Gold Canyon below.

He recalled one of Danielle's friends, that hippie Janis with all the beads who lived up in Sedona and made sculpture from random junk. If only Janis could see this – his barricade with its odd arrangements. The chaotic yet purposeful placement, the juxtaposed earth-colour rust and bright plastics. It was as artistically pleasing to him as anything he'd done in his life. All it needed was a name. *Materialism as Defence Mechanism.*

Not bad. Or how about *A Lot of Crap That Doesn't Mean Shit Any More.*

Yeah. Second one was better.

Now he followed the barricade, alert for any sign of a breach. Nothing. In the back yard, he could hear the generator chugging in the shed, activated by the timer he'd rigged to save gasoline. He paused to admire the Superstitions to the north, the blue sky clear of clouds and vultures. No aircraft, either. He'd long stopped bothering to be on guard for military planes or Blackhawks; that first summer, he'd dash back into the house at the first drone of a distant engine, but the Air Force had discontinued flyovers three years ago. Jet fuel shortages had pretty much grounded the fleet. And besides, there weren't any more survivors to rescue, anyway.

Satisfied that the yard was safe, he continued to the other side of the house, crossing behind the empty concrete pit that had been the pool. At the back corner of the property was Danielle's unofficial garden – nothing she'd planted herself, just a fenced-off section of wild flowers. Yellow evening primrose and purple vervain sprouted there on their own. He'd always appreciated them for the fact that they thrived no matter how he neglected them.

He stopped as he turned the corner.

Something had sprung the trap.

Twenty feet ahead, the white signal cloth waved to him from where the fibreglass snare pole bent over the barricade, pulled by an unseen weight on the other side. The pole was still. Whatever was caught in the snare wasn't putting up much fight.

Marco took a deep breath and set down the baseball bat, switching the Glock to his damp right palm.

Another coyote. A bobcat.

Jesus Christ. Did he want it to be her, or not?

Near the base of the snare pole rested a worn wooden ladder. He set it against the barricade, then hesitated. No noise from the other side. He gripped the pole and tugged. It swayed towards him and then away, a natural momentum, nothing forced. But still the end dipped towards the ground outside the wall, the cable taut. Definitely something there. He continued up the first few rungs, sweat chilling his armpits, his crotch.

He held his breath and stuck his head over.

Danielle . . .

. . . was not there, not smiling up at him with a putrid face and black crusted lips, the way she did in his awful nightmares.

He laughed once, not amused, feeling the pressure rush from his lungs.

At the end of the cable was an arm. A man's arm, hairy, torn from the body at the humerus above the bicep. Flies swarmed around the fresh exposed meat and the knob of bone. The jackrabbit carcass Marco had left as bait was gone. Around the wrist, the wire loop cut a bloodless purple trench – the more you pulled, the tighter a snare got – and Marco guessed that the corpse had simply yanked hard enough to escape, minus one limb.

He glanced around. Wherever the thing had wandered next, he saw no sign of it.

He set his Glock on the wall ledge, needing both hands free, and hoisted himself forward. His abdomen rested atop the barricade as he reached for the wire, his body stretched flat, an awkward distribution of his weight. Immediately he realised his mistake – almost a premonition, 'zombie sense' again – and with a startled reflex he hooked his foot around a rusted metal pole poking from the barricade rubble, an old red stop sign . . .

. . . or else he would have toppled when the corpse attacked, striking from the shadows outside the wall.

The dead thing had been hugging the blind spot along the base, hidden from view – yes, Marco should have checked there, he always did, but this goddamn time he hadn't, because he was distracted, and sick, and exhausted, and heartbroken – so that when Marco leaned out, the thing hissed and leaped straight up at him. Its rough fingers clamped his wrist and yanked him a foot over the wall. He yelled out in surprise – heard his jeans rip against the concrete, felt his ankle twist painfully under the stop sign. His free hand slapped at the wall, seeking the Glock.

Couldn't find it. Couldn't turn to look.

He shouted, cursed, his face burning with frustration.

The corpse tightened its grip on his wrist. And pulled.

2.4

Marco hung at the waist over the barricade, looking down into the eyes of a tall male corpse with thick grizzled eyebrows and a small knobby chin. Its corneas were red and disgusting, pooled with blood, and its gaping mouth had no tongue – but sure as hell the teeth were all there, gnashing and slicing at the short distance between itself and Marco.

The left arm was gone, a ragged stump. It didn't care. With its remaining hand it raged against Marco, thrashing, hanging its weight on him, and Marco watched in horror as his own forearm inched lower and lower towards those wild snapping teeth. A bite would be fatal; the Resurrection transmitted through large wounds. A scratch might not kill you – but if the teeth broke deep into the skin's hypodermis, the bottom layer where fat blood vessels crisscrossed the body and your red stuff really pumped . . . well, if that happened, you were fucked. Big-time.

Christ – the thing was strong. Fingers like a handcuff. Cold. Unbreakable.

Marco resisted, pulling back as if curling weights in the gym. The tendons in his neck bulged, and his bicep shook. With his free arm he grabbed hold of his elbow for extra leverage but, as he did, he felt himself slide farther out across the wall, his balance thrown even more out of whack. He arched his back desperately, keeping himself as high as he could, terrified the thing might jump and bite his face.

The muscle in his arm boiled. He fought back a growing panic, an excruciating need to release. If his strength gave out, his arm would be hamburger – and so he twisted his torso, trying to summon power from all points of his body and direct it to his wrist.

His arm dipped lower. Lower.

The corpse dug its heels into the desert, grunting like a

boar. Brown spittle from the thing's rotten mouth peppered Marco's hand. Marco squeezed his eyes shut and concentrated. He continued to slip forward, losing an inch at a time to the dead man pulling him.

Behind Marco the stop sign had pulled loose from the barricade – no good now, unable to moor him in place. The sign's broad metal face clattered against the concrete, then cut into the bend of Marco's knee as he teetered at the brink of the wall. Only his upper legs supported him. His waist, his chest, his face dangled out into nothing.

The congestion in his head drained to a spot behind his eyes, an intense pressure that dizzied him, almost emerged as vomit. Feverish sweat squeezed from his pores.

Fight this, he thought. The fire in his arm, his spine, unbearable.

He was going down.

'Fight this,' he gasped.

He would die today, finally.

No. Not today.

He opened his eyes and stared at the corpse. It watched him in return, its pasty face too close to his own, close enough to touch if Marco unarched his back; the dead man's right eye had burst from exertion, and blood oozed like tears down its cheek, along its broken nose, into the gaps between its jagged teeth.

For a moment Marco pitied it, even understood it – a creature fighting to survive, not really so different from himself. And then he aimed and swung his upper body down like a mallet, pounding his forehead square into the dead man's skull.

A bright flash blinded him, sharp pain, but it cleared quickly and he saw the corpse sit hard on its ass, releasing his wrist, its mouth rounded into a shape of surprise. Marco's chest whipped downwards, slamming the wall, knocking his breath away. He hung there, suspended, his left leg caught around the stop sign that extended into the blue sky above him.

Shit. He needed that sign.

He jerked his leg, hard as he could, wincing at the bite of metal into his skin. He heard the corpse grunt, and so he swung his arms blindly to ward off the attack he couldn't see coming. And then the sign popped free from the wall and crashed atop him as he fell to the solid earth.

He scrambled to his feet and turned just as the corpse rushed him. He dodged and delivered a rough kick to the thing's back, sending it face first to the ground again. Its half-arm flailed as it rolled, kicking up dirt and a bad, shit-like stench. Marco wheeled to find the stop sign.

There – in a bed of brittlebrush. He bent and grasped the green metal pole with both hands. The corpse righted itself into a crouch, tensing, now up and staggering towards him.

Hurry, Marco thought. He swung his shoulders and drove with his legs; the sign's weight snapped his arms taut, popped his elbows as it grated forward, dragging on the ground.

He wrung himself in a frantic circle, gaining speed; the sign scrabbled along the rocky soil then lifted off into space – slicing sideways like the blade of a giant octagonal axe, sailing across a panorama of red hills and plump cactus, the majestic Superstitions in the distance.

As his body spun he lost sight momentarily of the corpse, heard nothing but the hollow whistle of the swinging blade, heavy in his hands, and then his line of vision wheeled forward again, and there was the corpse, lunging at him, crazed.

The sharp edge of the stop sign caught it at the neck . . .

. . . slashed upward under the jaw . . .

. . . burst out the other side. Marco didn't even feel a check on the pole.

In one fluid motion, the head tumbled into the air, cut

free, and Marco continued his swing around again, another complete circle, arriving back just in time to see the headless, one-armed body topple. A spasm of black goo spurted from the neck-hole.

Marco relaxed his arms and let go. The stop sign skidded along the dirt and crashed back into the brittlebrush. He stumbled a few steps, letting his momentum subside, then stood shaking in place. His breath rattled through the congestion in his throat. His hands hurt. The rusted pole had sawed two bloody lines across his palms, the kind that would sting for days. He wiped his arm across his forehead, feeling the fever.

Should've gone to bed an hour ago.

He walked to where the decapitated corpse lay, a foul pile of brown clothes, its legs and single arm splayed out in three different directions like a broken, soiled doll. The head rested on its side a few feet further – face turned away from Marco, as if insolent.

'Hey, come on,' Marco said. 'Nobody likes a poor loser.'

He almost smiled. And then, just as abruptly, his eyes singed, tears hot on his lower lashes.

Quit screwing around, he thought, blinking. *Get back in. Another twenty corpses probably heard the racket, and they'll be sniffing around.*

He crossed to the shadow of the barricade, passing the sign where it had settled. The white letters flashed at him from the red octagon.

STOP

'I'm trying,' he answered. 'I really am.'

2.5

Dripping sweat, Marco circled the property outside the barricade and unlocked the main gate. He let himself back into his yard and returned to the snare pole, where the ladder remained propped in position. Climbing to the top, he reeled in the cable and removed the arm.

It was an eerie weight, still floppy at the elbow. Touching it seemed to release a reserve of foul odour. He crinkled his nose and flipped it over the wall. It landed near the headless corpse.

Returning to the backyard, he entered the shed and pulled a plastic bin from a shelf next to the generator. He lifted the lid, and the stink of dead rabbits assailed him. Their matted bodies lay in stacked rows, about twelve that he'd poisoned out in the scrub before the Montana trip. He pulled one carcass off the top and brought it back to the snare to reset for another night.

Sometimes he grew impatient, considered setting up traps all around the barricade. But the fear of filling the air for miles around with the smell of meat, attracting more corpses than he could handle, always convinced him otherwise. The last thing he wanted was a feeding frenzy.

One lucky winner per day. That was the limit.

Except he hadn't gotten lucky yet. No Danielle.

With a mixture of disappointment and relief, he finished his security check and headed back to the house. In the kitchen he scrubbed his hands, his wrists, his forearms all the way up to his raw elbows, scrubbing sadistically with soap and peroxide until there was no trace of the sticky feeling the corpse had left where it grabbed him.

His head felt clearer now, his throat less tender, so perhaps the Sudafed had done some good after all. He rubbed his eyes, and the bloodshot veins scratched against the eyelids. No monsters in the yard, which meant he could put sleep back on the agenda.

Upstairs, he replaced the Glock and bat in the closet. He wondered what the rest of Joan Roark's day would be like while he slept. He imagined her, too, crashing in bed, perhaps with a nice dose of Valium.

With a pang of conscience, he realised that he hadn't reported back to Benjamin.

Shit.

Marco looked longingly down the hall towards the bedroom. The doorway beckoned, dark inside, the shades drawn, and he could almost feel the foam mattress conforming to his exhausted body. But he also knew that his friend was probably desperate for his call. The Montana trip had been longer than most others, and by now poor Ben might be thinking the worst – that Marco's stripped bones were lying somewhere on a nameless mountain.

A quick check-in, that's all, Marco decided. *Hello, my guts weren't eaten, goodbye.*

In the office he booted up the computer and waited for the satellite to locate a signal. Sometimes it took long minutes before the dish on the roof found a signal still reachable from the West, but today he got lucky; by the time he'd settled in his chair, the webcam window had opened and Benjamin's phone line was ringing on the speaker.

Marco waited. The phone continued to ring. One minute, then two. He checked the time. Almost nine – he'd never had trouble calling this early before. Benjamin usually picked up fast, or, when he wasn't home, the calls forwarded to his cell. Ben lived alone in Pittsburgh. His wife Trish – Danielle's sister – had died during the Resurrection. Badly. Corpses had wrestled Trish from an Evac truck fleeing Scottsdale as Ben watched, screaming, restrained by Evac soldiers. He'd been relocated to Pennsylvania and languished for three years in Survivor Housing – state-subsidised tenements built by the Garrett administration to handle the influx of jobless evacuees. Finally, last spring, Ben had been able to afford his own house on the city outskirts. Bought and paid for with 'Corpse Cash', as Ben called it. Income from twenty-six contracts.

Actually, Andrew Roark made twenty-seven.

The phone rang again. Fidgeting, Marco longed for the days before the Resurrection when an unanswered phone didn't seem sinister. Now you never knew *what* the hell to think.

Could be Benjamin was just in the shower, or the can.

Sure. Or maybe there's been a new outbreak of the Resurrection, Marco thought, tensing. *And now the other half of America is fucked, too.*

The phone rang another fourteen times. Marco counted.

Each ring shook his nerves a little harder, and he began to feel his flu symptoms battling back. The sweat, the pressure behind his eyes. *Come on, Ben.*

Then a jarring click, and Benjamin picked up.

His face popped immediately on screen, close, soft-skinned and red, wearing the black wire-rimmed glasses that made him look like a beatnik poet. Ben was an artist, a painter. He'd shaved his head since Marco saw him last; he ran a hand over his scalp of blond stubble.

'Jesus, Marco,' he said, shaking his head.

'You had me worried,' Marco scolded. Absurd, but true. The instant he said it, he realised how easily frazzled he was becoming. He definitely needed the upcoming hiatus.

Benjamin's blue eyes widened. 'Fucking jeez, *you* were worried? Yeah, I get it – for two minutes you weren't in total control. Try waiting three *weeks* to hear from you, asshole.'

Both men fell quiet, and Marco sensed that Benjamin felt as shitty as he did.

'Sorry,' Marco said. 'That was a bad hello.'

Benjamin shrugged. 'It's okay, man, sorry too. I just didn't hear from you, that's all.' He leaned back, hands behind his head, studying Marco. 'You lost more weight.'

'Yeah, probably.'

'Not good, man. You have to eat.'

'Can you not sound like my grandmother?'

Benjamin frowned. 'I'm serious, Marco. You look like a prisoner of war. Like that guy Rambo pulls out of the water cage in *First Blood, Part II.*'

Marco laughed. He and Benjamin were the same age, but different in so many regards.

'Whatever you just said makes me glad I never watched movies,' Marco retorted. 'But okay, point taken – I promise I'll eat a few more Power Bars.'

He slowed as he spoke, noticing Benjamin's gaze dart somewhere off screen. And then he realised that something actually *was* wrong – he'd been right to worry. He hadn't noticed it at first, but Benjamin's face seemed stiffer than normal, the lines at the corner of his eyes longer.

Tension.

'Everything okay?' Marco asked.

'Yeah, man.' But Marco could hear the distraction in his voice.

'Okay then,' Marco said. 'The Roark funds cleared, right?'

This time he was certain Benjamin flinched. 'Yeah, no problems with that.'

Too quick, too vague. Ben was always jumpy about the money – he didn't report the income, since neither he nor Marco actually knew if what they were doing was legal – but not like this. Marco watched as Benjamin briskly scratched the back of his head.

'So how was Montana?' Benjamin asked. 'I assume Roark's done.'

'If you call it that,' Marco said. 'The trip was hard. I had trouble finding him – three different stakeouts. It's like that old expression about lost things, they're always in the last place you look. Plus it rained the whole way back, and now

I'm sick. The end. You can have the details tomorrow. Right now, I really just want to crash into a nice, soft bed.'

He cleared his throat, watching Benjamin fidget. Okay. Enough with the guessing game. 'So how about it, Ben – can you please just get the nerve up and tell me what's wrong?'

Benjamin froze, his mouth open. Then he sighed. 'Shit,' he said.

Over the speaker Marco heard a murmur. Voices.

People. There with Benjamin.

Marco's index finger flew to the power button and hovered. 'Friends over for coffee?' he asked. He smiled bitterly.

Benjamin held his palm up. 'Relax, Marco,' he said, 'it's nothing bad – I took care of it. It's just some men here to talk to you, that's all. New clients.'

'New clients don't come talk to us. You go talk to them.' Marco swallowed and squeezed the sides of his keyboard. He closed his eyes. 'Goddamn it, Ben.'

Benjamin sat up straight, defiant. 'I didn't *invite* them here, for Christ's sake. They found out about us. About you. Come on, man, you think I want house calls?' He shook his head and settled back. 'They've been here a whole week. Almost broke down the door to get in. I explained how it works . . . how I never know when the hell you're due back. So they just stayed here – in my *house* – and waited for you. I didn't have a choice.'

He pointed a thumb off screen. 'You'll see why when you meet Mr Personality here. And why I was going fucking nuts when you finally rang.'

Marco stiffened. 'Don't put anyone else on, Benjamin.'

'Marco, man, you don't get it.' Benjamin's face loomed larger. 'I love you and all, but I *don't . . . have . . . a choice*.' He reached for the cam and twisted it. On Marco's screen, the camera panned sideways around Benjamin's cluttered art studio. A glimpse of walls splashed with colourful, Pollock-type paintings, white tarps, free-standing easels . . .

Men in black riot gear, holding guns.

'Oh,' Marco said. Immediately he understood.

Another set of rules was about to get handed down.

THE BALLARD CONTRACT

3.1

The image on Marco's screen convulsed as if broadcasting an earthquake. Alarmed, he scrambled from his chair and knocked his webcam up to face the ceiling. He had no idea who was about to pop up on his desktop – but goddamn if *they* were going to see *him.*

The image settled, and in the frame appeared a pair of liver-spotted hands, folded, resting on Benjamin's studio table. Seconds later the camera shifted again, and someone adjusted a light, and there Marco saw a man in his late fifties, seated at the table.

The stranger was attired in a blue dress shirt with a white collar – the telltale wardrobe of an asshole, in Marco's experience. The man's hair was white as well, mid-length, combed behind his ears; his eyes were an inch too far apart, his mouth too wide for his jutting jaw. He looked vaguely like a piranha. Marco instinctively disliked him.

'Henry Marco,' the man said, pronouncing each syllable and letter precisely. His voice was cool and soft, almost ladylike. 'Are you there?'

Marco cringed. He hadn't heard his full name in years, not since Danielle. Even Benjamin shunned it, by some unspoken agreement between them.

'Yes,' Marco answered. He coughed.

The man squinted at the screen. 'Hiding? No need,

Doctor Marco. If you're worried about being identified, it's too late for that. I have over a dozen photos of you already in a dossier right in front of me. More photos, in fact, than I have of my wife.'

Marco waited, reluctant to talk. Not without a better grasp of what was going on here. The man obviously knew his name, knew enough to track him to Benjamin's studio. Had even called him *doctor*. But Marco wasn't about to get bluffed into revealing anything unnecessary. Nothing more than what the man had already deduced on his own.

As if reading Marco's thoughts, the white-haired man held up a small yellowed photo by the corner. Marco saw himself in a tuxedo. He recognised the event. A fundraiser for the American Association of Neurologists, a year before the Resurrection.

'You see, Doctor Marco, you're not as mysterious as you think,' the man said. 'And I always come prepared to class. Shall we compare notes? Henry Carson Marco, born 1976, Philadelphia, to Albert and Caroline Marco.' The man's eyes were fixed to the camera, citing details apparently from memory. If he read from a paper off-screen, he hid it well.

The man continued. 'The year 2006, graduated Weill Medical College, Neurology and Neuroscience Department, entered your residency at Cedars-Sinai Hospital in Los Angeles. The year 2010, married actress Danielle Pierce—'

'You can stop,' Marco interrupted. 'I get the point.'

'Yes? Then show yourself, and let's introduce ourselves like polite adults.'

'You go ahead,' said Marco. 'I'll just listen for a while.'

The man shrugged. 'However you'd like. I suppose it is my turn, in fairness, since I know your name. Mine is Owen Osbourne, Interim Director of the Office of Operations Coordination. We . . .' He gestured with his head to the left, then the right, acknowledging the others in the room as his hands remained folded on the table. '. . . We represent the Department of Homeland Security.'

Marco had perked up at the introduction. He recognised the man's name. Owen Osbourne had been one of the prominent New Republicans, back when the party first gained traction. *I knew you were an asshole.* 'Those men with you,' Marco asked. 'Are they police?'

The man shook his head. 'Federal officers, under my command.'

'Am I in trouble?' Marco asked.

The man – Osbourne – regarded Marco, not even blinking. The thumbs of his interlocked hands tapped against each other slowly, five or six times. 'I've heard,' Osbourne said finally, 'that people refer to you as the "Zombie Hitman".'

The non sequitur annoyed Marco. 'You didn't answer me. Am I in trouble?'

'Doctor Marco. If you're pushing for an answer now, then "yes and no" is the best you'll get.' Osbourne spoke as if admonishing a child. His nostrils twitched, and he exhaled. When he resumed, his voice had cooled again. 'So, please. My curiosity first, then yours. Let's back up, can we? I apologise for showing off – that heavy-handed reading of your biography. And referring to your wife was perhaps a low blow.'

Marco ignored the man's last statement. 'Fine. So what are you curious about?'

'I'm curious about the Zombie Hitman.'

Jesus, Marco thought. Was that really what people were calling him in the Safe States? How awful. Knowing Benjamin, the name was probably something he'd cooked up to help sell their services. Something 'catchy', Ben would say. 'Marketing.' Marco could protest, but he really had no control over what tactics Benjamin used to obtain leads.

'How did you hear about me?' he asked Osbourne.

Osbourne unclasped his hands and lay them flat on the table. He leaned towards the camera and spoke intently. '*Doctor Marco.* I'm attempting to be polite – under the pretence that this is a friendly conversation, which, as intelligent men, we both know is untrue. So, for a moment, let me set the pretence aside. If you ask *one* more question before answering one of mine, I'll have your friend Mr Ostroff here sent to prison.'

The threat echoed in Marco's mind as he studied the ugly man on his screen.

Osbourne waited. There was no emotion in his eyes.

Like a piranha, Marco thought again. *Deciding when to attack.*

3.2

From off screen Marco heard Benjamin.

'Come on, man,' Ben urged, addressing Osbourne. 'We're not doing anything wrong. Marco, just talk to the guy. He wants to use us. He told me.'

Marco sighed and hung his head, consulting the dull hardwood floor. Maybe he was getting defensive for no good reason. Maybe Benjamin was right.

Just talk to the guy. See what's up.

'All right,' he decided. 'Fine, then. How can I help you today?'

Osbourne settled back. 'Well. Please begin by clarifying what you do.'

'The short answer?' Marco asked, not bothering to hide his impatience. Why the interrogation if this asshole already knew?

Because he knows less than he's letting on. So stick to the basics. No harm in that.

'There are forty million corpses roaming the Evacuated States,' Marco began. 'Everybody who didn't make it out during the Evacuation. And they were all once somebody's mom or dad or sweetheart or best friend. So the survivors – the loved ones in the Safe States – contact me.'

'For what purpose?'

Asshole, thought Marco. 'I return the corpses.'

Osbourne looked at him quizzically. 'Return them?'

'To the dead. To the *really* dead.'

'Kill them again, you mean,' stated Osbourne. 'And people *want* you to do this? To loved ones?'

Marco shrugged. 'It's better than knowing Grandma Bessy is out here, stumbling around in some kind of nightmare, alone, and rotting, and hungry for raw meat – suffering. Unable to enter heaven, maybe, if you believe that. So compassion and concern are part of it. And then there's closure. The well-defined ending. Same reason people go to wakes and funerals. Seeing the coffin – knowing it's really over – allows them to move on.'

Osbourne nodded. 'And so Mr Ostroff finds these people living in the Safe States and offers them your services. How do you know where to find them?'

'Almost everybody's lost somebody. Ben just asks around, discreetly.' Marco studied Osbourne's face. The man had no wrinkles on his forehead, no creases. The unnatural facade of cosmetic surgery. Above the mouth, the cheeks were pulled too tight.

And who did you lose? Marco wondered.

'Yes,' Osbourne said, giving nothing away. 'But what I meant was, how do you know where to find the *corpses* you've been contracted for? They could be anywhere.'

'Not really.'

'What do you mean by that?'

'The world is a very big place,' Marco said. 'But people

live small lives. Most of us spend ninety per cent of our time in four or five locations – home, work, the park near our house, our favourite bar. The geography is hard-wired into us, so those are the places I start with. Give a corpse time, it'll usually show up where it would go normally. So I go there, too. Except . . .' Marco paused. 'Sometimes they don't show, and then it gets a little trickier. Then you have to consider *emotional* geography.'

'Emotional geography?'

'Locations with sentimental value,' Marco continued. 'Emotion strengthens the hard-wiring. Again, the home is usually top of the list, but beyond there, it's places like, say, the beach where you proposed to your wife, or the resort where you honeymooned. The hospital where your first kid was born. Like I said, someplace that meant something to you. I find out all I can about each target from the client – the loved one, I mean – and then I go hunting.'

Osbourne shifted in his seat and crossed his legs, one knee neatly below the other. 'Are you saying,' he asked, 'that the dead remember their lives?'

'In a sense. I wouldn't say it's a conscious recall. The human brain is complex – memories of things that happen to us are stored in the neocortex, but there's strong evidence of an association process taking place first in the limbic system—'

'Doctor Marco,' interrupted Osbourne. 'Now you're the one showing off. Please, without the medical terminology.'

'Sorry. Basically, our memories are stored in the higher section of our brain, the part that only more evolved mammals like humans have. But experiences in our lives that take place under strong emotion are tagged before they're stored, by a more primitive part of our brain – a part that predates our evolution, back to the lower animals. This primitive brain is a pretty scary place. Aggression, rage, hunger . . . all the basic survival instincts originate here. A resurrected corpse seems to have lost function of its higher brain, and now it's being governed by the primitive brain. Ever heard of Dudley and Stephens?'

Osbourne raised an eyebrow. 'No.'

'Cannibals. A big criminal case in the late 1800s, in England,' Marco explained. 'Three men in a lifeboat after a shipwreck, facing starvation, killed and ate the cabin boy. What happened was that their malnourished bodies conserved energy by shutting down the higher brain, then operated out of the lower brain. The reptilian brain, it's often called. Evolved functions, like ethics and compassion, went right out the window. The men's reptilian brains saw a simple choice – eat a boy, or die. So they ate. These corpses aren't much different.'

'Interesting. But I'm waiting to hear how their memories work.'

'Well, there's clearly still a little juice – bioelectricity, that is – trickling between the brain systems. Barely, but there must be. So that wire between the reptilian brain and the higher brain is still live, and now and then a few lights go on. Remember, these things are dead, but there's still a trillion megabytes of data stored in the cells of their brains, a lifetime of information. So maybe they see a quick highlight reel, and they just follow the pretty pictures, out of instinct. Maybe they *want* to feel alive again.'

The corner of Osbourne's lip tensed, and Marco thought he might smile. But he didn't. Instead he waved his hand, and an officer appeared on the screen to place a glass of water on the table. Osbourne raised it and sipped, swishing the water in his mouth. When he finished, he ran a finger along his lower lip to wipe away an excess drop.

Then he folded his hands again.

'Thank you, Doctor Marco,' he said curtly. 'That was

informative. As I said earlier, my curiosity, then yours. We've now reached your turn. So. Beginning with your first question, you are not in trouble, provided you remain as helpful as you've been.'

'You want to hire me,' Marco guessed.

'Yes,' conceded Osbourne. 'I've discussed finances already with Mr Ostroff. A generous contract, and the income would be exempt from the usual Survivor Taxes.'

'Wow. Are you sure you can afford that?'

The director ignored him. 'What I did *not* tell Mr Ostroff are the mission details.'

'Which are?'

Osbourne's grey eyes squared off with the camera. 'I'd be happy to tell you, Doctor. But I won't tell it to your ceiling. Please adjust your camera so that I may see you.'

Damn. Marco bent his neck, cracking the joints. What the hell. He supposed it didn't matter. He reached and lowered the cam back to himself. Osbourne nodded.

'Much better. I dislike speaking into a void.'

Marco half laughed. 'You still are.'

'Perhaps,' Osbourne said, undeterred. 'You certainly do look sicklier than your photos. The conditions there must be hard on you.'

'Best shape of my life. Let's talk details.'

'Such a trooper. Very well, the details. I need you to find a person – a corpse – on the West Coast. Sarsgard, California. I assume you travel wherever required?'

California. Marco's stomach churned. *Shit.* He hadn't been back to Cally in three years. He wasn't sure his heart could handle another trip there.

'Yes,' he said without enthusiasm. 'I travel. I assume Benjamin factored that into the price he gave you.'

Osbourne waved a hand dismissively. 'Yes, yes. I'm not here to haggle.'

'Good, then. California will take time. The more populated the area, the more careful I get. The slower I go.' Marco rubbed his throat, exhausted from all the talk, as if the mere mention of California had overworked him. 'Look,' he concluded. 'You heard my story. Family and friends, all that. So then – who exactly is the "loved" one I'm supposed to put a bullet in for the US Department of Homeland Security? Something tells me it's not Grandma Bessy.'

'Very perceptive of you,' Osbourne remarked. 'No grandmothers. You're looking for a man. A doctor by the name of Roger Terrence Ballard.'

Marco stiffened.

Osbourne studied him a moment, then continued. 'I'll assume you want to know everything I know. This Doctor Ballard was last seen at a medical prison centre in Sarsgard, the week after the outbreak. The centre had been overrun by then, the inmates all resurrected, but radio reports indicated that a small number of survivors, Doctor Ballard included, had barricaded themselves into a guard room. A subsequent rescue mission by Evacuation forces failed, with unfortunate casualties – Doctor Ballard received a severe bite wound on the arm, in fact, and the rescue team was unable to reach his position to extract him. They were forced to retreat, leaving him behind as a loss. Bites are one hundred per cent fatal, of course, but quite frankly we don't know if he resurrected, or if he was devoured before he had the chance. But, just to be safe, I'd like to contract the "Zombie Hitman" to go in for a look.'

Marco's mouth was sour, the bad aftertaste of old Tang. He'd missed half of what Osbourne had told him, unable to absorb it, his mind busy regurgitating a single thought.

Roger Ballard.

Roger Ballard.

'I know him,' Marco said flatly.

Osbourne nodded. 'Yes,' he said. 'I know you do.'

3.3

'Is that why you came to me?' Marco asked. 'Because I knew Roger?'

Director Osbourne frowned. 'I've come to you, Doctor, because you know how to find corpses. That's your expertise. It was a happy coincidence that Ballard's name showed up during your background check. I presume your personal knowledge of him will be an advantage.'

'You saw Roger's name in my file, and you thought it would make me *want* to help you? Jesus. Are you as loyal to your friends?'

'I thought it might make you more useful,' Osbourne said without blinking. 'But to your point, Doctor Marco, you yourself said that this is an act of mercy – *compassion* – for those people you care about.'

Marco snorted. 'Don't bullshit me. You don't care a damn about Roger. That's not what's behind this. So what is it then? What reason?'

'A matter of national security.'

'Yeah? And what does that mean?'

'Why should that matter to you, Doctor Marco? You're a professional-for-hire.'

'It matters to me. I don't take every job offer.'

'You're referring to the Giancomo contract. A mob boss ordering hits on corpses of an enemy family, purely out of spite. You turned him down last year.'

'Fuck you,' Marco barked. His forehead tingled with fever. 'I guess you do know everything, right?'

'I told you at the beginning, Doctor. I come to class prepared. And, as a matter of fact, I also brought something for show and tell. Perhaps you'll find this motivating.' Osbourne pushed his chair back from the table, and another man's arm reached into the frame. On the blue sleeve a patch was visible – DHS in stitched yellow letters.

Marco heard four or five faint mouse clicks, and the window on his screen went black. A second later it lit up again. The view had entirely changed.

What he saw now was grainy video of a prison cell block, black and white, silent, captured by a security camera from a mount on the top floor. To the right stretched a grated walkway along a row of darkened open cells, overlooking an identical balcony on the floor below and, underneath that, a long rectangular mezzanine. Hundreds of slow-moving prisoners in charcoal jumpsuits milled about in the open area, wandering in and out of doorways.

'Sarsgard Medical Prison, twelfth of March 2014, eight days post-outbreak,' Osbourne's voice intoned over the video. 'Footage retrieved from the central security system during the failed rescue attempt. I thought you might be interested in one of the highlights.'

Marco concentrated on the prisoners. Corpses. Their faces were bleached, featureless at this distance, but Marco recognised the herky-jerky gait, the slight sideways loll of their heads.

Exhaling, he took in the scene. Torn-open bodies of guards and convicts littered the floor, ripped livers and intestines flung about like trash. Trails of shining black liquid painted the floors. He could almost smell the piss, the shit, the stench of infection and rot. In corners around the mezzanine, the dead huddled like gangs, squatting, crawling over one another to pull meat from some carcass they'd dragged aside. Thank god for lack of audio, omitting the crunch of gnawed bones and the smacking of moist mouths spilled over with blood.

Along one wall Marco saw a pair of uniformed legs – a guard, still alive under a pile of feeding corpses, fighting, kicking for his freedom – convulse and stiffen as a dark stain spread from his crotch.

Marco shifted in his chair. He hadn't seen a death like that in years. At least nowadays the corpses had run out of people to eat in the Evacuated States.

Well, almost. They still have me.

From the far end of the corridor, a commotion captured Marco's attention. The door to a stairwell flung open, and out onto the balcony scrambled three men. Alive.

'Three brave heroes,' Osbourne said.

The men rushed fifty yards forwards along the walkway, towards the camera. Two of the men were uniformed soldiers, their chests thick with bulletproof vests, faces hidden behind Plexiglas riot masks; they swung heavy-looking automatic rifles haphazardly as they ran. The third man looked different – spectacles, torn white shirt, light pants. Black-spotted bandaging swaddled his left arm. The men abruptly stopped just feet from the camera.

The spectacled man's mouth opened in horror.

'Roger,' Marco said. He wasn't surprised. Of course he'd expected this – why else the video? Still, he couldn't stop a sick weight from rolling over in his stomach.

'Yes,' Osbourne said simply.

The three men reacted to something off camera, something ahead of them on the walk; they tripped backwards two or three steps then turned and bolted in the direction they'd come. But the stairwell door batted open before they could reach it, and corpses poured out. The dead jammed the walkway, clambering towards the men.

Roger and the guards wheeled once more, knocking into one another, comedic and horrifying at the same time. Panicking. At the bottom of the video screen, an out-of-focus shadow moved into frame, approaching from underneath the camera.

Heads. Shoulders.

More corpses, cutting off the other end of the walkway.

The men were boxed in.

The first soldier faced the onslaught of dead prisoners from the stairwell. He held his gun like a baseball bat, a two-handed grip on the barrel. Marco understood. Out of ammo. The soldier hauled his gun back and stepped into his swing; the butt of the rifle connected squarely with the first corpse in the pack, a giant bald convict with a bulging tattooed scalp and an eyeball dangling halfway down its cheek. The blow tore the corpse's lower jaw clean off, not high enough for a kill; molars and black drool pumped from the wound as the corpse grabbed the soldier with two huge hands.

The massive corpse hugged the writhing man to its chest and bit at his face; its upper teeth glanced off the Plexiglas mask, but the soldier was doomed. In seconds the mass of other corpses caught up, surrounded him, tore at his legs and arms. Marco winced as a long-haired naked prisoner, shoulders chiselled with muscle, crunched down on the back of the soldier's unprotected neck. Blood spurted, showering the mob.

'We suffered significant casualties,' Osbourne commented. 'In fact, we now use this particular Evac as a negative model in training exercises. Conservation of ammunition being a point of emphasis. "One brain, one bullet", the new motto goes.'

Marco didn't answer. He watched Roger Ballard and the remaining soldier race along the balcony, pulling on cell doors, hoping to find one they could duck into and slam shut behind them. But no luck. The doors were locked open.

The walls of corpses closed in from both ends. Only a

few yards away. Terrified, the soldier held his gun out in front, arms straight, as if he could push back the attack.

Ballard's mouth moved, yelling out to the soldier. The man didn't respond.

Ballard shouted one last time, then broke towards the balcony railing. A hundred grey, putrid hands reached for him as he vaulted over the rail with a wild kick of his legs, heels in the air, the tatters of his white shirt fluttering in the air behind him.

Then gone. Disappeared.

The drop must have been thirty, forty feet. Wherever he landed – alive, or twisted and broken on the concrete below – he'd vanished from view of the camera.

The lone soldier stared at the railing where Ballard had gone over. The man's shoulders rocked forward, then back, then forward again, indecisive. By the time he decided, he was already dead. Just as he lunged towards the edge of the walkway, the corpses swarmed in from the left and the right, swallowing him into their mass. Their weight was crushing, pressing him from all angles; he couldn't even struggle. He stood in place as if caught in a vice, pinned straight up, his screaming face hidden behind his mask, until moments later his body exploded in a frenzy of teeth and clawing nails. Shreds of uniform and skin rained over the monsters like confetti. Blood like fireworks.

And corpses – everywhere now, every balcony, hundreds more than before. Gore-soaked, surging in the mezzanine, driven mad by the kill.

The prison riot from hell.

Marco shuddered. The video mercifully disappeared from the screen, and the reappearance of Osbourne's ugly face was pleasant by comparison.

'Call me when you get there,' Osbourne said.

3·4

The sun had shifted in the sky behind Marco, entering through a different window in his study and casting a glare across the computer screen. Now the bottom half of Osbourne's face was too bright to be seen clearly. Only his eyes appeared sharp, pointed at Marco. Marco stared back. The asshole was challenging him.

A few seconds passed. Finally Marco sniffed, clearing the congestion in his nose. 'Thanks for the nice movie,' he said. 'But what even makes you think I can do this? If a full Evacuation Squad couldn't get out of there alive?'

'For starters, Doctor Ballard may not still be there,' Osbourne said. His voice was calm now, reassuring, once again reminding Marco of a parent addressing a child. 'He may have wandered off, just as you suggested. Emotional geography, correct?'

'Not if he's trapped in there. In a prison.'

'The entire facility was a breach by the end, a large hole in the perimeter. He could easily have exited. But if not, don't sell yourself short, Doctor Marco. You've been surviving quite well for years out there yourself. You must have a few tricks for evading millions of corpses. Or at least excellent luck. Either way, you have experience that we admittedly do not.'

'Yeah, I'm a real expert.'

Osbourne shrugged. 'You'll have help, of course.'

Marco stopped mid-breath. 'Help? As in?'

'Military, Doctor Marco. Special Forces, RRU – Resurrection Resistance Unit. Even as we speak, I have a team on standby in a secured position, several miles from your home, under orders to rendezvous with you tomorrow and escort you to Sarsgard. They've been surveilling your home for a week now, awaiting your return.'

Motherfucker, thought Marco. Frowning, he pinched the missing notch on his left earlobe, the old dog-bite injury, until he realised that Osbourne was watching. He lowered his hand. Was he being set up? Some kind of trick, maybe? Catch him off guard, take him into custody without a fight? He doubted he was worth the trouble, but still . . .

'I don't want help,' he said.

'Non-negotiable,' Osbourne stated bluntly. 'They're going with you.'

'They're going *without* me. I'm not taking the job.'

Osbourne scoffed. 'Nonsense. You are essential.'

'And what exactly gives you that delusion?'

'If Ballard is *not* still in that prison, then you are indeed essential. Roger Ballard was a very private man, with no family or friends on record. As far as my sources indicate, you were his closest acquaintance. If his corpse has escaped and wandered off to some location with personal meaning, then your insights into his character will guide us.'

Marco laughed. 'You think I have insight into Roger? Then you really *don't* know shit.'

'You're proving my point, Doctor. I need you to locate the Ballard corpse. If you're concerned about the mission's personal nature, you needn't pull the trigger yourself. The RRU will handle everything once Ballard is found. They have specific orders, and know what to do.'

'But you won't tell me *why*.'

Osbourne sat, motionless as a statue. Even his lips barely moved. 'No.'

'I don't get it . . .' Marco said. 'I don't get why you need Roger returned. And I get nervous when there are things I don't get.' He shook his head. 'I decline your offer.'

A pause. Then Benjamin's disembodied voice startled Marco. He'd forgotten Ben was there, listening to everything. 'Marco, think a second—'

Osbourne cut off him. 'Mr Ostroff,' he commanded, pointing a strict finger without turning his head. His eyes remained on Marco.

Marco heard muttering in the background.

Osbourne resumed. 'Doctor Marco, allow me to be clear. You chose to violate the original Evacuation Order and therefore are no longer a citizen of the United States. Your business across the Safe Border with Mr Ostroff violates the Commerce Security Act, which technically makes you a terrorist and Mr Ostroff a treasonist. It's within my official power to imprison Mr Ostroff – or, unofficially, to make him simply disappear. Yet I'm choosing a more generous option, because I recognise the value of your services. Not just to me here and now, but to the future. I'm not heartless. I realise what you offer survivors, and what it means for our national rebuilding. And I'm willing to allow it, on the side, you understand, not a public endorsement. Hidden funds have been approved for this contract. But don't mistake me – this is not an *offer*. You will do what I say.'

Marco waited. 'Or . . . ?'

Osbourne uncrossed his legs and sighed. 'Doctor, really. I'm attempting to spare us the embarrassment of hard facts. But you seem determined to make it awkward, so . . . You will do what I say, or Mr Ostroff will be shot through the head. You can even watch him die on the camera. If I were required to write a report, I would explain that he had attacked a federal officer during his arrest. But I'm not required to write reports.'

Marco closed his eyes. His stomach lurched. 'Ben, are you still there?'

Was it a bluff? Would they really kill Benjamin . . . ?

'Yeah, man, I'm here.' Benjamin sounded unsure, too. He cleared his throat. 'The money's good, Marco. It's good.'

'And,' said Osborne, 'there's one more thing to consider. Your wife.'

Marco's eyes snapped open, and Osbourne went on. 'You're there looking for her, aren't you, Doctor Marco? That's the reason you stayed behind. And I can tell right now by that haunted look on your face that you haven't found her. How long has it been? Four years? Most of your contracts take, what, a month? Why has this one been so delayed?'

Marco swallowed. 'I don't know,' he said hoarsely. He really didn't. He rubbed his eyes, remembering how tired he was. How good it would feel to be in bed right now, the covers pulled over his head. The darkness.

'Four years,' Osbourne repeated. 'Perhaps you've begun to wonder if you'll ever find her.' He raised an eyebrow, and Marco wanted to bury a fist in that smug face.

A moment later Osbourne continued. 'But I don't mean to be gloom and doom. I'm sure you'll succeed, eventually. Either way, whether you do . . . "return" her, as you called it, or whether one day you decide to abandon the search, then what? You missed the Evacuation Deadline and broke Quarantine, and therefore you can't ever be admitted to the Safe States. You'll simply wander out there, forever, until something eats you, or you become a zombie yourself. Which brings me to a very special incentive. What people call "the icing on the cake".'

Marco had the sense of Osbourne digging through his mind, like a gardener with a fork, turning the soil, each repulsive word wriggling like a worm in the ground. He recoiled from the image. But those words persisted, doing what worms do, aerating the dirt. And he understood that what really repulsed him were the thoughts they unearthed – ideas forming so long in his subconscious, but buried, even as the years wore him away at the surface.

Why has this one been so delayed . . . ?

Four years . . . ?

Perhaps you've begun to wonder . . . ?

He realised that Osbourne was waiting.

'Tell me,' Marco said, surprised at the neediness in his voice.

Osbourne leaned forward, his palms flat on the table in front of him. 'Amnesty.' The director's bony fingers flexed, and he spoke again. 'A free pass into the Safe States when the time comes, when you're ready. Rejoin civilisation, restart your life. With the living.'

Marco cleared his throat. 'Why would you include that? The icing?'

'In case I've misjudged your fondness for Mr Ostroff. In case you don't value his life, or the money. I'm motivating you with one thing I'm certain you do care about. Coming back.'

'I care about Ben. But you're wrong about the last part. It doesn't matter.'

'I think it does, Doctor. I think it matters to you very much. You don't really want to stay out there forever with the dead. But without my help, you're stuck there.'

A chill rippled beneath Marco's damp shirt. Goddamn it, he was cold. And tired. His head barely felt connected to his body, as if his neck had simply let go. He needed more Sudafed, more expired fucking Sudafed that probably didn't work any more.

'I can get you in,' Osbourne said. 'This can all be put behind you.'

Not just the Sudafed. Nothing worked any more. Everything out here was just one big expiration date.

'Find Roger Ballard.' Osbourne's voice washed over him. 'Find him, or Mr Ostroff dies today. Find him, and give yourself a future. That is the truth. Not the offer.'

Marco turned his chair to face the window, and for a moment the view of the Superstition Mountains was gone, and he imagined a glimpse of the ocean instead – the Atlantic, whitecaps churning off the coast of Maine, a rusted red lighthouse, the day he proposed to Danielle on the beach. He wanted to fall asleep, remembering those things.

And then he wanted to wake, just like Joan Roark would wake tomorrow and start over.

'All right,' he said. 'I'll return Roger.'

Osbourne smiled for the first time, his piranha teeth bleached an unnatural white. Marco almost laughed. These days, everyone he met wanted to eat him.

THE CHINESE ASSASSIN

4.1

Kheng Wu – *Ken,* he'd taken to calling himself among Americans – trotted up the trail, hating the Arizona desert heat. Hating himself, too. He'd allowed a year of living in the US to soften him, betrayed by too many workouts in the air-conditioned fitness centre back in Boston. He'd forgotten *this* – this pure and primal punishment, his lungs afire like two ovens, sweat wrenched from him by the outdoor sun. Longingly he recalled the military marches of his youth. Such true tests of endurance. He'd been a volunteer soldier for the People's Republic of China – eager to serve and win honours, to grow beyond the confines of his impoverished village in Qinghai. His brothers had held back, awaiting conscription. But not Wu. At eighteen he'd bid farewell to his uncle and reported to camp in Shenyang; there, for weeks with little sleep and no mercy, he'd slogged steep mountain paths with a fifty-pound pack biting into his shoulders. All the LifeFitness treadmills in America could never match those lessons.

Today, older, thirty-eight, he gritted his teeth and ordered himself up the trail.

Twenty metres to his rear, a small cluster of corpses staggered in pursuit. Sixteen dead men and women; he counted repeatedly, afraid to lose track of a single one, their faces parched almost black like charred bodies from a fire scene. They'd been following him the past twenty minutes, ever since the old campsite on the north side of the Superstitions.

He'd been picking through the smashed canvas tents half buried in the red dirt. Across the parking lot sat the United States military truck – the truck he'd been tracking for days. The Chinese Ministry of State Security had included GPS coordinates in the intelligence dossier, but the given location had been miles away; pinpointing the American RRU team had been more difficult than anticipated. And yet, after all the effort, here was their truck, an old 7-Ton model parked carelessly in the open. Perhaps the Americans had assumed – *typical arrogance*, Wu noted – that nobody was alive on this side of the continent to make stealth necessary.

He'd marked the site as a waypoint on his Droid GPS, then replaced the unit in his daypack. In the far corner of the lot leaned a filthy camper, its front end dug into the ground where a car had unhitched and driven off without it. From inside Wu heard hollow pounding. Someone had trapped the dead within; the door was padlocked, the windows too small to crawl through. The corpses had withstood years inside, rotting. Withering in a makeshift prison, the stifling heat, no food or water. *Remarkable*. Wu often marvelled at the dead's ability to survive.

If 'survive' was the proper word.

As usual, he couldn't help but pity them. He fetched a large rock from a nearby fire pit and hammered at the lock. Fingernails scrabbled at the other side of the door.

When the lock broke apart, Wu retreated a few metres and waited. The door batted open, and almost at once the air surrounding the trailer soured. His nostrils stung. He hoped for the hundredth time that the briefing he'd been given last month by MSS was correct – an assurance that the infection was not airborne. But perhaps . . . at this close distance . . .?

Before he could second-guess himself, a corpse lurched from the dark interior, teetering onto the top step. It was male, naked and grotesque; the head of its penis had pooled with rotten blood and bulged between the thighs like a horrible purple gourd. Its stomach was a shiny hard balloon, full of gas, distended to the point of almost bursting.

Wu ran his fingertips along the rounded handles of the two deer-horn knives on his belt, ready to draw if necessary. The deer-horns – *lujiaodao*, in his language – were still his most trusted weapons. He'd mastered them in Beijing; his first year in MSS had included an intense study of the Baguazhang martial arts. The double blades curved around his fists like two razor-sharp crescent moons – perfect for combat at close quarters, especially if surrounded, enabling him to swing in graceful circles and slice apart the necks of multiple attackers at once.

He'd been warned against using traditional weaponry for this mission. Flesh damage did nothing to stop the resurrected dead; by now everyone knew that the brain itself must be decommissioned. A bullet to the head. On Wu's back was a Chinese AK rifle, supplied by MSS, which he had no intention of using. The cold feel of the knife handles was enough to put him at ease; the blades could disable a corpse without causing it more harm than required.

The naked male corpse locked eyes on him.

The corpse snorted once, a wet sound like dislodged phlegm, followed by a burp of black goo onto its chin. Slowly it descended the steps towards Wu. Its stiff, uncooperative legs tilted it off balance, nearly pitching it onto its face. Before it reached bottom, another brittle figure emerged from the doorway – a female corpse in a muddy bikini top and tattered shorts. Its scalp dangled in meaty strips from the exposed skull, and remnants of red braided hair, thick like filthy ropes, swung side to side as it, too, hobbled down the steps.

Wu stepped back again, ready to turn and leave, hike back to his own sparse camp in the mountains. The shambling corpses were no real danger. At a brisk pace he could lose them in minutes. But another motion from the trailer stopped him. A third corpse – another male, and then behind it a fourth and a fifth filed out. The trailer had been packed full, and Wu experienced a sharp flashing vision of his own living quarters as a boy. His four brothers and two sisters, asleep with tangled limbs on the rough wooden floor of his uncle Bao Zhi's shack. The rain at night tittering on the red and white metal roof above – a sheet of uncut aluminium, imprinted with Coca-Cola logos, stolen from a shipment to the bottling plant in Sichuan.

Again Wu felt a twinge of sympathy for the dead campers.

The first corpse had drawn too close now, near enough so that Wu could hear its teeth clicking. The body's navel protruded obscenely, popped outward by the pressure of gases swelling within the gut. Unrattled, Wu jogged ten steps in reverse, his eyes still on the trailer. Even more corpses than before. Sixteen total.

Still he felt unthreatened, confident in his ability to evade as long as the dead remained in a group. Wu wasn't like the American soldiers he'd been assigned to track; they were fools, too quick with their rifles, popping off with enthusiasm at every corpse they encountered. A day earlier he'd observed them in their truck, whooping and hollering as they'd shot corpses for sport, like some hideous safari. The sight had disgusted him. A dishonour to the dead.

And a waste of bullets. *But that is the American way*, Wu had thought harshly.

Squander what you have, until everything is gone.

He'd be glad to return home to China after the mission. Since last summer he'd been embedded in the Safe States – a sleeper agent on the East Coast, awaiting unspecified orders from Beijing. He knew never to press for details. America was in disarray, and a political firefight was mounting; he'd assumed MSS wanted him near the chaos, his skills available if some unforeseen need arose. For restless months he'd lingered, wondering how he might be deployed – surveillance? assassination? – but Beijing had remained frustratingly silent.

And so he'd endured. He'd taken up residence in the former garment district of Boston's Chinatown, renting a one-room apartment in a converted hosiery factory. He knew no one, lived quietly. In the mornings he trained alone at the Boston Sports Club; in the afternoons he enjoyed meditations in the bamboo and rock gardens at the Chinatown Gate, or strolled through bustling markets, or browsed quaint, tea-scented shops. The proprietors intrigued him – descendants of poor Chinese sojourners, he imagined, crossing the oceans a hundred years ago. America had been their dream. Now the dream was shattered, and Wu wondered how many Chinese Americans longed secretly for a return to the now-thriving homeland.

The thought saddened him.

His own immigration to America had been faked with surprising ease. For all the New Republican tough talk, the Safe States' international borders were soft and weak. The watchdogs were distracted. Too many eyes on the Mississippi strongwall, hypervigilant against the dead menace staring back across the Mississippi River. One set of falsified documents and a bribed INS official, and Kenny Wu joined the payroll of Green Solar, a Boston manufacturer of solar energy modules. Green Solar had partnered with China before the Resurrection to build a photovoltaic plant in Mongolia; now

MSS had the executive board under its control, and a dummy position had been effortlessly arranged for Wu in the New England office.

He never once visited Green Solar in Boston; no questions were asked. He followed the business through press releases, watching as the States scrambled for new energy options; the oil trade here was hugely compromised, with Texas under the Quarantine and the Middle East finally shaking off its American oppressor. Wu relished the American downfall – the anguish, the confusion, the desperation sweetening as the Chinese economy vaulted to the top of the world. He'd savoured the anxious looks on white faces in the cobbled Boston streets. *How could this happen to us?* they seemed to ask. *To other people, yes. To other countries. But not to us.*

You had your time, he wanted to tell them. *Now it's our turn.*

Finally, last month, Beijing had transmitted its orders. The mission was far more glorious than Wu could have expected; his heart bounded as he'd decoded the brief from his Droid. Two days later he'd entered Canada through New York. Even here, at the top of the Safe States, the borders were closed indefinitely to Americans; all roads north had been sealed off using massive cargo containers from the shipping yards, each the size of a truck trailer, loaded with cement and stacked two high. But another well-placed bribe had afforded Wu a ride on a police boat across the tip of silent Lake Erie, late past midnight, with the fearsome Niagara Falls a whisper in the distance. From there he'd trekked west, then south into the Evacuated States; the mountainous forest below Calgary had pressed his survival skills to the limit, across a vast obstacle course of sheer cliffs and unending trees that the Canadians saw no need to guard. At last, over the border again, he'd hot-wired a Pontiac and motored the remaining miles to Arizona. When the Superstition Mountains grew large on the horizon, he'd ditched the car; the loud engine threatened to forewarn the enemy as he travelled the lone highway towards the GPS location.

Now, poised here at the base of the Superstitions, these thoughts about the Americans had given Wu his idea. The enemy's camp was located high in the mountains as well, a mile beyond his own. He'd studied them at sunrise that morning from a hidden point along the ridgeline. Five soldiers. Two dark-skinned men, three whites, among them a muscular man with silver-stubbled cheeks. *Grey Beard,* Wu had dubbed him, and he appeared to be in command. Wu didn't know their actual names. The names did not matter. Now that he'd at last located the American team after weeks of hard tracking – during which he'd half starved for lack of proper supplies, burrowing and sleeping in holes under boulders like a mangy desert fox – Wu was more than ready to complete this first stage of the mission.

Exterminate the Americans. Then move on to his next target.

Doctor Henry Marco.

'Hey,' Wu said to the nearest corpse. '*Gen wo zou.*'

Come with me.

4.2

The dead male's eyes widened, pink and veiny. From twenty paces away it staggered towards Wu, one skeletal hand outstretched – or not quite a hand. A thumb and four mangled nubs where the fingers had been bitten off. Wu turned, satisfied the corpse would follow, and jogged ten steps towards the entrance of the mountain trail. He paused at the trailhead, beside a brown wooden sign etched with faded yellow letters:

LOST DUTCHMAN STATE PARK
TRAIL 53. SIPHON DRAW 1.6 MILE
FLATIRON 2.4 MILE
STAY ON TRAIL. STAY SAFE

Wise advice, Wu thought.

He waved encouragingly to the pack of corpses creeping up behind him.

'*Guhn whu zoe*. Follow me!'

And they did, farther and farther up the trail. All he had to do was keep a safe distance, stop every dozen metres to let them *almost* catch up, keep them interested. Each time he allowed them close enough so that he could see their shrivelled faces hungering for him – black tongues hanging from black mouths like dogs – and then he sped up again, trotting out of reach as behind him the corpses barked grunts of frustration. He'd led them almost two miles now. Once again he found himself admiring the dead. They were persistent. Refusing to accept defeat.

The trail wove upward around a series of switchbacks, cutting between yellow carpets of desert marigolds and the rough ashen stubble of unflowered brittlebrush. A spiny-feathered bird, a roadrunner, dashed across the path into the scrub to the west. Gradually the crags in the surrounding cliff seemed to separate, and a massive peak angled into view, still far above.

'Flatiron', the peak was called, where the Americans had established their lookout onto the valley. Down where Wu stood, the trail dipped into a smooth rock basin, worn by the elements; on the opposite side, the rock sloped upwards again, leading to the base of a long natural staircase – steep, staggered plateaus of stone ascending another few thousand feet to the summit.

Long way to go. Longer than he'd remembered. He drew

a sustained breath and cursed. No lonely workout on the StairMaster in Boston could have prepared him for this.

He heard a pebble kick past his feet and realised he'd lost focus while bemoaning the climb ahead. The corpses had gained ground. With a scowl he resumed his climb, jogging forwards just as the slavering pack staggered into the basin behind him.

Anxious for the first time, he hurried to the start of the Flatiron staircase and skipped up the bottom step. For a hundred metres, all seemed well. The corpses were easy to outpace on the uneven stones, tripping over loose rubble and roots. The naked male flailed its arms and sprawled flat across the path, face first and hard; with an audible pop, its bloated stomach burst against the jutting rock, spraying a gassy jet of blood and slime onto the dirt. But the corpse rose quickly, teeth gnashing, stubborn and starving, its abdomen gaping open like a window into its gut. The other corpses, too – stumbling, rising, rejoining the chase without pause.

Midway up the steps, Wu began to worry. The dead hikers were tireless, moving as well now as they had half an hour ago. Perhaps they were even faster, as if spurred by frustration. He didn't know whether they experienced pain – whether the dead's physiology subjected them to the same fire of lactic acid that consumed living athletes – but, if so, they ignored it.

His own legs, however, burned like torches. He was aware of moving slower, no longer outrunning the corpses. They trailed closer now, overtaking him metre by worrisome metre.

He pressed a hand to his rib and upped his effort. He considered ditching the corpses – abandoning the plan by leaving the trail and cutting across the mountain, where the terrain would be too severe for them to follow. But then he spotted the small white mark on the red cliff wall. It was the scratch he'd made that morning to identify the turnoff point to his camp, about two hundred metres into the cliffs above. He knew the Americans weren't much farther ahead.

Better, then, to finish what he'd started.

He pulled a canteen from his daypack and swigged the last mouthful of water, then refocused on the trail ahead. He recalled Shenyang, those endless marches without pity. The group leaders barking insults at the stragglers. Wu had learned to keep pace, for fear of shame – or punishment. He could do the same now. '*Qian jin*,' he mumbled, wiping his forehead.

March.

March and suffer. Same orders he'd followed his entire life.

4.3

The Arizona sun burned hotter, as if the trail led straight to its core. Wu wet his dehydrated lips with his tongue, tasting salt. His lungs craved more oxygen. With great difficulty he rationed himself on quiet sips of air, no loud panting – sound carried too well along rocky peaks. If the Americans heard his approach up the mountain, the plan would fail.

A minute later, Wu heard the Americans first.

Deep voices, full of curses and laughter, echoed loud and unrestrained between the crags surrounding the unseen enemy camp. Once again, the soldiers had assumed that they were alone in this wilderness, with no need for stealth or caution.

Sensing the advantage, Wu calculated his attack. He knew the trail would wind him around the next ridge, placing him just beneath the American unit. The Americans had pitched their tents on a small plateau, in a crevice ten metres above the path. Staying on the trail, coming from below, was no good for Wu – certain failure. The enemy would have a superior position, with five guns firing down on him and the corpses as they struggled up to the plateau.

Which left only one option. Attack from *above*.

The American camp was close now. Wu could distinguish words from the voices reverberating off the cliff walls.

'Fuck, Nelson, you fuckin' cheat, man!'

'Oh, bullshit I cheat! Just cuz I'm the only one who knows how to play.'

The dead heard the voices, too. The corpse leading the pack – the naked male who had emerged first from the camper – lifted its chin, and Wu watched the bloodshot eyes dart back and forth between the echoes.

A noise like wet bubbling sounded from the corpse's throat, then sputtered. The others hungered forward; the promise of more meat had sparked them anew. Their faces trembled with something like lust, and a guttural moan emanated from the pack, low but growing louder.

Wu tensed. He hoped the Americans were too distracted to hear.

Back to his plan. There was no time to deliberate – not with sixteen corpses closing on him fast. How to reach the camp? He'd have to bypass the trail, find an alternate route that would take him above the Americans. He envisioned the terrain he'd seen while spying on the Americans, then rapidly mapped a course to his right over a rocky outcrop. *Yes.* On the other side, tall brown crags would funnel him and the corpses downwards onto the plateau.

Steep, but workable. Confident again, he turned and scrambled five metres up the hard-packed side slope. He paused there, perspiring, leaning into the mountain, his heel planted against the root of a scrub bush to prevent himself from sliding down.

'This way, this way,' he urged. The dead hikers needed to be redirected from the trail.

Except the corpses didn't listen.

The naked male staggered past Wu on the trail below, not even turning its head. Three more corpses followed, and Wu realised with dismay – and respect – that the dead were more intelligent, more logical, than he'd presumed. They'd lost interest in him, drawn instead to the louder Americans. With a larger population of prey ahead, Wu was no longer worth the effort.

He scooped a handful of pebbles from the ground and slung a dirty cloud at the passing corpses. One rock glanced off the shoulder of a teenage male in a red baseball jersey. The youth rolled its head briefly on its neck but pressed ahead without changing direction. The corpses marched on. Wu hissed a quiet curse. He was losing them up the trail.

No, he thought. Arms out for balance, he stutter-stepped back down the slope, spilling onto the trail and almost knocking into one of the dead stragglers. The female in the bikini growled, snatched at him, but Wu ducked and popped up running, keeping to the path's edge.

In seconds he'd passed half a dozen corpses. The air was humid with their stench, forcing his unsteady abdominal muscles to retch. He spat a mouthful of gummy brown saliva onto the path. A few strides later, he'd overtaken the naked male for the lead – just short of the curve in the trail that would carry them under the Americans.

He swung around in front of the male, an arm's distance apart. His skin tingled. The thrill, the awe of being *this* close to a living corpse was still new, still amazing to him. The dead man's red eyeballs ogled him, and he could only guess how he might appear in the corpse's vision; he had the sensation of being watched from a sacred temple that no man could enter alive.

Up until a month ago, he'd never even seen a corpse first-hand. During the outbreak, he'd been stationed in

Beijing; his initial encounters with the dead had occurred in dark briefing rooms, analysing unsteady news video or satellite photos of mobbed, death-ridden cities. The Resurrection had brought America its comeuppance, and the rest of the world watched. Later, stationed in Boston, he'd kept his television fixed on Fox News, where the dead were nonstop political fodder; the same iconic footage played again and again, rolling on screen as New Republican pundits ranted about the need for vigilance. The videos immortalised episodes from the outbreak – tagged with sensational names like California Z-Day, the Denver Death March, the San Antonio Massacre. 'Mother Reaper' was the most indecent – a shock media favourite, typical American garbage. In it, a dazed young mother stumbles past the news camera, carrying the decapitated body of a five-year-old boy. Ominous groans rumble in the background. *They pulled his head*, the woman says without emotion, and the camera goes black.

Wu had watched it all, mesmerised. Unafraid.

He wasn't afraid now, either.

Without hesitation he hopped forward and slapped the corpse hard on its shoulder, a satisfying smack that left a white handprint on the violet, festering skin. The male huffed in surprise; its lips tightened to a snarl. Wu pulled away and cut back to the edge of the trail.

He paused there, hoping. Slowly, to his relief, the male pivoted and staggered in his direction. The corpses behind it followed, steering the pack around towards Wu.

He had them again.

Just to be certain, he let the first few corpses creep near – too near, arriving in a mass of outstretched arms and gnashing teeth, frustrated, hungry for him . . .

Close enough. Wu stepped away and skirted the path, using the higher slope as safe ground, just beyond the reach of the crowd. On the uneven surface, his ankle buckled, nearly twisting him fatally downwards – *Idiot!* he scolded himself – but he stabilised and moments later had retraced the trail to his chosen attack point. He charged again up the slope.

This time the dead followed, bent at the waist, clambering over the bottommost rocks on all fours, as if they couldn't decide whether to be human or animal. Wu met eyes with a Native American corpse, the roots of its rotten upper teeth exposed where the top lip had been torn away. It slinked towards him, its fingers dragging over the red boulders, leaving black, bloody skid-marks.

Wu wheeled and pumped his legs uphill. His quad muscles screamed like overheated pistons, moments from locking up. He stifled the need to cry out; instead he clenched his teeth and his fists and fought the pain, until at last there was only sky above him, no more burning canyons, no more cliffs. A surge of pride carried him the final ten strides to the peak.

He'd beaten the mountain. *Now the next fight.* He staggered over the summit and braked a few steps down the other side, careful not to kick pebbles that might skip down the slope and give him away. The Americans were about fifty metres below, a direct descent from Wu's perch.

He'd calculated perfectly.

He appraised the camp. He'd tracked the Americans for days but had never ventured so close. Two small tents huddled against the western rock wall, next to four sandy backpacks. The soldiers formed a rough circle in the centre of the plateau, squatting on rocks they'd rolled in from the edges. In their tan shirts and desert-brown camouflage pants, the men almost looked like rocks themselves – dirty, solid, earthen. They hunched over a backpack positioned on the ground between them, a makeshift table. Playing cards were spread out on the surface.

The Americans' guns lay on the rocks at their feet. They'd be able to arm quickly, but the slight delay was all Wu would need. He couldn't help but smile. All the advantages seemed his. Even his earlier adversary, the sun, had now switched its allegiance – casting his shadow backwards up the slope, away from the camp, to prevent any possible last-second detection.

One of the white soldiers flipped over his cards. 'Read 'em and weep, bitches.'

'Un-fuckin-believable. Now I *know* you cheat.'

The white man – the one called Nelson, Wu remembered – pointed a finger. 'Guerrero, man, I'm seriously gonna beat your ass if you don't quit with that shit.'

Guerrero brushed Nelson's hand away, and the soldiers hollered with laughter.

Wu heard the crunch of dry dirt behind him. Corpses, reaching the top of the Flatiron peak, spilling over, hurdling down towards his back.

His hands swept his belt, then flew up into a fighter's stance. The crescent blades of his deer-horn knives glinted in the sun. Like predators, licking their lips for blood.

Wu inhaled once, then launched himself down the slope, towards the Americans.

Time to show his hand.

Read 'em and weep, bitches.

4.4

The first moments were chaos – exactly as Wu had hoped. Ten feet above the camp, running madly, almost in freefall, he kicked off from the steep mountainside – each frame of action distinct in his mind, seeing himself pinned airborne over the Americans, their round Western eyes startled white by this creature attacking from the sky, its talons curved and shining – and then he crashed across the hard earth, somersaulting once into the circle of soldiers. Cries of '*Fuck!*' and '*Shit!*' exploded around him, ricocheting off the rock walls. He lashed out with his left leg to kick at a black HK416 assault rifle lying unattended on the ground and, as the weapon clattered away, Wu vaulted to his feet and split the soldier Nelson's neck with his deer-horn knife, lengthwise along the base of the jaw.

The backsplash of blood against Wu's face was sweet-smelling and cool – a strange refreshment in the desert heat. Nelson grabbed his spouting throat and crashed onto his back, legs thrashing.

'*Fuck you!*' someone screamed.

The canyon roared, and a bullet cracked the rock behind Wu. Dropping flat, he grabbed the backpack – the soldiers' makeshift card table – then spun up on one knee and thrust the backpack out before his body, just as another bullet tore into the pack with an audible *WHUMP!* Playing cards and tufts of green fabric twirled in the air. Ahead of Wu, the soldier called Guerrero steadied a Beretta M9 in his hand, his face livid and red, measuring another shot as the other men scuttled for their guns.

Glancing up the slope, Wu dumped the pack and his deer-horns, then grabbed for the AK on his back. But the long climb had weakened him, and the Americans were fresher, faster. The barrels of HK416s sprang like black vipers from the rocks, coiled and quick in the soldiers' hands. All eyes on Wu. He braced for a torrent of bullets . . .

. . . but just then the corpses swarmed the camp.

Guerrero took the first hit. He stood with his back to the mountainside, squinting across his gun at Wu, so that when the naked male corpse dropped onto him from behind, Guerrero was completely unprepared for the attack. Off balance, he buckled forward.

'Fuck . . .' he coughed.

Five metres away, the grey-scruffed commander was the first to react. '*ZOMS!*' he bellowed and fired a thunderous barrage up the mountain, ripping dirt and stones from the hillside. The teenage corpse in the baseball jersey blasted backwards off its feet, brains erupting from its skull. In camp, the other soldiers forgot Wu, spun their guns to the new attack.

The corpse crunched down on the back of Guerrero's head.

'*Fuck!*' Guerrero roared. Two more corpses piled onto his legs, tackling him to the ground. Behind him the dead continued to stumble down the slope, tripping, falling, popping up again. With a vicious jerk the male corpse ripped away a strip of Guerrero's scalp. The meat hung like a hairy rectangle of bacon from its jaws, dripping blood.

Guerrero began to scream. And didn't stop.

Past him, the dead poured into camp. The soldiers pedalled backwards, their weapons bouncing from target to target, choosing carefully.

'*Cut 'em up!*' shouted Grey Beard.

Now, Wu thought, snatching up his deer-horns, and sprinted at the older man. He'd rushed half the distance when the soldiers fired their guns in unison, and the tremendous hammer-blow of sound almost knocked Wu to his knees. Above him, under him, the red mountain thundered like a volcano, crossfires of echo that made his organs tremble, his eyes water.

On the hillside, a row of corpses – the bikini woman, the Native American – thrashed and fell, spilling a slop of meaty chunks and blood like black oil. Wu staggered, the stink of gunpowder in his head, remembering again his boyhood in China and his uncle Bao Zhi, the fireworks they'd set off in a barrel behind the shack each year to scare evil spirits away. He almost laughed now at the memory as he rushed towards the pack of advancing corpses. *The dead cannot be frightened. Only men.*

The gunfire lulled, and Grey Beard yelled, '*Again!*' and Wu made one decisive stride forward and plunged his knives with all his strength into both sides of the old soldier's neck. The man barely had time to react. One final order – '*Cut 'em up*' – wheezed across his lips, and then the deer-horn blades snapped together, severing his windpipe, nearly decapitating him. His head flopped to his chest, held to his shoulders only by spaghetti-like strands of spinal cord. The body crashed to the dirt.

Wu's ears rang. More gunfire, screams, Guerrero wailing the last of his life away as the corpses peeled the meat from his legs, his ribs, his skull.

The dead surged ahead, overwhelming the camp. A withered male corpse with tattooed forearms dropped itself atop Nelson, straddling him, and plunged its hand into the soldier's gashed neck, all the way to its wrist, tearing the trachea free. Another gurgling scream.

Behind them, the naked corpse dug its teeth again into the back of Guerrero's scalp.

'*GET . . . THE FUCK . . . OFF!*' Guerrero shrieked, the words barely intelligible in the awful pitch of his pain. He jammed his Beretta into his mouth and fired. The bullet punched out the back of his head and through the left eye of the feeding corpse, shattering its cranium. Both Guerrero and the corpse flopped face down, motionless, black blood mixing with red.

Two soldiers remained. And nine or ten corpses, by Wu's quick count.

'*Pull back! Pull back!*' bawled one of the soldiers, a white man with a dark stubbly face and bleached yellow crew cut. He'd taken cover behind a boulder along the edge of the clearing. From there he fired off a burst of errant shots, showering the camp with dust and debris from the rocky slope. 'Baines! Get down the goddamn trail, re-engage there!'

The second soldier, a black man, giant and muscular, squeezed off three rounds from his handgun – his HK416 was nowhere in sight – at the approaching corpses. He scored just a single headshot before his gun emptied, a metallic *clack*.

'*Roger that!*' he screamed.

Wu's eyes widened. He couldn't allow their retreat. If the soldiers escaped to the trail . . .

He'd never recover them. The mission would fail.

He felt a pull on his sleeve and turned. A trembling elderly female in a nightgown stained with urine and blood had him by the elbow, steadying itself as it drew towards him. His fist tightened on his knife . . . but instead he tugged his arm free and pushed, almost gently. The corpse tripped backwards over the plateau edge and plunged to the trail ten metres below.

Wu didn't linger on the sound of its awful wailing. He had no time. The two soldiers were backing towards him, drawing the mob of corpses. He chose quickly. Springing forward, he launched into a tight cartwheel – whipping himself end over end, both palms planted on the hard soil – and hammered a kick between the shoulders of the bleach-haired soldier.

The man crashed forwards into three dead hikers, their weathered packs still belted to their shoulders, the straps cutting pus-filled trenches in their flesh. Within seconds the corpses had locked arms around the man and pinned him to the earth, their teeth carving and ripping.

'*Pozzo!*' shrieked the black soldier. Reflexively he yanked the trigger on his handgun twice before remembering the clip was empty. He stood frozen as more corpses advanced.

On the ground, Pozzo screeched in agony, fought, struggled to his feet – a man with his face shredded beyond recognition, all red and pink pulp, eye sockets pumping blood – before two more corpses joined the feast, dragged him back to the soil.

The last soldier set his eyes on Wu. '*Motherfucker!*' he snarled, then lowered his giant shoulders and charged. Wu squared for the attack, ready to dodge, to strike with the deer-horns, but the soldier was quick and well trained. At the last moment he swerved, deflecting Wu's swinging fists, then caught Wu off guard with a crushing uppercut. The steel barrel of the Beretta in the man's hand cracked Wu's jaw like a punch from a rivet gun. He staggered backwards, dazed, the sky and mountaintops orbiting around him. In a smooth motion the soldier caught him under the elbows and spun him. Strong hands clamped behind Wu's neck.

Wu struggled, but the chokehold was unbreakable, and he couldn't bend his arms to slash with the deer-horns. The man outweighed him by a hundred pounds. He shook Wu violently like a toy, wheeled him to face the last corpses – three males, their cracked lips foamy with blood and bile, just a few metres away. Coming nearer.

'Your turn, chink,' the soldier growled. 'Lunch time.'

4·5

Hot, mad fear blazed a path through Wu's suffocated chest. He cooled it rapidly – he had faced death often in his life – but another fire caught instead, burning his throat, his ears. *Shame.* He had failed, beaten by this American. A great opportunity for his homeland . . . soon to be lost.

He could smell the man's swamp-like breath, the tang of unwashed skin and sour sweat. The corpses reached for him – so close now he could smell their smoky hides, too. His eyes shot over their heads. Beyond, he saw the hillside where he'd led the charge down to the camp.

A corpse with a blood-crusted moustache grabbed Wu's vest, stretched its jaws wide.

'Yeah, bitch,' grunted the huge soldier. He leaned Wu closer to the snapping teeth.

No. Wu pushed back with his mind, resisting the shame – a useless emotion inhibiting thought. *China is the giant now. Not America.* He strained to remain rational.

America . . . is . . . dead.

His eyes widened. The hillside seemed distant, perhaps twenty metres away. Which meant he must be near the ledge, where the old female had fallen over.

Dead hands brushed his hair, his face . . .

'*Zhongguo!*' he screamed, the glorious yell he'd perfected as a young soldier.

China!

Swinging both legs up, he planted his boots on the chest of the corpse before him, then kicked off with every fibre of muscle left in his control. The corpse toppled away, and in reverse Wu and the black man stumbled an off-balance step to the rear, then another step – and then came the sound of scraping dirt and sliding rocks, and gravity shifted, and Wu found himself facing the blue sky. The merciless sun hung over him like a vulture, and there was the sensation of falling, a buoyancy in his gut, and the soldier screamed and the cliff walls rushed past and . . .

CRACK!

Pain! And the unmistakable snapping sound of bone. Wu's breath ejected in a single harsh blast; beneath him the soldier cried out. They'd plummeted off the ledge backwards, so that the American slammed first into the stony ground – his body a buffer for Wu, absorbing the worst of the impact. The man's ribcage had collapsed. His chokehold on Wu went slack.

Wu rolled off, testing himself for damage.

Bruises. Nothing worse.

But the soldier lay gasping in agony, legs spasming, his giant body performing a macabre dance on the ground. Back broken. Blood flecked from his mouth with each difficult breath.

Wu stood and gazed up to the ledge of the plateau. Rotten faces peered over the edge, regarded him sullenly. Then turned away. They had enough fresh meat above.

Wu's chest swelled. He'd beaten the Americans. His confidence was solid again, his body electric with same thrill he'd felt at eighteen, donning his first crisp uniform in Shenyang; alive with the realisation that he belonged to something big, something important and great.

China would lead the world. And he, Kheng Wu, would make it so.

A dry scraping brought Wu's attention back to the trail. The elderly female corpse he'd pushed over the edge was now at his feet, dragging itself along the dirt. Both its legs had snapped from the fall; the knees bent at grotesque angles, and sharp bones stabbed through the oozing skin. Wu hopped to the other side of the paralysed soldier and trotted five metres down the trail.

'No,' the soldier huffed as the female pulled itself onto his chest.

From this spot on the trail, the view was spectacular. The Americans had chosen their lookout well, situated in a gap on the south side of the Superstitions. Below, the desert rolled out in a flat carpet of orange soil and purple flowers and mute needled cactus, unfurling to the Gold Canyon a few kilometres beyond. Adobe houses dotted the foothills. Wu studied them.

Somewhere in those hills was Henry Marco.

Behind Wu the broken soldier screamed, a shrill sputtering

plea. The elderly corpse had bitten into his face, tearing free a huge flap of bloody skin from his nose to his ear.

The soldier screamed again, unable to move as the corpse plunged its cold fingers deep into his eye and began to gnaw on his exposed cheekbone. A horrible crunching sound.

It would be a long and difficult death for the American.

Wu concentrated, planning his next move.

Now it was Henry Marco's turn.

MEETING STORIES

5.1

Marco first met Danielle nine years ago, in line for the return desk at Tech Town. It was a Saturday in November, a month after his birthday, and he'd finally gotten around to returning the gift his mother had sent – a new cell phone, a sexy silver bar with a touchscreen and bright-lit graphics. He had absolutely no desire to keep it. He was perhaps the last man in California without a cell phone; try as he might, he couldn't overcome his loathing for the damn things. *The fast food of conversation*, he often groused. *Empty calories, people calling each other with nothing to say, just because they can.* For God's sake, the last thing he wanted was a bustling social life, never mind a portable one. And so he'd vowed never to own a cell, despite the way people reacted when he didn't have a number to give them. Gasps, widened eyes. Like he was some kook with long curly fingernails saving his piss in jars.

'I'm at the hospital sixteen hours a day,' he informed new acquaintances, secretly enjoying their outrage. 'You wanna reach me, all you need to do is have an aneurysm.'

Yet this phone, his mother must have believed, was wonderful enough to change his mind. He hadn't even removed it from the packaging. It came with a note that read, *For my hermit*, with a hand-drawn smiley face and her phone number written below.

For three weeks he'd debated keeping it, opening the

account just to make her happy, even if he never intended to make a call. But he was stubborn and, on top of that, he found himself lying awake one night, stressed by the idea of another phone number to memorise, as if seven more digits would burst his brain. And so he'd finally decided to just return the goddamn thing. Take the money and order his mother a nice vase of Christmas poinsettias instead.

He had no idea where she'd purchased the phone, but Tech Town seemed as good a bet as any, and he knew there were locations near her condo in Philly. The store nearest Marco was in Glendale, and so on that Saturday he'd blasted through a workout on the rower at the gym, and then, feeling hurried, shortened his usual shower to an unsatisfying three minutes. Back in the car, smelling of inadequately rinsed peppermint shampoo, he turned west out of the garage, chagrined at the loss of an hour from his only free morning that week.

At Tech Town, the parking lot was a claustrophobic environment of slow-moving cars and SUVs circling like sharks in an aquarium. He hadn't anticipated the early holiday rush. Now doubly annoyed, he darted his Audi to the first parking spot he saw.

Inside, the clerk at the return counter was a beefy kid, early twenties with messy blond hair and a poorly knotted tie. He watched Marco approach.

'Hi,' Marco said. He laid the cell phone in its plastic package on the counter.

'Hello, sir.' The kid's soft cheeks were cloudy pink and razor-burned. He wore a name tag with no name on it pinned to his blue vest. *Hello I'm*, it teased. 'How can I help you?'

'I received that as a gift,' Marco said. He smelled peppermint and realised with embarrassment that it was wafting from his scalp. He took a small step backwards. 'I'd like to return it, please.'

'All right, no problem,' the kid said. 'Do you have your receipt?'

Marco hesitated. 'Well, no. It was a gift.'

'Oh,' the kid said, sounding crestfallen. 'You need a receipt.'

Shit, Marco thought. 'Even for gifts?'

'Yeah, I'm sorry.' The kid pointed somewhere behind him, presumably to a sign posted someplace Marco couldn't see. 'Returns have to have a receipt.'

'Even for gifts?' Marco repeated, thinking perhaps the kid hadn't absorbed the logic. 'That can't be. People return gifts all the time.'

'Well . . .' the kid said, and the razor marks on his cheeks flushed a deeper pink. 'See, that's just the policy for phones. It's because we don't know if it really came from here.'

'But you sell them, right?'

'Yeah.'

'Then does it really matter?'

The kid absently slid the phone along the countertop. 'Well, I know you're not like this,' he said confidentially, and Marco realised the kid was trying to be cool with him, 'but lots of times, people just pick stuff off the shelf and, like, try to walk over here and return it.'

Marco took a deep breath. The peppermint cooled his sinuses. 'So what about after Christmas?' he asked, switching arguments. 'People can't return presents they don't want?'

The kid paused. 'Well . . . I never worked here for Christmas.'

'Right,' Marco said. *Figures*. 'Is there a manager here, then, that can help me?'

The kid raised his hand halfway. 'I'm assistant manager.'

'Right,' Marco said again. 'So is the manager here?' The question presented itself more rudely than he'd intended, and he saw the kid stiffen. *Oh well. Friendship's over.*

Unsmiling now, the kid – the assistant manager without a name – reached for a phone mounted behind the counter. He punched a few buttons and listened into the receiver. Marco waited, feeling stupid. In the next department he could hear a wall of televisions all tuned to *SportsCenter*.

'Hey,' the kid said into the phone. 'Is Mr Lang there? I need him for a return.'

'Thank you,' Marco said as the kid hung up the receiver. His head buzzed with a vague sense of wrongdoing. What if his mother didn't even get the damn thing at Tech Town? He turned from the counter, avoiding the kid as he silently rehearsed his argument for Mr Lang.

At least a minute passed before Marco noticed a woman ten feet away, waiting next in line for the return desk. What struck him first was the oddness of her hat – a straw sun hat with an enormous brim and outlandish pink flower, bigger than his fist, sewn to the side. The hat's weaving had come undone in spots, with haphazard stalks poking out here and there, and he couldn't decide if she looked more like a crazy gardener or Huckleberry Finn. The brim hid her upper face, revealing only two glossy lips and a slender chin. She wore a white skirt with a ruffled yellow blouse; her breasts were demure shapes, small and tantalising.

She raised her chin, and, as the hat tilted, he realised that she was watching him.

She was remarkably attractive. Her eyes seemed to display an intelligent curiosity in him, as if he'd just said something fascinating and philosophical; her eyelids were tinted lightly with eyeshadow, a faint lilac luster, almost but not quite a glitter. She had a model's face, perfect for an artist's sketch-book: a sleek nose and cheekbones captured with confident strokes, and short auburn hair tucked back behind her ears. Three small jade earrings dotted each lobe.

'Hi,' she said, startling him. He blinked two or three times reflexively, as though she'd swung a flashlight on him, before he was able to answer.

'Hi,' he said. So much for fascinating and philosophical. He debated which would make him feel more idiotic now – turning back to the desk to wait awkwardly, or chit-chatting with this woman who'd just caught him ogling. He wished Mr Lang would hurry his ass down.

'I heard what you were saying,' the woman said. 'About your phone.' Her head ducked into her shoulders, and she smiled sheepishly. 'Sorry, I eavesdrop everywhere I go.'

'Oh,' he said. He glanced backwards. The kid was typing on his keypad, not paying attention. Feeling bolder, sensing he'd gained a sympathiser, Marco faced the woman again. Yes, she truly was attractive. Her face had a pixie-ish quality, with strawberry cheeks and a nose angled up at the tip; she was in her thirties, yet she emitted the airy glow of a teenage girl. And yes, her eyeshadow *did* glitter, a delicate twinkle that would have annoyed him on anybody else – but on her it charmed him somehow. As if he'd received a sprinkling of her pixie magic.

'They won't let you return it,' she said, as though to clarify the situation.

'No, apparently not,' he confirmed. 'Not without a receipt. It was a gift.'

'It's a nice gift,' she said, and he felt a momentary betrayal, as if she were trying to convince him to keep the phone. Perhaps she noticed his mouth twitch, because she immediately added, 'You shouldn't need a receipt. Hardly anybody makes you have them any more.'

'I'm making that same argument,' he said, pacified. 'I may call on you as a witness.'

She encouraged him with a smile. 'Actually, that's what I wanted to tell you. I was standing here in line, listening, and

I couldn't believe it. I just bought that *same* phone here. The exact same one, last week. Look.' She reached into her purse and pulled out a duplicate model.

'Really,' he said, not quite seeing her point. 'You're returning it?'

'Oh, I like mine,' she replied. 'I'm here for something else, a CD. But what I mean about the phone is that I have the *receipt* for it, right here, still in my purse.'

A moment passed, during which he heard the unspoken suggestion. She grinned, biting her bottom lip in a way he'd later come to recognise as a harbinger of her mischief. Again he sensed an aura of girlishness, the teen tiptoeing out the back door after her parents fell asleep.

'Wow,' he said at last. 'There's a clever thought. Actually – you know, it would actually work, I think. It might be wrong, but it would work.'

Her mouth rounded, and she pretended to appear insulted. 'It's not wrong,' she protested. 'You didn't really steal that phone, did you?'

'No.'

'Exactly. So it's not wrong. If anything, it's righting a wrong done to you.'

He glanced back at the kid. Still not paying attention. 'Should we be whispering?'

'Oh, he doesn't care,' she said, flicking her hand at the counter. A smoky crystal sat in a copper ring on her pinkie. The other fingers were bare.

'All right,' Marco agreed. 'I'd really appreciate it, if you really don't mind.'

'Of course not,' she said. 'I was going to throw it out, but it had some other things on it, so I figured I better keep it a little longer. Now I'm glad I did.'

'Me, too.' He let that statement hang a second longer than

necessary, then held out his hand low. 'Quick. He'll be here any second.'

She laughed and handed him a small white slip of paper from her purse. 'You have a knack for drama,' she mused. 'Don't tell me you're an actor.'

'God, no,' he said too strongly. Her eyebrows lifted, and he sensed he'd made a gaffe. 'What I mean,' he began, but before he could soften his stance, a voice spoke up behind him.

'Sir, you had the phone?' A middle-aged man with a moustache now stood at the counter.

'Yes, that's me,' Marco said. He held up the receipt – the 'Receipt of Destiny', Danielle later referred to it – and rattled it in the air. 'You won't believe what I just found.'

Minutes later he had his refund, sixty-five dollars. On the receipt the kid scribbled out the cell phone in red pen before passing it back to Marco. Marco rejoined the woman in line.

'Thank you again,' he told her. 'I owe you. Here you go.' He offered her the receipt, but she pushed it back into his hand, shaking her head.

'Keep it,' she said. 'Oh god, this is the embarrassing part.'

She crossed her eyes and put a hand to her forehead, laughing. 'Okay, I'll just say it. You didn't notice, but I wrote my number on the back. Before I even spoke to you, when I was waiting in line. It was all part of an intricate plot.'

Marco blushed. The receipt quivered in his hand, like a magic-trick prop that might burst into flames. He resisted an urge to turn it over, check to see if she was telling the truth.

'Oh,' he said. His heart quickened a few beats. 'Thank you.' The stupidity of his words appalled him, yet she seemed pleased. She smiled beautifully, as though she'd been saving her prettiest face for the right moment, and held out her hand.

'You're welcome,' she said brightly. 'I'm Danielle.'

He crammed the receipt into his pocket, then reached back to her. Her hand felt like a soft leaf in his. 'Henry,' he said.

And that was how he'd met Danielle. A great 'meeting story', she liked to call it. Every marriage has its mythology, and Danielle delighted in telling theirs. She was an actress, he learned, with credits in movies he vaguely recalled – *Photo Album* and *Pearls* and *Next to Nothing* – although he'd never been much of a moviegoer. Her Hollywood friends were a mystic bunch, always marvelling at the machinery of the universe. At dinner parties, whenever conversations turned to the topic of fate, Danielle offered her meeting with Marco as proof, while he played the straight man – interjecting to argue it was only a coincidence, at which point he'd be drowned out by boos, and somebody usually hit him with a sofa cushion.

And that was the irony: rejecting the cell phone had brought him Danielle, his living, breathing, beautiful lifeline to the world. Before Danielle, he'd had nobody. *A hermit*, his mother had called him, and her assessment wasn't far from the truth. But with Danielle came friends, parties, plans for a family . . . Except now Danielle was gone again.

And without her, life was hell on earth.

5.2

The silver dome of the Maricopa train station harnessed the morning sun, shooting off a white flare that Marco could see from two blocks away in his Jeep. Ahead of him Route 347 wavered with a hazy heat. The morning was already hot. Twenty-four hours had passed since his negotiations with

Osbourne; afterwards he'd shut down the computer and made a beeline for bed, plummeting to the mattress like a defeated boxer to the mat. He slept a feverish sleep that sucked him deeper the more he tried to rise out of it, as if he were struggling in a vat of warm mud. Somewhere in another reality, distant, not his own, he heard gunshots, explosions. He slept through the afternoon, the evening, the night again; when he'd finally opened his eyes this morning, he felt healthier. The soreness in his throat had relented, his sinuses were clear, his airways alive once more with fresh flowing oxygen. He relaxed, suddenly aware that he'd been concerned; but there was definitely no Resurrection in his body. *No raw meat for me.*

And so he'd gotten up. He boiled water in the fireplace for a quick wash, then dressed and packed his gear and firearms. Out the door just after seven. He'd finally succumbed to Osbourne's plan – reluctantly, but at the same time perhaps grateful for the extra manpower – to meet the Resurrection Resistance Unit in the town of Maricopa, an hour south.

Roger Ballard, he thought now for the hundredth time as he drove. He frowned, still rattled by last night. The dredging up of that name. What the hell was Osbourne plotting? Why the need to return Roger? '*National security*' was all that Osbourne had offered.

Something's not right, Marco fretted. *I should've said no.*

But then again, he didn't really have a choice. Osbourne was a true bastard. The threats had been bad enough, Marco thought, but using Danielle like that to manipulate him . . . Christ, he'd practically been on his knees, begging for the job. He scowled now, remembering the questions Osbourne had put to him. The same cruel questions that loomed over him every day out here in this wasteland, beating down on him like the sun.

Why haven't you found her? Why is this taking so goddamn long?

Christ, he'd tried, staked out a hundred spots she *should* have been. The wedding chapel in Hollywood. The resort in Carefree. Their first apartment in LA, and the coffee shop they'd gone to for a first date. And the Arizona house, of course, four years there, waiting for her to show. He'd looked everywhere, every place that meant something – that *should've* meant something to her. Unless he was wrong . . .

His chest ached. He didn't want to doubt her.

Perhaps you've begun to wonder, Osbourne had commented.

Yeah. Perhaps.

The image of her empty Honda flickered at the back of his eyes, ghostly and half formed. It appeared to him often in moments like these, particularly when he was tired and depressed. And always more images followed, and once they began they were hard to stop – *himself in his Audi on the first day of the Resurrection, speeding madly across town to rescue Danielle from the unfathomable chaos of screaming people and broken glass and ambulance sirens and dead monsters chasing him, and suddenly he slammed his brakes and there was her Honda, crumpled around a splintered telephone pole, her silly licence plate YIN•YANG mocking him as he sprinted across the street, dodging corpses – No no no, he thought – bloody brown handprints on the open doors, the engine still hissing and steaming – No no no fuck fuck fuck – the driver's seat soaked with guts, loops of intestine, half a bitten liver, the floor mats submerged in blood – her red footprints exiting the car, disappearing into the desert, and he'd never seen her again . . .*

'Stop!' he said, and slammed his fist on the car horn. The brazen honk broke the daydream apart, sent the unwelcome thoughts scattering. 'No more,' he ordered.

Immediately he regretted the reckless horn blow. *Don't announce yourself, asshole*, he thought, forcing his concentration back to the road, watchful for what he called 'early risers'. Corpses never slept – but after a nightlong chill in the dark, sunlight seemed to trigger a higher state of activity in some. Probably another echo of their lives, distinct to personality and habit. Just after dawn you were likely to find white-haired corpses staggering along sidewalks, the elderly out for a sunrise stroll. Dead kids, too, acting on impulse to catch a school bus, maybe, or deliver papers. He'd once had to bolt from a corpse in jogging shorts; the calf muscles on its right leg were chewed off completely, just a grey stick of bone crammed into a crusted Nike sneaker.

Early risers were no real danger, not while driving. There were never many of them. But smacking a corpse in the road could damage the Jeep, maybe knock a part loose under the hood. And the last thing Marco needed was engine trouble.

His plan was to drive to Maricopa and join with the railroad tracks past the train station; steer the Jeep up the gravel embankment and drop right onto the tracks. Then follow the rails all the way to Los Angeles with the RRU tailing behind in their truck.

Bumpy, yes, but the surest way to cover long distances.

He'd thought up the trick two years ago. On highways in the Evacuated States, you were almost certain to run into a 'ghost jam' somewhere along the drive – thousands of empty cars and trucks clogging the road at unpredictable points, abandoned during the Evacuation. Terrified drivers caught in standstill traffic, forced to get out and run when mobs of the dead came swarming up the ramps, choking off any escape. Entire families became easy meals.

Now half the roads in America were just miles of rusting metal and sun-baked bones, impossible to pass. Crawling with hungry dead, too. He'd tried once to hike through on foot. Big mistake. He'd been lucky to reach an overpass, jumped into a river to escape a hundred corpses.

So – railroad tracks were the answer. No traffic, no getting lost. Just straight shots from Point A to Point B, over all kinds of terrain. Big cities, thick forests, grand mountains, you name it. Marco had plotted today's course on the map before leaving the house. Pick up the rail at Maricopa, then 400 miles west, exiting Arizona, up towards Los Angeles. He'd ditch the tracks far enough outside the city, before the area turned too population-heavy and dangerous.

The Maricopa train station glinted in the sun again, closer now. The station was a tourist attraction of sorts – an actual dome railroad car from the classic California Zephyr line, unhitched and deposited alongside the eastbound tracks, converted into a steel depot. He'd visited it once before the Resurrection – not as a passenger, but on a self-guided sightseeing tour he and Danielle had taken five years ago. Back when they'd first moved to Arizona.

Those first few weekends they'd bought travel books, explored the scenic driving routes, introduced themselves to the highlights of their new state. On that morning they'd toured the Gila River Heritage Center, absorbing Native American folklore and mysticism; Danielle loved it, while in Marco's opinion it was a large overdose of feathers and turquoise beads. Afterwards they'd followed the itinerary west to Maricopa, to the famous Silver Horizon train station.

Interesting, Danielle had commented, sounding unsure what else to say. It wasn't very exciting, really – just an old metal husk in the desert. They'd driven past the station without stopping, then eaten lunch at a run-down pizza joint a few blocks down the street.

Marco frowned. That pizza place.

He wasn't far from it now, just another intersection or two. Worth checking out? Finding her there would be a massive long shot – it was just a place where they'd eaten once, no special significance, and he couldn't remember a single thing they'd talked about during the meal – but then again, you never knew what might bubble to the surface in a dead brain.

And Christ, he was running out of places to look. He'd even revisited the Gila River Heritage Center a year back. Nothing there except a few dozen Maricopan Indian corpses lurking in damp earthen homes, crawling out to bite at him.

But no Danielle.

He turned left and coasted into the small station parking lot, opposite a dingy auto-parts store and a ramshackle Mexican restaurant called *Papi's*. The air bogged with a smell like excrement, thick and nauseating. Outside his bug-spattered windshield the grey depot greeted him, looking lonelier than he remembered it, a coach car divorced from its train. He peered farther up the street. Somewhere off in that direction was the pizza place.

In his chest he felt the faint tug that always accompanied these glimpses of possibility – pulling him along, almost impossible to resist. He sighed. If he *didn't* check this restaurant out, he'd spend the next month convinced she'd been there, sitting forever in one of those cheap red vinyl booths, waiting for a shitty vegetarian pizza that would never arrive from the kitchen.

At the thought, his eyes glossed.

That did it. He had to go look.

He swallowed uncomfortably and swung the Jeep through a clumsy U-turn in the parking lot, the tyres crunching as they stirred the gravel. He'd pop over to the pizza place, get back here before the RRU showed.

Back on Route 347, he drove a block. Darkened storefronts and shopping plazas beckoned from the roadside, their windows bleak with dust: a plumbing supply store, a grocery market, a laundromat. His eyes darted in and out of each. He felt his mind racing ahead of the Jeep, rehearsing his entrance into the pizza shop.

Footsteps loud in the foyer. The crackle of brittle linoleum under his boots. He steps into the dining area, and there she is. Danielle at a round table. Her face is wrapped in shadow but he knows her immediately. Her hair is still short, still the red-brown of autumn but stiff like straw. He speaks her name softly. She turns to him, a dry rasping in her throat . . .

A sudden squeal, loud and jarring, made him jump.

His eyes shot to the rear-view mirror in time to see a green truck skid through the intersection behind the Jeep. Towards the station. Fast.

And burning.

Jesus shit Christ!

The truck – a military transport – was on fire. Flames surged across the hood, whipping over the canvas roof like the mane of a demon animal, thunderclouds of black smoke fuming from the cab. The tyres screamed again, and the truck pitched left, bucking the kerb, slamming head-on into an electric transformer box outside the train station. With an obscene screech of metal ripping metal, the truck rocked on two wheels and then rolled entirely onto its back – crushing the roof, showering sparks outward as the steel frame grated the cement.

It flattened a grove of brown prickly bushes and stopped fifty feet from the station, its tyres spinning in the air. The fire poured upwards through the wheel wells, igniting the dry brush into stalks of red and orange, and the tyres began to bubble, and the smoke turned even blacker.

Marco sat dumbfounded, staring into his rear-view mirror. The entire crash had played out with such speed, he hadn't even turned to look through the back window.

He turned now, his heart galloping. And that's when he saw the man in the wreckage.

Upside down in the driver's seat, hands pounding the windshield.

Stuck in a death chamber as the flames raged into the cab.

5.3

With utter hopelessness, Marco observed the burning truck, the driver roasting alive. The wreck was an inferno, rescue impossible. And then he blinked twice – *what the hell*, he shrugged, *never know till you try* – and kicked his own ass into action. He slapped the gear in reverse and twisted to see through the back window as he stomped the gas, and with a frantic squeal of rubber the Jeep launched like a backwards torpedo down the street.

For half a second it shot towards the burning truck – then knifed sideways, off course. The metal pole of a streetlamp rushed at him through the rear window, and he jerked the wheel, and the Jeep swerved again, missing the pole and a mailbox before slamming the kerb opposite the station, launching him vertically in his seat; his head cracked against the overhead interior light and his teeth knocked together with an alarming clatter of enamel.

Scalp throbbing, he thrust the Jeep into park and reached for his bag. *Goddamn it.* The gear had dumped all over the passenger-side floor mat, a mess of maps, flashlight batteries, ammo, foil bags of freeze-dried beef, chicken and veggies. And his gun, the Glock, somewhere in the jumble. Furiously he searched the floor, the back seat, the crevice between the side door.

No gun. Couldn't find the fuckin' gun.

He heard a wail from the burning wreck of the military truck.

Screw it, he thought. *No time.*

He scrambled from the Jeep and gasped. Even here, twenty

yards from the truck, the heat was fearsome, as if a massive hand had reeled back and slapped him full force the moment he emerged. He slit his eyes to see. A churning cloud of red and black fire raged from the upside-down truck, stealing up the sides, snaking through the exposed underbelly of cylinders and pipes. The air was oily with the funk of burning tyres, and the smoke grated his eyeballs like sandpaper.

He inhaled, but his throat rejected the air, wracking him instead with a fit of foul-tasting coughs. *Christ.* He wrestled his T-shirt from his chest and covered his mouth with the soft cool cotton. Sucking for air, he circled around the truck to the front cab, where he'd seen the man trapped. The windshield was spider-webbed, blackened with soot. Impossible to see inside.

A burst of flames billowed sideways from the wreck, stoked by a passing desert breeze. He crouched and edged closer, risking a view into the driver's window.

'*Hey!*' he shouted.

Through the curtain of smoke, a hand slapped the glass. The palm pressed pink and bloody against the window. Then it pulled away and slapped again.

'*Hang on!*' Marco yelled. He bundled his shirt around his fingers and grabbed for the scalding metal door. The handle turned without effort, but the door rattled only an inch in its frame. The crash had buckled the doors, rendering them inoperable. Deep in the smoke on the other side of the window, a red glow began to throb like a heart. The seats had caught fire. The man's hand clawed the glass with a new, heightened vigour. Through the murk Marco glimpsed a terrified face – a bald black man, thrashing, his mouth prised open in pain.

Marco's thoughts reeled. If he had the Glock, he could shoot the glass out.

Or a tyre iron. Back somewhere in the Jeep; he'd have to dig for it.

Or use his fists. Or . . .

Boots. His heavy-duty, size 12 boots. Serious shit-kickers – he'd stomped enough corpse skulls these last few years to know.

Dropping, he crawled to the front of the truck and rolled to his back, knees squared, taking aim at the already cracked windshield. The upside-down hood loomed above him, crumpled open an inch, hissing angrily – radiator ruptured, steam seething out. The stink of gasoline was everywhere, an invisible timer counting critical seconds.

How long till the tank blows?

Till the whole truck goes up in a fireball? And me with it?

He kicked as hard as he could. Pain laced up his shins and resonated in his knees, but the glass held. He kicked again. The windshield buckled, sagged inward along a dozen fault lines but did not break. Stinging sweat ran into his eyes as he kicked a third time. The glass at last buckled, and his left boot punched a hole straight through into the cab.

He felt the trapped man grabbing at his foot, slipping off.

'*Hold on!*' Marco shouted. '*Almost done!*'

He pedalled his legs furiously until the hole had widened, a jagged mouth two feet across, vomiting ugly charcoal fumes. The smoke engulfed Marco. He batted it from his face, hacking, lungs revolting. How the hell could the man inside *breathe* . . .?

Forceful hands clamped down on his ankles. And pulled. Marco slid a foot forward, deeper through the broken windshield.

'*Hey!*' he called, surprised.

Hidden in the smoke, panicking, the man hauled again.

'Wait . . .' Marco said as he bounced forward, seeing his body disappear into the hole up to his waist. He felt his canvas pants bunch, flames ripping at his calves . . .

. . . cold hands seizing his shins.

At once the frigid, familiar shock of dead skin against his own electrified the nerves in Marco's legs, surged up his spine, lit him with terror.

'Oh fuck,' he sputtered.

Not a man in the truck – a fucking *corpse*.

Get it off! Every tendon in his legs went wild at once, and he kicked madly, desperately, blindly. His lower body was lost in the black smoke-storm beyond the windshield; he couldn't see his own feet, had no idea how near his flesh came to the dead man's teeth. He felt his shin crack against hard bone, the corpse's jaw or forehead perhaps, and he cried out in horror, certain for a millisecond he'd been bitten. And then a muscular arm coiled around his knee, and the corpse dragged him another half-foot into the smoke.

The heat was livid, agonising. Fire seethed along the green surface of the hood, two feet from his face, a terrible whistle in his ears. In seconds he'd either burn to death or be eaten alive.

Determined, he slammed his hands to the windshield, locking his elbows to keep from being pulled through. The glass itself had become another monster, superheated. Red blisters bubbled across his palms and broke instantly, leaving raw rosy puddles, and he screamed. But he had no choice. He strained against the windshield, arching his back, fighting the rotten weight attached to his legs. His arms shook. He gained an inch back in his favour, then six inches.

But then an ashen hand struck from the smoke, seizing him just above his knee as a beastly growl cut through the fumes; a moment later the corpse's head broke into the clean air. The skull was burnt hairless, the brown skin melted away in white gummy patches. One eye socket was empty, hollowed out, wafting smoke.

Gasping, Marco snatched his hands from the hot windshield and planted them on the pavement, crying out again as tiny squares of broken safety glass ate into his torn skin. From the wreck a hurricane of fire swallowed the corpse's face. The flames shot over Marco's bare chest. He bucked with a rush of adrenalin, fuelled by the pain, and wrestled another few feet back onto the pavement. His boots cleared the windshield, the soles spewing greasy noxious smoke.

The corpse hung on, stubborn. Its head thrashed from side to side like a panicked animal's, its lips pulled and snarling. Its other arm sprang from the wreck, grabbed at the glass, hoisted itself forward until finally the dead man's huge body crashed atop Marco's shins, pinning him.

The corpse was on fire, flames consuming its back. Blackened tatters of a military uniform clung to its char-broiled muscles – a soldier. Its single eye fixed on Marco, and he felt its fingers dig tighter, the pressure mounting until he swore his kneecaps would pop apart.

Strong fucker.

Marco strained, fighting panic himself. No good. The corpse had too much weight on him now. The soldier was at least two fifty, a real badass of sinew and strength. It had clawed farther up Marco's body, mouth stretched wide, snapping down . . .

. . . but with his quickest reflex, Marco lunged just ahead of the bite and jammed his thumb squarely into the corpse's empty eye socket, hooking the orbital bone. The corpse's head jolted to a stop. It chopped at the air, fighting, unable to connect with the meat on Marco's legs.

Marco drove his thumb deeper, felt it sink into an awful squishiness inside the skull. Black juice splashed from the hole. Marco cringed; he knew from experience that the cuts on his hands weren't big enough to suck the Resurrection into his veins – he'd stopped worrying about nicks and scrapes years ago – but Jesus, he still hated corpse blood anywhere on him.

C'mon, quit bein' a baby, and focus, he thought. *Now what?*

A mangled cry from up the street answered him.

He twisted his head, following the sound.

Four more corpses had emerged from the auto-parts store on the corner, shuffling towards him, wet hungry noises gargling in their throats.

The burning corpse crushed Marco with its full weight. With a quick strike it seized his free arm and slammed his wrist to the pavement.

Marco cried out. Couldn't move. As if his entire body had been nailed to the ground.

The corpses closed in for the kill.

5·4

Marco wrestled furiously for his life. He buried his thumb farther into the dead soldier's orbital socket, desperate to pry the corpse away, but it had him pinned solid – teeth snapping at his neck, inches from his pounding jugular vein. Fire rollicked on the corpse's back. A stink blew from its lips – not breath, but shit-smelling gas forced from the lungs as it slammed Marco against the pavement. Marco gagged, turned his eyes again to the side street.

The four other corpses were almost on him. Thirty feet away. Three males in torn mechanics' coveralls, and a female – *no*, the corpse with long black hair was male, too, a naked Maricopan with skin like grey leather and purple gashes on its stomach. It snarled at Marco.

Now twenty feet away.

Now less.

Marco bucked, whipped his legs, yanked at his trapped arm, tried to roll the corpse sideways. No good – the thing was too goddamn strong, impossible to keep hooked much longer. Marco's thumb trembled, bent backwards. Pain spiked up his wrist.

Gonna break, he thought.

Fragments of dead skin flaked off the burning corpse's arms and chest, swirled like embers past Marco's face. The flames raged above him, around him; he tasted salt and gasoline on his tongue; his ears filled with the roar of the fire, the hiss of the ruptured engine, the grunts of the monster atop him. It was too much, all of it. For a moment he felt himself lost in the chaos, a sensory overload of smoke and death. Then he blinked, and blinked again. Regained focus.

'Screw this,' he wheezed.

He looked up, and the other corpses had arrived. Crawling towards him under the hood of the overturned truck. Hideous faces crusted with old blood, black gummy drool.

Just five minutes ago he'd been safe in the Jeep, focused on Danielle. Now he felt a new burning in his eyes, and he battled back tears. *Sorry, Delle.* He'd always called her 'Delle'. A joke between them: he was too busy for her entire name. Had to be shortened, one syllable only. Then off to his next appointment, his next patient. *Sorry, Delle. I wanted to find you.*

But he'd run out of time for her. Again.

Frustrated, he screamed with all the air he had left, choked off with a gasp as the burning corpse grabbed his throat, and the four other dead males crouched over him, and he wished that the truck's gas tank would just fucking explode *now*, end him quick . . .

. . . and then a loud *whump* changed everything.

It happened fast, confusing him in a dozen ways before he made sense of it. He'd been bracing for the first cold touch of dead fingers, the first agonising rip of flesh from his body, when suddenly on all sides of him the four corpses crashed to the pavement, face-planted and twitching as if they'd been hit with a shovel, all of them at once. Christ, the truck *had* exploded – no, not exploded, but toppled onto the corpses;

no, not the whole truck, just the hood, he realised at last. The heavy hood had popped and swung down hard from above, clubbing the corpses across the backs of their skulls, dropping them. Only the fiery corpse atop Marco had been low enough to escape the blow. Unfazed, it snapped at his shoulder. Marco twisted, avoiding the bite, shocked to be alive still.

The scorched green metal hood hung a foot above his head.

Then it began to lift.

And locked back into place on the truck.

What the fuck? Marco craned his neck, trying to get a look up behind him.

Around him, the corpses struggled to rise, stunned but not finished.

At the edge of Marco's vision, a figure loomed. Another corpse stooping under the truck. But different somehow. Nimble, quick-footed. Hopping between the fallen dead men. It leaned in, and Marco flinched. But the hands didn't grab for him. Instead they struck at the soldier and just as quickly darted away, leaving a white nylon rope strung from the corpse's ankle.

And then an even bigger shock . . .

. . . a voice, speaking close behind Marco's ear.

'Hold on,' it said. A curt command, odd sounding.

'I can't . . .' Marco began.

Too late. The pain in his hand boiled over; he gasped as he lost control. His thumb popped from the dead man's socket, and the corpse, now unstoppable, lunged for his neck . . .

. . . but instead it jerked backwards, teeth connecting with nothing. Behind it Marco saw the rope snap taut, a straight line vanishing from view. Dragging the corpse. The huge dead man launched in reverse, biting at Marco's chest, hips, legs as it went, unable to connect, but at the last moment it lashed out a strong hand and caught Marco's boot.

Oh shit, Marco thought. Time for a ride.

Together they bounced from beneath the truck, and Marco had to contort to avoid a blazing puddle of oil as he and the corpse skidded onto the street. His mind was a daze of fear, relief, adrenalin. Bewilderment. His eyes followed the rope: fifty feet away, it coiled once around a telegraph pole and – holy Jesus goddamn Christ – there was a *man*, more dreamlike than anything real, a lean little man running back towards the truck, the rope slung over his shoulder as he hauled on his makeshift pulley, moving the giant corpse twice his weight.

The man pulled even with Marco. He was Asian, young, mid-thirties. Dressed in military fatigues, soaked with blood around the shoulders and chest. He nodded at Marco, but the gesture was nothing friendly; his eyes were hard and serious. An automatic rifle crossed his back.

A thought sped towards Marco's lips – *use the gun!* – but before he could speak, the corpse howled and swiped at the passing man, releasing Marco in the confusion. The man skipped easily over the corpse's swinging arms and continued up the street, still pulling his line.

Marco rolled twice and rested on his stomach, panting, his shoulders skinned. The corpse flopped away in the opposite direction, the pavement grating a trail of bad meat from its body. It slammed the telegraph pole where the rope looped, and with a grisly *snap* Marco heard even from a distance, the dead man's knee snapped the wrong way – crumpled around the pole so that its toes flattened against its front thigh. Roaring, it writhed there, broken, sizzling with flame.

Marco stared, transfixed. A hand grabbed his shoulder.

'Up,' said the Asian man, beside him again. 'Here come more.'

The four fallen corpses had recovered, crawling from beneath the truck.

'I-I see them,' Marco stammered, his throat hoarse from

the flu, and the noxious smoke, and the stranglehold clamped on him by the soldier corpse. He scrambled to his feet.

'No,' the man said. 'Not them.' He slapped Marco twice on the back, hard, and pointed at the silver-domed train depot. '*Them.*'

Dozens of bedraggled corpses flooded through the station doors. Across the parking lot.

'Oh,' Marco said. 'Them.'

5.5

Wu was not impressed by Henry Marco – at least not the Henry Marco standing here, half dazed outside the Maricopa station, a husk of the man Wu had seen in photographs. The intelligence dossier from MSS had included personnel files hacked from the defunct mainframe of St Joseph's Medical Center. Colour photos taken before the Resurrection – Doctor Henry Marco in a white coat, handsome, well groomed. His eyes had been sharp and intelligent, and on his mouth a reserved smile demonstrated politeness for the camera, nothing more. He had appeared fit, healthy in body and mind. 'Cunning', the dossier had warned. An 'adaptive thinker' with 'strong survival instincts'.

Wu saw nothing of that now.

This Henry Marco was barely more than a corpse himself. Blood and black ash layered his face. Oily sweat streaked his forehead, drawing lines in the ash before dipping into dark hollows under his cheeks. His ribs jutted from his sides. His eyes were tired, unfocused, and he teetered on his heels. This Henry Marco was weak. He would have died, if not for Wu's help.

Wu frowned. Either MSS had been wrong, or the years out in this punishing environment had ruined Marco, depleted his strength and vitality so that now he was nothing.

How can the mission possibly need this man?

Briefly he considered putting a bullet in the American now, then setting off to complete the objective on his own, leaving the doctor's bony carcass for the dead to gnaw. But he bristled at the thought of so much wasted effort – the weeks journeying to Arizona, the enormous risks taken to remove the RRU squad and intercept Marco here in Maricopa with the burning truck.

And, most important, his orders from MSS were explicit. Get Doctor Henry Marco to Sarsgard Medical Prison – alive, by force if necessary. If the primary target – Roger Ballard – wasn't at Sarsgard as speculated, then Marco's personal knowledge might be critical. Disposing of him here, ahead of schedule, would be a flagrant disobedience, foolish and dangerous. If, for any reason, the mission failed, and MSS learned Wu had deviated from instructions . . .

He recalled agents he'd known in Beijing, deactivated and convicted of treason. Kneeling on their raw knees in concrete rooms. Pistols levelled at the backs of their heads.

'Let's go,' he barked at Marco, frustrated.

The corpses from the train station had reached the closest kerb, a mob of rancid men in stiff-collared shirts and women in crusted blouses. A blue-uniformed ticket agent missing its lower jaw pushed through the crowd. Its tongue dangled, wriggling like a fat worm.

Marco blinked like a man coming out of a trance. 'My Jeep,' he ordered. The authority in his voice caught Wu off guard, and when Marco turned and bolted, Wu hesitated for the shortest moment, reconsidering. *So* . . . perhaps this *was* the Henry Marco described in the dossier after all. Wu frowned, uncertain about whether the realisation pleased him. He bent and grabbed up his daypack where it rested on the pavement, then sprinted after the American.

The orange four-wheeler sat lopsided on the next corner,

half up the kerb, its bumper crashed into a black trash can. The engine was still running. Without hesitation, Marco ducked into the driver's seat and reached across to throw open the passenger door; Wu dived inside just as the corpses reached the Jeep. The dead ticket agent slapped the hood, its tongue bouncing.

Marco grabbed the wheel, then let go, hissing. 'Fuck,' he said and flexed his hands. His palms were burned and bloodied, sticky-looking. 'That hurts.'

'I can drive,' Wu stated. His tone was factual, not sympathetic.

'No,' Marco said. 'You're shotgun.'

Wu frowned, not understanding. *Shotgun?*

'Passenger seat,' Marco said, and Wu bristled, feeling the American had read his thoughts too easily, but there was no time for ego as the corpses piled and pressed against the vehicle, and the Jeep swayed from one side to the other, then back. The passenger-side window was a few centimetres open; grey fingers waggled through the crack.

'Go,' Wu said, annoyed. 'They'll break in.'

Marco answered with a gun of the gas pedal, and the Jeep squealed, its tyres seeking grip on the asphalt. With a shudder it surged from the kerb, chucking corpses aside, rolling over others; the ticket agent disappeared underneath, and the cracking of bones played loud in Wu's ears as the Jeep gained speed. It broke from the crowd without trouble and hit the street, fishtailing as Marco fought the wheel with his damaged hands. Wu watched him, curious. The American stared ahead, his face scrawled with a pained expression.

A sudden roar of sound and light brightened his face, and the Jeep rocked.

The gas tank of the overturned truck had exploded – a dark red fireball mushrooming from the undercarriage, sweeping the street. The nearest corpses vanished, consumed by the cloud; others vaulted forward, hit hard by the shock-wave. A moment later the fire collapsed on itself, spitting out corpses that burned like walking torches as they staggered after the Jeep.

'*Shit!*' Marco yelled.

He wrenched the wheel, and the Jeep zigzagged between burning dead men and body parts as if racing a slalom course. Wu slammed twice against the passenger door, grimaced but said nothing. A block later they'd escaped, sailing westward up a side street, past a rickety wooden water tower. Wu observed the receding train depot in his side mirror, the metallic roof shimmering with red heat; below it on the street, unlucky corpses stood wrapped in shrouds of flame. One by one, they flopped to the ground and grew still. Smouldering away to ash.

Silently Wu bid them goodbye.

His plan so far had worked, much to his relief. Twenty hours ago, back on the mountain trail, he'd stood at his lookout above the Arizona desert, fresh from exterminating the American special forces team. A few metres behind him, the paralysed black soldier screamed pitifully as the old female corpse peeled apart the man's face. Wu concentrated, blocking out the screams. His rifle weighed heavy on his back, as did his conscience. A single bullet could end the man's suffering – but Wu needed the Resurrection to saturate the bloodstream, pumped by a beating heart. A quick death would not work. And so Wu waited. Patient. Preparing his next move.

Defeating the Americans had been a clever use of force. But Henry Marco would require more.

Wu had paused then, noticing a sudden silence in the mountain air. The soldier had gone quiet – dead – and only the moist smacking of the elderly female's mouth persisted. If the man's body was not consumed entirely, he would resurrect in any time from minutes to hours; it varied, based on some unknown variable between individuals – blood type? Immune system? Metabolism? Scientists had not yet unlocked the secrets.

But one thing *was* known: the dead repopulated by stealing numbers from the living. The old corpse, while alive, had likely been a mother, perhaps a grandmother. Now, resurrected, the female would be a mother again, this time reproducing in a manner that defiled nature.

Which was exactly what Wu's plan required.

With ease he'd rolled the frail female aside with his foot, sending it down the embankment into a nest of saguaro bush; it stuck there, wailing. Dragging the soldier was harder. The man was large, nearly twice Wu's weight. He grabbed the man's ankle and heaved; the big body scraped a few feet along the trail. At least they'd be going *down* the mountain.

He'd dragged the man a dozen metres before he realised what his plan was missing. *Idiot.* With a scowl he looked behind himself towards the encampment.

He had to go back.

Cautiously he'd climbed the slope, poked his head over the low-lying rocks. The camp was a slaughterhouse, blood and innards and glistening flanks of fat and meat spread along the red clay of the mountain. Ten or so corpses squatted around the dead Americans – *Nelson, Guerrero, Pozzo,* he remembered – but to Wu's good fortune, the headless grey-bearded sergeant lay off to the side, unattended. Wu crept into the clearing, keeping close to the rock wall. The corpses didn't look up, lost in their own racket of crunching bones, snapping tendons, slurping juices. Wu held his breath. Gingerly he rolled the sergeant's body to the edge of the plateau and dumped him over. The corpses didn't seem to hear.

Down below, Wu had worked with haste. He switched into the sergeant's bloodstained uniform, at the same time alert for the slightest twitch of the black soldier's motionless body.

What would he do if the big man leapt up, snarling . . . ?

But his luck held. Three hours later, he had the soldier strapped safely into the passenger seat of the American 7-Ton truck. The man had resurrected soon after; its one remaining eye sprang open, hungry and wild, as the big muscles thrashed uselessly against the seat belt, the broken body unable to move from the waist down, its hands tied with rope.

With the captured corpse, Wu drove to the address he'd located in his Droid GPS. Henry Marco's house. From a hidden driveway up the road he'd spied on the home; it was sprawling, once lavish and proud – *a rich American home,* Wu thought with disdain – but all beauty had since faded, and the castle had been transformed into something resembling a junkyard with vast walls of rubbish and scrap metal. As Wu waited, the sun set. He spent a sleepless overnight in the truck. Beside him in the dark, the dead soldier grunted and hissed, and the truck cab filled with a ripe stink of flesh and gas. Even the open windows did little to diffuse it.

'I'm sorry,' Wu confided to the corpse – Baines, its name had been. Guilt beat like a second heart in Wu's chest. 'I mean you no dishonour.'

The Baines corpse growled and chattered its teeth.

'It must be done,' Wu explained. *Bao Zhi would not approve,* he thought. Bao Zhi, his uncle. Wu rubbed his bloodshot eyes, freshening them.

'Thank you,' he told Baines, and then did not speak again for the remainder of the night.

In the morning he'd snapped fully alert when Marco had departed the house. Driving behind at a safe distance, Wu had followed the American doctor to Maricopa. But when

Marco's Jeep had unexpectedly departed the train station without waiting, Wu paled, worried he'd lost his chance. Thinking fast, he doused the front seat of the truck with lighter fluid and lit it . . .

. . . cut Baines free with a quick snap of his knife . . .

. . . then pointed the truck at the train station and bailed out through the door.

Crash, flames, Marco to the rescue. The action had escalated far more alarmingly than Wu intended; his impulsive fire-setting had endangered the American, and what had been meant as a distraction to gain trust became a near-fatal error when the doctor crawled under the truck.

But Wu had corrected the mistake. The two men were now travelling together.

With no more corpses in sight, the Jeep slowed and followed the avenue running parallel to the train tracks. Marco whistled, a hollow sound, and his jaw relaxed. He nudged his knees against the steering wheel to hold it in place, then uncurled his hands. 'Son of a bitch, that stings.'

Wu surveyed the Jeep. Supplies and gear littered the floor and seats. He kicked aside a flashlight that had rolled up against his ankle, then cleared aside a few crinkling maps.

'Is there a med kit in this mess?' he asked with disapproval.

Marco threw him a look. 'Yeah, somewhere. A gun, too.'

'Somewhere,' Wu mocked. 'Wonderful. Perhaps I'm sitting on it.'

Marco glanced into the rear mirror and squeezed the brake. The Jeep rolled to a stop, half a kilometre from where they'd begun. The scream of the fire had vanished, and only the rumbling engine remained. Marco slapped the Jeep in park, then turned in his seat to face Wu.

'So,' he said. 'I assume you're my military escort?'

Wu's eyes hardened as he stared back at the American. 'Yes. I am.'

Gen wo zou, Wu thought. *Come with me.*

5.6

Marco cast a sarcastic smile at the soldier next to him in the Jeep. 'So, you're the army,' he observed. 'I thought there'd be more of you.'

'Be glad there was me,' the man answered dryly. 'Or you'd be dead.'

'True – or then again, I'd be on my way to California right now, happily by myself, if you hadn't come along and crashed your fucking truck.'

The man glared at Marco, jaw tensed, but he said nothing.

'So what happened?' Marco prompted.

'We were attacked.'

'Ah. And you weren't prepared for that? God bless the military.'

The soldier's eyes sharpened over his high cheekbones. His eyes were green and unusual, a contradiction to his otherwise Asian features. Marco had never seen such a combination.

'You listen,' the man instructed. 'My team is *dead* because of orders to help you.' His speech was unaccented, indistinguishable by dialect. 'You'll show *respect.*'

Marco blushed. He knew he was being an asshole, for no good reason other than his contempt for Director Owen Osbourne. Contempt for this entire damn job. But lashing out at the soldier wasn't fair – especially now, after the man had just risked his life for him.

'Okay,' Marco said, exhaling. 'You're right . . . sorry. And I'm sorry for your, uh, team, too.' He fumbled, not sure what else to say. 'Thanks for saving my ass,' he added.

The soldier studied him, then leaned back against the seat, seemingly pacified. 'Don't thank me. Thank DHS. We wanted to go without you.'

'Sounds familiar,' Marco quipped. He regarded the soldier's dusty brown uniform. The shoulders and chest were caked dark with blood.

The soldier read his look. 'Not mine,' he stated. 'Baines – your wrestling partner back there in the truck – bled out on me.'

'So what happened?' Marco asked again.

The soldier shrugged. 'We were up in Lost Dutchman, running recon on your house. At sun-up this morning, a pack of zoms ambushed our camp. Corpses. Baines and Pozzo had watch. They whooped us awake, but too late. I heard crashing, sat up and saw a corpse crawling through the tent flap. I flipped the blanket over its head and escaped out the back.'

He swallowed. 'Outside Baines was down, being chewed. Pozzo was already torn apart. Twenty, thirty corpses. I grabbed the guns and ran to Baines, kicked a corpse off, and got him up. Guerrero, my rifleman, came charging, firing, bullets kicking off rocks – a miracle he didn't shoot *me*. Then he was piled on, went down screaming, nothing I could do. Hard enough just keeping Baines on his feet. I didn't see anyone else, but Nelson's tent was shaking, he was screaming, too . . .' The soldier trailed off, as if contemplating some private thought.

'You got Baines out,' Marco said.

The man nodded slowly. 'Yes. Propped him up, pulled back down the trail. Luckily the dead didn't follow. They had enough. I escorted Baines to the truck, bleeding bad, but I thought . . .' He rubbed the back of his neck. 'I don't know what I thought.'

'He couldn't have made it,' Marco said, trying to help. 'Not after he was bitten.'

'I know that,' the soldier said. 'But I couldn't leave him.'

'So you drove him here?'

'Had to catch up to you. Baines resurrected before I even knew he was dead. I wasn't thinking. I should have stowed him in the back, but I had him up in the passenger seat so I could talk to him, maybe keep him focused. We were doing eighty just outside town – suddenly he grabs for me and tries to take a bite. I barely held him off. Baines was big.'

'I noticed.'

The soldier continued in a flat voice. 'I pulled my pistol, but he knocked my hand and the shot hit the dash. Must've punched the engine, caught the oil. Before I knew it, the truck was on fire, with a giant corpse all over me. I managed to stomp the brake once or twice, then got my hand to the door latch and popped it. Bailed out backwards, almost broke my spine rolling on the road. The truck went another hundred feet and crashed. And that's where you joined the party.'

Marco studied him, perplexed. Throughout the retelling of the team's death, the man had seemed curiously untouched. Maybe he was a tough bastard, burying his emotions – or maybe he had no grief to hide. Indeed, there was an air of cold functionality about him, like a decision-maker who operated by logic rather than heart. He was small, slighter than a normal RRU soldier – the complete opposite of Baines, but his eyes were striking and fearless. Intelligent. In the silence Marco sensed a thousand calculations taking place behind each intense green iris.

And that's when Marco realised the soldier was measuring him as well.

A chill rippled through him – a hunch that the man was holding something back.

Well, no shit. Of course he's holding back. God knows his exact orders, or what Osbourne told him about me. About Roger.

So be careful, Marco reminded himself. *Wait and see before you get too chummy.* He almost flinched when the soldier extended his right hand, blood-smudged and gritty.

'Ken Wu,' the man said. 'Sergeant First Class, RRU.'

Beneath the gore on the man's uniform, a military patch was just discernible. Three pointed gold stripes above, two rounded stripes below.

Marco nodded and shook the outstretched hand. 'Henry Marco here,' he said, forcing a smile. 'I guess you knew that, right?'

The soldier – Wu – did not return the smile. 'I've been briefed.'

'Yeah, well. I hope your brief was more informative than mine.'

Wu frowned. 'Mcaning?'

'Meaning, what the hell are we doing?'

'I was told that you'd been apprised of the target.'

Marco scoffed. 'Target? Yes, Roger Ballard – a friend of mine, by the way. But I'm sure your director told you that.'

'You and the target were co-workers, yes.'

'Jesus, stop calling him that.'

'Ballard.'

'Yes, Ballard.' Marco sighed. 'We worked at the hospital.'

The comment seemed to interest Wu. 'And how did—'

'Shit,' Marco interrupted. In the rear-view mirror he'd seen motion.

Seven or eight corpses had caught up from the train station, lurching doggedly towards the Jeep from a block away. A dead male in a business suit led the crowd, smoke wafting from its jacket. It dragged its foot sideways, broken at the ankle.

'We have to get going,' Marco said.

Wu twisted around in his seat. 'I agree.'

'Great,' Marco said wryly. 'Your approval means

everything.' He popped the gear into drive, and the Jeep rumbled forward.

Wu sat silent for a moment. Then he spoke, his eyes fixed on the road ahead. 'This is a military operation, Doctor. Remember that.'

Marco drew a deep breath, his forehead burning as if he were still under the fiery truck. *Fucker.* He could tell he was going to hate this. For the past four years, every decision had been his own; nobody to approve or say otherwise. But now this – Wu, Osbourne, the United States fucking government telling him what to do, running his ass from here to California.

I was better off alone, he seethed. But then another thought whispered in his head.

Quietly, almost sadly:

Hey buddy – you gonna be ready for society if they ever let you back?

Or have you been 'alone' out here too long?

The thought sobered him.

'All right then,' he said, swallowing his anger. The Jeep sailed up the street, heading west, the early sun behind them. Racing them to the left were the railroad tracks, bound off by a chain-link fence. Marco eyed a crossing, one block ahead. 'California, here we come.'

Right back where I started from, he thought.

'I have a GPS—' Wu began.

'Don't need it,' Marco said, and swerved the Jeep through a gap in the fence. The vehicle skidded across a narrow bed of gravel, jounced twice very hard – sending both men briefly airborne, supplies flying – and smacked down onto the westward train tracks.

Marco shot Wu a devilish grin. 'I know the way there.'

Just don't ask me if I know the way home.

DEAD MAN'S SWITCH

6.1

Hours had passed, and the sun had climbed from behind the Jeep to a point high above, and then gradually nosed ahead as Marco drove west along the tracks out of Maricopa. Progress was slow – twenty miles an hour, tops. The terrain beside the tracks was frequently undriveable, extreme with rocks and abrupt hazardous ditches, and Marco often had no choice but to steer directly onto the railway. The haggard wooden ties pummelled the Jeep from below. Every few minutes a tyre swerved against a rail, and the men banged sideways in their seats.

On the passenger side Wu scowled, massaging his temple.

'Headache?' Marco asked.

'I'm fine,' Wu replied. He blinked and concentrated straight ahead.

Marco suppressed a grin. A long drive on the tracks was punishment on the body, the constant shockwaves hammering bones and sinew. Wu had no idea how sore he'd be tomorrow.

'Sure,' Marco said. His own neck was knotted tight; his entire frame throbbed with various degrees of pain, from the dull bruising in his legs where the giant corpse had fallen on him, to the sting in his burned hands, to the dry itch of his smoke-irritated eyes. 'I'm fine, too.'

They were crossing the hottest corner of Arizona, the

Sonoran Desert. Around them sprawled harsh, waterless miles, tangled with prickly pear and burro weed. No human population – no corpses, thank god – just rattlesnakes, tarantulas, even jaguars farther southwest. Distant brown mountains caged them in. By mid-afternoon the dashboard thermometer read a hundred and ten outside, and even with the windows rolled up and the A/C cooling, the Jeep felt stuffy, brooding with an atmosphere of sweat and unspoken worry. The sun proved unstoppable; it reached through the windshield and pressed its hot hands on Marco's forehead.

Ahead of the Jeep, a speckled iguana skittered across the tracks and disappeared into a scramble of red rocks. Wu turned his head to follow it.

'That would have made a good meal,' he remarked. 'How are you for rations?'

Marco gestured to the back seat. 'Jerky, water, MREs I grabbed from abandoned army trucks – plenty for me. I'll share, but I wasn't planning on a dinner guest.'

'I don't need your help.' The condescension in the soldier's voice was obvious.

Marco bristled. *Fine, asshole. Go hunt a fucking lizard.*

Wu seemed oblivious to the insult he'd caused. He turned from the window and cracked his neck with a spiritless motion, to the left, then the right. 'How far are we?' he asked.

Grudgingly Marco returned his attention to the tracks. Far ahead, the heated desert seemed to warp the rails and melt them into shimmering air. Beyond the window to his left lay miles of rippled sand dunes; saguaro cactus towered taller than telephone poles, ending where the horizon erupted into the Gila Mountains, a row of rough summits.

They'd passed through the Gila Bend station about an hour ago. Marco had eyed the concrete platform with distrust, but to his relief nothing crawled from the overhang to intercept them, and the Jeep rolled through without incident.

'Probably close to Yuma,' he guessed now.

He'd already reviewed the intended route with Wu, popping open the glove compartment a few miles past Maricopa to tug out a collection of railway maps. He'd handed Wu the thick rubber-banded stack and tapped a creased yellow brochure on top.

SUNSET LIMITED, it read. This was the Amtrak line running westward into Yuma, then across the Arizona border and up through California. Marco had shown Wu where they'd ditch the tracks just past San Bernardino, then back-road the remaining miles to Sarsgard.

Wu had given the map a cursory scan. 'Agreed,' was his only comment, spoken in a tone that suggested he would have chosen differently if he'd been consulted sooner. He returned the stack to the glove compartment and snapped the latch shut.

They drove on, mostly in silence. Marco wasn't yet sure what to make of Wu. The sergeant hadn't said much since leaving Maricopa, busying himself instead with returning Marco's spilled gear to its proper storage. 'Your weapon,' he'd observed once chidingly, then reached down between the seats to retrieve the lost Glock; he'd hung the gun in its holster on the neckrest behind Marco. For miles afterwards he'd stared forward through the windshield, as if in a trance – back straight, hands on his knees, inhaling deeply through rounded nostrils. On the backseat rested his Army daypack, beaten and brown with a single shoulder sling. Strapped to the side were two scary-looking knives, curled like half-circles with the handle in the centre.

'Cool knives,' Marco offered. 'I'm guessing those aren't standard Army issue.'

'I brought my own,' the sergeant said without looking.

'Out here, we're allowed to embellish.' His lips pressed tight together, signalling lack of interest in the conversation.

'Well, I like 'em. Maybe for my birthday I'll get me a pair.' Marco stole a sideways glance. On Wu's left cheek a shiny bruise had blossomed, glazing the skin from his jawbone to his ear. Evident in the middle were white knucklemarks.

He'd been punched recently. Hard.

Marco frowned. *Punched by who?* Wu hadn't mentioned it. Only his struggle with the dead man, Baines. *Guess Baines gave him a good whack?*

Again a thought stirred in Marco's head that Wu wasn't telling him everything.

Crap. He hated to admit it, but Wu made him uneasy, a discomfort that went beyond the natural awkwardness between a soldier and a civilian. Sitting there in silence, Wu gave the eerie impression of a jack-in-the-box, placid and uneventful, baiting you to turn the handle – nothing happens, except you feel a little more tension, and then you keep turning and turning, until . . .

Marco sighed, loosened his grip on the steering wheel.

Fine, fuck him then, Marco thought.

And fuck Osbourne, too, that New Republican asshole. Whatever was on the secret agenda of these two dickheads, all that mattered to Marco was returning Roger, then getting the hell home. Alive. With all his body parts still attached. *So let Wu think I'm incompetent, or a jerk, or a hindrance to the mission. Or all of the above. Don't matter to me.*

Marco knew better. *Give it a day, and I'll be the one saving his ass.*

He noticed Wu watching him with interest. Quickly he erased the scowl that had crept onto his lips. *Poker face, Henry,* he thought. 'Definitely close to Yuma now,' he said, conscious of the flush in his throat, and pointed off to the right, eager to draw Wu's green eyes off him. 'Those mountains there are the Harcuvars. Fortuna Foothills is right under. Nice place to live.'

'Not at present,' Wu observed.

Marco ignored him, contemplating the dry brown peaks instead. A memory popped into his head, surprising him. 'First time I ever saw Arizona,' he said, 'these mountains made me think of that old Hemingway story. The title. 'Hills Like White Elephants'. Except here the hills are like big golden cats. See what I mean? Cats, crouched down with giant muscular shoulders, like they're ready to pounce. And we're just squeaky little rodents.'

Nostalgia tugged at him, and he remembered more. 'We nearly bought a house here. In Fortuna.' For a moment he actually lost track of himself, forgot why he was here now, forgot that it was Wu sitting next to him. He felt good, just talking – not about corpses, not about contracts – just shootin' the shit. He almost laughed when he realised he was making small talk.

'So where are you from?' he asked Wu. 'Before all this, I mean.'

Wu's gaze seemed to scale the Harcuvars, disappear into the mountains. The corner of his mouth twitched. 'Far,' he said with a hint of regret. He paused. 'Boston.'

'Miss it?'

The sergeant's expression went cold again. 'No.'

Marco sniffed. 'Jeez, sorry. Didn't mean to get personal.' He let a few awkward seconds pass, then tried again, not ready to let go of his remembrance. 'Anyway, Arizona takes some getting used to, but it's beautiful in its own brown, rocky way. I guess out here you really feel like you're someplace . . . different, I don't know, than wherever you came from. Which can be a good thing. We ended up picking a house over in the Gold Canyon. Man, what a view, not like LA at all. The Superstition Mountains were practically our backyard.'

Ironic, Danielle had said. *You living here – the least superstitious man I've ever met.*

Wu answered only with a dismissive nod. His focus had settled again on Marco.

'Tell me,' he said, his voice serious, all business, 'about Roger Ballard.'

Marco's neck knotted tighter. Small talk was officially over.

6.2

The question about Roger had slapped Marco out of his reverie, kicked him back to the present. Danielle was gone again. The Jeep crunched through a patch of spiny ocotillo plants, and he tugged the wheel back onto the tracks. Wu eyed him expectantly.

'Roger?' Marco said, clearing his head. 'Oh.'

The resentment he'd felt minutes earlier returned in force. He didn't feel like discussing Roger. *Screw it*, he thought. *Wu and Osbourne are keeping secrets. Why can't I?*

'Go ask your boss,' he answered. 'Osbourne knows everything.'

Wu considered this. 'I see you're reluctant to share. But the answer could be useful.'

Useful. Osbourne had chosen the same word yesterday to describe Marco. Again Marco rankled at the idea – himself a tool in another person's hands. Doing their work.

Wu seemed to read his thoughts. 'I hope you realise I'm in the same position as you, Doctor. I'm NCO – non-commissioned officer, meaning I have no top-level intelligence. If you think I know all the tricks of this mission, I don't. I'm just a bullet fired from a gun, same as you.

We don't decide the direction or the target, or know why the trigger was pulled. We just go and hit something. Personally, I'd prefer to know more about what we're hitting. About Ballard.'

Wu stopped. Bumps of sweat dappled his forehead. He wiped them away with the back of his hand, then fanned his fingers before the air-conditioning vent. 'From what I can tell, Doctor, we both feel saddled with an unnecessary partner. But I think we underestimate each other. I do know that Uncle Owen considered you a highly skilled individual.'

Marco blinked. 'Uncle . . . ?'

'Director Osbourne,' Wu clarified. 'No relation to me. "Uncle Owen" is simply Osbourne's nickname in the media. You don't follow the news?'

'I've been a little out of touch lately. So why "Uncle?"'

'A reference to Uncle Sam, I suppose. The face of American bravado. A patriotic icon protecting the nation's interests.'

Marco laughed, a sharp bark. The Jeep rattled over a gap where four or five rail ties had torn loose from the tracks. 'Yeah, perfect. That ugly piranha on a poster. *I want you.*'

He grinned but was surprised to find Wu stone-faced next to him. He'd sensed a bit of fun in the banter, as if perhaps the sergeant were finally warming up – but clearly not. The sergeant's frosty green eyes regarded him, unblinking.

'Right,' Marco said, uncertain. He coughed and cleared his throat. 'But I still don't understand. Why is Osbourne an icon?'

'Osbourne was head of Homeland Security at the time of the Resurrection. More or less, he founded the New Republican movement the year afterwards – deflected all the blame onto

President Garrett. Got Hoff elected with all his bluster and finger-pointing. And on top of all that, the Evacuation was Osbourne's idea. The Safe States are his brainchild.'

In his head Marco heard echoes of New Republican speeches, hot with vitriol and threats, pushing laws through a weakened Congress. *Without a vaccine for the Resurrection,* they railed, *the West is lost. Poisoned beyond hope. The Evacuated States will remain closed.*

The Safe States are America's future.

Let us protect you. Give us power.

Stay afraid . . .

Just then, the sergeant cut off Marco's thoughts.

'So,' Wu said, 'Roger Ballard.'

Marco scowled. 'Jesus, you don't give up, do you? I'd rather talk politics.'

Wu fixed Marco with a grim look. 'Doctor Marco. Any mission can succeed or fail on the basis of a single detail. As a doctor, I think you'd agree. Would you operate without first demanding to know each symptom? No matter how small it might seem?'

Marco grimaced. 'All right. I get where you're going.'

'You value details as much as I do. So tell me about Ballard, and I'll tell you what I *do* know about our mission. Is that fair?'

'Depends who goes first. Are we using the honour system?'

'Honour is everything to me.'

'Right. "Death before dishonour", all that. Careful what you wish for.' Marco ran his tongue along his teeth. The talking had dried his gums. He reached between his feet for his canteen and guzzled a swig. He badly wanted to pour the water over his scalp, rub it through his grungy hair, but instead he offered the canteen to Wu. The sergeant declined with a slight shake of his head. Marco recapped the water and returned it to the shade below the seat.

'All right,' he declared. 'Fair deal. Honour system. I go, then you go. And nobody leaves out any of the interesting details.'

'Agreed.'

'Good. Now, the truth is, you might be getting the worse end of the bargain. I don't really have a lot to tell about Roger.'

'But you did know him.'

'Yeah,' Marco conceded. 'I knew him. We were both on staff at Cedars-Sinai. The hospital in Los Angeles. I was in the Neurology department – you probably knew that already – and Roger was in Encephalopathy. You probably knew that, too.'

'He was a brain doctor,' Wu said.

'Brain disorders. Diseases.'

'How long did you work together?'

'Um, let's see. Roger began at Cedars-Sinai . . .' Marco squinted, as if he could see through time. It had been the year he'd married Danielle, and the year his mother had died.

'. . . In 2010,' he finished. 'Then I left for Arizona in 2013. So three years.'

Wu's lips pressed together. He appeared focused. Marco imagined this new data being logged somewhere in the man's mind for later analysis.

'And you were friends?' Wu asked.

Marco stiffened. He shifted in his seat and checked the rear-view mirror; old driving habits were hard to break. Nothing to see behind the Jeep but endless scrub and train tracks.

He sighed. 'Friends. Yeah, in a way, I guess. Back at the start.'

'The start?'

'The start of his residency, yeah. We were both from the

East, me Cornell and him Yale. People said he was kind of a prick – I don't know, we got along. He was actually a lot like me, but a more extreme version. He was me in a funhouse mirror. You know, distorted, everything more out-of-whack. I've never been that great with people, but Roger, he was practically a hermit. He had no family, kept to himself. He was smarter than me, too. Smart as hell, and in a way, that was maybe his problem. The human brain absolutely mesmerised him – what made it go, or what made it stop – but never the human. If you asked him about a diagnosis, he'd talk you under the table. But ask how his weekend went, and you'd get nothing. One or two words. Three, if it was a long weekend. He wasn't being a dick. He just didn't think it mattered.'

'But he considered you a friend?'

Marco shrugged. 'I don't know. Respected me, I guess. Judged me as competent. In Roger's mind that qualified as friendship. And I'm no chatterbox, either, so probably he was more comfortable around me than other people. Like I said, we got along.'

'Yes, at the start, you said,' Wu observed. 'But not the end?'

The Jeep had crossed another four miles of the Sonoran, and on the north edge of the desert a miniature display of buildings and homes and a trailer park now dotted the landscape. Yuma, far ahead. To either side of the tracks, the desert tilted at steep angles; Marco centred the Jeep and eased off the gas. The vehicle slowed and bounced with greater deliberation. Marco felt his head lighten. He remembered his last day at Cedars-Sinai.

Goodbye, Henry, Roger had said. And Marco had ignored him, kept walking.

Dizzy, Marco gripped the wheel tighter. His hands hurt, the burns still raw, but at least the pain anchored him. Jesus, the ride was making him nuts. He waited another few moments, allowing the weight of his body to return before answering Wu.

'No, not at the end,' he admitted. 'By the time I left, not at all.'

'And why was that?'

'Because . . .' Marco began. He stopped; his tongue seemed to slide backwards into his throat. 'Things got different,' he continued self-consciously, feeling his ears burn. '*Roger* got different – moodier all the time, more withdrawn. Like he'd gone deeper into his own dark cave. You'd see him in the hall, or the cafeteria, looking very preoccupied, and his eyes would just glance off you like you didn't even register. Even me. He'd walk by and not say hello.'

And neither would I, he added silently.

'Why did you leave?' Wu asked. Marco shot him a guarded glance. How much did the sergeant know already? But Wu's countenance was blank, implying nothing.

'I had a great opportunity in Arizona,' Marco answered. 'At St Joseph's.'

Roger Ballard appeared in his mind. The bony, rectangular face, prematurely wrinkled, wire-frame glasses not big enough to hide the heavy dark bags under his eyes. Thick brown hair combed straight back on his head. Sallow cheeks tapering to a narrow chin, and his top lip not quite centred, formed just a bit to the left like a permanent sneer.

Whispering something.

'One creepy thing,' Marco remembered. 'He mumbled to himself a lot near the end. You'd see him at his desk, his lips moving, but he wasn't talking to you.'

'Talking to himself? Odd.'

Marco nodded. 'Rumours started around, like maybe he was having a problem – drinking, or some drug. Because . . . well, here's what you need to know about Roger. What pushed him over the edge, I think.' Marco's mouth was dry again. 'Something bad had happened.'

Wu cocked his head, interested. 'Bad. To Ballard?'

'Well, bad to a patient. But it affected Roger. People said it was his fault.' Marco took a deep breath and steeled himself. *Say it.* 'A baby died.'

Wu's eyes narrowed.

'*Hypoxic ischemic encephalopathy,*' Marco continued, the words turning over in his stomach. 'Birth asphyxia. Not enough oxygen to the brain—'

'Look,' Wu interrupted. He pointed through the windshield. 'Ahead on the tracks.'

Marco snapped up straight in his seat. '*Shit,*' he said and hit the brake.

6.3

A silent unmoving train blocked the tracks, lifeless and weathered like the cast-off skin of a snake. A hundred yards long, eleven cars connected. Far ahead, a titanic locomotive rusted on a curve in the rails. Faded pink and green stripes ran the length of the cars, powdered with windblown dirt. Grime covered the windows.

Marco crept the Jeep to a stop fifty feet behind the last car. He let the engine idle as he contemplated the dead train. 'It's the Sunset Limited,' he said.

Wu scratched the back of his head. 'How far from the next station?'

'Yuma. Not that far.'

'Any reason a train would stop here?'

'No,' Marco replied. 'Only bad reasons.'

Wu rolled down his window and listened to the desert. 'Seems quiet,' he observed.

Neither man spoke. Wu was right. Outside, the Sonoran

napped through the angry heat of daytime, nothing but the churning of desert bees and the faraway call – *kee-u, kee-u* – of a Gila woodpecker nesting somewhere in the shade of a cactus.

Half a minute passed. Then Wu asked, 'Does it have a dining car?'

Marco frowned. 'The Sunset? Sure. They all—'

He stopped mid-sentence, understanding Wu's interest. Immediately he regretted his answer. Too late. Wu nodded and opened his door.

'Wait,' Marco said, disapproving. 'What are you doing?'

'Getting a look.' Wu swung himself out of the Jeep and reached into the back seat. 'I assume this train wasn't empty when it left Gila River?'

'Safe assumption,' Marco grumbled. Both his hands remained on the steering wheel. 'The Sunset holds two hundred passengers, I bet. Probably two fifty. Plus the crew.'

'I see.' Wu pulled his daypack and the AK from the back. He untied the knives and hooked them to his belt, then slipped the gunstrap over his shoulder.

Marco tensed. The hum of the Jeep trembled up his legs, begging him to drive. 'Hold on,' he protested. 'Just get back in. We'll go around it.'

Wu leaned through the passenger door, shook his head. 'You have your rations, Doctor. Here's where I get mine. But I'm not reckless. We'll do a quick recon. If it's clear – and only if it's clear – we can raid that dining car's galley, in and out in three minutes, loaded with enough food to last us both the next week. Or would you rather risk a supermarket in the middle of the next town? How many corpses in Yuma? More than two hundred, I'm certain.'

Marco opened his mouth but had no answer. Wu's point was valid. The supplies in the Jeep would take them halfway only; when those ran out, they'd have to replenish somewhere. At least out here, the train was remote. Much safer than a trip into town.

'You're wasting time, Doctor,' Wu continued. 'If there *are* corpses on that train, we should make our move before they know we're here. In case they're as hungry as we are.'

'Funny,' Marco said. 'Look – some advice. There's no such thing as "easy" around here. I'm talking from experience. One minute seems fine, the next is all-out fucked. These corpses have a way of . . . I know this sounds crazy, but a way of *outwitting* you. Maybe because we overthink, and they just go on instinct, but I've seen some very smart people get their heads torn off because they underestimated a few rotting bodies.'

He hesitated. 'Your unit, for example.'

Wu's face darkened.

Marco reconsidered. 'I'm sorry,' he admitted. 'That came out harsh.'

'I appreciate the honesty.'

'Believe it or not, I don't want you to die a horrible death.'

Wu said nothing, simply stood and adjusted the rifle on his back. He left the Jeep and trotted four or five steps towards the tail of the train. 'Let's go,' he called back over his shoulder.

Shit, Marco thought, relenting. *Okay then.*

He couldn't let Wu risk it alone. However arrogant the man might be, however strange, however huge a dickhead, he'd been a lifesaver back at Maricopa. Wu was fearless, no doubt – a definite big-time ass-kicker.

The video of Sarsgard Prison flashed in Marco's memory. A thousand blood-soaked corpses, wild and rioting. He shuddered.

The truth was, he was going to need Wu's help at Sarsgard. And right now Wu needed his, whether the soldier wanted to admit it or not. *We don't have to be best buddies,* Marco thought. *But, Jesus, we oughta stick together.*

Marco tapped the gas and rolled the Jeep forward, pulling next to Wu. 'Hey,' Marco called through the open window. 'All right, you win. I'm coming with you.'

'Leave the Jeep,' Wu said curtly and continued walking.

Marco rolled his eyes. 'Holy Christ, it's hard to be nice to you. Stop acting like a teenage girl on a hissy fit for a goddamn second, and listen to me.'

Wu halted. He turned and regarded Marco with scepticism.

'Just get in,' Marco said. 'We'll drive up next to the dining car and leave the Jeep there. Engine on, ready to drive. No sense parking this far back.'

Wu considered, then a moment later nodded. 'Agreed,' he said, opening the door, and climbed back into the passenger seat.

Carefully Marco steered the Jeep off the tracks and onto the sloping desert terrain. The Jeep dipped to the right, and Marco heard his bag of gear slide across the back seat. Wu pressed his hands against the dashboard, steadying himself.

The Jeep crawled alongside the train. Each dark car was massive, the size of a house. The rear car was a double-level sleeper; centred in the middle was an open doorway through which Marco saw metal stairs ascending into shadow. He kept his boot steady on the gas pedal, and the Jeep passed the opening with no protest from Wu. *At least he's got some sense,* Marco thought. Entering the train at the tail end – walking up tight-quartered passenger cars to the diner – would be *way* the hell too risky, and Marco wasn't feeling quite that suicidal. *Not today, anyway.*

The Jeep continued past a windowless baggage car, and beyond that were four metal-ribbed coaches lined with portholes of dirt-caked glass—

Something moved.

Through the grime of one window, a flash of white skin. Then darkness.

'Aw, shit,' Marco said, craning his neck. 'Did you see that?'

Wu nodded. 'We won't go near that car. The diner is up ahead.'

'You said only if it was clear. That didn't look clear.'

The Jeep pulled even with the impressive lounge car. The vessel loomed above them. Marco watched it creep past, eleven dark windows staring back at him like a set of alien eyes. Thick observation glass rounded the upper deck, designed to give riders an unobstructed view of California mountains and sparkling stars on desert nights. All wasted now. Even from below, Marco could see streaks and spatters of what looked like dried black mud on the skylight glass.

Except it wasn't mud.

'There's guts everywhere,' he announced.

The dining car rattled up beside them.

'Stop the Jeep,' Wu said. 'We go in here.'

6.4

Marco winced at the crunch of rusted metal. In the quiet desert, each sound seemed a hundred decibels louder, a screaming wake-up call to every possible corpse on the train. *Jesus Christ, this is stupid.* He held his breath and wedged the crowbar deeper between the black panels that connected the lounge and the dining car, bending the material apart.

The diner had no exterior doors, so breaking into the small walkway between cars was the simplest way inside. Marco had volunteered for the job, attacking the lower corner, the only area he could reach. The corridor was raised ten feet off the ground, joining the upper levels of the train; he'd hoisted himself up by the outer grab-rails and established an unsteady foothold along a rubber-tubed electrical cable. From this awkward perch he could barely get leverage on the crowbar; the iron handle pushed back at him, almost chucked him to the dirt below.

'Do it fast,' Wu ordered. He sounded annoyed. 'Slow makes more noise.'

'So does talking,' Marco snapped. 'Shut up, please.'

He rocked the crowbar back and forth into the seam where the panelling bolted to the car. His grip was painful. On the fourth or fifth pull, he felt the burn blisters on his palms pop, and a watery serum leaked between his fingers. *Motherfucker*, he hissed to himself. The panelling shook and bounced to the sound of loose chains jangling.

Drops of his sweat splashed the metal, drawing dark wet spots in the dust. And then at last the panelling peeled apart with another hideous squeal.

A narrow shadow opened, large enough to fit through.

'There,' Marco breathed. Exhausted, he hopped down. 'We're in.'

'Not yet,' Wu said. 'There's still the diner door inside.'

Twenty feet behind them, the Jeep idled on a sandy dune where the desert dropped off steeply from the tracks. Marco had parked at a precarious tilt, the sand loose beneath the wheels as he fishtailed to a stop. Hurriedly he'd armed himself with the Glock, then rummaged in the back for the crowbar and a flashlight. And his duffel bag to cart whatever food they'd find.

Might find, he reminded himself. *Could be nothing.*

The more he thought about it, the more this idea sucked.

'Hey,' he said, turning to Wu. 'You ever throw a rock at a hornet's nest?'

Wu frowned; he seemed not to understand. Marco continued.

'Like when you're a kid, right? You find a hornet's nest, and it's all quiet and peaceful, and for whatever idiot reason that makes sense to a kid, you throw a rock. And then you better run like hell when a thousand pissed-off hornets come shooting out to sting your ass to death.'

Wu stared blankly. Marco sighed. 'Right . . . so maybe we had different childhoods. But my point is, right now we're standing outside a giant, metal, quiet hornet's nest. So before we do this, let's take a second and ask ourselves – are we really sure we want to throw a rock?'

Wu considered this. 'Doctor,' he said, 'were you ever stung?'

'Well, no . . . I always got away.'

'Exactly,' Wu said. 'So do I.'

The matter apparently settled, he grabbed the handrail and, with graceful ease – weightless, deft like an acrobat, each limb in perfect synch with the others – scaled the train exterior and slithered his upper body into the torn panel. For a moment his legs hung from the hole, and then he kicked and the darkness swallowed him.

Marco tensed, waiting. Then he saw the flashlight click on. Wu's voice, muffled, called to him. '*Clear. Come on.*'

Marco set the crowbar down, then reconsidered and picked it up again. With the Glock holstered and the crowbar tucked under his arm, he climbed, not like Wu at all, clumsily, banging his ribs as he flopped and wriggled his way into the crack.

Goddamn it. No style points there, he thought, rolling onto his back.

Inside, the atmosphere was cooler, out of the sun but musty and oxygen-depleted; Marco battled the urge to stick his head outside again for a fresh gulp of air. Instead he blinked, his eyes adjusting, the afternoon still bright on his retinas. He rose to his feet and bumped against Wu, who stood sweeping the flashlight high and low, measuring the space they'd entered.

The short connector was about three feet long, just enough for both men to fit shoulder to shoulder. Dust hovered in the flashlight beam, and ghostly spider webs laced the corners. Seed shells littered the floor around a ball of dry leaves where some desert mouse had once nested.

Wu cast the light over Marco's shoulder. 'That's it,' he said. 'This way.'

Behind Marco was a closed metal door, a window in the middle. The flashlight's reflection in the glass burned like a sun in a starless universe. A small placard read DINING CAR in dirty red letters; next to it sat a large rectangular button. PRESS. The door had been hydraulic – hit the button, the door slid open. Wouldn't work now.

'There'll be a release somewhere for emergencies,' Marco said, scanning the jambs. 'Like power failures. Or when resurrected corpses eat all the people on board.'

On the frame above the door he found it, a small inset panel with a sticker.

In Case of Emergency:
Open this Box
Pull Red Lever Down
Slide Door Open

Wu leaned across Marco and popped the lid. His hand reached for the lever.

'Wait,' Marco interrupted. 'Let's have a peek first. Turn off the light – there's too much reflection.'

Wu replied with the slightest of nods, and Marco heard a *click*. The antechamber fell dark, barely fed by light from the cracked panelling. In another few moments, Marco's eyes had once more adjusted. He squinted into the window to the dining car. Even here, inside the train, the grime and debris on the glass were thick, hard to see past.

He rubbed his elbow on the glass, then cupped his hands around the cleared swathe and peered again. Still no good. Too much shit on the other side, mucking it up. He registered a few dark edges of tables. The rest was pure black.

He raised a fist and rapped three times on the window.

Behind him, Wu spoke up. 'I thought you said no noise.'

'If anything's in there, I'd like to know now. *Before* we open the door.'

They waited. Nothing.

'All right then,' Marco said. 'Pull that bad boy.'

Wu yanked the red lever, and the door shuddered once. 'Try it.'

Flushed with sweat, Marco wrestled the crowbar into the padded edge of the doorway. Even unlocked, the door was stingy – years of caked filth in the runners had almost cemented it shut, but he threw his shoulder against the bar, and the door popped open, too hard, too loud, dirt grinding in its gears. It rattled halfway, then stopped.

Marco aimed his Glock into the gap. The stock felt slick in his palm.

The darkness seemed alive, grumbling back at him. Buzzing. Sounded like . . .

Click. The flashlight leaped on, cutting a beam into the dining car.

Flies. Thousands of flies, exploding in and out of the light, a repulsive black cloud that swirled and bounced, split in pieces, merged again. Marco flinched. *Disgusting.*

Wu swung the light lower. To the floor.

Bodies.

6.5

The centre aisle was a graveyard – a slaughterhouse killing-floor of torn human limbs and ribcages and mummified heads with screaming mouths captured in final poses of pain and terror. Men, women. Small skeletons, too, chiselled with bite marks. Children. Thirty, forty people caught here in an attack, making a last stand as corpses overtook the train. Bodies piled in the booths, too, gutted while they'd hidden under tables or struggled to break the windows.

'Welcome to the dining car,' Wu announced. His voice was unamused.

A sludge of blood and offal carpeted the floor, inches thick. But solid. Hardened with time. The bodies had been dead for years, dried now and colourless. Spines torn apart, brains gnashed. These victims been devoured too quickly, too completely to resurrect.

The stench was old, too – a fusty, stomach-turning gas, molecules of dissolved soft tissue bogging down the air. Marco coughed, hid his nose in the crook of his elbow. The sight sickened him, and at the same time propelled his heart faster.

'Fuck,' he said. 'We should go back.'

'Why? These bodies aren't moving.'

'Come on, man,' Marco urged. 'What do you think happened here? Food poisoning? The train must've had its own mini-outbreak – some passenger with the Resurrection punched everybody else's ticket, too. The corpses that did this are someplace onboard. Guaranteed.'

'I understand, Doctor. Thankfully, we only need this one car.'

'Jesus Christ – how many safety lectures do I have to give you today?'

Wu brushed past, knocking Marco's shoulder as he stepped through the doorway into the dining car. The flashlight poked deeper into the darkness, illuminating more ghostly tables cloaked in grey tablecloths and a waiter's station halfway up the car.

'*Wu*,' Marco growled. 'Get the fuck back. We have to go.'

Wu continued forward, stepping over bones.

Asshole. Right here was exactly what Marco hated – stupid military bullshit that gets everybody killed. He considered retreating to the Jeep, leaving Wu. Just sit out there and wait for the screaming to start. But then what? Rush back to the rescue? Drive away?

His neck flushed, ashamed. *Don't be a pussy*, he thought. He shook his head and sighed.

Whatever. I guess this stupid military bullshit is contagious.

He flexed his fingers on the crowbar and stepped over the gap in the connector, rolling his eyes at a small white sign.

WATCH YOUR STEP

Yeah, tell me about it, he thought. His boot crunched down on the crust of blood in the entryway, and the smell of death thickened. He followed Wu up the car.

Around him, a thousand flies rose and dived, bouncing off his face as he tried to swat them. He clamped his mouth tight to keep them out. He couldn't help but marvel at how long they must have existed here, chewing nests into carcasses. Generations of flies. Each surviving days at a time, doing its part, picking the dead clean. Laying eggs. Dying so the next can be born, repeating over and over, four years here in this same train, shut off from the world outside. The first generation had seen the carnage, had feasted on fresh blood and moist, shivering organs. But these flies knew none of that.

This is all normal to them, Marco thought. *The only life they've known.*

Hatched into a land of silent bones.

How long, he wondered, *until it's like that for us? A generation? Nobody'll even remember this planet before the Resurrection.*

Disheartened, he moved carefully, but stumbled once, stepping hard on a brittle femur bone that broke underfoot with a grisly *crack*. He grabbed hold of a table edge to steady himself, and the stiff fabric of the tablecloth bunched in his fingers. In the dim light he saw a dark blotch on the cloth. An old bloody handprint, small and female. He fixed his balance and kept moving.

Halfway through the car, he caught up to Wu at the counter of the small waiter's station. Wu stood examining a square hole in the wall, about a foot and a half wide. He shone the flashlight in. A narrow shaft dropped straight down.

'Dumbwaiter,' Wu said. 'For sending up food. The kitchen's below us.'

'Don't tell me. We're going to slide down it.'

Wu shot him a quizzical look. 'If you'd like, Doctor. I'll use the staircase there.' He gestured with the flashlight to a small flight of steps beyond the counter.

'Wise ass. Well, I'm glad you have at least *some* common sens—'

He stopped, snapped his head to the left. Squinted towards the far end of the car.

'What?' Wu asked.

'Shh.' Marco frowned and pointed up the aisle. 'Shine the light.'

Wu turned the beam. The door at the other end was open. A petrified mess of human forms lay sprawled in the doorway, preventing it from sliding shut.

Marco's gut went cold.

'Would've been easier to come in that way,' Wu observed.

'Hold the light there,' Marco told him, extending his arm

with the Glock out in front. He ventured another few feet, eyes fixed on the open door, his head bent.

The buzzing of flies engulfed his ears. He batted them away.

There was something else. Something he needed to hear.

A few feet further, past the stairs, he heard it again. A heavy thump.

Then a whispery sliding. Then a thump again.

Footsteps.

His pulse pounding, he focused on the rectangular doorway. Felt himself jump when a pale hand reached from the shadows and grabbed the frame.

A slender feminine hand.

His mind leaped. *Danielle . . .*

No, he scolded himself. *Not Danielle, dumbass.*

An older female corpse slithered through the door. A black dress hung in tatters from its bony body, exposing shrivelled tits. It goggled at Marco, ice-white eyes sunk deep in its skull. Strands of brittle silver hair dangled in its face.

And it wasn't alone.

Two, three . . . four corpses creeping in, and more behind them; pasty figures swaying in the dark of the adjoining car. Shambling into the diner.

'I *knew* it,' Marco muttered. 'Fucking *knew* it . . .'

Without pause he aimed his Glock straight into the middle of the female's forehead, tightened his finger on the trigger . . .

Behind him the flashlight clattered to the floor.

Blackness overtook him as if he'd been thrown into a sack, and he lost his mark on the corpse. 'Christ!' he shouted, more pissed than frightened, and spun around.

He couldn't see shit. 'Wu!'

On the floor, the flashlight rolled in a lazy semi-circle, sending light into the wall . . . then rolled back to face the waiter's station.

Wu—

Suddenly Marco wasn't pissed at all. Suddenly he was pretty fucking alarmed.

Wu was there, slammed against the counter, thrashing, wrestling with a heavyset corpse – a fat monster in a soiled conductor's shirt, ticket punch bouncing from its belt, its face a vicious white snarl. It slung its bulbous arms around Wu's neck, squeezing him towards its teeth.

The tables, Marco realised stupidly, his thoughts spinning like tyres in mud, trying to grab hold. Hadn't checked beneath. The corpse must've crawled out. *Jesus Christ.*

'Doct—' Wu began, but his hands slipped from the counter. He crashed to the floor, kicking up bones, and the dead conductor pounced on top of him.

Marco choked the crowbar, bit his lip. *Here we go. Head-bangin' time.*

He charged a single step . . .

. . . and faltered as the older female clenched its hands on his shoulders from behind. Before he could whirl, the corpse pitched itself against him, and he stumbled to the left, surprised – surprised again when his ankle buckled under him, and the floor opened like a pit, and all at once his vision spun topsy-turvy.

With the female corpse pinned to his back, he toppled down the unlit stairwell.

Down to whatever waited in the shadows below.

6.6

White fireworks ruptured the blackness, pain lighting the nerves in Marco's visual cortex as he crashed sideways down the stairs. He hit the last four steps on his chest and slid as if being scrubbed on a washboard, his teeth clacking, the female corpse screeching in his ear. Halfway down, the stairwell turned; Marco and the corpse met the wall with a terrible *snap* – brittle bones splintering into toothpicks under the female's skin – and they flipped, a tangle of hot and cold limbs, their foreheads knocking. For an instant the corpse's mangled lips were so close to his own that he could have kissed it. Horrified, he planted his foot and shoved off.

He felt himself airborne again, this time falling backwards, somersaulting down the second short flight of steps. He landed with a thud on his ass. The floor was wet, soaking through his pants in moments. His boots slipped as he scrambled to his feet.

Christ, the air reeked here, fierce like ammonia. His eyes flashed left, right, straining into the dark. Waist-high countertops. Cupboards, shelves, the deep basin of a sink.

He'd found the kitchen.

Feeble light trickled into the room from a single glass pane – a muck-covered window on the opposite wall, facing west out of the train. He hadn't detected it earlier from outside; the Jeep had driven along the unending chain of cars on the east, where the diner's bottom level had appeared windowless. *Nice going, genius,* he grumbled. *Woulda been a lot fuckin' easier to break in here, through a window. Next time, check the* other *side of the train.*

Frustrated, he gave himself a rapid check-up, bent and unbent his arms, flexed his knees. Sore but nothing broken; probably just a few more bumps and bruises for his collection. And, thank Christ, he'd held onto the Glock and the crowbar, two reassuring weights in his hands.

The female corpse hadn't forgotten him. It faltered down the last step, grunting, arms outstretched. A marble-sized diamond crowned its ring finger. Fleetingly, Marco pondered the fate of its husband. One of the mummified bodies upstairs, or another walking corpse on board?

Or had the husband escaped?

Fuck it, Marco decided. *Nobody escapes.*

Incensed by his own nihilism, he lashed forward and rammed the point of the crowbar up through the female's nose – the easiest path to the brain, he'd discovered years ago – until he felt the tip punch past the nasal cavity and lodge in the prefrontal cortex. In a single motion he wrenched the bar, ripping the brain in half, and twisted the female's head around on its shoulder until he heard the vertebrae in the wrinkled neck groan and shatter.

The corpse flopped to the floor.

Shadows lurched on the staircase. More corpses coming.

'*Wu!*' Marco screamed up the steps.

No answer. Then a crash.

Marco backed away. A cluster of corpses rounded the corner, descending into the gloom.

Enough dark, he thought. *Let's turn the lights on.*

He wheeled, the Glock ready in his right hand, and fired one bullet into the filthy pane on the western wall. The gunshot thundered in the small kitchen, the reverberations so intense he heard knives and ladles on wall hooks chattering against themselves.

The glass exploded. Sunlight flooded the kitchen.

Much better.

He blinked, ears ringing, and shaded his eyes with the gun. Suddenly he understood the putrid smell he'd noticed in the darkness.

The floor was a stew of liquefied rat bedding, turds and piss; he'd stumbled into a nest. So that's how this post-apocalyptic world worked – flies ruled the top level, rats below in a subkingdom of spoiled vegetables and cupboard perishables. Along the counters, brown hairy bodies scurried for safe crevices, terrified by the light and noise.

Not a bad idea, he reckoned. *I could use a crevice myself.*

A dead couple emerged from the stairwell, a male and

female decked in red sweatshirts emblazoned with University of Arizona decals, followed by another male, and another. Daunted, Marco retreated around a stainless steel island occupying the centre of the kitchen. He passed three shelf fixtures stocked with canned soups, fruits, pasta – *Wu's gonna have a feast, if he's not already dead* – and stopped at the broken window. Shattered glass crackled underfoot.

The window wasn't big, but it was big enough for an escape. With the crowbar he hurriedly crushed out the remaining glass and swept the shards from the sill.

The male corpse rounded the island, faster than the others. Marco lifted the Glock and fired, sending the rats into a fresh squealing panic as the corpse rocketed backwards, its face caved in, pieces of skull spinning across the island tabletop like broken eggshells. Black ooze spewed over the Arizona logo on its chest, soaked into the cotton.

The female stepped over the body. Corpses continued to march downstairs. The kitchen had filled – ten, fifteen, circling the long counter towards him.

Time to get the hell out.

'*Wu!*' he called one more time, hopeful. Nothing.

Dammit. Marco hesitated, but there was really no choice. He grabbed the sides of the window and heaved his upper body through the opening, all the way to his waist . . .

. . . then screamed as rotten hands grabbed at his face. Corpses, outside, on the ground. He dangled halfway out of the window, terrified, certain his momentum would drop him into the crowd. Fifty or sixty dead passengers from the coach cars. They must've heard the Jeep, disembarked – he remembered the open exit at the rear sleeper – and mobbed here beside the diner, drawn by the commotion. The window was eight feet off the ground, thank Christ, or he would've been lunch. Gasping, he kicked his legs and squirmed back into the kitchen.

So much for an easy exit.

Ten bullets left in the Glock. Wouldn't even make a dent in the crowd outside. Not much help here, either. Corpses packed the kitchen and, on the floor above, he heard more creaking footsteps, more raucous gargles and moans. His heartbeat ticked like a stopwatch.

Think fast.

The female in the sweatshirt touched his shoulder.

Faster!

He dropped and spun under the steel tabletop. *Shit*, he thought, immediately second-guessing himself. *Bad move, Henry.* The corpses had the island surrounded. Peering out from underneath, he saw dead spindly legs blockading him on all sides, like the bars of a cage.

The female corpse in the sweatshirt bent under the table, a ratty ponytail of hair dangling from its head. Marco shot it through the cheek. The ponytail snapped like a whip as the head tore backwards and the corpse crumpled.

Nine bullets left.

Need a new plan, let's go, let's go . . . His hands vibrated with adrenalin. His mind raced through twenty bad ideas in a second, and then he had no more seconds left. The corpses had figured him out – poking their heads under the table, smacking their dry mouths.

They'd crawl under and drag him out screaming.

Grim-faced, he gathered his legs under him like a sprinter at a starting line, ready to dash out from the table, make a mad rush to the staircase. Knock through a few corpses, pop a few with the Glock, hope for the best upstairs. No other option.

He tensed, flexed and—

'*Doctor!*'

Marco froze.

'*Doctor! Can you hear me?*'

Wu. His voice distant, hollowed.

'*Hey!*' Marco yelled back, surprised at the relief in his

own voice. A dead hand touched his foot, and he yanked it away; the corpses were on all fours, under the table, coming for him.

In the kitchen, he heard a loud clattering, a banging of metal. Something falling.

'*The dumbwaiter!*' Wu's voice shouted.

Marco puzzled, not understanding.

'*The dumbwaiter!*' Wu repeated. '*Look!*'

Gotcha. Marco didn't answer – didn't have time. A thin, broken-nosed corpse wriggled towards him from the front. He shoved the Glock between its lips and pulled the trigger. Its brain exploded from the rear of its head, and before the body even hit the floor, Marco was scrambling over it, his fingers slipping through the chunks of wet grey matter.

Eight bullets now in the Glock. He prayed he wouldn't need them.

Corpses closed in from the left and right; he felt a tug or two on his shirt, but none too firm, and he pulled free, skittering out from beneath the table. Standing, whirling, he frantically scanned the kitchen. The banging had come from . . . *there.* In the wall, a small closed door. To his left, another wave of the dead mobbed the stairs, a march that never seemed to end. He high-stepped over two corpses still halfway under the table, their legs kicking, and flung open the dumbwaiter.

Jackpot.

The AK-47 lay in the narrow chute. A gift from Wu up above.

The sight of the gun strengthened Marco at once, an instant detoxification of the fear in his bloodstream. He was clear again – back in command.

'Thank you,' he said and snatched up the automatic rifle.

He wheeled first to the corpses advancing from the stairs, unleashed a barrage of steel core bullets that tore through necks, popped heads like balloons. The gun kicked ass. He'd never fired an AK before; his shoulder would be a giant purple bruise tomorrow, slammed again and again by the kickback after each shot, but he didn't give a shit. It felt fucking *good.*

The roar was ear-splitting, and all else was impossible to hear. His eyes told him everything he needed to know – corpses breaking apart, holes punching through walls, pots and pans flying off hooks, the kitchen floor sloshing with black blood and rat urine.

When the last corpse dropped, he released the trigger, dizzy, out of breath.

His eardrums throbbed, still echoing. He swung the gun around the room, body to body, on the lookout for movement. The slightest twitch, and he'd let rip again. Nothing. He checked under the island tabletop. Good there, too.

He limped to the open window, where the dead passengers outside were battling to climb into the kitchen. He wasn't worried. Corpses couldn't climb for shit. He paused there above the sea of discoloured waving arms, feeling like a rock star, like the goddamn Beatles pulling into Liverpool station to greet the fans. *They all want a piece of me*, he thought grimly.

He considered opening fire, but that would be senseless. He had no idea how much ammo an AK clip held, and these corpses weren't an immediate threat. Not worth the bullets.

Better to go find Wu, get the hell back to the Jeep without being seen.

But first, rest. He sagged against the table; his body felt fifty pounds too heavy.

This day was catching up on him. Big time.

He let a minute pass before he ordered himself up. *All right, lungs. Back to work.* He was ready to backtrack upstairs, grab some canned fruit on the way out, when a massive jolt pitched him sideways – nearly threw him face first into the rat shit.

He dropped immediately to one knee and grabbed hold of the tabletop.

His entire body shook. The fruit cans rattled on the shelves.

At first he thought he was crazy. He had to be wrong.

But seconds later, he knew he was right.

The train was *moving.*

6.7

In the corridor behind the locomotive cab, Wu threw the knife-switch – the large metal tong connecting the battery to the train's starter circuit.

Would the power be drained? After all this time, would it be as dry as the desert . . .?

A soft crackle reassured him. His fingers danced over the circuit-breakers, flipping pegs as he went. He hadn't operated a train in almost twenty years, and yet the movements were automatic and gratifying. His chest swelled, and briefly he felt himself transformed – a teenage soldier again in the People's Liberation Army, manning the disaster-relief train through slashing rainfall and underwater fields, a national hero risking death to evacuate women and babies from the Yangtze River floods – and then he blinked, surprised. He missed that life. Back before he'd been chosen for MSS. Now, no more saving lives. Now he *killed* for the good of China.

He frowned and focused on his task.

He hit the switch labelled *Fuel Pump*, then scrambled to the engine room and primed the diesel's fuel system; once the air was flushed, he cranked the lever, and the starter motor growled. Hurrying, without waiting for the system to pressurise, he released the handbrake and cranked furiously until he felt the train shudder and roll. Then he jogged to the cab – leaping over the two carcasses in the corridor, the mangled bodies of two engineers fused together into a single slop of decomposition – and freed the set of double brakes on the control stand. All set. He pulled the throttle towards him, locking it into the first notch.

The entire train rumbled under his boots.

To his rear the main generator bit into the traction motors, and the locomotive lurched forward, slow, still picking up the weight of all the cars behind it. Four or five corpses blocked the track ahead, snarling at him through the window; their grey faces didn't even register surprise as the train dragged them under, ground them like meat.

He inched the throttle another notch.

Crawling through the desert. Picking up speed.

Wu nodded, satisfied.

Ten minutes earlier, he'd been pinned beneath the conductor corpse in the dining car, struggling against death. Marco had plummeted downstairs to the kitchen, the female on his back. *He'll die*, Wu had thought. The words bubbled in his mind, then burst and were gone.

Nothing he could do about that now. Nothing but fight to survive himself.

And so he'd rammed his knee up into the conductor's groin, but the corpse didn't flinch. Instead it raged and snarled and clawed atop him, crushing him into the floor of the dining car. The dried-out bodies of massacred passengers surrounded him; old bones splintered and broke beneath his back, stabbed at him through his shirt.

Close combat with the dead was difficult, Wu realised; blows that neutralised human enemies were useless on corpses that didn't feel pain . . .

Frustrated, he hooked his hand under the conductor's neck. The flesh was overripe, squishy like bad fruit, and his fingers sank in with ease, all the way to his knuckles. The corpse grunted, infuriated, unable to get its teeth down for a chunk of Wu's face.

Wu twisted for a look up the aisle. More corpses coming.

From the kitchen below, a gunshot roared and glass shattered.

So Marco wasn't dead yet.

Wu blinked, annoyed at the distraction. *Focus here.* He needed a weapon, something to beat back the attack, club the conductor – not kill it, of course, unless his own death was the only other option. The AK-47 on his back was tangled with his daypack, impossible to pull. With his free hand he yanked at his deer-horn knives, but they were lodged in his belt, pinned by his hips.

What else, then?

A metre from his right shoulder, the flashlight shone towards him on the floor. The beam spotlighted the conductor's grim complexion – pickled skin, veins thick as liquorice bulging under the surface, a black spider web across its jaw and cheeks.

Wu grabbed at the flashlight. Missed it.

Another gunshot exploded in the kitchen.

Then Marco's voice, faint but urgent. '*Wu!*'

Wu ignored him. *Focus.*

His fingers closed on the flashlight.

From the conductor came a sound like an alley dog growling, its throat curdled with disease; it grabbed Wu's wrist and yanked, breaking his chokehold under the chin. His eyes widened as the corpse lunged for the kill. For an instant the open jaws struck down at him, ropes of saliva stretched like brown taffy between the teeth, the tongue swollen and black . . .

He rammed the flashlight into the corpse's mouth as hard as he could.

The metal barrel punched through the top row of decayed teeth, lodging deep into the throat. The corpse bellowed, a cry muffled by the thick flashlight. The bulb end protruded from the dead man's stretched lips. Wu squinted, half blinded by the bright beam, and pounded the end with his palm. The blow drove the flashlight another five centimetres deeper.

Yellow pus oozed around the barrel, dribbled down the corpse's chin. It jerked away, surprised, fumbling for the light. Wu gasped as the heavy weight lifted from his chest; on the same outward breath he coiled both legs and planted his boots on the dead man's chest, then shoved. The corpse flipped backwards, smashed into a booth as Wu leaped to his feet.

He swung the AK-47 from his back and held it sideways in front of him, one hand on the barrel, the other on the stock, then charged the corpses advancing single file up the aisle; the rifle caught the lead corpse – a young black male in a Hawaiian shirt – smack across the chest, and the corpse reeled back, toppling the others behind it.

A third gunshot screamed from the floor below.

Now, Wu thought, *it's time to help the American.*

He glanced ahead. Corpses packed the narrow stairwell descending to the kitchen. He needed another way. Instantly he knew the answer.

The dumbwaiter.

Hollow moans sounded through the open metal shaft. Wu bent to the square hole and called. '*Doctor! Doctor, can you hear me?*'

For a moment, nothing. Then, '*Hey!*'

Wu fed the AK-47 through the opening and let it drop, heard it bang to the bottom. No other choice but to use the firearm, he reasoned. It was the American's only hope. '*The dumbwaiter!*' Wu yelled twice. '*Look!*'

And then he bolted. He didn't know if the rifle would do any good – if the American could even reach it – but he had risked enough. The rest was up to Marco.

A strobe of light swept over his shoulder, danced on the

walls. The dead conductor was up again, the head of the flashlight a bright beacon in its mouth.

Wu pulled his deer-horns and hopped onto a tabletop in the nearest booth, then leaped to the next booth, the next table, safely passing the corpses in the aisle, heading towards the open door at the north end of the dining car. Towards the engine room.

His real reason for boarding the train. Not the lie he'd told the American.

Wu wanted the locomotive.

At the dark doorway, he hesitated, peering into the next car. The lounge. Without the flashlight, his vision was weak, but he sensed no movement, no hungry shadows. He stepped over the mound of bodies and dashed straight through the lounge. The door at the opposite end was open, and streams of sunlight beckoned him into the next car. A coach, the windows smashed. Behind him, somewhere lower, he heard the pounding beat of gunfire.

The AK. Marco.

Wu sprinted through the coach car – then stopped halfway.

Out of the windows he saw a mass of corpses, rioting, swarming both walls of the train. Twenty metres back on the dune, corpses surrounded the Jeep – *invaded* it, crawling inside, tearing the seats – as if they'd detected a scent of life, some trace of Marco and Wu still present. And then, as Wu watched, the Jeep shifted on the unsteady sand, too many corpses climbing and pulling, and with a slow motion the entire vehicle flipped and rolled twice, a groaning orange ball of metal and broken, flopping limbs and crushed bodies, down to the bottom of the dune.

Wu remembered Marco's warning. *Pissed-off hornets.* The American had been right – but that no longer mattered. Good riddance to the Jeep.

Without further hesitation he'd flown up the aisle and run

through the next coach car, to the final door. The engine room. The door was open half a metre; he'd wedged his shoulder into the gap and heaved it wider, then slipped through.

And brought the locomotive back to life.

Now Wu removed his daypack and dropped it to the floor. He felt suddenly buoyant, unburdened by the weight of all his gear. From a few cars behind, he heard the AK-47 rattle off another volley. *Marco.* The doctor was upstairs, alive. Wu's shoulders relaxed. With some surprise, he admitted to himself that Marco's survival was preferable, at least until the mission was complete. The doctor's instincts did, indeed, seem useful.

And, of course, Beijing wanted Marco alive, too.

For a short while longer.

Outside the front window, sand dunes undulated on the horizon. A century and a half ago, poor Chinese labourers had laid the first cross-country railroad through these same Western deserts; they'd perished by the thousands at the behest of the American government, slaving for minuscule wages, only to be cast aside when the railroad was complete. Banned from white society, denied citizenship, scorned and branded with the hateful slur 'coolies'. Wu stirred. He hoped the spirits of those Chinese were watching now; he hoped they felt honoured at last, witnessing their bloodstained tracks convey him on a mission to serve the homeland.

The Sunset Limited rolled half a mile from where Wu and Marco had boarded; in the rear mirrors Wu saw the rioting corpses fall farther behind, shrinking into the desert until they were just another texture like dirt or cactus or rocks. The overturned Jeep was a speck, too. Then gone.

Marco's gear and supplies gone with it.

A smile hardened on Wu's mouth. He glanced at his own

daypack resting against the console. Everything he needed was right here at his feet.

Kheng Wu was in control again. Not Henry Marco.

6.8

Bullets bursting from the AK-47, Marco advanced through the remaining coach cars, mowing down corpses. The train swayed from side to side, making it difficult to aim; he fell against seats, wasted bullets – too many misses between headshots. Just as the AK sputtered, the clip empty, a flashlight blinded him from ahead.

'Wu, goddamn it,' he began, but stopped.

The dead conductor charged down the aisle, its mouth stuffed with the burning head of the flashlight. Marco threw the AK down, came up firing with the Glock; his first shot missed, but the second bullet shattered the flashlight, exploding the batteries out the back of the conductor's skull. The fat corpse stumbled two more strides then collapsed in a mound.

Waste of a flashlight, Marco thought. *Way to go, Wu.*

He retrieved the empty AK and shouldered it for later, assuming Wu had more clips, then pressed ahead with the Glock. He dropped five more corpses – five headshots, leaving a single round in the Glock – and arrived, ears throbbing painfully, at the locomotive.

Inside the door, two bodies blocked a narrow, blood-painted corridor – the train's engineers. They'd fossilised in mid-struggle, one atop the other. One's ribcage had been torn open, organs ripped loose; his hand gripped a screwdriver buried into the other's skull. Marco imagined the scene – the first engineer resurrecting, assaulting the second.

Killing each other at the same moment.

Teamwork at its best, Marco thought, stepping over the

bodies. Then again, who was he to judge? *My partner just left my Jeep in the fucking dust two miles back.*

The car lurched beneath him as he stumbled up the corridor, past fat pipes and gauges and loud hulking engines the size of refrigerators. The corridor widened at the end; at the locomotive's nose sat Wu at a tall stool behind a console of dials and levers, gazing out through the windshield, absorbed in his thoughts. His hand rested on the throttle.

'What the hell are you *doing*?' Marco demanded.

Perhaps Wu flinched; Marco wasn't certain. The soldier swivelled halfway around on the stool. 'Removing us from danger,' he said, much too matter-of-factly.

Marco stared in disbelief. 'Oh yeah? And what about the Jeep?'

'Upside down, being torn to scrap metal, the last I saw. This was our only escape—'

'Bullshit,' Marco cut him off. 'Stop the train. We're going back.'

'Impossible. Too many corpses.'

'Jesus, Wu, use your head. All my shit was in the Jeep – my bag, and all my gear and supplies. Maps. My *guns*.'

'You're carrying two guns now, Doctor. How many do you need?'

'More than two, asshole.'

Unperturbed, Wu swivelled back around. Through the windshield the scenery had begun to evolve as the train streaked towards Yuma. Paved roads cut lines in the desert, telephone poles appeared alongside brown cactus husks. The tracks passed a lonely liquor store with smashed windows. A begrimed red car sat outside, abandoned, doors rusted open.

'I won't need a gun,' Wu said. He spoke without looking at Marco. 'Only my knives. You have two guns. The rest of your belongings, however, are a loss. I'm sorry.'

Marco seethed. *You don't sound sorry one goddamn bit.*

'Listen,' he said, controlling himself. 'I mean really listen. I warned you about boarding this train – you ignored me. Twice. Now you suddenly decide to play choo-choo on your own fucking whim? That was *my* Jeep. I *need* that Jeep.'

'Your Uncle Osbourne will replace it. A gift from the United States government.'

'You're missing my point. Do *not* make any more decisions without me.'

A suburb of tan adobe houses had appeared out of the western window, and beyond that an old golf course, the once-green grass now a dead brown rug. To the east lay a small shopping centre. The parking lot was a wasteland of overturned shopping carts, interspersed with haphazard mounds of rags and bones – human remains, picked by vultures.

Wu clicked the throttle forward one notch, and the train slowed. 'We'll keep our speed low through town,' he said. 'There may be blockages on the tracks.'

'*Wu*—' Marco began.

'Doctor,' Wu interrupted. 'I'll ask you again to remember that this is a military operation. In which case, who makes the decisions? The uniform with the most stripes – and in that regard I outnumber you three to zero. Back there I observed through the window as fifty corpses overturned your Jeep. There was no time to ask your opinion. I made the decision.'

'Great choice, Sarge. Should I salute you?'

Wu rose from the stool. 'We're both quick thinkers, Doctor. It's our strength. But sometimes . . . sometimes, we do what the moment requires and accept the consequences later on. Like losing the Jeep. Or nearly being killed by a corpse you pulled from a burning truck.'

Marco's forehead had been packed with pressure, like an overheated boiler. At the mention of the burning corpse – his own fuck-up back in Maricopa – he imagined a pop, the steam leaking out, his anger retreating.

Shit. Score one point for Wu.

'So,' he said with an effort to stay pissed. 'We all make mistakes, is that it?'

'I didn't make a mistake.' Wu brushed past him down the corridor. Without missing a step he hopped over the dead engineers and dragged the rear door closed, securing the locomotive. 'I assume you shot the corpses between here and the dining car?'

Marco sighed, exasperated. 'Yes.'

'Most of our passengers disembarked at the Jeep. But there may still be stragglers in the back coaches, so we'll keep the locomotive locked for now. I can disable power to the other cars but keep it for ourselves here in the cab – this way we can run the A/C, work the lights at night. Later, if the train is quiet, we'll make a supply run to the kitchen.'

Marco rubbed his eyes, barely listening. *Run to the kitchen. Sure. A little midnight snack.* He laughed humourlessly.

The tracks had entered the centre of Yuma. Outside Marco saw crumbling offices and apartment complexes. Forlorn gas stations. Silent hotels, and hollowed-out restaurants that seemed to echo with whispers. The train crossed beneath a highway overpass – packed with a ghost jam of cars, dead-locked bumper to bumper, left to rust in crooked lanes – and then rumbled into a concrete canyon running half a mile alongside two sets of parallel tracks. Ahead stood a shadowy parking garage beside a dull, sand-coloured building.

The train station.

'Shit,' Marco mumbled.

The platform was packed with corpses dressed in torn collared shirts and slacks, others in scummy baseball caps and shorts. Their eyes widened at the train's approach – god knows how long they'd been waiting – and greedily they pressed towards the edge of the platform. The entire first row of dead commuters toppled to the tracks. The hundred-ton locomotive roared through, crushing them to pulp; Marco didn't even feel the impact.

'We're safer this way,' Wu said, returning to the control stand. 'You see now? The Jeep was vulnerable. We'd have never made it past that station, not with all those corpses. Instead we just roll along. For the next three hundred miles, we're invincible.'

'Yeah . . .' Marco said, trailing off. Beside the main console was a second, smaller control stand; he sank onto the padded stool and set the AK down at his feet. The foam cushion felt . . . *great.* He swore he could take a nap right here, sitting up straight.

He pinched his earlobe, rubbed the notch of the old dog bite, reflecting. Wu was right about one thing. The train *was* invincible, an unstoppable force; as long as they kept moving, they were safe from attack. A hundred frenzied corpses? Didn't matter. Bring 'em on.

He sighed and shut his eyes, closing his senses to everything but the rhythmic rocking of the train. Sure as hell smoother than the Jeep over desert rocks.

Within moments he felt his resolve soften. Succumbing to the momentum, to the forward motion – this non-negotiable, unswerving line, predetermined by the lay of the tracks. Hurtling him ahead to California, towards a past he doubted he was ready to face.

But that's what this was about, wasn't it? Face the past. Get it over with.

You're avoiding. Danielle's voice echoed in his head, weeping. Twisting his heart. *You're always avoiding, Henry. It's not fair. It's not fair to me . . .*

He defended himself. *No, I'm not. Not this time. Full speed ahead.*

Yes, he would allow this. Surrender control. Sit back and enjoy the ride. And anyway, he hadn't been in control for years, had he?

Finish this and go home.

He repeated the thought, more slowly. *Finish and go home.*

That's all that mattered. *Who gives a fuck how you get there?*

For the first time that day his neck muscles loosened. Maybe this idea was good. And anyway, it was nice – not worrying about getting eaten for once.

'Okay,' he said, opening his eyes. Finding them moist. 'What the hell. Punch my ticket to LA. We can stop at the Jeep on the way home, right? By then the corpse party should have ended. I busted my ass to find all that gear. I'm not giving it up so easy.'

Wu shrugged. 'We can try.'

'Wow, thanks, Sergeant. I can tell you really care.' Marco bent and unlaced his boots, eager to stretch his feet, feel some air on his toes. 'But how about we take a lesson from our two funky-smelling friends in the hall – let's try to get along, okay?'

Wu considered the dead engineers, each murdered by the other. Nodding, he glanced at Marco, then turned his attention back to the tracks.

'Don't worry, Doctor,' he said evenly. 'I'm not ready to kill you yet.'

INTRUDERS

7.1

The night sky in the desert never seemed quite real to Marco – not with the stars so exaggerated, so large and bright, and the blackness too low-hanging, as if a billion miles of space had somehow compressed against the horizon. Danielle had once asked him, *Can you feel that?* as they reclined on their balcony, savouring a summer night. Her voice was hushed, reverential, what he often jokingly called her 'New Age wonder tone'.

The universe touching the Earth, she'd said.

Marco hadn't even teased her that night; he secretly *did* feel it himself, a screwed-up perception that the heavens were impossibly nearby. As though you could simply reach out and stir the stars with your finger, or walk to the desert's edge and hop off into the cosmos with a kick of your feet. It was a sensation entirely different from LA, where the constant glow of city lights muted the stars and shunted the universe away.

Out here in the unpopulated desert, you lost the people and gained back the stars. Long ago, before the Resurrection, Marco had believed that was a good thing.

But now . . .

Now maybe a few more people would be nice.

The train chugged through the night, chewing miles of Southern California desert. Marco lowered his eyes from the window. Sitting on the floor of the locomotive, stiff and cramped, he bent his legs towards him and rested his head on his knees, then sat up again. As utterly exhausted as he was, sleep wasn't coming easily. At least he'd had a decent meal before bed. Canned carrot soup. Cold and congealed, but still better than another night of dried jerky. He and Wu had gathered supplies from the kitchen without trouble; Marco had been thorough with the AK-47 on his first trip, and the only corpses they saw were slumped in brain-beaten heaps. But just to be safe, he'd dragged shut the rusted door at the back of the diner; it snapped into its latch with a satisfying squawk. If there were any hiders in the rear cars, they weren't going anywhere.

In the locomotive, Wu ruled the control panel. He'd dimmed the lights; the night rendered him a shadow against the window, a silhouetted extension of the controls. His hand appeared fused to the throttle. If the sergeant was tired, he showed no sign of it. He perched on the stool as though he'd been bolted to it, solid and straight, his lower jaw as taut as his posture. He'd stripped from his bloodstained military shirt, down to a white tank top, revealing a fighter's physique, lean and muscled. Pale scars blemished his shoulders in long narrow lines, almost like the lashings of a whip, but Marco had been reluctant to enquire.

Shortly after sunset, Wu had slowed the train to a crawl. 'We wouldn't be wise to reach Los Angeles County in the middle of the night, in the pitch-black,' he'd reasoned. 'We'll pace ourselves and approach slowly. At this speed we'll arrive after dawn.'

Made sense to Marco. Ten miles an hour was just fast enough to keep any desert-roaming corpses from seizing a grab-rail and hauling themselves aboard.

For now, the two men could relax. Sit back and catch some slumber.

And God, I need it. Marco closed his eyes. His body swayed, his shoulders jostling below his heavy head as the locomotive rocked him to sleep like a gentle mother. He and Wu had agreed to take shifts. Two hours each. One man napping, the other on watch, tending to the train's alerter – the 'dead man's switch', Wu called it, a safety mechanism that disabled the train if the engineer was unresponsive for anything longer than twenty-five seconds. In the darkness Marco heard a soft bell and then a demure *tick* as Wu tapped the alerter button. Beneath him the train wheels clacked a monotonous beat against the tracks, an endless metallic lullaby.

California, he thought, half dozing. He'd been happy there once. He and Danielle in California. Before everything went to shit.

Would any of this have turned out different? he wondered. *If we'd stayed?*

If we'd stayed. His thoughts skipped to the tempo of the tracks.

If we'd stayed. If we'd stayed.

But they hadn't stayed. They'd fled, hoping for better in Arizona. And now he didn't belong back here, back in Cally. An intruder, that's what he was, sneaking through an open window at night. His heart rang loud behind his ribs, like an alarm sounding.

He'd felt the first pang right after Yuma, just across the Colorado River. The train had exited Arizona finally, met at the border by leafy eucalyptus trees along the California tracks. He'd last travelled this way three years ago – the summer after the Resurrection – before he'd gotten caught up in all this crap, before his first contract, before he'd become . . . what did Osbourne call him? '*The Zombie Hitman*'. Before that.

He'd just been a scared man, nothing more, sweeping the west coast for Danielle.

Christ, what a summer that had been. Through late winter and spring he'd dug in at the Arizona house, labouring over his barricade, enslaved by the conviction that she'd return there. She hadn't. But he'd begun to notice things on his supply runs into town. Blue-vested corpses shuffling through Walmart . . . dead males in blood-soaked jerseys, camped in sports bars . . . rotted young mothers slouching on playground benches, empty eyes watching empty swings. All with such a palpable expectancy – he could *feel* them waiting for god-knows-what – that a growing suspicion took hold in his head, telling him their movements weren't random. That perhaps these mindless mechanisms of dead flesh and bone weren't so mindless.

Perhaps they were . . . nostalgic? Wistful? As crazy as that seemed . . .

Finally, on a sweltering July night, he'd pulled out his maps.

His checklist had been exhaustive – four typed pages, a catalogue of remembered date nights and theatres and Café La Bohème and yoga retreats and organic markets and Disneyland and public parks and the Ritz-Carlton and studio movie lots where she'd made her films. And then, hopeful, he'd packed the Jeep and headed west.

He'd started at the top of the list. Tech Town, where they'd met.

No Danielle there – only the young assistant manager, dead and hungry, mustard-coloured pus bubbling from its burst lips as it crawled out from behind the return counter. Disappointed, Marco had filled his pockets with batteries and escaped.

In total, hundreds of miles covered. Hundreds of memories. Each tarnished as it came up empty, just another meaningless place in a meaningless world. Yet when he'd reached the bottom of his list, he'd started back at the top. He had to be sure.

The California search had taken three months.

Here in the train, the soft bell sounded again, followed by the quiet *tick*.

Marco's head dipped.

Swooning, he saw himself in his Jeep, heading back to Arizona after that last California trip, defeated, befuddled, aching for Danielle. The radio crackled with nothing but angry static, but he refused to turn it off, shouting instead over the noise, apologising to her as he drove drunk for two days straight, weaving across lanes of forever-empty highways with only himself to kill. Begging her to come home – to be dead with him.

Home. Arizona. They'd moved there a year before the Resurrection. A year after . . .

He faltered; couldn't bring himself to complete the thought, not even in a dream. *California's too much*, he'd told her, the safe way to phrase it, summarising words he wished to avoid. The position at St Joseph's had opened in Phoenix, an amazing opportunity for him. For *them*. Things would get better, he'd believed, Danielle would be happy. They'd stop arguing so damn much. But he was wrong about that . . .

Her voice, her bewitching alto, descended on him in the dark locomotive, dreamlike, a night bird swooping down to sit on his shoulder. Sharp talons. It hurt.

You knew I didn't want to come here, she said.

Bullshit, he answered. That was his line, the script always the same. *You said—*

I moved for you, Henry. I gave up my career—

Christ! That's revising history, Delle, you weren't getting parts—

Oh I wasn't? You asshole—

You said you wanted to be near your sister—

You know what I really wanted. You're avoiding, Henry.

Bullshit, I'm not—

You said we'd try again—

I know what I said—

I wanted—

Well, I never promised—

A man's voice cut in, loud and urgent. *I can save Hannah.*

Marco jerked awake. His damp shirt clung to his clammy skin, and he shuddered. The locomotive had turned cold and inhospitable while he'd slept, refrigerated by the desert night, the floor unforgiving, like a mortuary slab. Blinking, he rubbed his hands together and settled his fast heart with long, deliberate drags of air that stretched his lungs to capacity. He was thankful for the chilled air – shocking him to full alertness, locking his wild nightmare back into whatever subconscious cage it belonged. Unable to harm him until his next sleep. Still, even as the sounds and images faded, and his pulse slowed, and his breath evened, he couldn't stop shivering.

He couldn't forget Danielle's words stabbing him. Fragmented arguments, lodged inside him now like splinters under the skin.

And the last voice in his dream, the man's voice.

That voice had been Roger Ballard.

Marco swallowed. Funny how his dreaming mind had paired Roger with Danielle – stitched them together, ganged them up against him in a war of words.

I can save Hannah.

But you didn't, Marco mused. *You fucked up. We both did.*

He felt his stomach clench. This trip to California was screwing with him. Again he had the sensation of rushing headlong towards . . . what?

Towards something terrible.

'You're awake.'

Wu's austere voice jarred Marco. He'd almost forgotten the sergeant was present, immersed in the shadows up front.

Jesus, please tell me I wasn't muttering in my sleep.

'Yeah,' he answered. 'Bright-eyed and bushy-tailed. Want your turn?'

'No.'

'C'mon, I'll tuck you in. I'll sing you a song.'

Wu stepped into the dim light. His face was carved with concern.

Marco sat up, alarmed. 'What's the matter?'

Wu pointed into the midnight world beyond the window.

'We're being followed,' he announced.

7.2

Marco gawked, paralysed by the report that Wu had just given. *Followed?* For several slow seconds the word skimmed atop the surface of his comprehension – important but lacking meaning – then broke through with a crash into his deeper brain.

'By *who?*' he demanded.

'I don't know,' Wu answered frankly. 'They're not with me.'

Wide awake now, Marco struggled to his feet and almost doubled over; his legs had cramped during the uncomfortable hours on the floor. Steadying himself against the wall, he hobbled to the window and pressed his palm against the cold glass.

Outside, the night sky was still at full power, still perplexing, the blackness bright with starlight. The terrain lit up with an unexpected clarity. Silver ironwood trees and patches of desert scrub stubbled the land. A hundred yards of track gleamed ahead in the locomotive's spotlight; beyond that, the full moon bore down like the oncoming beam of another train. Only the distant mountains were obscured – rocky ridges lurking at the desert fringe like an audience in a dark amphitheatre, encircling the stage, ready for the next performance.

Marco scanned the landscape. His neck crawled with the eerie sensation of being observed by someone unseen. He leaned until his forehead tapped the window, stealing a view as far back as he could along the vast length of the train. The glass fogged as he gulped anxiously. Didn't matter. He couldn't see a damn thing anyway.

'Where?' he asked, impatient.

'Straight behind. In the mirror.'

He squinted into the tall rear-view mirror bolted outside the glass. In its depths bobbed a dot of sharp red light – the back end of the train – but beyond that, nothing. A washed-out reflection of himself hovered in the window, frowning.

'I can't see shit,' he said. He was about to pull back when Wu cut the locomotive lights, and the cab went truly dark; without the backlighting, Marco's reflection vanished, and at once he was able to discern shapes where none had been. And there it was – the tiniest, coal-coloured fragment in a grey sea of sand, half a mile behind. From this distance Marco wouldn't have noticed it without Wu's guidance; at a glance the speck could have been a rock or a tumbleweed. A minute passed before he was even convinced it was moving – keeping pace with the train, purposely hanging back at the outer range of eyesight.

'Some type of all-terrain vehicle, a four-wheeler,' Wu concluded. 'A quad. He's followed us for the last quarter-hour, perhaps longer. I detected him once the sand turned paler. An error on his part – he should have remained on the tracks. Better cover.'

'But who *is* it?' Marco asked again. 'I mean, are you sure it's not your men? Maybe Osbourne sent backup.'

Wu shook his head. 'If that were RRU, he would have caught up and made contact by now. This individual is stalking us. Poorly, but his intentions are clear.'

'Oh yeah? And what are his intentions?'

'He wants to know where we're going.'

Marco exhaled, exasperated. 'Jesus Christ, can you stop with the half-answers? *Why* is he following us?'

A pause. Without the interior lights Wu's face was a silhouetted mystery, but Marco sensed the sergeant was regarding him with disdain.

'Really, Doctor,' Wu said at last. His tone had changed from concern to admonishment. 'Did you think we're the *only* ones hunting Roger Ballard?'

Marco blinked. 'What . . . ? What are you talking about? Who else—'

'Other political interests. Governments.'

Marco backed a step from the window. 'Oh shit,' he said. The realisation hit him like dynamite blasting through dense rock. He bumped into the stool behind him and sat.

Nice job, Henry, he thought, shaking his head. *What the hell've you gotten yourself into?* Other nations – *how many?* – were hunting Roger. Goddamn son of a bitch. He'd been an idiot not to predict this. 'National security', Osbourne had said. *Of course.* If US Homeland Security was playing this sick game, then there'd be other pieces on the game-board, too, other governments with Roger on the agenda. Marco's mind raced to catch up with the implications.

This isn't a contract, he realised. *It's some kind of world war.*

But for Christ's sake, why? And what if he didn't win?

'So who is it?' he asked yet again. The urgency had faded

from his voice; he heard only resignation. 'North Korea? Iraq? Chi—'

Wu interrupted. 'Any of those, perhaps. Or others. It doesn't matter. They all want the same.' He brushed past Marco to the control panel. 'Move.'

'Sure. Sorry to bother you,' Marco griped. He surrendered the stool, moved to the opposite console. The empty can of carrot soup he'd eaten for dinner sat by the base. He gave it a rude kick, gratified to hear it bang away into the shadows and roll down the corridor.

Unfazed, Wu grabbed the throttle and yanked it towards him a notch. The engines in the hallway groaned louder; the train kicked forward, rocking Marco backwards on his feet. Wu waited twenty seconds then upped the speed again. Two minutes later he had the train barrelling at ninety miles per hour. He consulted the mirror and nodded, satisfied.

'Gone,' he declared. 'Quads top out at seventy, even the military grades. He won't catch up now. He'll be cursing himself.'

'But . . . I mean . . . he won't just give up, will he?' Marco asked.

'No,' Wu admitted. 'He'll stay on our trail. I suspect he knows who you are, and that you're tracking Ballard. However, I doubt he knows our destination is Sarsgard, or he wouldn't need to follow us – he'd be there already. Therefore, we still have the advantage. We'll abandon the train at San Bernardino, as planned. But I can rig the alerter so the locomotive rolls on without us. He'll follow the tracks, not realising we're not onboard.' Wu sniffed. 'He'll find the train crashed at the LA terminal with a million corpses to greet him.'

Marco squeezed his raw eyes shut. The revelations swirled madly around him like sheets of paper in a tornado, and he desperately wanted to snatch them up, assemble them in proper order. 'Okay – let me get this straight,' he said, his eyes snapping open. 'This guy's a spy, right?'

Wu flashed an annoyed glance. 'Foreign operative, yes. I would think so.'

'On the same mission as us? To kill Roger?'

'Yes.'

'But why? Why does everyone want Roger's corpse returned?'

Wu cocked his head to the side, furrowed his brow. Marco sensed him contemplating an answer, deciding whether to serve up another half-truth or a flat-out lie. At last the sergeant appeared to make up his mind. 'That's not all they want.'

'Meaning?'

'Meaning that killing Ballard is not the end-objective.'

'Goddamn it,' Marco declared. He'd had enough. He strode to the opposite side of the control panel and grabbed the throttle, squeezing until his knuckles whitened. He half expected Wu to slap his hand away. Instead the soldier's eyes narrowed – not a look of surprise, but curious, interested to see what Marco would do next. Marco met his gaze, refused to waver.

'Enough vague answers,' Marco said, his cheeks broiling. 'Remember our deal? Honour system. I gave my report, now it's goddamn time you gave yours. Or should I stop this train and let our new friend catch up? Maybe *he'll* be nice enough to explain what's going on.'

The corners of Wu's mouth constricted. In the unlit cab his face was more shadow than skin; black, bottomless pits loomed where his green eyes had glinted hours earlier. The two men held their positions at the console, each measuring the other, motionless except for the sway of the train. Finally the alerter's soft tone broke the quiet.

Ping.

A pause, and then it rang again, and then again – *ping ping ping* – like the bell at the end of a boxing round, instructing the fighters to separate.

Wu's hand emerged from the darkness around his waist. The deer-horn knife gleamed in the red glow of the control instruments. Without blinking, he rested the blade on the console – slowly, deliberately, inches from Marco's outstretched wrist.

'Let go of the throttle, Doctor,' Wu said.

Marco held tight. 'Or else . . . ?'

Wu said nothing.

Ping ping ping. The bell rang and rang. Any moment now the safety brakes would engage automatically and drag the locomotive to a stop.

Ping ping ping.

With an unhurried movement, Wu released the knife and pressed the alerter button with his empty hand. The bell ceased.

'Let go of the throttle,' Wu said, 'so I can tell you important details about Roger Ballard. Details I'm sure you don't know.'

Marco exhaled. 'So,' he said warily. 'You're honouring the honour system?'

'Of course,' Wu answered. 'I've said so already. Honour is everything to me.'

Marco nodded, unhanded the throttle, flexed his fingers.

'Okay,' he said. 'Tell me. Why does the world want Roger?'

7·3

'After you moved to Arizona, did you ever hear from Doctor Ballard?' Wu asked. He sat atop the stool, monitoring the rear mirror.

'Well, no,' Marco admitted cautiously. 'That . . . wasn't

something either of us would have wanted. Once I left LA, that was it. I didn't keep in touch. Not with anyone.' Slumping against the cold wall, he grunted and slid down to rest his tired ass on the floor. He crossed his knees in front of him and gazed up at Wu like a kid ready for story-time.

'So then you aren't aware that Ballard quit his residency. Four months after you left.' Wu delivered the news without shifting his attention from the window.

'Roger . . . quit?'

'Abruptly. He announced his resignation on the morning of the twenty-eighth of September 2013. Ten minutes later, he was gone. Down to the hospital lobby and out the front door and never returned. Left his diplomas hanging on the wall in his office.' Wu spoke with the matter-of-fact inflection of a military briefing. Detached, dispassionate.

Roger quit, Marco marvelled, still absorbing this first detail. Guilt nipped him with sharp little teeth. He should've known this information already, should've remained better attuned to what he'd left behind. Obviously Roger had been in pain over what happened.

But the truth was, at the time, Marco didn't give a shit.

And maybe, just maybe, he'd *wanted* Roger to suffer.

'But why?' he asked Wu.

'No reason given. He simply announced he was leaving. And not only leaving the hospital.' *Ping*. Wu swivelled from the window and tapped the alerter. 'Ballard vanished.'

Marco flinched without knowing why. 'I don't understand.'

'I mean, Doctor, that he abandoned his apartment as well. His clothing, his furniture, his belongings, all left behind. Hospital security discovered his blue BMW in the parking garage. Also abandoned. He'd driven in that morning, but evidently departed by another means. Even his bank accounts were discovered untapped. Not a dime withdrawn. A missing persons report was filed by hospital administrators since, as you know, Ballard had no next of kin to pursue the matter – but mysteriously no action was ever taken, either by the LA County police or the Federal Bureau of Investigation.'

'Jesus Christ . . .' Marco trailed off. 'So where was he?'

'From the twenty-eighth of September 2013 onwards, no one knew.'

'And yet,' Marco prodded, 'something tells me Owen Osbourne knew.'

Wu nodded, although his stern expression was not encouraging. 'Perceptive, Doctor. Yes – Ballard had been recruited in high secrecy by the Department of Homeland Security. Osbourne organised the disappearance and the cover-up.'

'Great,' Marco flared. 'So we're cleaning up some mess Osbourne made. He pisses all over floor, then sends us out with the mop?'

Unrattled, Wu considered Marco's remark and then turned once more to the window. 'It's a much bigger mess than you think, Doctor,' he replied at last, gravely. 'Osbourne was busy cleaning it, too. Which brings us to why we're here.'

Marco shuddered. *A much bigger mess.* The link between Roger and Osbourne disconcerted him, along with the feeling that he, too, was trapped in the same spider's web – that the wisp of silk binding Marco to Roger also tied him to Osbourne, weaving them all together into a dizzying circular trap. And somewhere, hidden beyond his understanding, waited the spider – the reason for everything, the logic spinning the web.

And suddenly he guessed what it was.

Jesus, Roger.

Jesus fucking Christ.

'Tell me why,' he said. His throat rasped. 'Why Roger was recruited.'

Wu placed his hands square on his knees. 'You seem to know already, Doctor.'

'The Resurrection.'

'Yes,' Wu confirmed. 'The Resurrection.'

Marco rubbed his eyes, dumbfounded. His fingertips were frigid in the night air, and he could feel rough veins scratching below his eyelids.

'Osbourne needed a skilled research neurologist,' Wu continued. 'Ballard was the best in his field, and so Osbourne selected him to contain the Resurrection.'

Marco blinked, reabsorbing the dim light. 'Contain? As in "stop"?'

Wu nodded. 'That was the intent. Before the outbreak.'

'Hold it – back up again,' Marco said. He had to slow this down, understand it better. 'How did Osbourne know about the Resurrection before the outbreak?'

Ping. The alerter bell sounded, and Wu slapped the button with his palm. He seemed irritated by the interruptions to his narrative. 'Summer 2013,' he announced brusquely. 'Federal agents working for the Department of Homeland Security received reports of an unknown encephalopathy with highly alarming symptoms taking hold in the population of a high-security medical prison – and yes, Doctor, before you ask, it *was* Sarsgard Medical Prison, our current destination. The Sarsgard physicians had never seen anything like it. A near-total neurological shutdown, followed soon after by necrosis and ceased functioning of heart, lung and other major organs. All this while the patient apparently still survived. Of course, it was soon determined—'

'They actually *were* dead,' Marco broke in. 'But they walked around and ate people. You can skip all that, I've heard it before. Get to the part about Osbourne and Roger.'

Wu scowled. 'I'm getting there, Doctor. At the time of these reports, Sarsgard incarcerated a number of international terrorists – three members of the Islamic Jihad Group, one soldier of the Lebanese Asbat an-Ansar, and a high-ranking officer in the Japanese Aum Shinrikyo. As you recall, this was a time of heightened precaution against terrorism in America. The concern – the fear – was that one of the jailed terrorists was a carrier for some biological weapon. An engineered virus, perhaps, or bacteria.'

'So Osbourne wanted Roger to take a look.'

'Yes. Osbourne anticipated that Sarsgard was just the beginning – an accidental preview of an impending widespread bio-terror attack. A doomsday weapon to be released throughout America, with no possible way to predict where or when it would happen, or who would deliver the blow. Osbourne needed a vaccine ready or, even better, a cure, when the time came. In the meantime, the events at Sarsgard were a highly guarded secret.'

Marco hung his head, combed his hand through his unkempt hair. His fingers came away sticky with soil and sweat and gummy corpse blood from the day's kills. Repulsed, he wiped his hand on his canvas pant leg and stood, aching.

'Okay,' he said. 'Roger disappeared after I left for Arizona. That means, what? He was hiding here six months, trying to figure out what the hell makes the Resurrection tick. Obviously with no luck. It outfoxed him – which, knowing Roger, must've been agonising. Millions of people killed by a puzzle he couldn't solve. And it killed him, too, in the end.'

'He was close to a solution when he died. That's why Osbourne needs his corpse.'

'Yeah. That's the part I don't understand.'

'You will soon, Doctor.' Wu's finger hovered over the

alerter button, anticipating the next chime of the bell. 'The truth is . . .' he began, and even the alerter seemed to hold its silence, hushed, awaiting his next words. Wu shook his head gravely.

'Roger Ballard's corpse is *not* like any other corpse on earth.'

7·4

Marco felt his forehead screw tight, baffled, needing more. Wu obliged him.

'I'll explain,' Wu stated before Marco could ask, his tone once again official, a reporter of facts. 'During the first rescue attempt at Sarsgard four years ago, Ballard's lab was overrun by his dead patients. His research was destroyed. All Osbourne had to show for his efforts was a smattering of reports that Ballard had provided prior to the outbreak. Since then, Osbourne has had a team of scientists in the Safe States attempting to create a vaccine, but with no success.'

Marco didn't see where this was going. 'Roger's a tough act to follow,' he offered.

'Osbourne would agree with you. He'd been losing hope. But two months ago, that changed.' Wu paused, as if feeling a change himself. 'Two months ago, Homeland Security detected a trespass into the encrypted mainframe of their database. A computer break-in. Someone, somewhere, had managed to hack into Roger Ballard's personnel file. Luckily, as the hack was in progress, the CIA tagged the hacker with an invisible string code. Like an old-fashioned tracking device, allowing them to secretly follow the hacker's subsequent activity.'

'Okay . . . and then?'

'Within seventy-two hours, the unidentified hacker had

trespassed into several additional government sites, including the US Correctional Department's private files on Sarsgard. To the CIA, the threat was obvious – espionage, some foreign power digging for information. Seeing what they could learn about the Resurrection, and Osbourne's attempt to develop a vaccine.'

Marco puzzled, still not getting it. 'And now they're looking for Roger . . . because?'

Wu delivered him a curious look. 'Before I answer that, Doctor, I should first mention that in addition to the government mainframes, the hacker was also observed breaking into email accounts. A dozen or so. Accounts belonging to former associates of Roger Ballard. Presumably the hacker was looking for information Ballard might have leaked to an outside contact.'

The hair on Marco's scalp stirred. Something about the way Wu was watching him . . .

Wu continued, a coy note creeping into his voice. 'For example, one notable break-in occurred on the mail server for a certain hospital in Arizona. St. Joseph's.'

Oh, shit. Marco's head buzzed.

'And there,' Wu said, 'with the CIA watching, a most incredible discovery was made.'

Oh, holy shit. You have got *to be kidding me.*

Wu nodded. 'Yes, Doctor. You've guessed.'

Marco groaned. 'Roger emailed *me*?'

'You're surprised, understandably. Osbourne was surprised, too, to say the very least.'

'But – when? I never . . .'

'You never received the email, Doctor, because you had already fled the hospital. Ballard's email to you was sent the day following the rescue attempt at Sarsgard, more than a week after the public outbreak of the Resurrection. You were gone by then – in hiding, fighting to survive yourself, no doubt. Society was in freefall, the country in chaos. Ballard's email simply vanished into a discarded, forgotten server. Like an artefact of a lost civilisation.'

Marco rubbed his face, his hand a cold hard weight against his cheek. Roger had tried to contact him? For what? *An apology? A farewell?*

'What did he say?' Marco asked. He had to know, of course, but goddamn, the answer scared him. His stomach flexed; he swallowed back the anxiety rising up his throat.

'I explained that Ballard's research on the Resurrection was lost during the raid,' Wu said. 'As it turns out, that was not entirely true. He sent a partial summary to you, Doctor.'

Marco blinked. 'Me?' He puzzled for a moment. 'Why me?'

'An interesting question. The CIA's theory is that Doctor Ballard believed he could trust you. He apparently did not share the same high opinion of Owen Osbourne.'

Marco scoffed. 'Well. I don't blame him for that . . . but still . . .' His thoughts swam, as if he'd been plunged beneath black frigid water, choked off from logic and reason. *Jesus Christ, Roger, why? Why do that, after all the shit you caused me? Why me, of all people, can't you just leave me fucking out of it – I don't want your bullshit, you crazy asshole—*

And then his mind broke to the surface again, and he sobered.

'Fine,' he heard himself say, his voice oddly flat. 'So now the million dollar question. What was in Roger's research that sent Osbourne hunting across America to kill his corpse?'

Wu leaned forward, just perceptibly, on his stool. 'Ballard's email revealed just how near he'd been to discovering the vaccine. Remarkably near – far closer than Osbourne had imagined. Are you familiar with DNA vaccination, Doctor?'

Marco shifted, frowning. 'A little. An experimental method for developing a vaccine. The idea is to take blood cells from a healthy person, and then inject a virus or bacteria directly into the nucleus. Into the DNA. The cells divide, and you do it again – and again, actually, hundreds of times. You need a ton of generations of mitosis. Finally, if it works right, a new nucelotide for white blood cells might evolve, specially adapted to kill the disease. It's like placing a special order for custom-made antibodies. But that's only if it works right. Nobody's perfected it yet.' He paused. 'Of course, you're about to tell me that Roger perfected it. Typical Roger.'

Wu nodded. 'He was close, yes. And what else do you suppose I'm going to tell you?'

'That the healthy blood cells Roger used for the experiments were his own.'

'You do know your friend well.'

Marco couldn't help but bristle. 'I'm not sure about the "friend" part. But I do know that Roger could be a goddamn idiot. Take any risk for science.' His voice had turned bitter.

Wu seemed not to notice. 'Ballard detailed his process in his email to you. Over a period of seventeen weeks, the doctor collected blood samples from himself and implanted the nuclei with the Resurrection under a microscope. Then he'd reinject the cells back into his bloodstream, hoping they'd divide and propagate – hoping to create genetically altered blood using his body as a breeding ground. His objective was to convert his entire system to the new DNA.'

'Yeah, that sounds like Roger,' Marco repeated. 'And it worked?'

'Not quite. Not enough to be used as a vaccine. But after countless cycles of injections, Ballard did report that infections occurred noticeably slower when his blood was mixed with corpse blood in a Petri dish. He believed he was very close to success. Another month or two, he might have evolved the correct antibodies. He simply ran out of time.'

'During the rescue attempt. He was bitten.'

Wu nodded again. He seemed on the verge of speaking, but instead he swivelled on the stool and reached below him into the shadows. From underneath the console he dragged out his daypack and unzipped a side pocket, then reached inside and handed Marco a small bundle of papers, two or three sheets, crisply folded. The locomotive swayed below Marco's feet. He took a breath, unfolded the papers and, his eyes straining in the moonlight, surveyed the first page.

He wasn't surprised at all. An email.

From: R Ballard
To: Henry Marco
Date: 13 March 2014, 10:36 AM

Henry, this is important. As you know by now, an outbreak has occurred.

Marco stopped, already annoyed. *Typical Roger*, he thought again. No 'hello' or 'how are you'. Sure as hell no 'I'm sorry'. Just drill straight to the facts, skip past everything human.

Grumbling, he flexed his jaw and scanned the remaining pages. Indeed, the facts were all there – or a summarization, at least, of all that Wu had told him. The experiments, the DNA, the antibodies . . . but not enough detail to replicate the process. Osbourne must've been *pissed*.

The last sheet ended with a few short, emotionless lines of text:

```
My bite wound is severe. The Resurrection
is too strong for the current antibodies.
My body is shutting down. Becoming a
corpse. Take care of my notes, Henry.
– Roger
```

Marco sighed and refolded the papers. 'So he knew he was dying.'

'And wished to bequeath you his knowledge,' Wu added. 'Before he resurrected. The trouble is, we need more than a hastily written email.'

Marco shuddered. His anger had gone cold, and beneath his shirt, his skin had turned clammy and damp. He didn't want to imagine Roger's last moments: his thin face shading blue, gangly limbs all racked with agony . . . reaching out to Marco with some insane last wish.

'So Roger's blood is evolved,' he said unsteadily. And then suddenly it all made sense, as if the paper bundle in his hand was an X-ray, a window into total darkness, revealing every hidden bone. 'Roger is the missing link to the vaccine,' he continued, now certain, now clear, almost challenging Wu to dispute him. 'But first, Osbourne needs Roger's DNA. So we're on a hunt to collect some super-Ballard-blood for Osbourne's boys in the lab.'

'Now you understand,' Wu said.

'And our new friend, the stalker back there on the quad. He's after the same thing?'

'Yes,' Wu agreed and, reminded of his concern, cast his eyes to the rear-view mirror. Finding no cause for alarm, he refocused on Marco. 'Osbourne realised that whoever had hacked into Ballard's email would attempt to retrieve a sample for themselves. He ordered you – *us*, I should say – to locate Ballard's corpse first, before anyone else. It's a race.'

'With Roger's head as the finish line.'

'Very clever, Doctor. The good news is, you're still in the lead.'

'Yeah. Well. I don't like it.' Marco chewed his lip. 'And anyway, why fight over the vaccine? What does it matter who gets there first?'

Wu raised an eyebrow. 'Think, Doctor. A vaccine for the Resurrection represents a major shift in world politics. Right now only America has fallen. However, governments worldwide are in frantic preparations for an outbreak of their own. The nation that learns the secret to controlling the Resurrection would do more than ensure its survival. That nation would vault to the top of the new global paradigm, an instant superpower. The vaccine is a gold mine, worth trillions to the economy in production and distribution. And its political worth is virtually infinite – a supreme bargaining chip with other governments, allies and enemies alike. Any infected nation needing the vaccine would have to beg at the feet of its master.'

'And if the master doesn't want to share,' Marco mused, 'everybody's screwed.'

'Quite.' Wu studied the rear mirror again. 'So now you see why we're being followed. And why we can't stop or go home. Osbourne desperately wants his great American comeback. The last thing he can allow is another country beating him to the Ballard corpse.'

'Great. And what if none of us can find Roger?'

Wu stared, deadpan. 'Then Osbourne never lets you stop looking.'

Marco grimaced. Outside, the black sky had softened to a listless grey as dawn approached, and the stars sank back into the unknown universe. In another hour the sun would rise and rule the desert again with a tyrannical heat. Nothing could stop it.

His shoulders sagged. He had a feeling he wasn't ready

for whatever the next twenty-four hours would bring. Everything he'd just heard was incredible – the stakes so high, he could barely believe his own involvement. World power? Genetically altered blood? He'd listened intently, seeking some false note, some indication that Wu was making this shit up as he went. But no. Wu's answers made sense, seemed to snap into place with Marco's own intuitions.

So Wu was telling the truth. Except . . .

Except that Marco's mind buzzed again with the same thought he'd had earlier that day in the Jeep – a nagging sense that Wu was hiding something.

But what? What else could there be? The sergeant had answered every question – held nothing back, explained everything. Marco stirred. *Everything.*

His ears popped, congestion clearing like a cold little bomb going off in his skull. And then he knew – knew what wasn't right about this.

Wu knows everything.

'So just one more question,' Marco said. 'For First-Class Sergeant Wu.'

Wu had returned to monitoring the rear-view mirror. At the mention of his rank, the muscle in the side of his jaw flexed. 'Yes?' he asked tersely.

Marco hesitated. He took a bolstering breath, then fired. 'Who are you *really*?'

Wu half turned – avoiding eye contact – and focused instead out of the window, as if studying something far away. Marco was certain his suspicions were correct. The man knew *way* too damn much for a sergeant, shouldn't have had answers to *half* this crap . . .

But just then Wu's eyes bolted wide.

'*Down!*' he shouted and threw himself to the floor as Marco looked on, stunned . . .

. . . and without further warning the train's windshield

exploded, a hot sandblast of shattered glass against Marco's left cheek, and a small metal gas canister banged into the cab, spewing orange smoke that clawed his eyes and invaded his lungs, and he cried out in pain as the smoke filled him, burning, choking; he couldn't breathe, he had to *escape* . . .

But too late. The sky turned black again; night had won and extinguished the sun, and Marco crumpled, unconscious and lost within the orange gas filling the train.

7·5

Marco was awake. Or not. He couldn't decide.

Sitting in his office at Cedars-Sinai.

'I can save her, Henry.' Roger Ballard planted his fists on Marco's desk and leaned forward, not quite threateningly but with such intensity that Marco edged backwards in his chair. The rectangular lens of Ballard's eyeglasses assigned his face an extra austerity, an accent to the bony ridges of his cheeks and chin. Behind the glasses Ballard's pupils flickered with excitement. Marco sensed his hunger.

Then he noticed the black veins spider-webbing under Roger's grey skin.

Marco shuddered. His mind was a fog, thoughts drifting slowly through the murk, then gone again before he could capture them. He squeezed his eyes shut. Confused.

'Wait,' he said. 'Roger is dead. Aren't you, Roger?'

'I can save Hannah.' Ballard's lips were unmoving as he spoke.

So this was a dream. A dream, right? Marco glanced down at his desk. Atop the familiar green blotter was his desk calendar, scribbled with appointments, notes, reminders. He squinted. He couldn't read a single word.

Ballard spoke again. 'I can save—'

Marco interrupted. 'No, Roger. You couldn't. You tried, but it didn't work.' He didn't mean to sound angry, but he did. Angry and blaming and bitter.

Ballard jerked as though he'd been slapped, and suddenly Marco's cheek stung. Somehow he'd felt it, too. Pain electrified the side of his head.

'The asphyxia is severe,' Ballard explained. 'But if we cool the brain beyond—'

Marco stopped him again. 'It didn't work. You shouldn't have done it. You made it too cold. The metabolic strain was too great. She died.'

Ballard shook his head. 'No, no. I can save her, Henry.'

'You killed her,' Marco spat. He felt his body pulling away, changing locations against his will, as if he were being dragged, and now he was standing in the hallway outside the Special Care Neonatal Unit. He wanted to enter, but the door to the treatment room was locked, the knob unyielding. Suddenly the door shook. He heard shouting voices on the other side. Then the shouts stopped, and the knob clicked. The door opened, and Roger's decomposed corpse shuffled out. Its face was stricken, anguished. 'Pulmonary haemorrhage,' it said. 'Brain dead.'

'Why, Roger?' Marco pleaded. 'Why did you do that?'

Ballard studied Marco. He seemed lost. His mouth opened, groping for words.

'You shouldn't have emailed me,' Marco groaned. Then winced as another whiplash of pain lit up his cheek.

Wake up. Slap. Slap.

Slap.

His eyelids cracked open, even as his eyeballs still rolled in his head. The sky was pink now, early dawn, the horizon tilting like a seesaw, up then down. His head felt stuffed with wool, a fat mass packed between his ears, soundproofing his skull; he heard nothing but muffled noise, a scraping, the sound of someone retching – himself, he realised, warm vomit splashing his chin – and he remembered being grabbed by his feet and dragged over dirt, a hundred years ago maybe, or only just a few seconds.

His thoughts were sluggish; he could feel them clinging stubbornly to the very bottom of his consciousness, and he waited dumbly, minutes and minutes, for each to lose its grip and rise – float to the surface and pop like bubbles so their meaning could escape.

Slap.

Someone had just struck him across his bruised cheekbone.

'Wake up.'

The voice was like a pair of sharp scissors, cutting through the wool in his head.

'Roger?' he asked, disoriented. *Still a dream? No. Yes. No.*

'Wu?' he tried.

He was lying on his spine, his arms stretched back behind his head. He stared at his feet far away. His eyes refused to focus, and blurred contours made his legs seem confusing. He tried to sit himself up. He couldn't. His arms were stuck; he didn't understand. A hazy figure hovered over him, the rough shape of a man. *Wu?*

'Birth asphyxia,' Marco mumbled. His lips were numb. The complex syllables were difficult to push across. 'Hypoxic . . . ischemic . . . encephalopathy.'

'What'd you say?' The sharp voice again.

Marco continued, concentrating yet woozy. 'Neonatal condition – newborn babies – born not breathing. No oxygen to the brain. Roger induced hypothermia. Standard treatment, cool her to thirty-three degrees Celsius, three days. But Roger went lower. Risky. The asphyxia was severe. He wanted to save her, no brain damage. But. She died.'

'Roger who?' demanded the voice. 'Roger Ballard?'

Marco wet his lips with his tongue. His head pounded

with pain, but his ears were crackling, clearing. He felt a cool morning breeze freshen his forehead. His words smoothed, flowing easier. 'Roger wants to keep the brain alive. Without oxygen.'

He stopped and frowned. His eyes had firmed, and at last his surroundings took solid shape. He was laid out amidst a tangle of grey branches and bushes on a rugged embankment of desert earth. The dirt was bone-white, a paler bleach than Arizona. Twenty feet down, the hill bottomed out onto a bleak two-lane highway. Telephone poles spooled off forever to the north and south, and smaller roads broke away from the main highway, skulking towards distant houses and ugly structures that looked like industrial warehouses. He saw rotting bales of hay stacked at intervals across parched fields. He was on the outskirts of some remote California town.

Across the road he saw a dilapidated shingled building, more like an oversized shack, hunkered in a dirt parking lot filled with ghostly sun-whitened cars. Orange cones marked the corners of the lot, and around the perimeter a half-assed fence of nylon rope was strung between rusted metal posts, decorated with small plastic flags of blue and yellow and red. He squinted at the building. Over the entrance, burnt neon tubing looped and twisted to form the word *Bill's* and a giant mug of foam-headed beer.

A bar.

This was wrong. It took Marco another moment to realise why.

'Why aren't we on the train?' he asked.

The simple question seemed to crash through the last obstructions in his head; suddenly he was sharp and rational, able to remember. '*Down!*' Wu had yelled, and then the explosion through the windshield, the metal canister, the smoke. Someone had gas-bombed the locomotive – knocked Marco halfway into a coma. His mouth was sour with the after taste of the toxin; he hawked and spat into the dust.

And then he realised why he couldn't move. His arms were handcuffed. Chained backwards to something above his head. Grunting, he wriggled his body, craned his neck.

He was shackled to the rear tow-bar of a quad. The vehicle was dirt-splattered and coffin-brown, splotched with desert camouflage – the size of a golf cart, but squatter, lower to the earth, with a scooped-out driver's seat and handlebars to steer. From behind, it looked like a mutated motorcycle with four monster tyres, each treaded deep for off-road traction.

'Wu!' he called, alarmed, snapping his head back to where he'd seen the shadowy figure.

'What the hell—' he began. Then sucked in a quick breath.

'You're not Wu,' he said.

The man crouching beside him was dark-skinned with a black nest of beard framing two cracked lips and disarrayed yellow teeth. A desert-coloured beret lay flat atop his head; he wore a green camouflaged military jacket and loose cargo pants, neither of which matched.

A soldier . . . maybe. He was too dishevelled, too haphazardly outfitted. Like some grunt in a guerrilla army, or a mercenary, perhaps. Sure as hell not US Military. On his breast pockets and shoulders, loose threads outlined spots where embroidered patches had been torn off, as though he had no allegiance to any flag, any division, any nation.

'Wu.' The man grinned. 'Who's that, yer friend?' His voice was deep. American.

Twisting on his chain, Marco scanned both left and right, his forehead steamy with a fresh sweat. No sign of Wu. He turned back to the soldier. 'Who the fuck are you?'

The grin vanished from the soldier's ugly mouth. He slouched forward and boxed Marco's left ear with a heavy backhand. All around him the desert flashed white; Marco scrunched his eyes, felt a tear dribble onto his lashes. The pain was familiar. He waited for it to subside, then reopened his eyes. He remembered the half-dreams he'd had while knocked unconscious by the gas, the sensation of being slapped. *Wake up.*

This jackass had been hitting him.

Now the man was scratching his knuckles on his beard, grinning again. His pale blue eyes shone with malice. 'None a' yer business,' he said. 'Fuck you, that's who.'

'Nice to meet you, too,' Marco muttered, his earlobe throbbing. Despite his tough talk, he was afraid – stricken with the sensation of being crushed, as if the four-hundred-pound quad had rolled over onto his chest. He swallowed dryly.

Oh god. I'm in deep shit here.

Over the horizon the sun had grown larger, coaxing more colour from the land. Yellow desert sunflowers winked cheerily from a patch near Marco's feet. He saw his Glock on the ground, and the AK-47, laid out beside a dusty brown daypack. Next to them was a gun that looked like a grenade launcher – probably used to fire the gas canister into the train. The soldier picked up the AK and carried it to the quad. On the side of the vehicle was a makeshift gun rack – a network of frayed bungee cords holding a shotgun, an axe and some sort of squat-barrelled machine gun. He added the AK to the collection, then returned and knelt beside his pack.

Marco hesitated . . . then dared to ask. 'Where's Wu?'

He braced, awaiting another punch for an answer.

The man ignored him. Instead he pulled a brick-sized walkie-talkie from a side pocket of his daypack and flicked it on. 'Conquest Three,' he barked.

A coarse voice crackled from the speaker. 'Conquest Three, what d'ya got?'

The soldier paced away, and Marco lost the conversation. A minute later the soldier returned, nodding. 'Hell yeah,' he finished. 'See ya soon.' He clicked the handset off.

Marco tried again. 'Where's Wu?'

The soldier held up his hand as if to say, *Be patient.* He returned the radio to his pack, then stood and grabbed Marco by the ankles. Before Marco had a chance to kick away, the soldier dragged him in a half-circle, orienting him feet-first up the embankment. Blood rushed to Marco's head, pushed against his eyeballs. Under his spine the ground was hard and stony; the chain on his hands jangled as he swivelled.

The soldier dropped him to the dirt with a solid thud.

'Your bud on the train?' the man asked, gesturing west past Marco's feet.

Marco looked. From his new position he could see up the hill, past the prickly scrub. There was the Sunset Limited. Motionless, dead on the tracks. The alerter had shut down the driverless locomotive. Orange smoke wheezed from a hole in the windshield.

'Wu, right?' the soldier said, smirking; the name seemed to bring him amusement. 'Yeah, found him taking a nap up there. The gas got him sleepy.' He made a gun shape with his thumb and index finger, then aimed the imaginary weapon at his temple and fired. 'Pow,' he said, and splayed his fingers wide to mimic splatter from his skull. 'Bad news. I shot Wu.'

Marco grimaced, felt his stomach contract. *Wu's dead.* The thought clamped onto him like another shackle, steel and inescapable, as certain as the chains on his trembling wrists. He was alone now. No way out. *Wu's dead and I'm fucked.*

A dull, sad weight hung from his heart; however ambivalent he'd been about Wu, he was tired, too fucking tired, of people around him dying.

Still smiling, the bearded soldier reached to his belt. From his hip he unclipped a keychain and dangled it theatrically, inches from Marco's face. A small black box danced at the tip of Marco's nose. It was a wireless control of some kind, with a round red button in the middle. Satisfied that Marco had seen, the soldier snatched the device away and planted his thumb on the button. Dried brown blood caked in the creases of his knuckles.

'Buh-bye, Wu,' the man said. Then squeezed the button.

A red bulb blinked three times on the box.

For a full second the desert seemed to hold its breath – silent, expectant – and then it exploded. From everywhere at once a massive hammer plummeted down on Marco's skull, pounded a deafening spike through his ears, and he cried out in pain as the locomotive erupted in a volcano-blast of flame – a tremendous ball of fire that grew and grew, giant and terrible, as if the sun had finally descended to swallow the desert. The locomotive rocked on the rails, and shockwaves tore down the hill to suck the air from Marco's lungs as a huge chunk of fire snapped off into the sky. Glass rained over the tracks. And then it was quiet again. The blackened shell of the locomotive settled into the earth, its sides bent outward, black fumes spewing from gashes in the steel. Small flames crackled between the wood rail ties.

A forty-foot piece of shrapnel.

And a coffin for Wu.

Marco clenched his eyes shut, his jaw hanging, his eardrums beating with horror.

Suddenly something hard clacked against his front teeth. Metal. The soldier had jammed the barrel of the Glock into Marco's mouth. It tasted foul and oily.

'Now,' the soldier said. 'You're gonna take me to Roger Ballard, right?'

His blue irises burned hot like gaslight. He twisted the gun painfully against Marco's tongue and wiggled his trigger finger.

'Or pow. Like Wu.'

The soldier laughed.

KILLERS

8.1

Wu pressed his body flat atop the stony ridge, hiding, blending; his warm skin harmonised with the clay, and the muscles in his biceps were edged like rock. He was a predator on the hunt, poised and watchful before the attack. He'd always been good at this, even as a boy – running down his brothers in games of Cat Catching Mice, played in the unpaved alleys of his boyhood village in Qinghai. He still knew the chant sung by the children:

What time is it?
Just struck nine.
Is the cat at home?
About to dine.

Kheng Wu had warrior's eyes, the townspeople had said. Green, the colour of legend. It was the hereditary mark of Crassus's lost Roman legion, soldiers who'd disappeared in Gansu two thousand years ago; they were rumoured to have wandered China as mercenaries, fathering exotic new bloodlines as they went. Surely young Wu had soldier-blood in his heart, pounding like cannon-fire, his rare green eyes sparking as he chased and dragged his quarry to the dirt. He was a born killer. Strong, ruthless – not cruel, but the games always awakened some part of him otherwise hidden. Once triggered, he was unstoppable, targeting his brothers with a fury that left them bleeding and breathless. Often he'd pinned Jiang – poor Jiang, the slowest, the easiest to outmanoeuvre and out-think – and pretended to devour him while the other boys cheered for the winning Cat. And then, sated, Wu had helped him up, and together they'd visited the water pump to wash the grit from Jiang's skinned elbows before returning to Bao Zhi's for dinner.

Now, all these years later, Wu was playing a deadlier game.

Thirty metres across the embankment he saw Marco, captive, handcuffed to an all-terrain quad. An unkempt bearded man in mismatched fatigues crouched next to the American.

Who was this enemy? For starters, he was no real soldier, not of any national force, Wu was certain. Everything about the man suggested he was renegade. *Militia?*

Yes. An extremist in a private army, Wu guessed; even before the Resurrection, America had been riddled with such nonsense, fools in love with their guns.

But this man had targeted Marco specifically – abducted him. And Wu had heard the soldier speak Roger Ballard's name just moments before.

What militia would possess such knowledge, so high-level?

Suddenly Wu knew. He squinted and studied the quad. It was a Boar model, wide-bodied, specially outfitted for military excursion. And there, tied to the front rack as he'd suspected . . .

. . . was a horse's skull, bleached stark-white and missing its lower jaw.

Horseman, Wu confirmed. His jaw muscles flexed. MSS had profiled Horsemen in his briefing – extreme survivalists, anarchists, a post-apocalyptic army holed up somewhere in the forests of California. Ex-military, most of them, highly trained and lethal; many were dropouts with criminal records, glad to see America fall. They'd ignored the Evacuation and now lived off the land – hunting, gathering – while ransacking civilisation's leftovers, stockpiling cash and jewellery and guns and drugs and whatever else they could scavenge from dark houses and dry skeletons. Mexico had a thriving black market for such ill-gotten goods; most of the desolate southern borders were easy to cross – huge unpatrolled gaps, no different from the days before the Resurrection – and the Horsemen reaped profits by transporting loot into Central and South America, the lower latitudes where the Resurrection had not yet travelled.

Wu frowned. Horsemen were dangerous. Worse, they had ties overseas; MSS had linked them with terror organisations in Kazakhstan and Iran. And now they, too, were seeking the Ballard DNA. Wu imagined faceless terrorists, watchful in the shadows, deciphering encrypted radio frequencies from the US, or worse, as MSS agents had relayed information to Beijing – knowledge discovered during China's hacks into the American mainframes.

Still, the terrorist intelligence was spotty, he reasoned, clearly lacking critical details such as Ballard's location at Sarsgard. The Horsemen were relying on Marco to lead them. They were like hyenas circling a lion's kill, hoping to steal a meal; the superpowers may have found the vaccine, but it was the Horsemen who planned to snatch it away at the last moment for a sale to terrorist allies. Horsemen were mercenaries – but they were fierce and good at their jobs.

Defeating this enemy would be hard. Very hard.

Which meant Wu could afford no more errors like the one he'd already made, back on the Sunset Limited. True, he'd known the train was being stalked, but carelessly he had assumed a single operative working alone. *Fool!* When Wu had accelerated the train to outrun the first Horseman quad, the driver had simply radioed ahead, thirty miles north.

The second Horseman had been ready with the gas launcher as Wu had driven into the trap.

And how many others were out there now? Patrolling up and down California? Converging across the desert to collect Henry Marco, even as Wu wasted time here wondering? One Horseman was bad enough. *Strike now, before more arrive.*

Half an hour ago the gas grenade had torn into the locomotive, and Wu had become briefly the hunted, not the hunter – scrambling for self-preservation, furious that the food chain had shifted against him. He dropped to the floor and stole a single deep breath, and seconds later orange smoke filled the cab. One lungful of clean oxygen – it was all he had been allotted, and all he would need. He scrabbled up the corridor on hands and knees, the smoke chasing him. He floundered over the mummified engineer corpses as somewhere back in the fog he heard Marco choke and crash against the console.

Nothing Wu could do about that now. His lungs bulged, his eyes burned. He reached the door to the next coach, slapped the button, and collapsed through the door as it opened. Tendrils of smoke reached after him, but the door closed, slicing them off.

Gasping, he rolled to his back. Tears beaded on his lashes, poison flushing from his eyes. From the train's undercarriage he heard the air brakes hiss, felt a check in momentum. The train was slowing. With nobody at the controls, the alerter had cut the engine and engaged the brakes.

He coughed up a bitter-tasting phlegm and, as his head cleared, so did his thoughts.

Marco.

The American was alive, without doubt. The gas wouldn't be lethal; Wu knew the stink of Kolokol-1, an old Soviet incapacitator still manufactured in black markets.

Knockout gas, of course. Deadly force would be illogical;

the enemy wanted Marco alive to lead them to Roger Ballard.

Wu stiffened and sat bolt upright.

The enemy needed only Marco. Orders would certainly call for Wu's immediate execution. He could flee and save himself . . . but if he were discovered missing on the train, an alarm would be sounded, the area scoured until he was found and terminated.

How, then, to prevent this? His mind whirled, grabbing at ideas, and in moments he'd cobbled together a plan – a risk, but a plan. But time was short. He had to act.

Bracing himself, he stood and elbowed the button on the door. As it groaned open, he inhaled, stockpiling his lungs again.

Then hurtled back into the smoke-filled locomotive.

The fumes grabbed him instantly, absorbed him into a ghostly orange gloom. He couldn't see beyond his outstretched arms, but he knew where to go, where to stop. The dead engineers appeared at his feet. Without pause he grabbed the top carcass by its shoulders and wrenched; it broke apart from the second body with a rude crack.

Good so far. Already Wu detected an ominous urgency between his ribs – his body begging him to breathe. *Hurry.*

Straining, he dragged the body to the front of the cab. Marco lay in a crumpled heap, unmoving, but Wu had no time to check for a pulse; he dumped the dead body next to Marco and rolled it on its stomach, face down on the floor.

His army gear jacket hung over the stool at the controls; he snatched it and, hastening, wrestled it onto the engineer. A decoy – believable enough in the murky room, provided it wasn't examined closely. Wu could only hope it wouldn't be.

The side door of the locomotive rattled in its frame, making him jump.

They were here. Entering the cab.

His lungs convulsed. *Go!* No time to seek his daypack in the mist. Desperately he clamped a hand to his throat, crushing his trachea shut – a single breath would render him unconscious, deliver him to execution – and dashed down the hall, knives bouncing on his belt. Just as the side door screeched open on rusted gears, Wu burst out the back exit, spilling into the connector between cars and ducking as the door shut behind him.

His mouth exploded open, fresh oxygen nourishing his body.

Gulping hungrily, he waited . . . thirty seconds passed . . . his deer-horns drawn, ready to strike if the door opened . . . if anyone pursued him.

Nothing.

Tentatively he stood and peered through the glass porthole.

The gas inside had thinned just enough to see down the corridor, all the way to the cab. He sighted a barrel-chested soldier – *just one,* Wu thought, feeling his hopes lift – outfitted in an olive-green uniform and a beret, muddling past the control stand. The man looked more like a monster, his face deformed by a black gas mask as he swept a flashlight through the cab. The flashlight beam stopped on Marco's unconscious face . . .

. . . hovered there as if considering . . .

Then continued a metre farther until the beam lit upon the dead engineer, face down and disguised in the American army jacket.

Wu tensed. Silently he cast his thoughts at the man.

Go ahead. Believe what you see. Be a fool.

The soldier bent and clipped a set of handcuffs on Marco's limp arms. Then he stood again and pulled a pistol from his belt; he aimed straight down and fired two shots into the back of the dead engineer's skull.

The blasts were like bursts of laughter in Wu's head. He smiled coldly, pleased with himself, as the soldier holstered his firearm and grabbed Marco by the ankles, dragged him to the open door, and lowered him outside.

Relieved, Wu turned and slumped against the wall. The stink of the gas had soaked into his shirt. He crinkled his nose and wiped his agitated eyes with his arm.

Ten minutes later, long enough to ensure that the soldier had abandoned the train, Wu had crept outside and found his perch on the embankment as the morning sun broke over the hills. The heat cracked him across the shoulders like the first lash of a whip.

He watched as farther down the hillside the bearded Horseman struck Marco with a violent backhand. Wu twitched. His veins swelled with a rush of liquid anger, and he frowned, curious at his reaction. Whether the American suffered meant nothing to him – or shouldn't, at least – yet somehow, Wu sensed, this was a violation. *An insult.* Yes, that was the explanation.

Henry Marco belonged to Wu, and Wu alone would decide the punishment.

He cut the thought short. At the moment it didn't matter. All that mattered was getting the American back alive before more militiamen arrived—

His eyes shot wide.

The Horseman had a detonator in his hand.

At once Wu recognised the logic he himself would have applied if he were the enemy. The locomotive had been wired to explode – *plastique*, he guessed fleetingly, *C4 or Russian PVV*, although it made no difference now – to render it useless to hostile operatives who might follow. The train sat ten metres up the hill, so close he could still smell the lingering acrid tang of the gas. His mind lit up with a single word, bright and brief like lightning – *move* – and then switched to wordless instinct; he flipped from the ridge, away from the tracks as the explosion tore open the morning and fire swarmed over the terrain he'd only moments before escaped.

For an instant the flash was blinding, and he threw himself down the embankment, betting that the Horseman would miss the sudden move – counting on the man's eyes to be covered from the blast. In mid-roll he regained his feet and sprinted to the grove of low-lying bushes near where Marco lay captured. He threw himself at their roots, merging with the shadows as metal hail from the exploded train clanged to the tracks.

He held there, panting, tense. But he'd gambled correctly; his leap to safety had gone unnoticed, and the Horseman did not attack.

Within moments the desert was calm again.

But not Wu. Inwardly he raged, cursing the Horseman. Cursing *himself.* His daypack had been in the locomotive, and his Droid. Destroyed now. He pinched his eyes closed and exhaled.

Focus, he counselled himself, listening to his breath. *Calm your thoughts. Focus ahead.*

He quieted his lungs and, like a sleek, soundless cat, circled the brush.

This, finally, felt right – being the hunter once more, ears buzzing, muscles eager, his nostrils wide and hungering for the sweet smell of the kill. He reached the edge of the brush and peered through the gnarled sticks. The mercenary soldier was three metres below on the hillside, crouched over Marco, a gun shoved between the American's bleeding lips.

'Or pow,' the soldier said. 'Like Wu.'

The Horseman laughed.

Smouldering, further insulted by the invocation of his name, Wu coiled the power in his legs. His body ached like a compressed spring, begging for release. *Not yet.*

He dug his fingernails into the rough earth and anchored himself there with the pain. Sweat prickled on his skin, evaporating away into the early desert heat.

He waited. *Patience.*

The soldier removed the gun barrel from Marco's mouth and stood.

Kill!

Unleashing his anger, Wu sprang – pouncing airborne as his eyes measured his prey below, marking the nape of the neck, the soft spot where the knives would plunge and rip . . .

. . . but the Horseman's senses were honed, too, reflexes quicker than Wu had bargained for and, at the sound of skittering pebbles, the soldier's head jerked, and the man spun . . .

. . . and as the gun exploded and the bullet bit his arm, Wu realised that he'd miscalculated, that this vulgar soldier was *not* prey but a perfect killer like himself, and with a thud of bone against bone, the two blood-soaked predators crashed down the hillside to determine whose throat would be torn, and who would live to hunt again.

8.2

Marco watched. Watching was all he could do – sprawled on the dirt, handcuffed to the quad – as the bearded soldier whirled with his gun upraised, and a fast-moving shadow struck from overhead, and the gun blasted, and Marco twisted away, confused, certain that the next bullet would come streaking right into his gut.

Instead the soldier hit the ground, tackled by . . . *a corpse*, Marco thought, his heart misfiring.

But no, thank god . . . it was *Wu*.

Wu! Alive, bleeding. *Shot*. The bullet had grazed him,

clipped off a chunk of his arm as it passed. The wound spat red droplets like a demonic sprinkler as Wu and the soldier tumbled down the embankment, caterwauling like animals as they went.

The two fighters somersaulted onto the desert highway and somehow landed upright, bouncing to their feet like an acrobat act gone wrong, each man streaked with blood but determined to perform. The soldier struck first – a powerhouse punch straight to the gory bull's-eye on Wu's left shoulder, the gunshot wound. Wu barked in pain and staggered backwards, and the soldier struck again, this time with the gun in his hand, hammering Wu across the jaw – a sickening *crack* that echoed in Marco's stomach – and Wu's legs seemed to go slack, and he toppled to his back. Without hesitation the bearded man raised the gun, aimed into Wu's chest—

'HEY!' Marco screamed.

The soldier flinched – barely, barely – his head cocking to the side for just the smallest fraction of time, but it was enough.

On the ground, Wu seemed to burst into fire.

A white-hot flash of light consumed him whole, stretched across the desert and then just as instantly retracted, and Marco saw Wu on his feet, the steel rounded knife blade in his hand, catching the sun. With a snap of his wrist, Wu sent the knife spinning like a lethal discus at the distracted soldier. The blade gyrated twice and clipped the soldier's gun hand.

The man yipped as his firearm clattered to the road and his fingertips tumbled and scattered, sliced off, his fingers spraying blood like hose nozzles. His thumb flopped and bounced at his wrist, held only by a disgusting meaty hinge.

In a burst Wu was up again, darting, sliding feet-first at his opponent. With a single fluid motion Wu kicked the gun where it lay, sending it into the brush off the highway, and followed with a chop to the man's ankles, toppling him to the pavement . . .

An ugly racket, a sound like splintering, distracted Marco.

The bar across the road. Bill's. The door had broken open.

Out into the daylight staggered a putrid-skinned corpse in a red plaid sleeveless vest, the crown of its head bald and peeling, long ratty hair clinging to the sides around its ears. Its mouth hung freakishly open, the bottom jaw broken and resting on its chest, exposing its entire bottom row of shit-coloured rotten molars and a tongue torn in two, each half wriggling obscenely independent of the other. It stumbled a few steps into the dirt lot, looking like a drunk venturing out to his car after a hard night's drinking.

A *very* hard night for this poor bastard.

'Aw, shit,' Marco groaned.

The corpse had drinking buddies.

The bar was emptying, a mob of the dead crowding out through the door, wakened by the explosion and the highway fistfight. Crossing the lot towards Wu and the soldier.

'*Wu!*' Marco shouted.

On the road the soldier had regained his feet. His gun hand was useless, spouting blood that hit the pavement in thick drops and congealed immediately in the dirt. But in his left hand he'd drawn a knife of his own, a hunting knife, thick and serrated, and he slashed at Wu like a madman. Wu dodged, shielded himself with his remaining knife, and the metallic *clang* of blade striking blade reverberated up the hill as the first corpse reached the highway.

Behind it followed a dozen corpses, with more emerging from the bar even as Marco eyed the door – milky-eyed males in mesh truckers' caps and cowboy hats and denim jeans dyed with blood and beer, some with necks ripped wide, others dragging their intestines behind them. Dead men who'd hunkered down for eternity at their favourite watering hole. A female, too, a barmaid in a short skirt, its thighs greased black and wet, a glass mug clutched in its hand. And at the back of the pack, a younger corpse, clearly underage, with scabs of crusted black acne and a knobby Adam's apple. Marco would have felt sorry for it, if he wasn't so scared shitless.

'*Wu!*' he cried again. '*Behind you!*'

But Wu wasn't listening – couldn't listen – as the bearded soldier swung again with his blade, cleaved the air just over Wu's ducking head . . .

. . . then lunged forward and drove his elbow into Wu's brow, just above the eyes; Wu's neck cracked backwards on his shoulders and he dropped again, sprawling to the ground at the feet of the oncoming corpses. The dead were just five steps away, reaching for the kill—

No!

The realisation that he was about to watch Wu die, so soon after reclaiming him alive, stabbed into Marco like a spur to a slow horse's ass. Adrenalin danced up his body, superheated and enraging. *Fuck the spectator shit. Do something!*

He snatched a fast, hard breath and yanked frantically against the chain holding him to the quad; it snapped taut and his skin bunched against the handcuffs, hot with pain, no fucking way to pull through without pulverising every bone in his hand. *Shit!* He struggled upright, his arms contorted back over his head for a better look . . .

. . . just in time to see Wu flip to his feet again, dodging the mulleted corpse that swiped at him. The dead horde mobbed the highway, still more coming, a line stretching from the road to the bar door, and Wu saw them all now, fifty hungry rotting drunks swarming as the enemy soldier rushed him again from the front.

He's done, Marco understood suddenly, certainly, horribly. But even as Wu's eyes widened in surprise, his body was already in motion – a high kick backwards, ramming the bald corpse square in the chest and knocking it to its bony ass, and then, so fast the separate movements blended impossibly into one, Wu lashed out with his opposite foot and booted the charging soldier right under the chin. The man staggered back, emitting a wet gargling noise as he clutched his throat.

Marco almost laughed in relief. *Holy shit, Wu. That kicked ass.*

The bearded soldier spat blood and snot onto the highway, then raised his knife into a fighter's stance, arm halfway extended, blade forward. Corpses had crossed from the parking lot onto the road behind, a double wall of death collapsing on both sides – no way out for the battling men. The soldier licked his lips and grinned; blood squirted from his wounded hand as he teased his fingers, waving an invitation to Wu.

The message was clear. *Let's finish.*

For an uncertain moment, Wu appeared too tired to fight. Drained. His shoulder was an eyesore of black and brown dirty blood; his chest grew and shrank as he gasped for oxygen. He teetered precariously as if his ankles might buckle out from under him. The crescent-shaped knife sagged in his hand, suddenly seeming to weigh more than he could carry.

And then, to Marco's astonishment, Wu hollered – an ear-splitting warrior's cry, long and furious, like a flame forging steel – and charged.

What happened next was madness.

Wu and the soldier exploded at each other, colliding as the corpses ran amok on the highway, a chaos of dead bodies and two fighters in the middle.

Marco couldn't believe what he was seeing, couldn't breathe, couldn't blink, *Christ* . . .

The bearded man struck like a scorpion, his blade over-swinging Wu's head by inches just as a ponytailed corpse lunged from behind, and the soldier spun in a circle and plunged the knife into the corpse's earhole, then plucked it free with a queasy sucking sound . . .

. . . as Wu dodged low and heel-kicked the leg of a scrawny biker corpse in a bandana and leather-studded vest. The dead kneecap tore loose and plopped to the pavement in a sticky puddle, but even before the corpse hit the ground, Wu was already up, his knife shielding his face as his opponent's blade glanced off with a high-pitched squeal . . .

. . . and then two dead males in baseball caps grabbed the bearded soldier's arms. The soldier slammed his elbows back like two sledgehammers, demolishing the soft dead nasal bones, leaving deep ditches in the corpses' faces as he pulled his arms forward again and snagged the tip of his knife into the gunshot wound on Wu's shoulder.

Wu bucked with pain . . .

. . . and more corpses surged from the left and right, tightening the circle, a three-way war between Wu and the soldier and a snarling mass of the dead.

All with the same mindless hunger. The same need to kill.

Marco's head dizzied; he hadn't taken a breath since the melee began, awestruck by the velocity of the action, the skill of the fighters. It was like watching a movie played somehow at two speeds simultaneously – the dead lumbering and heavy, the soldier and Wu quantum-quick, moving faster than light, slowing down time around them as they fired impossible punches at the corpses and each other. The stakes were all or nothing, and a single mistake, the smallest miscalculation of tempo or distance, meant death to the loser.

The thought overwhelmed Marco, and he gasped, air bounding from his lungs.

His mind cleared . . .

Oh shit.

Six or seven corpses had crossed the road and were climbing the embankment.

Towards him.

A nice easy meal chained to the quad.

8.3

The sight of the climbing corpses jolted Marco like a cattle prod. Frantic, he threw his weight against the chains; they jangled tauntingly and held strong to the quad bumper. He pulled anyway. Needles shot into his shoulders, and he dropped the chains. *Nope.* He scrambled awkwardly to his feet instead, contorting to keep his elbow from dislocating.

'*Wu!*' he yelled and immediately felt like an idiot.

Yeah, right.

No chance for Wu to bail him out this time – Wu had his own shitload of trouble down on the road. The sergeant was busy punching a skeletal black male to the asphalt, as beside him the enemy soldier grappled with a fat old corpse in a worm-eaten Dodgers jersey. In a burst of motion the dead barmaid joined the fight, slung its wiry arm around Wu's neck from behind. Wu's reaction was instant; he grabbed the beer mug from the female's hand and smashed the glass against its black teeth. Its gums caved in, it swallowed its teeth . . .

. . . as the bearded soldier carved a rancid blubbery strip from the fat corpse's belly, then turned and lunged, his knife a slick red point aimed at Wu's heart . . .

. . . but Wu twisted, lightning-fast, the female still draped on his back, and the soldier's blade sank into the corpse's brain stem instead.

Dammit. Marco needed another solution, fast. His eyes darted down the embankment, measuring seconds until the corpses reached him – *fifteen? twenty?* – then reeled back to his wrists, the unbreakable chain, the bumper, the quad . . .

Son of a bitch.

The answer was so goddamn obvious he cursed himself for taking this long to see.

The soldier's guns. Strapped to the ATV, not five feet from his hands.

The chain was plenty long enough to reach; he snatched up the machine gun, but the weapon was too bulky, too awkward to hold with his hands bound together. He'd never manage. *Shit.* Fine, the shotgun would have to do. Two shots.

Better than nothing.

If it was even loaded.

Grunting with effort, he wedged the stock against his shoulder and swung to aim down the embankment. The corpses were a tight group, just steps away, led by a loose-skinned male with a braided beard. Broken ribs like thorns pierced the skin beneath its right pectoral. Marco planted the shotgun sight on its forehead and fired; the kickback nearly knocked Marco on his ass, slamming him to the quad, but the shot was a bull's-eye. The male's head vaporised into a cloud of black mist; its body fell, muddying the dirt as its brain plopped out like pudding.

Marco didn't pause to congratulate himself. The shotgun erupted again, spraying buckshot wide, drilling holes into the underage corpse he'd seen earlier – *Did your parents know you were a drinker?* Marco wondered fleetingly – as well as the mulleted corpse next to it. Both crashed over backwards and tumbled downhill.

Two with one shot. Bonus points. *Nice.*

But the shotgun was spent, and four corpses remained – three males and a topless female with pierced tits that sagged to the belt of its jeans. The smell of burnt gunpowder tingled heatedly in Marco's nose, and his thumbs throbbed from the kickback. *Quit yer bitchin'*, he thought. The female attacked, and he swung the shotgun like a baseball bat. But the swing was weak, a lame-ass embarrassing little wave. *Fuckin' handcuffs.* The corpse grabbed the barrel of the gun and twisted it out of his hands.

Great. Time for Plan B.

The axe.

He snatched the weapon from the quad and was already in mid-swing back at the female when his eye caught a glint of metal from within the vehicle, a familiar shape and, as the axe completed its arc and chopped sideways into the female's ear, lodging firmly in the skull with a crisp clean *thwack*, Marco realised what he'd just seen.

Are you kidding me?

He whirled back to the quad even before the female hit the ground, spasming.

The key. The key was in the goddamn ignition.

With the male corpses ten feet away, Marco mounted the quad, dragging the chain over the handlebar. For the first time, he noticed the bulk of an animal skull – a burro? a horse? – tied with twine to the front of the quad like a demented hood ornament. *What the fuck . . .?*

Screw it, no time for that shit. He refocused on the quad's ignition. He'd driven a quad once before – an adventure tour in the dunes near Sedona, the year before the Resurrection. He and Benjamin. It had been a 'guys day out' while the wives, Danielle and her sister Trish, spent the afternoon at some silly thing called an *energy vortex* at a New Age centre in town.

Hey, Ben had asked him tentatively, buckling his helmet before the ride. *Are things okay?*

What do you mean?

Y'know, man. Things with Danielle.

Everything's fine.

Cause Trish said—

It's fine, Ben. Goddamn it. And with that Marco had started the engine, just like the instructor had demonstrated, and the deafening roar ended the conversation.

Now, dripping sweat, Marco re-enacted that first step. He wrenched the ignition switch to the 'on' position, then blinked, frozen, desperate to recall that afternoon's lesson from all the years of shit and misery since. His hands fumbled on the key. His mind was blank. The first corpse shambled up, and he kicked sideways, vaguely aware that he'd just snapped the dead man's knee. The corpse crumpled beside the quad.

Brake lever! There it was, on his left; he yanked the small red handle, and thank god it was like a release on his brain, and the rest came easy – check the fuel cock, push the starter button, feel the engine roar like a buzz-saw as his teeth chattered together. With the handcuffs on, he couldn't grip both handlebars, so he grabbed the right-side throttle between his palms and gunned the quad as the last two corpses attacked, and with a spitting of soil and pebbles, the wheels swerved left then right and then shot forward, through the grasp of the corpses, bucking like a wild bronco down the embankment as though the horse skull on the hood had come to life.

He almost fell, which would have killed him for sure, but with his ass half on the seat, half off, and his organs jouncing in his chest, he kept his balance and somehow steered. For a pants-shitting second he sailed airborne over a flat rock that angled like a ramp from the earth, then crashed down again with a crunch of metal and plastic and the chain whipping against the handlebar. Brisk air whistled in his earlobes.

Shit!

The highway sped towards him, the war zone, the battlefield below where the corpses and the soldier and Wu were taking each other apart, bit by fleshy bit.

His fingers eased on the throttle, slowing . . .

Ah, fuck it.

Wu needs help.

He crushed the throttle with both hands, and the quad rocketed ahead.

His senses seemed to speed up, as if powered by the engine; he heard and saw everything – the tortured wails, the knives carving skin, the black asphalt doused with fallen corpses and chopped-off arms and glistening blood-slicks, like a horrible traffic accident minus the cars, and other corpses still on the attack, Wu and the soldier fending them off in between punches and kicks to each other, *thwack thwack thwack*; more dismantled corpses – and then the quad shot to the highway, clipping slack-jawed corpses, sending them spinning with broken legs and backs.

The quad was like a knife itself, slicing the crowd, and Marco didn't swerve, *refused* to swerve, instead battling the handlebars to keep the wheel straight, every stubborn drop of adrenalin combusting in his head as he hurtled towards his target, locked in . . .

Hey Wu, buddy ol' pal

. . . twenty feet before impact, he glimpsed Wu drenched in blood, bedraggled, his eyeballs paled to a cool green mint, his arms locked with the bearded soldier's in a deadly stalemate. Each man's knife strained towards the other's throat . . .

My turn to bail your ass out

. . . the quad barrelled another ten feet, and something in Wu seemed to break at last, too much life pouring from his gunshot wound as the soldier's razor-sharp dagger pressed a red dimple into the lump of Wu's jugular vein . . .

Thank me later

. . . five feet away, the soldier whirled at the oncoming engine roar, his eyes round and white, his beard sopping with gore and chunks of skin . . .

Fuck you!

With a lung-crushing *whump*, the quad slammed into the bearded man like a four-hundred-pound battering ram, nose-diving forward onto its front wheels – and as Marco catapulted from his seat, his fingertips clinging to the handlebar, he wondered if this was maybe the shittiest idea he'd had in a long fuckin' time.

8.4

The impact launched the soldier airborne; he hovered two feet above the quad for what seemed like minutes, limbs splayed like a freefalling skydiver. And then time and gravity corrected themselves, and the soldier slammed down onto the hood as Marco pitched forward halfway across the handlebar, both men knocked windless, shoulders colliding . . .

. . . and for a terrifying moment Marco balanced like this, handcuffed arms pinned under him, stomach on the handlebar – the eerie horse skull on the hood grinning up at him, inches from his face as he rode the quad like a body board – and then the vehicle crashed down, the rear wheels banging to the road; he hooked his ankles underneath the aluminium seat frame and wrangled himself back in the saddle just as the quad swerved out of control. The other man wasn't as lucky. The bumper sucked his legs under, and he clung to the front hood, his fingers clawing the eyes of the skull, yowling as the vehicle scrubbed him over the asphalt.

In the driver's seat, Marco heard himself screaming, too. He grabbed the handlebar in a panic, no intent to steer, just a wild prayer to hang on. The quad sailed to the far side of the road, wheels crunching through the brittle weeds as it left the pavement and bounded into the dirt parking lot of Bill's. The mob of corpses fell behind, ten yards back, twenty . . .

. . . the immediate danger subsiding as the quad sped away. The soldier howled and slapped at the hood, the blood from his mangled fingertips smearing red on the metal, and the horse skull snapped apart, tumbled from the quad, smashed to a hundred white shards on the hard earth. Marco met eyes with the man; the soldier's face was blood-spattered and grotesque, hot with pain – a pain, Marco realised, that he had inflicted on this fellow human being, not a corpse who didn't care or feel when you broke its leg or chopped off an arm, but a *living, suffering man.* The knowledge sobered him like a bucket of cold water.

His adrenalin rush sputtered, and he snatched his hand from the throttle.

'I'm sorry,' he said. He spoke without thinking, then recognised how ridiculous he'd just sounded. *Sorry I ran you over and tried to kill you.* He choked the brake, and the quad skidded to a stop near a lopsided wooden porch, the entrance to the bar.

The soldier rolled from under the bumper as if he'd been spat out. He tumbled two or three times like a rag doll, then flopped onto his spine and rested there, limp and gasping, folded all wrong; his knees were bent sideways, and a spear-shaped bone stabbed through his left pant leg, just below the thigh. His skin was sticky – blood-wet, coated so thickly with desert dust that he looked like a lump of bread dough rolled in flour.

A hand grabbed Marco by the shoulder, and he spun in a panic.

'Wu,' he breathed.

The sergeant collapsed against the quad, his jaw slack with exhaustion. He'd escaped through the hole Marco had punched in the crowd of corpses. His once-noble cheekbones were battered and swollen pink, and his entire face was plastered from forehead to chin with viscous black blood. He looked like a mechanic who'd just gotten his ass kicked during an oil change. His breath came in short grinds that seemed to hurt going in, coming out. And, Christ, he reeked, every inch of him doused in death.

Marco grimaced. Back on the highway, the corpses had turned, heading back this way, into the parking lot. Only a dozen or so – Wu and the soldier had racked up the body count big-time – but these survivors looked hungry as ever, pissed off, growling and frustrated. Wu glanced stiffly over his shoulder.

'We have to go,' he huffed.

'No argument,' Marco said. He nodded to the groaning bearded soldier. The man had managed to push himself up to hands and knees and was dragging himself towards the bar door, hoping to find cover inside. 'Let's collect our new friend.'

Wu narrowed his eyes. Blood clouded the cornea around his left pupil. He glanced once more to the ragged corpses, then separated himself from the quad and half jogged, half limped to the downed soldier. He planted his boot on the square of the man's neck and drove his heel down hard. With an agonised cry the man collapsed back into the pebbly dirt. Wu bent, and Marco saw him pull something from the soldier's belt. A moment later Wu had returned to the quad.

'Your handcuffs,' he said, and held out a stubby silver key.

Marco exhaled, relieved. 'Good thinking. These kinda cramp my style.'

He winced as Wu grabbed the handcuffs rudely. The key clicked in the chamber, and the cuffs swung loose into Wu's hands. The chain slithered free, jangling happily. Marco exhaled. Shit, that hurt. He blew a cooling breath across the ugly scarlet gashes that the bracelets had sawed into his skin.

'Thanks,' he said. 'Now let's get the hell out—'

He didn't finish. Wu had turned back to the injured soldier, kneeling beside the man.

'What are you doing?' Marco asked suspiciously. Halfway across the lot, the corpses were advancing. Getting too damn close.

Without answering, Wu grabbed hold of the man's arm and began to drag him. The soldier screamed as his exposed broken femur scraped the ground. Wu dropped him five feet nearer to the building. There in the dirt was a square grate, a rusted sewer hole.

The handcuffs flashed in Wu's grip.

'Wait—' Marco protested, suddenly understanding.

But too late. Wu had snapped one cuff on the man's wrist. The other cuff clamped around the iron grate.

'*No!*' the soldier cried through gritted teeth.

Wu bent and spoke into the man's ear, quietly, beyond Marco's hearing. Marco paled; his pores flushed a new sweat onto his skin, freezing him, soaking him in horror. '*Wu!*' he blustered. 'We're not doing this!'

With a defiant glare, Wu hurled the key across the lot. It disappeared in the scrub beyond a stack of faded orange parking cones. Marco's stomach sickened.

Yes, apparently, they *were* doing this.

Wu hiked himself up onto the quad, sitting backwards in a small hollow behind the seat that was meant for supplies and gear. His legs dangled over the rear wheel well. Fearlessly he faced the corpses shambling towards him, ten feet away.

'Go,' he said, the command curt, without emotion.

No, Marco thought. His right hand twitched on the throttle, his mind reeling. The groaning of the corpses wafted to his ears, close, very close . . .

In moments he'd feel dead, sticklike fingers seizing handfuls of his hair, yanking him kicking and screaming from the quad . . .

I can't leave. I can't—

'Go!' Wu roared as a rotted beefy bartender in a vomit-brown apron threw itself at him, and that did it, like a whip cracking Marco's back – no time left to argue, no time for rescues, no time to do anything but accept the bearded soldier's fate; and with a frustrated cry of '*Fuck!*', Marco gunned the throttle and the engine screamed in terror.

The quad fired forward past the doomed man.

For an instant Marco remembered himself pinned under the truck in Maricopa yesterday, those bitter moments he'd believed to be his last. And then he felt his consciousness shift, suddenly able to see through the enemy soldier's eyes – these dwindling seconds of the man's life, the quad abandoning him, his hands chained to a makeshift feeding trough for a slavering pack of cannibals. No escape possible, and nothing but agony ahead – and then, just as abruptly, Marco recoiled from these thoughts, overwhelmed . . .

Thankful it wasn't him. Not this time.

'*Please!*' From far behind the soldier begged, his voice fading with distance.

And then the dead were on him and, for half a second, there was silence.

A horrible, stomach-turning silence.

And then the morning erupted with a noise that men

weren't meant to make. It was a high-octave screeching, damned and hideous, violating Marco not just through his ears but somehow through his skin. A nauseating scream that went on and on . . .

Keep going. Don't look.

. . . and on and on . . .

Don't look.

. . . as if it would last for ever.

Shit. Marco braked and turned in his seat. The corpses were peeling the man open, breaking him, cracking him like a lobster to suck out the juices – grey fingers plunged into his eye sockets, his nostrils, his howling mouth, prying the cheeks while others attacked his arms, his legs . . . tearing away pieces of rubbery muscle and entrails like pink stretchy gum, and Marco glimpsed the dead bartender gnawing the exposed broken bone as the soldier writhed and bucked, the last ticks of his existence devoted solely to pain.

And then, with a hellish *crack*, the man broke apart, showering the dirt with bone and brains and sloppy organs, and the corpses grabbed up their prizes like demon children playing piñata. His head detached and blood jetted from the neck, carrying with it a final wet shriek . . .

And then at last the man fell eternally, mercifully quiet.

'Show's over, Doctor.' Wu's voice.

Marco turned. Dazed.

Wu was speaking to him. 'Now drive, please. Or we'll be the encore.'

With a mechanical motion, struggling to think, Marco hit the gas. The quad swung through the parking lot entrance, out again to the highway. The morning sun was in full force now, the asphalt alive and undulating with heat. Leading away.

A thought materialised from the fog in Marco's mind.
I just helped kill a man.
And then a question.
So where do we go from here?

RESPECT THE DEAD

9.1

'Christ, that's awful.' Marco spat out a mouthful of the stale Snickers bar that Wu had rummaged from the minimart; the chocolate crumbled like powder, and the chewy centre tasted like caramelised piss. 'There was nothing else? Twizzlers?'

'The store's cleaned out, Doctor.'

Marco scowled. The hunger in his gut jabbed at him for the third time in a minute. He could practically hear his stomach begging. *Shut up and eat.*

He smacked his lips and bit off another chunk. Nasty.

He was leaning on the quad, parked under the overhang of a Mobil gas pump about twenty miles from the massacre at Bill's Bar. Escaping the last surviving corpses hadn't been much of a challenge. With Wu on the back of the quad, Marco had buzzed north along the dusty road, skimming the fringe of the paltry California town. Dead citizens shambled up the side streets, emerging from ramshackle homes, early risers in sweatsuits and raggedy robes – but the quad was just too damn fast, and the roaring motor caught their attention only long enough for them to see their breakfast escaping at fifty miles an hour. *You snooze, you lose.*

And anyway, Marco realised, the dead weren't the real danger. Not any more.

Crazy-ass soldiers and foreign governments had just jumped to the top of the list.

For fifteen minutes neither he nor Wu had spoken as the quad barrelled northwards, the sun ascending to the east. A white road sign offered minimal guidance. *CA 111N.* Marco registered it only dimly; his mind was stuck in a tar pit of remorse, scalding him alive as it sucked him to the bottom. The bearded soldier's hideous death-squeal nagged his eardrums, refusing to go silent. He'd heard that sound before, witnessed men die in equally horrible fashion – but this death was different in one monumental way.

I did it. I left him there. I fed him to the fucking zombies.

And Wu. The sergeant had clapped on the handcuffs without a moment's hesitation. Without mercy. Marco shuddered. *What the hell kind of man does that?*

Behind him on the quad, Wu had been just as silent, perhaps gathering his thoughts or diagnosing his wounds. Sure as hell not mourning his fallen enemy, Marco was certain.

But even if Wu's conscience was unharmed, the rest of him looked like hell. His face and arms were pasted with dark, sticky blood, and scraps of dead flesh clung to his stubbled chin like blobs of mincemeat. His eyes had swollen noticeably, and he seemed to flinch whenever he blinked. Across his shoulder, a short trench opened where the soldier's bullet had grazed him; the skin was red and black at the torn edges, burnt and bleeding at the same time. *Better clean that up*, Marco thought. With so much corpse juice spilled over Wu's face and arms, there was a real danger of infection through the carved-out gun wound.

He deserves it, Marco thought, then reddened.

Nobody deserved that.

The men drove on, wordlessly motoring up Route 111 on a course towards hazy, distant mountains. When Wu finally called out, shouting over the engine, Marco had jumped in his seat.

'*Pull in!*' He pounded Marco on the back and pointed to a haunted-looking gas station a hundred yards ahead, coming up on the right. The windows were dark, and tall grass spiked through cracks in the asphalt between the pumps. Beside the road a red sign with missing letters and numbers teased a few ancient gas prices.

UNLE DED 3 9. D SEL 2.8.

Meaningless now, in every sense.

Marco was in no mood for a stop, but Wu was right. They needed to regroup, figure out what the hell to do next. He swerved more rudely than necessary, a petulant answer to Wu's habit of ordering him around, and the quad coasted into the station.

He brought it to a rest between a quartet of beaten old pumps, two to the left, two to the right. His fingers tensed on the throttle, ready to peel out if some dead freak came charging around the corner in bloody gas station coveralls.

But nothing happened, no crazed attack. Marco killed the engine and scanned the neighbourhood – another sparsely developed ghost town, a bleak boulevard of low-end business establishments crumbling to dust in the desert. A grubby-looking Mexican bar, its brick walls painted a queasy light blue, sulked on the next kerb. Marco eyed it warily. He'd dealt with enough dead drunks for the day. Beyond that stood a shuttered pawn shop and a bail-bond office promising *24/7 Super Service* on a torn banner over its shattered glass door.

Across the road, shielded behind corrugated metal, was a large lot – a scrapyard, stocked with hulking rusted pipes and unrecognisable, multi-jointed farm machinery for which Marco couldn't imagine a purpose. Telephone poles and stray palm trees led away north. A block farther he spied a car dealership with silent Hondas corralled like steel cattle;

coloured ribbons hung limply from a towering flagpole missing a flag. The ribbons stirred in the breeze. Their motion was the only movement anywhere, as far as he could tell.

'Fill the tank,' Wu instructed, sliding off the quad. 'I'll look inside.'

'Inside? What for?'

Wu regarded him disdainfully. 'I've been shot, Doctor. In your medical opinion, should I look for a Band-Aid?' Without waiting for an answer he limped towards the minimart connected to the gas station. He spoke over his shoulder. 'My daypack was in the train when the cab exploded. My GPS is gone. I'll look for a map, too.'

He disappeared into the store, leaving Marco alone outside.

Prick.

Marco had tried pumping gas, but the station had no back-up generator, no way to start the suction in the pipe. Since the Resurrection he'd learned more about the inner mechanisms of a gas pump than any other man alive with a medical degree. But no luck today. The storage tanks were sealed, and even the pipe was dry when he cut the hoses – nothing but a rush of sweet gasoline fumes, lightening his head like a balloon. He tossed the separated gas nozzle to the ground, frustrated, and winced at the clatter of sound.

Jesus, asshole. Don't ring the dinner bell.

The pump was the old-fashioned kind, with a mechanical display counter that read *$20.96*. He reflected on the numbers, his imagination working. Some panicked man or woman had stood right where he was now, at this pump. When? The last days of the Evacuation? He envisioned them huffing with fear, pumping out the last meagre drops. He wondered how far they'd gotten with their twenty-one dollars' worth of gas.

Often in the past four years he'd been struck – disheartened, really – by these small leftovers of life, minor evidences that popped up wherever he travelled. It was like reading the first page of an incomplete novel. Turn the page, nothing but sheets of blank white paper.

Did the hero survive? Or die horribly?

He shivered, unsure whether it was better to know the ending or not.

From inside the minimart he heard Wu fumbling through the aisles, the crunch of broken glass under boots, the remarkably loud crinkle of foil chip bags. A sign in the window advertised $7.59 for a pack of Marlboros. A payphone stood beside the door, its cord ripped loose; the black receiver lay on the concrete kerb below. A ratty clump of hair stuck to the mouthpiece. Probably somebody had used it as a corpse-beater.

He wished Wu would hurry up.

Lying next to the phone was a crushed Styrofoam coffee cup and ten or twelve instant lottery tickets, all weathered and old. And unscratched, Marco noticed. Idly he picked one up. *Desert Dollars*, proclaimed gold type over a cactus shaped like a dollar sign. With his thumbnail he scraped away the silver squares. He'd won $2. He laughed humourlessly and let the ticket slip from his hand. It fluttered back to the kerb.

He squinted into the dark store, feeling his impatience rise. *C'mon, Wu.*

The minimart was quiet now.

Suddenly worried, he strained, listening, and heard nothing but the back-and-forth tide of his own breath. Somewhere a few buildings over, a crow cawed.

'Wu?' he tried. He spoke in a hush, reluctant to go louder.

He tugged at the netting on the quad and unzipped the bearded soldier's daypack. Hurriedly he rummaged through the contents. Water bottles, ammo clips, binoculars . . .

Here we go. His hand closed on his Glock.

But just then the minimart door swung open, and Wu emerged, carrying a plastic shopping bag. He dumped it on the oil-stained cement at Marco's feet.

'Not much left,' he reported. He bent and dug in the bag. 'But here. Eat something.' He produced the antique Snickers bar and handed it over.

Now Marco forced the last bite down his throat; the urge to vomit hit him hard, but he endured five or ten seconds, and it passed. Wu had returned to the plastic bag, and, as Marco watched sullenly, he pulled out a gauze square and a roll of bandage.

'No alcohol,' Wu commented, almost to himself. 'I'll disinfect with gasoline.'

Marco shook his head, and for the first time Wu noticed the severed gas nozzle lying where Marco had cast it. 'No gas?' he asked. His concern was audible.

'Not a drop,' Marco said. 'Not that we can get to, at least. Unless you happen to have a tanker's wrench-key to open the iron ground caps.'

Wu scowled. 'The quad's half full. That won't get us far.'

'True, but how far do we need? Any idea where we are now?'

'Salton, California. According to a business licence behind the counter.'

With paper towels Wu wiped the blood from his face and arms until he was as clean as possible without water to help, then plastered the gauze to the oozing groove on his shoulder. He hissed as he pressed it flat. A red circle bloomed within the white square. Next he unfurled the bandage and began wrapping it around his bicep, under his armpit, securing the gauze in place.

'I found the road maps to get us to Sarsgard,' he continued as he worked. 'Back roads only – the next hundred miles will be hot with Horsemen.' He noted Marco's puzzled frown.

'Horsemen, like our friend back there. A Californian militia, anarchists, linked to terrorists in Iran and Kazakhstan. You've never run into them out here?'

'No, I can definitely say I haven't. I haven't been to California in a while.'

'Consider yourself lucky. Horsemen are dangerous.'

'What's with the name? And the skull on the quad?'

Wu shrugged. 'A biblical reference. As in the Four—'

'Horsemen of the Apocalypse,' Marco finished. 'I get it. Conquest, War, Famine and Death. Very cute. So what are these guys – religious whack-jobs?'

Wu regarded him soberly. 'Don't let the name fool you, Doctor. It's self-aggrandising, meant to intimidate. The Horsemen don't care about God. They're thieves and looters. They want money and power, and they're exploiting the Resurrection for both.'

'Conquest,' Marco remembered. 'That's how the guy with the beard referred to himself on the walkie-talkie. 'Conquest Three.' I overheard him talking.'

'Yes,' Wu said. Consternation had crept into his voice. 'They want Ballard, too – they just don't know where he is. They need you to guide them.'

'Gee, I wish I was this popular in high school.'

Wu ignored the joke. 'That Horseman radioed in our location, so we'd better move. No doubt the others are headed this way. We bought ourselves only a little time by killing the scout.'

The reminder of the bearded soldier's execution stung Marco anew. To Wu, the man's murder meant nothing – just a bit of strategy designed to provide an advantage. It was logical, yes, it made sense . . . and yet it chilled the blood in all four chambers of Marco's heart.

Wu gave his bandage a final tightening tug, then clamped on the metal clips. Marco watched, not bothering to help.

Probably he should feel grateful; Wu had taken a bullet to rescue him from the enemy soldier – the Horseman. And yet, Marco knew instinctively, there was no altruism in Wu. He'd saved Marco for his own selfish reasons.

And what exactly *were* those reasons?

Marco remembered his question on the train, right before the gas grenade.

'So you never answered me,' he said now. 'Who are you, for real?'

9.2

Marco observed as Wu tensed, and the sergeant's eyes avoided his.

'And what do you mean by that, Doctor?' Wu asked, checking his bandage.

'You're not some regular Joe Shmoe sergeant. All that shit you fed me, "we're just the bullets, not the gun" crap. Seems like you know a hell of a lot more than you let on. Sorry if I sound naive, but everything on the train sounded pretty damn top secret. Not the kind of information the Army hands out to grunts.'

Wu patted the bandage and gingerly lifted his arm, testing its mobility. He winced. 'Relax, Doctor,' he said. 'The truth isn't as sinister as you make it sound.'

'So what is it?'

'I'm MI – Military Intelligence.' Wu looked him in the eye. 'Planted with the RRU team sent to meet you. Osbourne wanted critical insight to inform all military decisions. That's my role. It doesn't affect your role, or our relationship. In fact, it's so unimportant that it's not worth the effort to hide it from you, since you guessed. Does that satisfy you?'

Marco watched him warily. Bit by bit, he was forming a complete picture of this man, Ken Wu. He couldn't decide whether he liked it. The feeling that something wasn't right had been dogging Marco since yesterday, a constant irritation like a small jagged rock in his boot. But now, at least, Wu's confession helped explain matters.

'Do I still call you "Sergeant?"' he asked.

Wu shrugged. 'If you'd like. It was my rank, prior to MI.' He bent and returned the medical supplies into the plastic bag, organising the contents.

Marco chewed his lip. He wasn't quite ready to forgive and forget. Still reverberating in another corner of his mind was the bearded soldier's death scream.

'What did you say to him?' he asked Wu.

Wu looked up, puzzled. 'To whom?'

'The Horseman. Before you left him there, you said something in his ear.'

The temperature of Wu's skin seemed to drop, and he gazed at Marco with frosted displeasure. Again Marco sensed calculations clicking and whirring behind the man's green irises, as if circuit boards existed where his brain should be.

'I told him,' Wu said flatly, 'that it was my duty to destroy him.'

'Wow.' Marco made a sour face. 'Very patriotic of you.'

'I sense you disapprove, Doctor.'

'Of leaving him to die? Fuck yes, I disapprove of that.'

'Our lives meant nothing to him. He received no worse than he would have handed us.'

'So you killed him, just like that.'

'Yes. I've killed many men like him. Enough to know when it's required.' Wu's eyes flared a warning, as if expecting a challenge.

But Marco already sensed himself backing away. *I can't do this,* he thought. *I'm in over my head. So goddamn deep you'd need a submarine to find me.* He regarded Wu through what felt like a hot mist and swallowed miserably.

'I never killed anyone,' he said. 'Until today.'

The admission seemed to catch Wu off guard. The soldier frowned.

'Not anybody living,' Marco continued. 'Only corpses. What I mean is, I never took anybody alive and made them dead. I only do "dead to deader", and that's tough enough. Like Cassandra Pearson – she was a dead fourth grader. That was the hardest. She was . . . sitting on the roller coaster at Knotts Berry Farm, not moving, just sitting in the station, waiting . . .'

The corners of his mouth tugged tight. *Why am I telling him this?*

Because, he realised, *it feels good to confess.*

'Anyway,' he said, cutting the memory short, regrouping, 'today tops that. I mean, I know he was a bad guy, or whatever. But . . . he was alive, still a normal man, and I . . .'

He sighed dismally and gave up. 'Oh well. Shit happens, right?'

Wu's face clouded. He bent back to the bag, fished out a handful of road maps and carried the bag to the quad, stashing it in the side net. When he turned to Marco again, his countenance had shifted. The bent shape of his lips almost suggested empathy – but too guarded and too austere to be kind. He handed Marco the maps.

'Find Sarsgard,' he instructed, then studied the highway in the direction they'd come. 'We've been stationary too long already.'

Marco thumbed through the maps, distracted. A Rand McNally road atlas of California and a few smaller folded maps. Palm Springs . . . Victorville & Barstow . . .

He froze on the third map in the pile.

Hemet & Perris.

His heart quickened. Hemet, California.

Jesus, how close was he to Hemet? The other maps slipped

from his hand as he knelt and spread the crinkling paper on the cement. *Hemet.* Right there. He tapped a tiny black dot with his fingertip and felt himself flush with the discovery. Next he scanned the alphabetical index of city names. Salton . . . Salton . . .

There.

He eyeballed the distance to Hemet. Ninety miles, maybe.

Should he try?

Of course he should try. How could he not? Excitement mixed with a sick, reluctant weight in his stomach.

But you don't really want to go there, do you?

He ignored this and focused back to the map. Sarsgard Medical Prison was much farther north; Salton to Hemet would be a huge detour, steering them south on a lonely sojourn through desert mountains before carrying them north again.

Could add half a damn day to the trip.

Then again, Wu *did* say back roads.

He became suddenly conscious of Wu watching him. He cleared his throat and gathered up the map, tucking it under his elbow. 'We'll stay on this road here, Route 111. Not much choice right now, but we can ditch it a few miles up, then go hide ourselves on some quieter roads off the beaten path. I'd say two hundred miles to Sarsgard.'

Oh, and we'll just happen to be passing through a town called Hemet. I forgot to mention that. I'll let you know when we get there.

Hemet. Danielle's hometown, where she'd been born, where she'd grown. Where both her parents were buried. The cemetery where—

He almost yelped in surprise when Wu grabbed his wrist, yanked him down behind the nearest gas pump.

'Ow,' he griped, the cuts on his arm sizzling. 'Right where the handcuffs—'

'Shh!' Wu cut him off, pointing to the highway a hundred yards from the station. Marco peered through the gap between pumps. He saw nothing.

But then he heard it.

Engines.

The desert heat turned cold on his neck.

The noise was faint, like a mosquito, but within moments it was larger, angrier, a swarm just around the bend in the road, approaching from the north.

Run, Marco urged himself. *Duck into the minimart, go now . . .*

But before he could move, five Horsemen quads buzzed into view, racing towards the gas station. The drivers appeared fierce and alien; dark motorcycle goggles obscured their faces, green helmets capped their heads. They were a ragtag army, no two men outfitted the same; one wore desert fatigues, the next a thick motorcycle jacket, while a third sported a pilot's jumpsuit, torn and blue, the wind whipping madly at the fabric. Slung across their backs were guns – mismatched rifles and black machine guns wielded like deadly scorpion stingers. Only their quads were identical, the same mud-coloured model driven by the bearded soldier. Probably all stolen from the same military lot. And on each quad's hood, a horse skull, bleached and cracked.

It's like a stampede from hell, Marco thought.

The fifth quad was different from the others – constructed longer, with a turret behind the driver's seat where a second man stood, lording over a machine gun mounted to the nest; the weapon was a Browning, massive, loaded with a seemingly endless belt of ammo. The gunman was solid and strong, too, in obvious command as he barked orders at the driver. Even from this distance Marco perceived the man's power. Unlike the ragged Horsemen, the commander looked sharp in a battle-dress jacket, black and braided red along the shoulder. His nose was large and dented, as though it had once been broken; his eyes were keen like a hawk's on a mountain crag. He was the only man without a helmet, and his bald head appeared chiselled from rock – sleek but hard-edged and too large in the cranium. The ridges of his lateral skull bulged outwards above his ears, stretching the skin like an extra inch of bone strapped to his head.

Shaking, Marco crouched lower, trying to make himself as small as he could. He felt Wu beside him, tense and breathless. Parked beside the gas pump, only partially hidden from the street, sat their stolen quad. It seemed gigantic, twice its normal size.

Shit. They're going to see, they're going to see it . . .

The five quads darted past the station, continuing south.

Wu exhaled. Rivulets of sweat had cleaned thin paths down his grimy forehead. 'We were fortunate just there,' he admitted. 'They're headed to the train, to meet their comrade. I doubt they realise he's dead yet. With more luck, they'll run into the same ambush of corpses. That would improve our odds.'

'I have news for you,' Marco said, his stomach still fluttering. 'Our odds suck, no matter what. Did you see him? That beast with the freaky head?'

'I saw, yes,' Wu answered. 'The Horseman squad leader.'

'Please say we don't have to fight him. He's scary.'

Wu didn't bother to answer. He stood and tested his arm again, lifting it as high as his shoulder would allow. Halfway up, he grunted. Biting his lip, he sat backwards again on the quad, his feet propped on the rear hitch.

'You drive,' he instructed. 'Before your friend Big Skull comes back.'

'Nice. Big Skull. Thanks for naming my nightmares.' Marco stuck the Hemet map into his back pocket. 'All right then.'

Here we go. Forget the Horsemen.
Onward to the real nightmare. The cemetery in Hemet.
A quick visit.
His chest tightened, constricting his ribs.
Maybe you're visiting, too, Delle?

9.3

Route 111 was an ugly line north out of Salton, dismal and depressing, a two-lane road intercut with blighted side streets that vanished into the fossilised silence of the desert beyond. Marco kept the quad at a low hum, hugging the shoulder, ready to dart off road if another Horseman convoy burst into view ahead. It was a tense ride. His jaw ached, and he was exhausted, and he caught himself slumping against Wu behind him. The two men sat back-to-back. Marco drove; Wu monitored the road already travelled, in case the Horsemen had doubled back after discovering their dead soldier at the train.

Or whatever was left of the guy – probably not much.

Marco focused his gaze ahead, doing his best to ignore the occasional human carcass lying mangled across the yellow highway lines. Lumps of parched skin and bleached vulture-picked bones. *Roadkill*, he thought, not amused.

On the outskirts of town he slowed and steered cautiously through a jumble of collided cars, eight or ten total, their doors rusted open, abandoned in haste. As the quad rolled past a red Ford pickup truck, a pot-bellied corpse in a cowboy hat popped to its feet in the truck bed. Its cheeks were bubbled with soft-looking blisters that throbbed; flies had laid eggs below the facial epidermis, giving birth to maggots. The corpse teetered, its arms extended as if it wanted help getting down. *Yeah, fat chance.* Marco goosed the throttle and zipped from the intersection. The corpse grunted and sat back in the bed.

Five miles later a blue sign for I-10 appeared, but Marco veered left. Stay on 111 a while longer, that was the plan. The interstate was too conspicuous. Too much danger. Big Skull – the name had stuck in Marco's head – and the Horsemen would be patrolling the major roads. And there would be ghost jams, too, he'd explained to Wu. Plus plenty more corpses.

Wu had agreed without even asking to see the map; he'd simply responded with a firm nod. 'Good. Let's go.'

As much as Marco hated admitting it, he'd felt bolstered, as if Wu's approval meant something. *Great,* he thought, cringing. *The cold-hearted killer likes me.*

Now Marco gathered a deep breath. At this pace they'd reach Hemet in about two hours. Part of him wished it would take four. Or eight. Or how about tomorrow?

Entering Palm Desert, his pulse jittered. This town had been higher-populated than the towns before, and the road ventured through a downtown district of tightly grouped brick buildings – strip malls, every recognisable retail chain from McDonald's to Gap, now vacant and haunted and threateningly close to the road. God knows how many corpses lurked behind dark glass doors and cash register counters, gearing to spring out. But the town seemed quiet. The next block was a black, eerie wonderland of burnt foundations and charred wood, a hundred thousand square feet stripped to a scorched skeleton. Must've been a bitch of a fire. Char and ash still lingered faintly in the air, pinning tiny needles into Marco's nostrils. He eased the quad past a gutted post office. Soot-smeared mail trucks ornamented the lot.

If there were any corpses around, Marco didn't see them. Which always made him nervous.

Perhaps Wu was feeling the same. 'Speed up,' he called, clapping his hand on the metal quad. 'We're far enough from the main road – engine noise is okay.'

'Horsemen might not hear,' Marco shot back, 'but I'd

rather not wake every corpse for five miles. If they hear us coming, they'll be waiting like a roadblock.'

Still, he revved the throttle higher, and as the quad kicked forward, he felt himself marginally relax. The breeze tickled his forehead, evaporating the nervous sweat. A rise of dirt-coloured mountains beckoned ahead. He turned left again, aiming upwards.

His heart lurched.

Gated communities, once attractive with manicured lawns and hedges, sat in ruin off both roadsides, the grass now like straw, the hedges overgrown into shapeless, dry-looking monsters. The street was scattered with corpses. A Hispanic male loitered beneath a palm tree, a pair of garden shears impaled in its neck. Cross-legged against a stone wall sat a scaly teenager in a black Oakland Raiders jersey, and a shirtless barefoot male in bloodied dress pants wandered along the kerb. Marco eased past them without trouble, then noticed another corpse ahead.

Oh, gross.

On the sidewalk a fat female sprawled on its round belly, naked and obscene, paying the quad no attention. Its eyes were fixed on the ground directly beneath its mangled nose. The corpse was picking black ants from a crack in the cement, stuffing them into its maw, crunching on them like popcorn – and, at the same time, ants marched in streams across the corpse's jiggly bare ass, pinching off minuscule chunks in their mandibles to import back to the colony to eat. Raw red craters gaped from the flanks of the buttocks.

The dead woman didn't seem to care. It was a fair trade. Food for food. They would continue trading until one side had no more left to give.

Marco shuddered and edged the speedometer faster before any corpses could draw near. The quad quickly exited the neighbourhood.

'How's your shoulder?' he shouted back to Wu.

'Fine,' Wu responded with such immediacy that Marco knew he must be hurting like hell. *Fine*, as in, *I don't want to think about it, so please shut up.*

Up into the mountains the road climbed, then climbed again, leaving civilisation; Marco nearly laughed when he considered how little that term now applied. The quad chugged its way higher, burning precious fuel. A brown road sign on double posts encouraged them onwards.

State Route 74
Pines to Palms Scenic Byway
Slow Traffic
Use Turnaround.

Turnaround, Marco scoffed. *If only that was an option.*

He'd driven this road before, but never here at the eastern end; he'd always approached from the other direction, driving with Danielle from LA out to Lake Hemet. On the map the road resembled a haphazard scribble, a crazy twisting roller-coaster ride through the San Jacinto Mountains. Driving it now, the impression held. The quad swung rudely, tracking the curves through a dizzying landscape of tumbled rocks and thirsty-looking brush. Steep cliffs dropped away from the left. Wu held tightly to the gear rack, at risk of sliding off. The roller coaster continued upwards. The landscape thickened with trees and forest. The views were stunning, and Marco was happy to let his mind slip untroubled into this majestic reprieve from the horrors below; at sea level, only death and corpses and pain awaited, but at this altitude the air was gloriously fresh-smelling, and the trees prospered without a care for the state of the manmade world. Sugar pines spiked high, two hundred feet tall, like quills on a massive porcupine's back; ponderosa pines decorated the skyline, their orange bark crisp in the sunlight. The San Bernardino Mountains saluted him from across the valley; small brown shapes stirred on the rocks, mountain goats picking their way along the crags, beyond the reach of any man or corpse.

And then, Marco realised, the ride had peaked, and the quad sank under him as gravity nudged him towards the handlebars, and Wu's back jostled against his own. The road was descending now. He tapped the brake and felt the check in his spirit.

Down again. He could sense the bottom dropping out from under him, the roller coaster hurdling over the apex of the rails, plummeting him back deeper into his thoughts than he wished to go. The road passed the turn-off to Lake Hemet. He and Danielle had picnicked here once, a hundred miles from Los Angeles, the year they met. He remembered her that day – wet auburn hair slicked behind her ears after an hour of swimming, and in her hand she held that ridiculous straw hat of hers, using it to shoo bees from her salad. She'd looked fantastic in a turquoise bathing suit, and he recalled sitting, flush and giddy, at an old wooden picnic table stained with bird poop, secretly hoping the other picnickers might look over and recognise her.

Hey everyone, look. It's Danielle Pierce, the movie actress. Sitting there with boring unpopular Henry Marco! The guy nobody liked in high school!

Danielle had always done that to him – inspired those silly schoolboy kind of daydreams. Stupid, but at the same time stimulating. Blame it on the pixie magic he'd sensed in her that first day at Tech Town; the damn stuff just never wore off.

And he'd loved it.

His palms flexed on the handlebars as the quad passed the lake. Almost worth a side-trip to check it out . . . see if she might be there now, still shooing bees. But he knew Wu wouldn't go for that – hell, they were *already* on a side-trip, and he hadn't even told Wu yet about his plan to stop in Hemet – and besides, he had a much stronger hunch burning in him now. Urging him to keep going. *Hemet. The cemetery. She's there.*

His stomach knotted. His eyes had been gathering tears from the wind beating his face, and now finally he felt two drops leak to the bridge of his nose.

Emotional geography, right? That's how he'd described memory association to Osbourne. The way your brain tagged your most powerful experiences, like pushing pins into a map so you can find them anytime. So nice and orderly, and the brain thinks it's doing you a favour. But there's one thing it doesn't realise.

Sometimes the emotions take you up – to happy places. To Lake Hemet.

And sometimes they take you down to places that hurt.

Places you don't want to go again.

The cemetery. She's there. I can feel it.

The ride was over. Route 74 had levelled out, free of the blanketing forest, and another mile up the road was Hemet, and his heart spasmed and he swallowed a bubble of vomit in his throat. *Because that's what you do at the end of the roller coaster,* he thought. *You try not to throw up.*

He considered the Glock holstered under his arm. One bullet left in the clip. Which was fine.

Danielle only needed one.

9·4

The quad jerked left then right, shaking Wu like a rat in a dog's teeth.

With bloodless fingers he clutched himself to the rear rack of the Boar, grimacing. At every skip in the road, every bump of rubble or fallen branch under the wheels, he felt his bones strike together like flint sparking fire. The gunshot wound on his left shoulder sizzled the worst, as if the bullet had torn a steam vent in his skin. He imagined boiling gas, rupturing outward. Any moment he'd whistle like a teapot.

Propped there, his head a dead weight between his shoulders, he felt old. Heavy and stiff. Tired. He was thirty-eight. In his life he had been shot twice, and whipped, and once impaled through the thigh with a bayonet in North Korea. He had been tortured, burned, had grains of sand placed under his eyelids. His thumb had been bent and broken. Yet never, he mused, had he felt so injured as now. *Sleep*, he rationalised. Sleep was the problem.

He hadn't slept in sixty hours. He might not sleep for sixty more. He still had a vast task ahead: locate and destroy the Ballard corpse, then collect a DNA specimen before burning the body to cinders – useless to other nations that might come searching. Then transport the prized DNA south into Mexico, across the same unsecure borders exploited by the Horsemen. There, in the unmonitored deserts outside Tijuana, an MSS recovery team would meet him.

The thought of it all exhausted him further. His Droid was gone, lost in the explosion at the train, leaving him no way to contact the team. He would need to seek an alternative solution. But first he needed strength. He closed his eyes and tried to feel his body healing, the wound patching itself solid. *Concentrate*. Globules of dazzling light swam in the darkness, bobbing to the quad's motion. He reached his mind out into the black and imagined strands of loose thread pinched between his fingertips; he tugged them tight and tied them together.

'How's your shoulder?' the American asked, breaking the trance.

'Fine,' Wu barked, annoyed. He was expert at mastering

pain – or, if not mastering it, then hiding it. Henry Marco had no right to ask. *Kheng Wu is in control.*

His hands tingled, and he realised he was gripping the metal tow-bars with such fervour that he'd cramped his blood. He eased his grasp.

The air cooled in his nostrils as the road ascended the mountains. For the tenth time he replayed in his mind the scene at the train. The fight against the bearded soldier, and his own close brush with death – saved only at the last possible moment by Marco ramming the Horseman with the quad. The American was quick-thinking, Wu had to admit.

Decisive. Ruthless when it counted.

He scowled. An unwelcome warmth had wormed its way into his head with each remembrance of the morning, shapeless and alien like a tumour. It was . . . *appreciation*, he realised, repulsed, instantly angry at himself. Yes. There it was, a raw gratitude towards the American for saving his life. He wished to reach inside his skull and pluck it out.

But he couldn't deny the truth. The American *had* rescued him. And, without that act, Wu would be dead, and China might be left to rot in a world of Resurrection.

Wu exhaled, understanding. Here in this wasteland, he and Marco shared one goal: to survive. And if survival meant working together against a common enemy, then so be it. *MSS is not always so wise*, he thought. In the far-removed, safe offices of Beijing, it was easy to preach nationalist absolutes and ideologies. But out in these grim conditions, perhaps those grudges should be suspended. Temporarily, of course . . .

His chin drooped, coming to a rest against his chest. *Sleep*, he thought again. He needed to rest, to recover. To heal. The coming hours would demand all he had.

With the mountains cradling him, he at last felt himself drift upwards, away from the physical pain, out of his body. Rising like a weightless kite. Far, far, far.

But away from his body, away from his strength . . . he was vulnerable.

I've never killed anyone, he remembered the American saying.

It's hard the first time, Wu answered, dreaming. The empathy in his voice surprised him. But this Wu was not thirty-eight. This Wu was nineteen, lean and fresh with sinew.

Who was your first? the American asked.

A man named Tenzin Dawa. A monk in Tibet. I cut his throat, for my homeland.

I see, the American said.

Yes. Dawa opposed the railway, the younger Wu explained. The Qinghai-Tibet Railway. That noble endeavour of China Western Development, two decades ago; in Wu's dream-rich mind he saw lustrous metal spanning mountains, engineered to bring industry and prosperity to undeveloped regions – his own boyhood home included – and yet Tibetans like the holy man Dawa had protested. The rails were iron shackles, they accused, a means of political control, souring Tibet with unwanted Chinese immigrants; Dawa had organised a coalition that grew too strong, too vehement, and MSS had judged that a covert intervention was required.

So you killed him, the American voice confirmed. *The monk.*

Yes.

Do you regret it?

I . . . I had orders. They were not mine to regret.

But afterwards, alone in your hotel – did you weep?

Yes. Yes, I did.

Wu jolted straight. Pain came rushing back into his flesh, and he embraced it. He sneered, smacked his lips, as if clearing a bad taste. Around him the vapours of his dream vanished, trailing off like the charcoal exhaust from the quad.

That had been long ago. A memory long banished.

Make no mistake, Doctor Marco, he thought now, fully awake, incensed.

Killing is easy.

I will show you.

9·5

For the first mile through Hemet, Marco recognised nothing, a comfortable numbness he knew wouldn't last. Like the brief second between cutting your hand and seeing the blood spill. It all looked familiar, unnervingly so – a shopping plaza, an Italian restaurant called Bella's, Rite Aid, a driving school, a Toyota dealership, even mundane details like stoplights and fire hydrants he knew he'd seen before. He could feel his memory slamming its shoulder against a closed door in his mind, determined to break out. He fixed his eyes to the road; the double yellow stripe between lanes had a calming effect, a sort of mindless preoccupation.

But warding off the memories proved hopeless. Too many phantoms here, especially downtown, wrapping their ghostly arms around him. He flinched, remembering. The Baskin-Robbins where he and Danielle had stopped for sundaes one muggy July night. The dinky theatre where they'd seen a second-run showing of her first film, *Next to Nothing.* Yale Street – her father had lived that way, a few miles south. The streets and buildings looked sad and lonely, subdued with litter and grime. Store windows were smashed.

Suddenly an odd shape caught his eye. 'What the hell?' he grunted.

On the sidewalk outside a laundromat was an armless corpse, lying on its back in a chunky morass of black blood and bile. It looked dead – really dead. Not moving. Its stomach had been torn open, scooped out, the organs stolen away. Gristled ribs curled wetly from the torso, and a massive chunk of its neck was missing, too, the brain stem severed. Flesh hung in tatters from the wounds. Bite wounds. Fresh. *Recent.*

'Interesting,' Wu commented. Marco jumped. He'd practically forgotten the sergeant was along for the ride; the last hour had been quiet, without talk. But now Wu was awake and alert. 'I didn't realise they fed on each other.'

'They don't. Not that I've seen. Must be a new trick.'

The cadaverous face gawked at the sky, its lips like stone, offering no answer.

'Let's get going.' Spooked, Marco accelerated west.

From somewhere a block up he heard another corpse howl, electrifying the hair on his neck. He scanned the sky; the day had turned uncharacteristically grey and overcast, missing the usual stage-light of California sun. But no vultures, thank god.

The yellow stripe stopped at the intersection of San Jacinto Avenue. On the corner a delivery van had crashed into the crosswalk sign. *Brach's Flowers*, it read on the side.

Marco held his breath and turned right.

'Doctor! You're off course.' Wu's disembodied voice behind him was like a reprimand from his conscience, boxing his ears. *Off course! Off course!*

He ignored Wu. A moment later he felt a crushing grip on his elbow.

'Route seventy-four went straight,' Wu growled.

'I know. I need to make a stop.'

'There's a gas station—'

'Yeah, that, too. But I need to check something first. Something else.'

For half a block more Wu held silent, although his disapproval seemed audible to Marco on its own, louder than the quad's gunning engine.

'Where are we going, Doctor?' Wu finally asked. The question was terse; Marco heard the implied threat. *The answer had better be good.*

Fuck you, Marco replied silently. Enough with Wu's bullshit. *I've got my own problems, and Roger Ballard's dead cold body can wait.* So could Wu and Osbourne. Jesus Christ, they *owed* him this detour—

A thin, razor-like pain lit up the skin on the back of his neck.

A knife blade.

Wu delicately dug the knife between Marco's first and second cervical vertebrae, just under his skull. Any harder, and the skin would slice open. *Hello, spinal cord.*

Son of a bitch, Wu, Marco seethed. *You're bluffing.*

'Wu . . .' he warned.

'I'll ask you again, Doctor. Where—'

'Right here,' Marco said, and braked the quad.

The green lawn of San Jacinto Valley Cemetery sprawled to the north as far as the men could see. The grass was overgrown but verdant, like a wild meadow framed by city streets and sidewalks and a red brick wall running the entire perimeter. From the tall vegetation poked solemn spires and crosses, the tops of granite gravestones. A wide cobble-stoned driveway beckoned them inside; two rows of palm trees flanked the path like giant pallbearers waiting to escort the next coffin to its plot.

Marco felt the knife leave his neck. He glanced back at Wu. The sergeant was squinting into the cemetery, his head cocked, an expression of combined suspicion and curiosity. Beyond the wall a blue butterfly jigged over the long stalks of grass.

At last Wu frowned. He fixed Marco with a gaze sharp enough to cut through any deceit. 'You have someone here,' he said. A clarifying statement, not a question.

'Yes,' Marco answered simply. Was there reason to say more? He wondered if Wu knew about Danielle, and if so, whether Wu thought he was crazy. He waited.

Wu inhaled and exhaled, his breath congested, the nasal passages likely clotted with blood. 'And after this,' he said, still clarifying, 'Sarsgard. No more interruptions.'

'Yes.'

Wu processed the information a second longer. 'Agreed,' he concluded, and with a stern finger he tapped his wristwatch. 'Fifteen minutes. Then out.'

'Agreed,' Marco nodded. Then paused. 'Thanks.'

Wu narrowed his eyes.

'Go,' he said.

Gratified, Marco edged the quad through the cemetery gate. Farther ahead the driveway disappeared between trees, past ornate mausoleums with Grecian columns and eternally sealed doors. He knew where the road led. Up a rolling hill, past the cemetery office and a serene-looking chapel with a golden-crossed steeple. He drove slowly, eyes sweeping left and right, feeling too cut off from the main gate. Deep in the cemetery, the city outside was almost forgotten. Nothing but willows and overgrown grass and sculpted angels on gravestones, watching him pass with smooth white eyes. Tree branches everywhere were hung with shrouds of vanilla silk; caterpillars had spun their nests, whitening the trees, giving the grove an almost wintry feel, despite the heat.

Where the road turned and began to loop back on itself, Marco stopped the quad. Off to the right a flagstone path met the road, leading into the overgrowth. The stone steps vanished a few yards deep, swallowed by unchecked grass and ivy vines.

'Here,' he said, more to himself than Wu.

He killed the engine. His ears rang in the sudden quiet. The odour of gasoline and oil wafted through a light breeze, and he heard Wu shift on the seat behind him. He studied the path leading out of sight into the vegetation. Nothing moved.

Wait – there, by a pink marble obelisk, the high grass bobbed as if disrupted by something passing through at ground level, unseen.

A hider, he thought, pulling the Glock.

He watched a few seconds more. The stalks grew still.

No, not a hiding corpse. Just the breeze.

'Time is ticking, Doctor,' Wu said. With a grunt and a wince, he slipped from the quad, then cringed. His beaten muscles had stiffened during the drive, Marco figured, and now the crusted bullet wound was cracking open again as he stretched his body.

Wu's nostrils flared as he holstered his knife. 'Lead the way,' he said.

'Hang on.' Feeling suddenly short of breath, as if under a great exertion, Marco grabbed the AK-47 from the gun rack and rummaged through the Horseman's pack. He palmed three full clips and slipped them into his back pocket. 'I know it's a cemetery, but some of these dead folks might be the "above-ground, walking-around" variety.'

With Wu trailing, Marco made his way up the path. The grass was waist high, soft and thick under his boots, and he saw no signs of corpses – no crushed stalks, no trampled vines alerting him that another pair of feet had trod this way recently. Spider webs, too, barred the path like miniature gates. He broke through them resolutely, telling himself this meant nothing – that of course Danielle could still be ahead.

Couldn't she? Yes, he told himself, if she'd walked in months ago and never walked out, and the grass had grown over her tracks and the spiders sealed her in.

His heart beat impossibly hard, too large for his body. A

giant red, pounding muscle, swollen so big it would break his ribs apart . . .

Every fifteen feet or so, a tombstone stuck its weathered head from the grass. Marco had always appreciated San Jacinto for not being a cemetery with a warehouse mentality, the kind that cram graves into every square inch. Here the plots were spread out, each gravesite separated by a modest expanse of lawn. The effect was more personal, more respectful. When you visited, you could believe the dead were at peace.

He rubbed the corner of his eye and swallowed.

Almost there. The AK rattled in his hands; he noticed he was trembling. He hated this, he hated this . . .

Please, Delle. Please just be here.

The path bent around a gnarled oak tree – he'd sat under that tree once with Danielle, cradling her into his chest, her tears dabbing his shirt . . .

. . . and fifty feet ahead were two gravestones, side by side.

Just the gravestones.

Danielle wasn't here.

He exhaled in a burst, a rush of air that choked off halfway into a tortured groan. His face seemed to catch fire, burning and wet at the same time.

Goddamn it. Goddamn it, goddamn it, goddamn it.

He managed to walk without breaking stride, hiding his anguish from Wu on the trail behind him. He focused on breathing . . . slow, cooling lungfuls . . .

That's okay. It was a long shot.

You'll keep looking, you'll find her. Plenty more chances.

By the time he reached the gravestones, he'd recovered . . . almost. And then his heart shifted again, sucked into a whirlpool of even greater force, down to an even blacker depth. Panic seized him.

He thought he'd be ready for this. He wasn't.

He stepped past the gravestone on the left. *Amanda Pierce.* Danielle's mother.

Then took a final step closer, stopping in front of the second stone.

Smaller, newer. A sculptured dove sat atop, its wings open, poised to fly.

The space around Marco stretched, adding distance, so that the gravestone at his feet seemed a mile from his pounding head.

And far, far below, etched in block letters, the stone read:

HANNAH ISABELLE MARCO.
7 DECEMBER 2012 – 9 DECEMBER 2012

His throat tightened. His stomach cramped.

He closed his eyes. The darkness was timeless, a fusion of past and present, and Danielle was suddenly beside him in that void, alive, the way he remembered her on that last morning in June, saying goodbye on the drive from California to Arizona.

The year after they'd buried Hannah.

We can't, Henry. We can't leave her here. Alone.

Baby . . . we're not leaving her. Your mother, your mother's right here.

Don't make us. Don't make me . . .

Delle. Baby, we have to go . . . I promise she's not alone.

She wants me here.

She wants you to be happy.

I'll never be happy.

His eyes flicked open, red and glassy. He sniffed and wiped his nose, not caring that Wu had arrived next to him. Fuck that. Fuck pretending. Let Wu see this – Wu, who didn't have a fucking emotion in his blood.

Beside Marco, Wu lowered his chin as he absorbed the gravestone etchings. He held his hands together in front of his body, the posture of a man paying his respects.

'Your daughter,' he stated.

'Yes.'

Wu nodded, pursed his lips. He hesitated and then spoke again. 'The infant, the baby who passed away under Roger Ballard's care . . . ?'

'Yes.'

Wu blinked, depositing the information into his lockbox, and responded with a step backwards and the slightest bow of his head. 'I'm sorr—'

A crashing of leaves interrupted him.

Both men snapped straight, whirled towards the sound. The high grass to the west whipped left and right, then split down the middle.

Something – something big – was charging at them through the grass.

9.6

No time to think. Marco whipped the AK towards the approaching attack; whatever was coming, it was coming fast, rifling through the green stalks. Beside him Wu sprang to a fighter's stance, hands up, knives gleaming atop his fists.

The men locked eyes. Wu nodded, his jaw clenched.

Here we go.

The brush burst apart . . .

. . . and a snarling yellow mastiff barrelled out, its fur caked and bristled, closing the distance with a furious thrashing of legs. Marco's stomach went weightless, as though he'd stepped off a cliff, a scream trailing from his throat. For a paralysing moment he forget about the gun in his hand; Frankie was all he could remember, the mongrel dog next door that tore his ear when he was seven, exploding through the hedge, tackling him . . .

I'm getting eaten

. . . and the mastiff, somehow it read his mind, knew he was weak and *chose* him instead of Wu. It leapt at Marco, jaws snapping towards his throat, and Marco braced . . .

. . . yelling out with surprise as the giant dog crashed sideways away from him, its ribs cracking against Hannah's tombstone. The mastiff yelped and rolled to the ground in pain.

Wu stood on one foot, his right leg extended; he'd booted the dog mid-air with a thunderous kick. He replanted his foot and cast Marco a puzzled look. 'Just a dog,' he chastised. 'They're not bullet-proof, in case you were wondering.'

Marco looked at the AK in his hands, felt himself blush. 'I don't like dogs.'

He stopped and frowned. Listened. The blush on his cheeks suddenly chilled.

Everywhere behind Wu, the grass began to shake.

'Dogs . . .' he said. *Oh Jesus.*

Lots of dogs. Slinking from the brush, fur raised, heads low like hunters. All sizes, all kinds – mongrels, black and spotted, ears pointed, muzzles slick with brown slobber, pure breeds, too, German Shepherds, retrievers, hounds, lips curled back to reveal long curved fangs. Thirty, forty, fifty dogs emerging from the cemetery hollows, a massive hungering pack. Fierce growls rattled within their necks.

Collars and dog tags on them all.

Pets, Marco realised.

Former pets. Gone feral, reverted to wild instincts. The Resurrection only took men and women; it left their dogs behind. No one to care for these creatures or put kibble in the bowls. He imagined the dogs in Hemet roaming the streets after the Evacuation, scrounging to survive. Then finally, driven by starvation, they'd banded together to hunt.

Feeding on squirrels, birds, cats . . .

With a chill he recalled the torn-up corpse he'd seen downtown.

So that unlucky bastard had been dog food.

The animals spread wide, a quarrelling half-circle around the men, awaiting some instinctual cue to attack. A filthy-coated Dalmatian darted forward, snapping, then retreated to the line. Then a second dog did the same. Then another.

Riling each other up. Any moment now they'd swarm.

'Too many to kick, Sergeant.' Marco's tongue was a chunk of dry wood.

'And too many to shoot,' Wu said. He gestured at a drooling Great Dane, big like a bear. 'Put a bullet in that one. Then run.'

'Right behind ya.' Shakingly Marco aimed at the massive dog. Its right eye was gone, the lid infected shut, seeping fluid. Marco hesitated.

Somebody had loved this poor animal once.

Sighing, Marco lifted the AK straight up into the air and fired.

The warning shot blasted a hole in the morning, loud and stupefying. The Great Dane dropped flat, its good eye rolling in terror; the pack of dogs scattered, ears pinned to their matted heads. Confused – but it wouldn't last.

'*Go!*' Wu slapped Marco's arm and bolted down the flag-stone path.

And then Marco fled, too, bounding in high steps through the grass, empowered with adrenalin and fear. Behind him he heard the baying of the dogs; they'd regrouped, refocused on the hunt. The soft earth sounded with the drumming of a hundred paws, and everywhere was the jangling of silver dog tags, chasing him, coming to drag him down from behind; he fired the AK wildly to the side, mowing a wide swathe of grass with bullets until the clip emptied, but this time the dogs weren't deterred, and the barking pulled closer.

He was losing his lead. The grass crunched under his boots, throwing him off balance. Twenty feet ahead, Wu sailed along gracefully, light like a deer, evolved in the art of escape. His wounds hadn't slowed him so much, after all.

Survival of the fittest, Marco thought, demoralised. *And Wu's winning.*

He wasn't even sure they were on the path any more; the grass had grown too thick to see the stones, and in his panic the trees seemed different, too; he didn't remember this hill, or that gravestone with the statue of a man holding a book . . .

'*Wu!*' he bellowed. '*Wrong way!*'

He swivelled his head frantically, seeking the path . . .

. . . and never saw whatever his foot snagged in the grass, a rock maybe or a fallen branch, pitching him ass-over-head to the ground. He cried out, horrified, and tumbled, somersaulted down the incline, thumping against a mossy gravestone at the bottom; he landed with his cheek to the dirt and a mouthful of damp grass.

Help, he thought, half-dazed . . .

. . . because in another moment the dogs would be on him, ripping him to shreds of wet, shivery meat, tussling over the scraps of his organs, just like the corpse in town.

He almost screamed when the first set of jaws clamped on his arm . . .

. . . except it was Wu, pulling him to his feet.

'Hurry,' Wu ordered. 'Over there.' He gestured to a modest white building a hundred feet ahead. The cemetery chapel. In the madness of flight they'd taken a sharper angle through the cemetery grounds, reaching the chapel from the rear.

At the top of the hill the crazed dogs streamed over the crest and charged down.

Frantic, spitting grass from his lips, Marco sprinted towards the chapel. He pumped his arms, running; he'd lost the AK in the fall, goddamn it, but that didn't matter now, *just get to the chapel, get to the chapel, please let the door be unlocked, please!*

He made it two steps ahead of Wu, his heart stuck between beats as he rammed the oak door, fumbled for the brass handle. The latch popped – *thank you Jesus* – and the door collapsed open; he spilled inside, Wu right behind, and flung the door shut.

Immediately the oak rocked with a barrage from outside, dogs launching against it, claws scrabbling the wood. Barks and howls thundered in Marco's ears.

'*Christ!*' Marco backed a step from the door and half collapsed, hands on his knees, chugging air. 'Do you think,' he asked, refilling his lungs, 'they'll stay or go?'

Sweating furiously, Wu shrugged. 'Go away, I would think. There must be some slower-moving prey out there in the graveyard. Corpses, like we saw in town.'

'I had the same thought.'

'The more urgent question is,' Wu said, 'are there any corpses in here?'

Sobered, the men turned their eyes into the chapel. They were standing in a small marble vestibule, next to a table stocked with pamphlets on dying and afterlife. A giant vase loomed in the corner, once full with flowers, now withered to petrified stems.

The lighting was dim, suffused with blue and red; stained-glass windows admitted a weak glow. Marco squinted against the gloom. The whole interior wasn't large at all – a single set of pews, six rows deep, facing a gargantuan statue of Christ on a cross at the far end, beyond a podium and a small brown altar. A red carpet led from the vestibule and then split in two, each path following a coiled radiator up the side aisles.

The air was stale and foul. Yellow-smelling, like a bedpan.

And something else. Marco sniffed. Something rancid, infected.

His jaw twitched.

There was a dead man in the front pew.

Definitely a corpse – its head leathery and bald, and on the back of its crown the skin had eroded to reveal a worm-holed patch of skull. It wore a collared shirt, above which the knobs of its upper vertebrae poked through the decomposed skin on its neck.

'Is it alive?' Wu asked, then frowned at the wording of his question. 'You understand what I mean.'

'Resurrected, yes,' Marco answered in a whisper. Despite his caution, the words struck loud against the vestibule's marble walls. 'Look – it's moving.'

The corpse's head bobbed, a feeble motion, down then up again like a sleepy man prodding himself awake. It moved three or four times, then went still.

'Why isn't it getting up?' Wu wondered.

'I don't know. We made a hell of a racket coming in.'

Outside, the dogs continued their siege on the chapel. Marco heard them racing back and forth along the walk, barking and hungry and very pissed off.

'Wait here,' Wu said and crossed the vestibule. He gave the door a strong tug, satisfying himself that it was shut solid. Just to be safe, he dragged the table over and, dumping the pamphlets to the floor – a hundred copies of *Coping with Loss* spilled across the marble – Wu tilted the table edge against the latch.

Then, knives readied, he returned to Marco's side.

'Go slow,' he said and stepped onto the carpet runner. Puffs of dust rose from the red felt under his boots.

'Hold it – what's your plan here?' Marco asked.

'Getting a look.'

Marco shook his head, uncertain. But damn, he was curious, too.

He pulled the Glock – one bullet left – and followed Wu into the church.

They crept softly up the side aisle, Marco alert for any sudden movement from the quiet corpse. The dead man's head bobbed again, once, but that was all. Pew by pew the men approached; Marco aimed the Glock into each row as they passed, anticipating an ambush – some dead pastor or nun to spring hissing from beneath the hymnals.

At the corner of the front row they stopped.

'Holy shit,' Marco muttered.

The corpse was elderly, a male in its seventies, its facial skin loose and sagging like an ill-fitting mask; its nose was bulbous, etched with purple capillaries. It wore a striped necktie with a fat clumsy knot draped down its bloodstained shirt. Its pants were bunched at the calves; black socks drooped atop its bug-eaten dress shoes, exposing two milk-white, hairy, rail-thin legs that barely reached the floor.

Tipped over beside it was an aluminium walker.

The corpse's filmy eyes were fixed on the cross behind the altar. Its parched lips smacked together, and the head bobbed once more. It didn't turn, even when Wu spoke.

'What is it doing?' he asked.

Marco felt a shudder twist up his spine. 'I . . . I think it might be praying.'

Wu studied Marco briefly. 'You're serious.'

'Well, I mean, not really praying – but stuck in the motion of it. He must've been the religious type. Church was real important to him. Emotional geography.'

Wu stared. 'Emotional geography?'

Marco shook him off. 'Never mind, long story. The short version is that for the same reason Roger Ballard is wherever he is, this particular corpse is here.'

Wu watched the transfixed corpse. 'Doesn't it wish to eat us?'

'I don't know. I'd assume so. But . . . maybe this is more important to it.'

Jesus Christ, listen to me, Marco thought. *What am I saying? This corpse found a higher calling?*

'Anyway,' he said, feeling the urge to back-pedal. 'Let's not stick our hands in its mouth. I suggest we retreat a few rows, and observe from there.'

Wu nodded. 'Yes.'

Thcy slipped back down the aisle and shuffled into the last pew. Outside, the dogs were stubborn; the world reverberated with a constant high whine and the occasional squall of animals fighting. Every few seconds intruded a scratching at the oak.

'Might as well get comfortable,' Wu said. 'We could be here a while.'

'Not too long, I hope. We're in trouble if the rest of the parish shows up.'

Six rows ahead in the darkness the old corpse quivered in pantomime worship, and Marco wondered . . . If God actually *did* exist, what the fuck was He thinking?

9.7

'It's a mean joke,' Marco observed. He sat alongside Wu in the musty wooden pew, hands folded in his laps, legs crossed at the ankles. The coloured light from the windows had intensified a few brighter notches up the spectrum; the sun outside had prevailed over the clouds. Marco guessed the time was around noon. His stomach had begun to gurgle again, an embarrassing loud complaint in the quiet chapel.

He pressed a hand to his gut and continued. 'A dead chunk of meat praying to a giant plaster replica of Jesus. Totally oblivious to the fact that *this* is its afterlife, and its God is fake.'

Wu stirred. 'From your tone, I assume that's your assessment of all religion.'

Marco laughed mirthlessly. 'Ha. Yeah.'

'You don't believe in God.'

'Not really.'

'I thought you bring peace to tortured souls. Isn't that your business?'

Marco flashed a bitter smile. 'That's marketing, my friend. Words chosen to sell a service. I doubt the corpses actually give a shit.' He hated himself the moment he said it. An immediate image of Danielle appeared to him – emaciated, mould-faced, suffering who-the-fuck-knows-where, with her guts torn out and the agonising need to eat raw skin . . .

He squeezed his eyes shut, erased the image. Blobs of light swirled in his retinas. Somewhere within the formless shapes he heard the Horseman soldier still screaming.

Had Danielle ever peeled a man apart like that?

Horrified, he recoiled, blinked his senses back to the chapel. The morning had beaten him down, he realised, given him a severe spiritual ass-kicking. His chest ached something fierce, as if Hannah's tombstone had toppled onto him, crushed his heart flat.

He became aware of Wu observing him curiously.

'Sorry,' Marco said. 'I'm kinda having a bad day.'

The men waited, serenaded by the baying of dogs beyond the stained glass. Five minutes passed, then ten. Wu's breath cycled slow and even, and Marco thought he might have drifted off to sleep; as far as he knew, the sergeant hadn't rested in two days.

Then Wu spoke.

'I come from a Chinese family,' he began haltingly, guardedly, as if some unspoken thought were hiding between the words. 'Very traditional. I was not given a name the day I was born. My uncle Bao Zhi had instructed my brothers and sisters to refer to me only as an "animal". Not because he was cruel – he loved me very much – it was simply his trick to fool evil spirits that were believed to kidnap human newborns. When I was several weeks old, he honoured me with my father's name, Kheng Wu, who had died before my birth. As a child, I was told that my achievements in this life would bring happiness to my father's spirit.'

The sergeant raised his chin, his eyes absorbing the stained-glass depictions of saints and holy miracles immortalised in the chapel windows. Marco waited, not sure what Wu was trying to tell him. Wu seemed to detect his uncertainty.

'My point, Doctor,' Wu continued, 'is that the dead do "give a shit", as you said. My uncle's culture perceives death differently than Americans. The traditional Chinese believe that the dead and the living exist together – side-by-side in the same plane, not infinitely separated dimensions like your Heaven and Hell. Our dead are not gone. They are here with us, literally, and even though they are spirits, they have physical needs.'

'Needs?'

Wu nodded. 'As children we prepared them food and water, left them toothbrushes and combs, burned "spirit money" into the air for them to collect and buy goods. If my uncle Bao Zhi were alive today to explain – he himself passed away years ago – he would perhaps tell us that, in the Evacuated

States, the spirits have assumed a physical form as well. Dead bodies that eat and walk. Frightening, but still we must honour them. Because the dead connect us to God.'

Marco pinched his dog-bitten ear, reflecting.

Spirits in physical form . . .

'So you're saying what?' he frowned. 'The Resurrection is some sort of Chinese afterlife? We should honour the dead by feeding ourselves to them?'

Wu shook his head disapprovingly. 'You misinterpret, Doctor. I don't pretend to understand the Resurrection. I'm only assuring you that there *are* spirits here on earth, real spirits. Some remain invisible, the way it has always been, and some now travel in rotting bodies – for whatever purpose the universe has deemed necessary.'

'And so,' he added, flexing his neck left and then right, 'I accept my duty to respect the dead. To hold them sacred the way my uncle taught me, the same way you respect life. This morning, for example. You were repulsed by me because I killed the Horseman soldier. You would have spared him, even though he posed great danger to us both.'

Marco flushed. He hadn't known Wu had read him so clearly.

'So now let me ask you, Henry Marco, corpse-killer-for-hire,' Wu said. 'Would it surprise you that I've never killed a corpse?'

Marco raised an eyebrow. 'What do you mean? Never?'

'Never.'

'Not once, since the Resurrection?'

'No.'

'Jesus,' Marco admitted. 'That's hard to imagine.'

'Not from my perspective.'

Marco frowned. 'Maricopa,' he said. 'You pulled the burning corpse off me, and I wondered why you didn't use your gun.'

'Yes. For the purpose of my own survival, I will confront a corpse, disable it if necessary – but to kill it would dishonour my father.' He shrugged, then scowled and put a hand to his shoulder, cradling the bullet wound as if to calm the pain. 'Men, however. In my life, I have learned to kill the men who oppose me, never to hesitate . . .'

He trailed off, woozy with fatigue and discomfort, his swollen lip curled in distaste. His eyes rolled back, the lids half closed in a trance. Perhaps the conversation continued on in his head; Marco didn't know, but the silence was immediately odd, awkward, like a lull in an argument. Sadly, Marco faced front again.

In the first row the elderly corpse bobbed its head – how many times more before the skull simply snapped from the spine and thumped to the altar? – and a pained, wheezing sound creaked from its putrid mouth.

Marco felt his gun holster rubbing under his arm.

He thought about the Glock, the single bullet it held.

He could just walk up there, end the corpse's misery. Put the muzzle right square against that brown patch of skull, and pull the trigger.

Would that really be dishonour? A violation? Was Wu right?

No. Marco couldn't accept that.

I'm helping them, he thought. *Returning them.*

But returning them where? countered some other voice in his mind, traitorous, subversive. *What if* here *is where they're supposed to be?*

No. He shuddered the doubt off him like a spider he'd found crawling on his skin.

Danielle needs me. My help.

When I find her, I'll return her. That's honour. That's love.

He sniffled up the loose snot in his nose as the pew creaked under him.

Then he cocked his head, realising why the silence had struck him as so odd.

'The dogs are quiet,' he announced.

It was true. The howls, the growls, the yelps . . . gone.

At the sound of Marco's voice, Wu was instantly alert. He bucked up straight in his seat and grabbed at his knives, his breath quick as if he were being chased. Marco wondered what things Wu saw in his nightmares.

'The dogs,' Marco said again, reassuringly. 'I think they left.' He slipped from the pew and crept to the vestibule, afraid to make noise that might summon the animals back. He put his ear to the oak door and listened. Nothing.

He jostled the table aside and then, hesitating, held his breath and clicked down on the brass handle. The door cracked an inch. He propped his shoulder against the wood, ready to slam it shut if drooling jaws came snapping through the gap.

Again, nothing. He peered outside.

The dogs weren't there. Tufts of torn fur rolled like tumbleweeds in a breeze over the walk, and dark fresh dirt lay in piles where they'd dug at the walls. Brown paw-prints crossed the road, disappearing into the brush. He scanned the shadows.

'All clear,' he determined. 'We should go now.'

'Doctor.'

The solemn note in Wu's voice made him turn. The sergeant was standing at the carpet edge, just inside the vestibule.

'What I explained about my father, and the dead,' Wu began, then stopped, then began again. 'I meant it to bring you comfort.'

The remark caught Marco off guard. He blinked, not understanding.

'I meant,' Wu said, 'that your daughter is not gone. She, too, is on this journey – travelling with you, watching over you. Petitioning the universe on your behalf, even when you say you don't believe. She is the reason you've survived this far.'

Marco paled. A chemical heat passed through his body, leaked into his eyes.

He remembered Danielle, that day at the grave.

We can't, Henry. We can't leave her here. Alone.

Delle. Baby, we have to go . . . I promise she's not alone.

'I'd like to think that,' he finally allowed. It came out strained and hoarse.

Wu's bruised face regarded him in the soft light, unsmiling but, for the first time Marco could recall, not unkind. The sergeant nodded, then straightened the knives on his belt with a solid tug, signalling an end to the talk. He brushed past Marco to the door.

'We'd better hurry,' he said. 'The dogs might circle back.'

'Yeah.' Marco rubbed his neck and turned for a final look at the pews. The pious corpse hadn't moved. It would remain here for eternity, prayers unanswered.

Briefly he wished he knew the corpse's name.

Maybe someday he'd come back this way on a job.

Peace be with you. What he used to say as a kid before leaving church with his dad. *Peace be with you. And also with you.*

Outside, the sun was bright now, the clouds evaporated. The men jogged down the looping road, their senses tuned for any indication of stray dogs or corpses. Once, wistfully, Marco glanced back up the hill towards Hannah's grave, tantalised by a fleeting hunch that he'd missed Danielle by minutes. *What if she showed just after I left?* he wondered but just as soon banished the thought, knowing it would only drive him mad.

Rounding the bend, he saw the quad a hundred yards ahead, undisturbed, exactly as they'd left it. The road ran straight through a suffocating tunnel of low-hanging pine branches and grass on either side. He faltered half a step, thinking he might be entering a perfect trap, baited with the quad . . . but what the hell could he do? He bolted the last hundred yards like a sprinter to the finish line, certain the dogs would come pouring through the trees and tackle him off the track. He reached the quad untouched.

'We should be clear,' Wu said, arriving behind him. 'I heard barking and what sounded like a corpse screech, back in the opposite direction. The dogs found lunch.'

'Poor dead guy. Even I feel sorry for it.'

'Check the map,' Wu said, stone-faced. 'We need to get back on course.'

Whatever glow had softened Wu back at the chapel was gone now, Marco noted. The sergeant was all business again.

'Gotcha,' Marco said. He, too, felt restored from the gloom of the church interior, reinvigorated by the fresh, grass-smelling air and the promising sun. He fished the Rand McNally map from his back pocket and spread it over the seat of the quad.

'How far until Sarsgard?' Wu asked.

'Hmmm . . . hundred miles, maybe.'

'Good. Get us there before dark.' Wu took up his position on the rear rack.

Marco refolded the map, settled into the driver's seat. It struck him that he was growing acclimated to Wu's curt orders, no longer as compelled to push back. Wu knew what he was doing, Marco figured. No point arguing.

But still . . .

'Y'know, there's a word we still use in civilian life. It's called "please",' he quipped. He didn't bother turning to see how Wu received the remark. 'Anyway, we'll hit the first gas station out of town. After that, it's a straight shot, no stops.'

He started the quad and swung a U-turn, heading back.

Sweat had plastered his shirt to his skin; he was eager to ride again and let the wind cool him down. Obliging, the quad picked up speed and skimmed along the cracked cemetery road. Seconds later they zipped through the main gate, back to the world of sidewalks and pavement and brick buildings. The shift was disconcerting; the city seemed more lifeless than the graveyard.

Driving away, he permitted himself one last peek backwards at the diminishing cemetery. One last goodbye to Hannah.

I love you. I'll visit again, I promise.

He cringed, guilty, uncertain whether he could keep that promise.

From the cemetery a small black dog with a white chest trotted onto the sidewalk, watching them go. Its muzzle dripped with dark meaty juice – corpse blood.

See ya, pup, Marco thought. *Sorry the whole 'man's best friend' thing didn't work out.* He gunned the throttle and sped through the empty blocks.

Next up, Roger Ballard.

Marco's eyes watered in the wind; his heart shrank. He knew one thing for sure.

He'd better focus on the task ahead, or Sarsgard Prison would eat him alive.

PRISON TERMS

10.1

In the mid-afternoon they hit traffic, five miles deep through the San Bernardino Mountains. 'Shit,' Marco groaned. '*Shit!*'

He released the throttle, and the quad coasted on the mountain highway. A quarter-mile ahead, there it was – a dreaded ghost jam. Big one. Hundreds of mute cars and minivans and eighteen-wheelers and rugged SUVs, now abandoned; the shimmering desert sun seemed to melt them all together into a single massive gleaming chunk, like a metal plug shoved up the highway's ass. Every lane was blocked solid. Steep rock walls leaned against the road on both sides, towering cliffs that were impossible to traverse. The men were trapped.

Muttering curses, Marco rolled the quad to the bumper of a Mazda convertible with California plates. The car had once been a sharp aquamarine blue, like a sleek shark, but now languished, discoloured and warted with rust. The top was down, the seats fuzzy with black lichen growing into the leather. No driver. One ratty brown loafer lay beside the open door.

Cracked with dry blood.

This is why, Marco seethed, *you don't drive highways, asshole.*

He'd fucked up, and he knew it.

I-215 had been his own dumb-ass choice. Buzzing out of Hemet, he'd perceived himself in a frantic race against time – a blood-crazed adrenalin rush from here to Sarsgard, and speed meant everything. The sun had taken too large a lead, dropping minute by minute towards the hazy mountain horizon, and Marco had cringed at the notion of not reaching Sarsgard by dark – spending the night in the desert, exposed and vulnerable.

No damn way, he'd vowed. *Not gonna let that happen.*

And so, an hour ago, he'd turned to Wu. 'We'll catch 215, the interstate north. No time to dilly-dally on the back roads – or risk getting lost.'

'Agreed,' Wu called from behind. 'Shortest route.'

The truth was, nightfall was the least of Marco's fears. He was maddeningly aware that somewhere behind the quad – or ahead? – the Horsemen were running the same race, hunting Roger. They'd be ruthless, vengeful for the death of the bearded soldier. *They'll force me to find Roger. Then they'll slit my throat.* He couldn't shake the image of Big Skull – the muscle-bound leader with the bone-heavy head – peering at him from the shadows of his mind, like a hunter half hidden in jungle growth. The man unnerved him, more than he wanted to admit to Wu.

But Big Skull wasn't even the worst problem.

Because, Jesus Christ, what if the Horsemen won this deadly contest? Grabbed Roger's prized blood for themselves – what then?

Wu had given him the answer already. The Horsemen would sell Roger's DNA to terrorists, Iranians, madmen eager to synthesize a vaccine. And God knows what they'd do with the formula once they had it – sell it on the black market, or demand some unholy ransom from the big nations. Or maybe just save their own asses while everybody else on the planet rotted.

Shit, no pressure there, he thought. *Don't fuck up, Henry, or bad guys conquer the world.*

He paled. The stakes were so high they dizzied him. His head ached terribly from lack of sleep, lack of food, and, most of all, too much goddamn worrying – like a vice had clamped on his brain, and every new minute felt like another crank on the handle.

Outside Hemet the quad had zipped past a desolate Walgreens. Dead shoppers meandered in and out of the drugstore's smashed entrance. Marco sighed.

Battling those corpses would *almost* be worth it for a bottle of Advil.

Expired Advil, he reminded himself. *Wouldn't even work.*

Besides, no way would Wu indulge him again, not with the sun getting lower, turning a bloodier orange in the west.

Just then, approaching on the right, the blue sign for I-215 had beckoned. And, like a gambler rolling dice, he'd steered onto the interstate, hoping to save time.

How depressingly empty it had appeared. Lost, forgotten. Bleached food wrappers and mouldering newspapers heaped against the concrete medians; the once-great road was now reduced to a three-lane repository for litter, with brown weeds sprouting from cracks in the pavement and white-striped orange construction barrels tipped over at haphazard intervals. The highway was a long, silent chute, fairly straight, with a vanishing point miles ahead. He'd scanned the distance, found nothing to alarm him – no quads charging south with their guns blazing. No vultures.

Good thing about highways, he'd thought. *You can see trouble coming.*

Bad thing is, trouble sees you, too.

He shook his head. *Quit scaring yourself. Just hit the gas and get this over with. Get through the mountains, then you can hide again in the back roads.*

For forty-five minutes he'd travelled north, his nerves popping hotly like camera bulbs each time he heard another motor roaring, but it was always his own quad, echoing back from a concrete overpass or the stone acoustics of the mountains. Once he almost braked, terrified, confronted by a roadblock of Horsemen military trucks ahead – and then realized sheepishly that it wasn't a roadblock *or* even Horsemen, but merely three burned cars crashed on their sides, bellies exploded outwards. They balanced against each other like a bizarre house of cards.

Thank god he hadn't hit the brakes. Wu would have ridiculed him without mercy.

The highway flowed like a dry river bed through Southern California towns, past glum billboards and cities dead of thirst, nothing moving except for tumbleweeds on streets. And up again into the San Bernardino Forest, the northern end this time – another thrill ride soaring between mineral-coloured cliffs and sugar pines and raw scrub. All the while, seconds ticked in his mind, an excruciating countdown. To what? He wasn't even certain.

And now this.

A ghost jam, a goddamn predictable *ghost jam*. He chewed his lip. In his Jeep the decision would've been a no-brainer – turn around and find another route, no other choice. But . . . the quad tossed another option on the table. Reluctantly he considered it.

He could fit between the outer cars, riding the shoulder of the breakdown lane.

Perfect, he thought. *I miss the Jeep.*

The Jeep made it easier to chicken out.

'Go,' Wu said, impatient. He'd also noted the gap.

'Yeah, yeah,' Marco said. 'I'm going.'

Even as he hesitated, he knew the Horsemen were closing ground. How far back? Ten miles? Five? Just around the bend, and any second they'd jump out and say boo?

Sick at the thought, he nudged the throttle. The quad

motored to the right shoulder and slipped into the narrow channel between the outer rail and a scratched-up SUV with flat tyres. A surfboard was strapped to the roof. He chugged forward, slow and careful, passing cars.

Empty metal shells. Except he knew that there were corpses here, somewhere, hiding; there were *always* corpses hiding, waiting to scuttle out of holes like nightmarish crabs for a meal.

The breakdown lane was wide enough but not a friendly ride. Loose dented hubcaps and corroded mufflers and torn-off bumpers scattered the road, as if some angry mechanic had gone on a rampage, spewing car parts everywhere. The quad's large wheels worked hard, trampling obstacles, jarring Marco's breath loose. Which was helpful, in a way; his chest had squeezed itself so goddamn tight, he kept forgetting to exhale on his own.

Behind him, Wu grunted in discomfort.

'Kinda makes you miss the train tracks, huh?' Marco asked.

'Are you watching for corpses?' Wu groused. 'Or thinking up clever jokes?'

'Both. I get silly when I'm about to be eaten.'

But the roadside debris was still kinder than the horrors in the abandoned cars. Human bodies, ripped apart. Half-eaten arms dangled out half-opened doors. Skeletonised drivers slumped against steering wheels, their lips torn off, teeth clenched in agony. Marco knew too well that when the dead came swarming through deadlocked traffic, you had two basic options – run like hell, or hide in the car. People who hid learned the hard way that a car was a perfect little coffin. You couldn't just roll your windows up, keep the corpses out like a summer storm. Smashed windshields were everywhere, the cars like open caskets interring mummified men and women. Between cars the pavement was studded with broken safety glass and gnawed bones. Torn shirts and pants and dresses lay in ragged mounds by the bumpers.

He froze. Did that body blink?

No. You're just being jumpy.

Fidgeting, he tried to keep his ears perked. The quad was too damn loud. No way to detect the click of a car door, the squeak of hinges. Dead feet scraping asphalt.

But so far, so good. He wasn't hearing those things because they weren't happening – right?

They'd progressed a mile when, holy shit, he *did* hear a scream.

High and loud, the cry pierced the roar of the motor and pimpled his skin with instant goose bumps. In the back seat, Wu twisted as the wailing died.

'What the fuck?' Marco gasped.

There. Ahead he saw it. A weathered Volvo station wagon, the rear window smeared black. On the bumper was a cracked sticker for the San Diego Zoo, a cute furry koala. The cry sounded again – disgusting, wretched, like somebody was gargling a throat of curdled milk. Awful. Marco drew even with the car and peered into the shattered back seat window.

A dead toddler glared at him. Strapped into a baby seat. Trapped.

Two years old, maybe three, its neck shredded open, its windpipe exposed. It wore stiff denim overalls and a blue-striped shirt doused with old sour blood; baby fat wobbled in white wormy strips under its chin. Its eyes were yellow-pale, like peeled apples.

Marco's stomach heaved. The toddler strained against the straps, arms outstretched as though it wanted to be picked up.

Jesus Christ, Marco thought. Numb.

In the front seat two adult skeletons – *Mommy and Daddy* – had been dragged halfway through the smashed windshield. Their legs hung over the dash. Their heads were gone. Eaten.

Jesus.

Christ.

The quad rolled past. Marco's mind reeled, trying to reset. As if somehow he could hit a button, erase what he'd just seen.

I should go back, he realised. *Return the kid, save it from that . . . that nightmare. Stuck forever in a car seat, crying. Except Wu would never let me . . .*

He was so distracted that when two dead hands popped from behind a sky-blue Lincoln and slapped the hood, he didn't even flinch.

A wrinkled corpse hoisted itself to a standing position and leaned on the car. An elderly male in a stupid fisherman's hat, a yellow lure hooked to the brim.

Hello, Grandpa, Marco thought.

His veins thickened, blood rushing. Suddenly, in the next lane, there came more movement – another corpse, female, slithering from beneath a black Nissan.

'We have corpses,' he announced to Wu, his voice rising.

'That's not all.' Wu grabbed his shoulder, turned him in his seat. 'Look.'

Far back where the empty highway hadn't yet met the ghost jam, familiar shapes fanned out across the barren lanes.

Five military quads, speeding towards them.

The Horsemen had caught up.

10.2

Marco was paralysed. The sight of the Horseman motorcade was almost dreamlike, a desert mirage that couldn't be real and, just as in a dream, his limbs were unable to move, obeying some secret logic beyond his control.

Except, of course, this shit *was* real – and in another minute the Horsemen would be here to stomp his ass dead.

A shock of panic reattached his nerves to his brain, and with a jolt he spun forward on the quad. The old fisherman corpse tottered around the Lincoln towards him. Black flies crawled atop the white scruff on its cheeks, like a second beard.

'Perfect,' Marco groused. 'Exactly what I needed.'

'Go,' Wu said, strangely calm. 'We have a good lead, as long as we hurry—'

He hadn't finished before Marco punched the throttle and the quad bucked ahead. The old corpse lunged as they went, missed, flopped to the road.

Ouch, Grandpa, Marco thought. *Broken hip for sure.*

The quad scooted up the narrow breakdown lane, clunking through the debris, zooming past cars on the left. Marco's teeth pressed together, his eyes shooting back and forth between the road and the graveyard of cars. Trouble. *Deep-shit* trouble. All around, corpses were rising, wakened from hibernation in their rusted dens, bleary-eyed, sour stomachs calling for meat. Heads popped from behind cars, from back seats, from truck beds, like kids summoned from hiding spots at the end of hide-and-seek. *Come out, come out, wherever you are.*

Stay focused, Marco ordered himself. *Do* not *fucking crash.*

'They've reached the cars,' Wu shouted over the engine. 'The Horsemen.'

'Thanks for the update – keeps me motivated.'

A burly trucker stepped around the cab of its eighteen-wheeler, and Marco accelerated, afraid the big male would block the lane; the quad beat it through the gap by a bare second, snapping off the corpse's foot as it stepped into the path of the buzzing wheels. Black blood splashed up and over the quad hood. Spitting, Marco wiped his face with his forearm.

Didn't want that shit getting in his mouth.

From somewhere far away, popping noises accompanied

the roar of the quad, bouncing back and forth against the cliff walls, and it wasn't until the rear-view mirror on a grey sedan right beside him exploded into shards that Marco understood the Horsemen were shooting. '*Fuck!*' he screamed and hunkered lower in his seat. 'They're shooting at us!'

'They're shooting at *me*,' Wu carped back, annoyed. 'They want *you* alive.'

'Hey, don't blame me— shit!' Fixing his eyes ahead, Marco slammed the brakes.

Wu banged against his back, cursing. 'What's wrong?'

'Dead end,' Marco said.

Ten feet before them, crashed sideways into the barrier, was a prehistoric-looking Cadillac – fins crumpled, pinned there by a black Lexus, and beyond that, a mash-up of more tangled fenders, five or six cars deep. A chain reaction of rear-end collisions as corpses had mobbed the highway and drivers panicked, floored the gas, and died even faster.

And now the mangled wrecks entirely cut off the lane.

Frantic, Marco wheeled in his seat, seeking another route. But the entire highway denied him, cars bumper to bumper, too tight for the quad to squeeze to the next lane.

The only direction to go . . . was back.

Fuck that.

Two hundred yards to the rear, the Horsemen had entered the breakdown lane, flying single-file up the sideline of the ghost jam. In their green helmets and goggles, they were like freakish insects, cold-blooded, a killer swarm. They zipped past corpses raging in the next lane; the dead were blocked by the wall of endless cars but fighting out, crawling under tyres, climbing hoods. More corpses than Marco had even imagined.

Christ, he'd driven right past them – stirred them all up.

'We can't fight so many,' he conceded, his voice glum.

The weight of an AK pressed into his chest – Wu was

shoving the last weapon from the gun rack into his arms. The sergeant stood next to the quad, knives swinging on his belt, the Horseman's daypack slung over his good shoulder.

'We're not going to,' Wu said, his eyes sharp and urgent. 'Run.'

And then Wu bolted, sliding over the hood of the sideways Cadillac, ditching the quad behind. Marco watched him go, stunned momentarily.

A grunt made him turn. The fat trucker corpse hobbled towards him. The stump of its missing foot dragged the road, etching a line of oily blood.

Marco hopped over the Cadillac and ran.

Gunfire exploded, and bullets jack-hammered the highway barrier to his right, spitting up concrete chunks. Wu dived for cover, scrambling to his left, between bumpers, into the middle lane as Marco bounded behind. *Jesus, Wu! You sure they aren't shootin' at me?!?*

He hastily measured the barrier, but right away saw that hopping it to scramble up the mountainside wasn't an option. Out there in the open, he'd be the easiest target on the shooting range. The Horsemen fired again, and bullet marks singed the asphalt a step away.

Then he understood. *My legs . . . they're takin' me down alive . . .*

Highstepping, he dashed up the middle lane, feeling like a bull herded into a corral with walls made of empty cars. He vaulted over a dead teenager as it wriggled out from under an old Camaro, barking, grabbing at his ankles; its black lip was pierced with a tarnished silver loop.

Ahead Wu cut left again as a mob of corpses charged down the lane. Marco ducked behind a lopsided white RV as the corpses ran past; he crept to the opposite side and emerged disoriented, almost forgetting whether he wanted to go left or right.

Right.

He ran, fixing on Wu ahead, determined to keep pace.

By now, he guessed, the Horsemen must have reached the Cadillac dead-end. Good guess – he heard a sudden shout, echoing unintelligibly off the rock walls. He imagined Big Skull, that massive domed head thrown back in a roar of anger, the taut skin sunburned a poisonous red. More shouts now, answering from across the lanes – *Five, take middle! Six, check left! Hump it!* – as the Horsemen, too, dumped their quads and spread out on foot.

As if to prove his theory, a bullet sizzled low past Marco, plunked the hubcap of a rusted Volkswagen. He whirled. There, a hundred yards behind him, crouched the Horseman in the pilot's jumpsuit; the soldier aimed a sleek rifle, its nozzle propped on a toppled motorcycle . . .

Shit!

. . . but before the gunman could fire again, a rotten biker corpse sprang from behind a car, sacking the Horseman as the rifle screamed skyward. More corpses piled on.

Marco didn't linger. He spun again and quick-stepped along the narrow corridor between cars, cracking his hip on side-view mirrors as he went.

Behind him he heard hideous screams and gibbering, and panicked gunfire rattled fast and faster yet. The tunnel of corpses was collapsing, he realised, crushing the Horsemen within. He'd inadvertently lured them into a death trap. *Like Moses and the Egyptians,* he thought giddily, *the Red Sea crashing down on Pharaoh's army. All I need's a white beard.*

Meanwhile, Wu was nowhere to be seen.

'*Wu!*' Marco shouted, anxious.

'*This way!*' Wu's voice boomed from the next lane, over to the right.

Another pile-up of cars heaped in front of Marco, and a filthy windowless van had wedged itself sideways, blocking the path. The back door of the van banged open, and seven or eight dark-haired corpses poured out, rushing Marco. *Crap.* He scrambled under the colossal trailer of an eighteen-wheel truck; the corpses snatched at his legs, but he kicked and kicked and rolled out the other side, and there was Wu, waving him on.

'*This way!*' Wu yelled again and pointed ahead.

The end point of the ghost jam. A hundred yards to go. The cars began to spread out, separated by larger gaps; the mountains ceased, and the road returned to the flat brown earth, a glum landscape rubbed raw of vegetation. Marco bounced on the balls of his feet and took off running. His lungs heaved, begging him to stop, but the screams of Horsemen being eaten alive cheered him on, bolstered him. He was winning the race.

He broke past the end, a state police sedan overturned on its roof, flipped probably during a hopeless effort to restore order during the Evacuation; instead, all the officer had accomplished was to stop traffic for miles. A skeleton hand hung limply from the driver's side window, a macabre welcome to the uncluttered highway beyond.

Back in the ghost jam, bullets chattered in rapid succession like a string of firecrackers. A collective agonising shriek, multiple men dying at once, echoed from the wrecks, penetrating to the core of Marco's brain before it cut off in a wet gurgle.

Another sound effect for his nightmares.

He kept running, a length behind Wu – promising his burning legs just five strides more, then five strides more, then five strides more . . .

The last of the gunfire stopped, swallowed up by the dead.

And then the desert was quiet again.

Wu stutter-stepped to a walk. 'Far enough,' he said, panting. 'Rest.'

Marco turned, surprised to see how far he'd run; fear and adrenalin had confused his internal odometer. The overturned police car was a speck, a mile off in the sun-glazed distance, the rusted traffic just another coarse texture blending with the dirt.

From here it all looked calm; no hint of the feeding frenzy going on inside.

The two men lingered. Watching.

Still calm.

'The Horsemen?' Marco asked.

Wu shrugged and resumed walking. 'We're safe for now.'

'Death by ghost jam,' Marco mused.

'Let's hope,' Wu said, although he didn't sound hopeful. 'Our concern now is reaching Sarsgard on foot. From our current location in the middle of nowhere.'

The barren earth scrolled east and west from the interstate, nothing but scrub and knobs of brittlebush drawing long shadows from the late afternoon sun.

'I've got the map.' Marco patted his back pocket. 'But I don't know if we need it – we're probably pretty close.'

He pointed up the road to a solitary white road sign, the lone manmade structure in the barren panorama. Black letters pronounced a stern warning:

CORRECTIONAL FACILITY AREA
DO NOT PICK UP
HITCHHIKERS

Wu straightened the daypack on his shoulder. 'Encouraging.'

'Yeah. I'd call that some good advice.' Marco glanced one final time back to the mountains. Nobody coming. But the sun was dropping steadily. He wiped sweat from his slick forehead and eyebrows. 'We'd better hurry.'

They quickened their steps, pushing north, Wu in the

lead. The muscles in his shoulder blades rose and fell as he walked, like those of a prowling animal. Flies buzzed around his soiled bandage. He brushed them away every dozen steps.

'Too bad about the no-hitchhiking rule,' Marco said dryly. 'We're gonna need a ride home after this. Arizona's a long walk.'

'First things first, Doctor,' Wu said without turning. 'We might not live long enough for that to be a problem.'

Marco said nothing. The soles of his feet hurt; he felt a damp, cranky blister on his big toe, rasping against the boot as he trudged. On the eastern horizon he saw buildings and a tall sign for a Circle K gas station, but the road curled west towards the sunset. A cinnamon-coloured hawk glided overhead, on the hunt for jackrabbits and ground squirrels. *At least the rabbits are smart enough to hide,* Marco thought. *Not like us idiots, strolling out in the open through the middle of Corpseland, USA. We're easy pickin's.* Anxious, he focused on his blistered toe. *Ouch. Ouch. Ouch.* At least this pain was tiny. Kept his mind off bigger troubles.

Twenty minutes passed, and then thirty. Neither man spoke. There was nothing to say. They were exhausted and hurting. They huffed as they went.

At last Wu broke the silence.

'There it is,' he said solemnly. 'Sarsgard.'

10.3

Standing at the intersection of two desert roads, gazing upon the vast structure of Sarsgard Medical Prison, Marco recalled the first time he'd seen the Grand Canyon. It had been a day's drive to the South Rim, the summer he and Danielle moved to Arizona. Nothing had prepared him for that first encounter – not photos in books, not television shows, not the abstract sketches of his own imagination. There he'd stood at the rail of a breathtaking chasm, as if five hours in the car had somehow transported him to an alien planet, sculpted in strata of dizzying red and gold and green rock. He'd never felt so dwarfed by nature, so powerless to change the earth in his lifetime. *Six million years*, he'd thought. *That's what it takes.* Danielle had leaned on his arm, and they'd wordlessly shared a strawberry ice-cream cone, absorbing the sight. And it had occurred to him that, in geological time, his own existence on Earth would be as fleeting as Hannah's – over so soon as to almost warrant never being born at all. He'd reddened, squelching tears, and kept the thought to himself. Danielle would've hated him.

Now, here, that same overwhelming feeling returned. The prison was a colossus, and he was an insignificant mite. So small and weak. Staring into another abyss.

'It's too big,' he told Wu. 'How the hell are we gonna find Roger in there?'

The prison complex dominated six hundred acres of desert, a solemn metropolis of red, block-shaped buildings surrounded by a towering concrete wall. It loomed on the northern horizon like a great ruin uncovered from an archaeological dig – bleak and menacing, reborn from the ground but unmistakably dead, dead, dead. Vultures blackened the sky above the slate roofs. Marco's innards chilled.

God knew what was waiting behind that wall.

Wu swigged the last gulp from his water bottle and squinted at Marco. They'd slowed half a mile from the main prison gate; Marco noted the hesitation in their steps, like boxers plodding out for the final round, resigned to a decisive beating. The sun scraped the mountains to the west, and the sky had darkened like a bruise, as if it, too, had been through an ass-kicking. Sunset was an hour away, at most.

Ahead, the long driveway stretched towards the prison, culminating in a massive, iron-latticed gate.

Even from afar, Marco could see the gate was shut tight.

'Let's not linger,' Wu said. 'We still need to locate a way in.'

'Osbourne said the prison was a breach,' Marco remembered. 'So there must be a hole, someplace we can't see. Maybe around back.'

Hiking towards the main gate, Marco grew reflective; he imagined how newly arriving convicts must have felt being transported up this very road into Sarsgard. They must have wondered: would this be their last look at the world outside? The road led in; it didn't always lead out. *I'm going to die here,* he predicted, then recoiled at the thought.

Fuck no. You're going to find Roger and return him. Let Wu collect his blood sample. Then you're walking outta here, a free man.

He blanched, remembering Osbourne's video. Thousands of rioting corpses.

Sure, no problem at all.

As expected, the main gate was impenetrable, the iron bars thick and tumoured with orange rust. And the wall, Christ, the wall put Marco's barricade back home to shame – sixteen feet high, topped with curls of angry razor wire. Impossible to scale, even if Wu's shoulder worked and Marco's hands weren't chewed with burn wounds.

The wall ran five hundred yards towards the sinking sun, then wrapped right, boxing in the prison grounds. Rising from the other side was a forbidding guard tower, a square-walled platform on iron stilts. A white siren roosted on the roof like a fat seagull.

As Marco watched, a corpse popped up on the platform – a dead guard, its blue uniform tattered, emotionless eyes deep in its sockets. It surveyed them with a slack expression. Cradled in its arms, upside down and awkward, was a rifle.

'Hopefully it doesn't know how to use that thing,' Marco said. 'Let's go that way. Around the perimeter.' He pointed to where the wall turned the corner.

'We won't have time to walk the whole exterior. Not before dark.'

'Not much choice. C'mon.'

They hugged the wall, avoiding the sightline of the guard tower. Even chimps could pull a trigger, Marco mused, and maybe the dead guard had enough leftover muscle memory to warrant taking a shot. As they passed below the tower, a dull *whump* sounded from the ground on the opposite side of the wall. Marco backed a step and craned his neck up. The tower was empty. 'I think the guard fell out,' he said.

'No fear of heights,' Wu noted. 'He leaned too far.'

Cautiously, the men hiked west along the barrier. Wu had been right about the unmanageable distance. Circling the entire compound would take hours.

But to Marco's relief, ten minutes were all they needed. Not far around the first corner, they hit the jackpot – a row of drab-green military trucks. Four 7-Ton models, armoured and solid, with six-wheeled drive for transporting troops and weapons cross-desert. All abandoned.

'MTVR's,' Wu noted. 'Medium Tactical Vehicle Replacements.'

'Cool,' Marco said.

Beyond the trucks was a large collapse in the wall, ten feet wide. Rubble littered the ground in melon-sized chunks, and bars of reinforced steel protruded from the blasted-apart cement like bent spider legs. The work of dynamite, Marco guessed.

'The first RRU squad blew this up, trying to get Roger,'

he said. 'That didn't go so well. But at least they made a nice new door.'

He readied the automatic in his hand and stepped cautiously to the breach.

Then poked his head through . . . half expecting dead hands to lash out and seize him, impale his face on the exposed steel rods.

But the complex inside was silent. Nothing moved. He swivelled his neck, checking the wall for hiders, then quickly assessed the layout of the enormous prison grounds. As much as he could see, anyway. Guard towers dotted the wall every few hundred feet; in the distance to his right he saw the fallen dead guard staggering towards him, its pace slow and excruciating, dragging its hand along the wall for support. Its rifle was gone.

Straight ahead, a broad no-man's land of dirt separated him from the first set of prison buildings – three grim structures a hundred yards away. They looked more like old factories than prison housing; the windows were grimy and broken, and conical brick chimneys stretched their long necks high. A narrow service road led from the factories to a small gas station and a water tower that looked cracked and empty. Beyond the last building was a softball field, the infield potted with rocks and sparse, anguished-looking grass.

And beyond that was the main compound – a modest outpost of what looked like administration offices, and the prison itself.

The cell blocks. The formidable red buildings he'd viewed from the main road. Three long buildings, each four storeys high, the windows bracketed with black steel bars. They were arranged in a horseshoe shape around a weed-choked courtyard, a maze of chain-link fencing that reminded Marco of a dog kennel. And behind that fence . . .

Corpses. Like caged animals. Dark figures shuffled behind

the chain link, jostling each other, skirmishing, barking. Marco chewed his lip.

Are you someplace in there, Roger?

Nervous, he studied the fence. At one end it hung open, a tear in the chain link. The corpses didn't seem to notice, milling back and forth without climbing through. No reason for them to leave the prison yard, he guessed. They were accustomed to it. *Lifers.*

Behind him he heard an engine cough. He turned.

Wu had assumed the driver's seat of the nearest MTVR. The sergeant frowned as the ignition sputtered, the gas old and oxidated. He tried again, and a third time. On the fourth attempt, the motor kicked to life. He leaned out the window. 'Get in,' he said.

'You sure you know how to drive that? You crashed the last one.'

Wu showed no smile. 'It's getting dark, Doctor.'

'Okay, okay.' Marco climbed into the passenger seat. 'Good idea. I'd much rather see the sights from a moving vehicle. The walking tour looks risky.'

Wu edged the truck through the gap, bumping over the rubble, and turned left to follow the interior wall. The sun had surrendered, and the prison grounds were dissolving into grey fuzz; a pale shard of moon was already present in the eastern sky. Even the vultures had left, gone to nest for the night. 'We're too late to go exploring the cell blocks,' Wu said. 'Not tonight – no light in there. It would be suicide.'

'You mean it's not already?'

Wu ignored him. 'You'll be happy, Doctor. There's an entire rack of guns in the cargo bed. Food supplies, too. I imagine you're as hungry as I am.'

'You're not planning a camp-out, I hope. In this truck?'

'No. Up *there.*' Wu braked the truck. They'd reached the

base of another guard tower. Unmanned. 'We'll be safe at night.'

Marco tilted his head to peer at the ladder. The hatch was open, inviting him up. 'Works for me,' he agreed. 'But *that* guy's not allowed.'

He pointed to the side-view mirror. The dead guard from the first tower was still staggering in their direction, one tortured footstep at a time.

'He'll draw a crowd under us,' Marco warned. 'There's a hole in the prison yard fence. If we attract attention, those dead cons will make a jailbreak.'

Wu pressed his lips together. After a moment's deliberation, he knocked the MTVR into reverse, and they rattled backwards over the rocky soil.

Ka-thunk.

Wu shifted the truck forward again. Marco glanced into the mirror. The guard was down, its legs cracked at the knees by the rear bumper. It slapped the hard earth with a mould-coloured hand, like a wrestler begging out of a fight.

'It'll stay there,' Wu said. He parked under the tower and killed the engine. 'Collect what you need, and let's go.'

The cargo bed was an arsenal wonderland – M16 rifles, M4 carbines, HK416s, pistols, sleek carbon-fibre models Marco had never seen before, all lined up ready for action. A stout shotgun caught his eye. He had no idea what it was, but damn, it looked like an ass-kicker, so he grabbed it, then tucked a smaller pistol into his belt. He could feel Wu's disapproval as he stocked up, but he didn't give a damn. Fuck Wu. Firepower was good. And food. Under his elbow he clamped as many MREs as he could.

Hands full, he clumsily ascended the ladder. At the top he looked back at the dead guard lying crumpled in the dirt. Its face was puckered, haggard; its knees bent at wrong angles, oozing black puddles like some awful melting candy.

I know how you feel, buddy, Marco thought. His muscles groaned as he climbed, pain spiking from every raw wound on his body. *I feel it, too.*

Like I've been hit by a truck.

10.4

Marco stirred in the dark, his head propped uncomfortably on a wadded wool blanket he'd found on a second supply run to the truck. Overhead the moon was a great round searchlight, affixed over the guard tower where he slept. Tried to sleep, more like it. He felt like a death-row prisoner, the night before execution; his mind throbbed, refusing to rest. The wooden platform grated against his vertebrae, and his ass was freezing, even with the blanket. The night air was sharp; the wool under his cheek was damp and cold with condensation from his breath. Unseen insects congregated in the roof beams, chirruping a creepy little tune, and once he felt a spider scuttle over his arm, sending him into momentary terror. Now he itched like mad, too.

Across the platform Wu was a silent dark mass. Maybe dozing, maybe not.

Up here in the tower, his legs cramped and restless, Marco remembered the tree blind twelve hundred miles away in Montana – the Roark contract, Andrew and Joan. How long ago had that been? A week? He shook his head. Impossible. He thought again. *Yes. A week.*

Holy shit.

Felt like a year. He wondered about Joan Roark, how she was doing. And what had *her* week been like? Had she told her friends that Andrew was dead – *really* dead? Or maybe she'd been too guilt-ridden, too ashamed to tell anyone she'd hired Marco.

He hoped she wasn't ashamed. He hoped she was doing okay.

In the distance a dead wailing sounded from the prison blocks, long and mournful like a lone wolf's howl. Marco shivered, buried his ear in the blanket to muffle the sound. He didn't want nightmares. Not tonight.

From Joan Roark his thoughts gravitated to Benjamin. How was Ben handling himself, stuck at his home in Pittsburgh with Owen Osbourne breathing down his neck? And the goons from Homeland Security? Poor Ben. Trapped with those assholes bullying him around his own house. Osbourne eating his food, shitting in his toilet.

Marco winced. Osbourne had threatened to kill Benjamin.

Please, he thought. *Let Ben be okay, too.*

The cry from the prison fell silent as the corpse lapsed back into whatever emptiness the night held for it. *Do the dead dream?* Marco wondered. Was that possible? Was a resurrected corpse like a sleep-walker, dazed, enacting some scene from its churning subconscious? A never-ending nightmare of carnage . . .

Squashed beneath his rib, Marco's left arm had begun to tingle; he tossed to his other side and felt his blood readjust. Damn hard wood. He'd be lucky to walk tomorrow.

More groans from the prison, louder this time, the pack joining in.

Those horrible, tormented voices . . .

Did one of them belong to Roger?

Sighing, Marco closed his eyes. He imagined an aerial view of the prison, the way vultures saw it. So that's what he'd finally become – a vulture, here to prey on the dead. *Find Roger, swoop down, put a bullet in his rotten brain.*

But what if he couldn't find him? What if Ballard wasn't even in this hellhole, after all the bullshit getting here? Marco fidgeted, flustered by the thought. *Where would we go next? Christ, I don't know. Cedars-Sinai?*

He strained, groping back through time for any

recollection of Roger's personal world, no matter how slight. Where would the compass in Roger's dead brain navigate him? Some secluded coffee shop, a quiet bookstore, maybe. Had Roger ever mentioned places like that?

Nope. Cedars-Sinai. That's all I got. Three years working side by side, and I barely knew the guy, like he didn't even exist outside work. Wow, Henry. Some great friend you are.

He sighed. *Then again, does it matter? If Roger's not here, we're pretty much fucked anyway. Wu and I are half dead. We don't have the strength to keep looking. I doubt we'd even make it to Los Angeles.*

Good thing I didn't offer Osbourne a money-back guarantee.

An hour ago Marco and Wu had hunkered down on the tower platform for a dinner of cold jerky. They ate in silence, too exhausted to do anything except shovel food into their destitute stomachs. Wu chewed deliberately, his eyes unfocused, lost on some faraway sight. Finally he shoved the last of the jerky into his mouth and opened a zippered pocket on his pant leg.

He pulled out a photograph, tossed it like a Frisbee to Marco's feet.

'What's this?' Marco asked.

'Sarsgard.'

Marco wiped his fingers on his bloodied shirt and picked it up. It was a grainy black-and-white view of the prison complex – the rectangular cell blocks arranged in a horseshoe around the courtyard. The picture had been taken from high above.

'Satellite photo?'

Wu nodded.

Marco squinted in the fading light, held the photo close to his eyes. The land between the buildings teemed with black dots. Corpses.

'How did you get this?' he asked.

'My briefing.'

'So which, if any, of these dots is Roger?'

Wu raised an eyebrow. 'Isn't that what you're supposed to tell me?'

'Okay, relax. Where's the hospital in this place?'

'Attached to the cell blocks. Bottom of the picture.'

Marco touched his finger to the photograph. A separate square building was joined to the cell blocks by a long connecting tunnel. The hospital. It sat on the opposite side of the horseshoe arrangement, away from the prison yard; he hadn't been able to see it earlier from his vantage point at the prison wall. He tapped it twice.

'I assume that's where Roger was conducting his work?'

Wu nodded again.

'Then if he's anywhere in this godforsaken place, he'll be right there,' Marco declared. 'You didn't need me to tell you that.'

Wu shrugged. 'I wanted to be sure we agree. The infirmary.'

'Roger worked around the clock when he was alive. That's where he would be now. And knowing Roger, we'll find his corpse organising the scalpels from small to large.'

'Getting to him will be difficult,' Wu warned. 'The only path to the infirmary is through the main block out front.'

'Through a thousand corpses, in other words.' Marco tossed his unfinished beef jerky over the edge of the platform. No more appetite.

He studied the photo. 'The exercise yard connects to the main block. We could take the truck and punch into the yard, then get our asses inside quick.' He sighed. 'Too bad Roger didn't like basketball. Would've been a lot easier if he were shooting hoops outside.'

His joke was lost on Wu. The sergeant eyed him blankly. 'Let's rest,' Wu said. 'We'll go at first light. Perhaps we can get past the crowd before they're fully alert.'

'Yeah, the best laid plans and all that. I wouldn't count on it.'

Now, lying on the floor, Marco's arm had lost sensation again. He wrapped the blanket more tightly around his shoulder and, settling back onto his crude pillow, stared out over the platform edge. Seen sideways, the world made even less sense. Across the prison grounds the cell blocks were black cut-outs in the night sky. All dark like pitch, except for the softest glow somewhere beyond the main building, a weak halo like a second moon hiding just out of sight – was dawn coming so soon? Christ, he hadn't slept.

His breath puffed cold and white, swirling like a dreamy fog before his eyes and then dissipating. And then again. He watched it come and go, a hypnotic cycle. As a kid he'd been fascinated by his breath on frigid days in Philly – not so much the wintry splendour of it, but the revelation that *this was happening all the time*, whether he could see it or not. Air that had been *inside his body* – touching his lungs! – was pouring out each time he flexed his diaphragm, and the low temperature was like a special lens, allowing him to view the invisible. Sometimes on a warm summer afternoon, he'd focus his eyes to the end of his nose and imagine the whorling blobs he knew were right there, his breath firing unseen into the world.

Before it enters us, air is only air, Danielle once told him, teaching him yoga on a Sunday morning in LA, their mats stretched out on the sunny floor. *But we change it to breath. Breath is life. It's you. Breathe out, and the universe absorbs you.*

I don't want to be absorbed, he'd protested.

She'd laughed, lovingly. *Too late, Henry. The universe has already claimed you.*

And now he was here, in this frozen dark corner of the universe, missing her like mad. He watched as his lungs emptied him across the prison grounds.

Breath is life, yeah? Well, I'm still alive.

For now.

His eyelids eased shut. Below him the floor seemed to soften, as if the wood were rotting under his weight, allowing him to sink into the planks.

Quietly, eerily, an image floated up from his subconscious.

The dead toddler in the car seat. It hovered in the black void, its throat savaged open, its windpipe flopped to its bloody chest like a detached hose. It reached its arms for him, same as it had on the highway when he'd driven past.

Just a little boy. A kid who didn't know enough to unstrap his seat belt, never mind comprehend the enormity of his death.

I should have returned you, Marco thought. *I'm sorry.*

The boy's face shifted. Morphed. A girl now.

And Marco's heart sparked and scorched like a burnt fuse, because somehow he knew that this girl was *Hannah* – Hannah, if she'd lived a few years more. A beautiful little girl with auburn hair and pixie magic in her eyes, just like Danielle.

Would it have been you? he asked. *You in that car?*

Hannah's corpse stared, her eyes like congealed milk. He saw that she was tucked into a cooling blanket, hooked to the Blanketrol machine they'd used at Cedars-Sinai. An endotracheal thermometer was lodged in her throat, and IV lines ran from her thin arms. On her ankle a blinking red light counted the oxygen concentration in her blood.

He almost cried out in horror, overwhelmed by the sight of her like this, again. His baby, struggling for life, stuck with tubes and cuffs and wires. He wanted to hold her, comfort her, promise her there was a reason for this miserable horrible world of shit . . .

He blinked. *I'm glad,* he said. *I'm glad you aren't here today.*

He stopped, shocked at his words. Then continued, tentatively.

I'm glad you were spared. Because this . . . this is worse than being dead.

And then his face crumpled, and he was awash in tears.

I love you . . .

The car seat floated closer, and Hannah reached her hand to him, and he took it. Her fingers were stiff and icy. She turned, and he understood. He was being escorted. Together they descended, down into a deep sleep, and she deposited him there . . .

And, exhausted, he slept, perhaps for the last time in his life – sequestered from the night chill and the cruel wood floor and the groans of the condemned, and thank god he didn't dream, and thank god he didn't have nightmares.

He slept.

The night passed.

At dawn he rocketed awake, thunderbolts in his blood—

Crack Crack Crack!

Beside him Wu was up, already scrambling. He kicked Marco hard.

'*Horsemen!*' Wu hollered, his voice a faint siren, nearly lost under deafening gunfire and the roar of oncoming quads, and vanished down the ladder.

10.5

The prison grounds were a mad circus – a thousand dead convicts in orange jumpsuits, red lips snarling, cheeks white and waxen like nightmarish clowns stumbling across the barren field. The air quaked, and three smoke-belching Horsemen quads screamed through the crowd, zigzagging, firing handguns as they veered – a death-defying act, part daredevil, part sharpshooter, dropping corpses to the left, right and ahead. A convict with a long wiry ponytail flipped like an acrobat as a bullet popped its rotten brain.

So, Wu thought, not surprised, *the Horsemen survived.*

Or some had, at least. Two standard Boar quads, and the double-manned quad with the gun turret. The giant commander Big Skull was alive – his body a brute muscle behind the Browning, his face a sneer as he rattled maniacal bursts of ammo into the field. Blood geysered from dead foreheads, bodies toppled. In the dirt the quads sawed brown circles as the wheels skidded, spun, reversed. Corpses surged from the cell blocks to replace the fallen – staggered through the torn fence, overwhelming the yard, the earthen battle-ground, the road between the buildings. More corpses than Wu had ever seen at once.

His fingertip touched the MTVR's starter switch.

And waited.

In his lifetime he had often stared across a battlefield, outnumbered. Never once had he hesitated to charge. Never had he doubted that he would win.

But this . . .

His heart panged with a sudden longing for his uncle Bao Zhi – an emotion he hadn't felt in many years, joined immediately by a memory of himself as an eight-year-old boy. Cross-legged on the floor in Qinghai, admiring the shoes Bao Zhi had cobbled for him. On each small shoe, a tiger had been stitched in orange thread to ward away evil spirits.

Bao Zhi had known how to outsmart the dead.

Bao Zhi's hand would not be trembling now . . .

Crack! A gunshot ripped Wu back to the present.

'*Hurry*,' he snarled up the tower ladder. What was *taking* the American?

The Horsemen zipped past the truck; they hadn't seen Wu in the driver's seat, but that would soon change.

He watched them go with a grim respect. These militiamen were resilient, and he . . . he had been far too optimistic. The highway corpse attack had only slowed the enemy down. They'd likely backtracked, sought out a longer route around the mountains. Yes, he'd suspected they would return – but the ambush now was unexpected, an aggressive strategy in the half-light before dawn. He imagined them walking their quads up the road last night, silent and careful, and camping outside the prison wall. Huddled in the cold, patient like rocks, counting the minutes until daybreak. Then they'd pounced. *Cat Catching Mice.*

With a scowl Wu mashed the starter switch. The truck cranked, a loud, obnoxious wheeze heard by a hundred corpses. The crowd broke, and a mammoth horde turned and teetered his way. He could feel their cold eyes brushing him; his skin prickled.

Fifty metres away on the nearest quad, the Horseman's helmeted head whipped towards the rumbling truck. Like a reflex, barely aiming, the driver flailed his arm backward and fired two bang-bang shots, wild and off-target. Beside the truck, a rung on the ladder sparked white with a metallic *ping*, and Wu heard the second bullet clang high off the tower siren.

A millisecond later, Marco's voice ricocheted down. '*Shit!*'

Wu popped the truck in gear just as the American came plummeting down the ladder, his toes stubbing the rungs, his gun holster looped on his elbow.

The single quad had pulled away from the other two. Dust mushroomed from its tyres as it chucked through a violent 180-degree turn.

Back towards Wu and Marco.

'Get in,' Wu snapped. He seized the steering wheel . . . *pain!*

. . . and released it with a shameful cry. His wounded shoulder had crusted over during the night, the skin red and infected around the crater of the wound, and now the pain was too livid to lift his arm. He grimaced and slid across the seat. As Marco flung open the passenger door, Wu caught the handle and yanked it shut.

'You drive,' he ordered through gritted teeth.

Marco sprinted to the driver's side. 'Thanks, Dad. Promise I'll be careful—'

A bullet whistled through the windshield, popped the seat between them.

'Oh shit,' Marco breathed. 'They're still just aiming at you, right?'

'Drive.'

The Horseman quad fired towards them like a missile, twenty metres away, ten, the driver's pistol held out like a lance, pointed at Wu's forehead . . .

'*Drive!*' Wu bellowed.

Marco gunned the gas, and with a vicious chawing of rubber on hard-packed earth the MTVR bounded ahead, bull-charging the quad. Wu threw his legs straight, braced for impact – but the driver spun left, avoiding collision by the length of an arm. The quad disappeared, reappeared immediately in the side-view mirror, chopping up dirt as the Horseman fought the steering for control. In seconds he'd recircled, now behind the truck.

'So much for tiptoeing inside,' Marco said, knuckles white on the wheel.

'What took you so long?' Wu demanded. 'In the tower?'

The American seemed embarrassed. 'Finding a gun.'

'*Look out!*' Wu cried.

They'd met head-on the first onslaught of corpses, the outer lip of a massive army. Stiff faces leered at Wu through the punctured windshield as Marco wrenched the wheel; the truck fishtailed, tilted on two left wheels, and as it tottered for a mortifying heartbeat, debating whether to tip or right itself, Wu glimpsed individuals in the crowd.

A sad-looking male with bent spectacles but empty purple eye sockets . . .

A skeletal black corpse with dreadlocks, its bony wrists handcuffed together . . .

A pockmarked face with a swastika tattooed on its shaved scalp . . .

. . . and then the truck slammed on all four tyres to the earth, and Marco cried out a curse, breaking Wu's focus.

The truck swerved east, skirting the dead, but the mob was shifting fast, spreading outward and outward in a widening circle. Behind Marco, the Horseman quad had gained ground, just metres back – and worse, up ahead, the other two quads had joined the assault; they'd skidded and turned, and were now hurtling across the field on a sharp diagonal to intercept the truck, Big Skull hungering forward in his gun turret, hellbent . . .

The wheel jerked in Marco's hands and the truck veered left, mowing a path through dead men; the side mirror brained nine or ten heads in a rapid burst.

Pa-tunk-tunk-tunk-tunk-tunk-tunk.

'Where are you going?' Wu demanded.

Marco answered with a harder punch of gas, and the engine's roar amplified.

Whump. The sound of a bullet punching the back of the truck. Wu scoured the side-view mirror. The Horseman was right there. 'Coming up the side!'

Wu faced forward again – and sucked in his breath. The two other quads sliced across the truck's path directly ahead; Big Skull howled as the Browning sparked in his grip, and a barrage of bullets puckered the hood, then bounced high and obliterated the windshield. Marco and Wu ducked. Glass rained like sharp confetti across their necks, the blasts rocking their eardrums.

'*Fuck!*' Marco cried and dragged the steering wheel, and the MTVR pitched hard right, whipping Wu sideways in his seat . . .

. . . and he heard a hollow metallic crunch, mashed with the needling scream of an engine rotor under his window . . .

. . . and he saw the third quad, caught under the truck, its front corner wedged behind the wheel well, the rubber tyres churning and smoking, black fumes pumping through the orbital sockets of the horse's skull strapped to the hood; the truck had sideswiped the Horseman, and Wu saw surprised eyes behind the driver's goggles as Marco stomped the brake. Beneath a shower of dirt, the conjoined vehicles pirouetted like dance partners; the truck spun halfway round, facing backwards now, and slammed sideways – the side dragging the quad – into the horde of rioting corpses. The man screamed, the dead swarmed.

Fifty clawlike hands clamped on the Horseman, wrestled him kicking from his seat. In the mirror Wu saw a hairy plump corpse bite down on the soldier's cheek, and then the man was gone, buried under a chaos of flailing bodies and greedy grunts.

Marco and Wu goggled at one another, momentarily stunned.

Wu spoke first. 'Smart manoeuvre, Doctor.'

'Thanks,' Marco gasped. 'It was kind of an accident.'

And then more corpses began to scale the quad, hoisting themselves up. A bloody hand slapped Wu's window, deposited a palm-print with no thumb.

'Better go,' Wu urged.

'Going!' Marco floored the gas, and the truck lumbered a slow ten metres, burdened by the bodies pressed against it and the quad mashed underneath; and then suddenly the scraping wheel well went silent, and the truck skipped ahead, lighter.

Wu turned. The corpses had wrung the quad free from the truck. They'd flipped it and were biting ridiculously at the smoking tyres, the scalding belly. Indifferent to the skin that peeled from their hungry mouths and stuck to the hot metal.

'What a pit crew,' said Marco as the truck sped off.

'Where are the others? The quads and Big Skull?'

Marco squinted into his mirror. 'Hmm. Don't see'em.'

'They must have gone that way, around the buildings. To the cell blocks.'

'Guess they don't have your satellite photo – that's the long way.' He swept his eyes ahead, found what he wanted. '*There*. The service road.'

The truck squeezed a tight turn and bounced onto the single-lane asphalt. Corpses swamped the path; Marco banged ahead – *ka-thump, ka-thump* – racking up hits, spattering the hood with black blood. A dead male in a shirt and tie, probably a prison administrator, bounced hard off the metal bull bar on the front grille. Yellow-gold sparks showered upwards like popcorn popping, coupled with the sound of scraping metal.

'Bumper's loose,' Wu warned. 'You don't have to hit every corpse, Doctor. We need the truck to last until we get there.'

'Right. If you see a road *without* a thousand dead speed bumps, let me know.'

Ka-thump!

The truck raced between the two nearest buildings, monstrous brick blocks with the sullen mood of abandoned factories. *Vocational Industries*, a white sign flashed. In the wide alley lay an overturned dumpster and something that looked like a ribcage attached to a spine.

Marco didn't slow, swerving instead around the dumpster, and seconds later the service road broke again into the open.

Straight ahead were the cell blocks.

The truck aimed into the cup of the horseshoe, the prison yard. Wu's bruised eyes flicked wide. *Impossible*, he thought. The yard teemed with the dead – packed tight with brawling, hungry, rotten bodies, a solid mass pressed up against the chain-link fence; one by one, corpses squeezed through the shoulder-wide gap in the fence, while the rest raged in captivity, shaking the metal with a horrific rattle that Wu could hear even above the truck's howl. Beyond the dead at the yard's inner end, the doors to the prison were tantalisingly open, a lightless void where the American mission had blasted its way inside.

Too many corpses, he judged. *Too many to get through.*

A hundred metres distant, where the road forked away to the north grounds, the black shape of Big Skull's double-quad rumbled into view, trailed by the single Boar.

'See?' Marco said. 'Ours was a shortcut.'

'Hurry,' Wu said, 'They're fast.'

'Don't worry, we've got this.'

'How? The yard is suicide. We need another way.'

He'd no sooner spoken than the MTVR accelerated and, as the speedometer inched past thirty, past forty, past fifty, Wu's heart kept frantic pace. He glanced at the American – the malnourished figure hunched over the wheel, his forehead furrowed and slashed, his skin slathered with every kind of filth, blood, sweat – and in that moment Wu judged that Henry Marco was the most relentless man he'd ever known.

'What are you doing?' Wu asked, quiet but stern.

Marco ignored him.

'*Doctor.*'

'Breaking into prison. What else?'

The yard rushed towards them at blistering speed . . .

. . . and gunfire erupted again as the Horsemen and Big Skull charged from the north, and Marco's unyielding foot pinned the accelerator to the floor, and the dead convicts behind the chain-link snapped their jaws, urging the truck forward, and Wu thought *No!* . . .

. . . and then every last thought in his head smashed to pieces as the truck slammed the fence at sixty miles per hour.

DEATH SENTENCES

11.1

Marco yowled upon impact, his mind vivid with imagined horrors . . .

. . . the truck somersaulting end-over-end in his thoughts, a green metal blur that broke apart on the asphalt, corpses peeling his pink wet meat from the wreck . . .

. . . but instead, thank Jesus God, that didn't happen, and the fence imploded, the two-ton truck trumping the weight of the corpses piled against it; the scream choked off in Marco's trachea as the chain-link crumpled around the truck's grille, and, as easily as snapping a twig, an entire thirty-foot section of fence ripped free from the posts, carried forward by the speeding MTVR. The prison yard rang with a metal hiss and the din of a hundred balloons bursting – damp, fermented air blasting from the convicts' dead lungs as the truck levelled them.

With the chain-link section pinned to the hood, the truck barrelled into the yard like a bizarre bulldozer, ploughing corpses into its elongated shovel; those who hit first clung to the fence, their gnarled fingers wrapped in the chain link. Briefly Marco locked eyes with a hardened male, a knife scar like a lightning bolt struck upon its ashen cheek; dozens more corpses piled behind it, amassing four or five deep as the truck raked a crazy, violent, high-speed path, knocking aside a weight rack, tossing dumbbells, skipping across the white stripes of a basketball court on a collision course with the brick wall ahead . . .

Marco screamed again.

The dead took the brunt of the crash, a fifty-corpse buffer between the wall and the truck; Marco cringed at the collective *CRACK!* of a thousand pulverised bones as heads popped from bodies like champagne corks. A hailstorm of rubbery corpse flesh plopped onto the truck hood, small diamond shapes chopped by the chain-link holes into bits like greasy cookie dough. The knife-scarred male's lips thrust open on impact; its stomach squirted from its mouth and dangled like an obscene giant purple tongue, dripping slime.

The steering wheel punched hard into Marco's sternum, slugging his breath away. His head swooned as the truck settled to a stop; his mouth opened and closed, gasping for air that wouldn't come. Five seconds passed until he'd gathered himself to speak.

'Holy . . . *shit!*' he spat.

Wu's face was a rictus of pain, his hand clamped over his shoulder. Fresh red blood trickled between his fingers. 'That – was foolish . . .'

'Yeah, my bad,' Marco cut him short. 'C'mon, we gotta go.'

Behind the chain-link a dozen surviving corpses wriggled, pinned harmlessly against the brick – but in the mirror Marco saw another orange-suited swarm staggering towards the truck; the dead rioters were returning for an easy meal here in the yard.

He scrambled from the truck. The dead were fifty feet away. No sign of the Horsemen yet, but the noise of their quads grew louder by the second.

And the fence was torn wide open, like a red-carpet welcome.

Dammit.

'That way,' Marco pointed as Wu joined him at the back of the truck. The prison entrance was ten feet ahead, a scorched rectangle where the doors had been blasted off by the RRU. He hadn't taken a step when a thunder-blast crashed down on the yard, and brick fragments exploded from the wall, peppering him like painful little bites.

'*Christ!*' he yelled, shielding his head with his arms.

At the open end of the yard, the Horseman quad had dragged to a stop. From atop the gun turret, Big Skull scowled across the sea of corpses.

'*Hit them!*' he boomed, his voice deep and savage, so feral a cry that Marco barely discerned words. '*Clear it out!*' On command, a second monsoon of bullets blazed from the Browning. Corpses burst apart, strips of orange fabric fluttered in the air.

Wu blew past Marco. '*Inside!*'

Maddened, Marco broke for the doorway at full sprint, sensing the Browning locked on his mad running legs, the steel rounds aimed to snap him apart at his knees . . .

Into the blackness he leaped, sprawling as his foot caught the top step. Bullets whistled overhead. He bounced up and ran through the intense dark. Wu's footsteps pounded ahead. *This is crazy*, Marco thought. *Reckless. Anything could be waiting in here*. Blindly he lumbered down a hallway that turned twice, arriving at a security checkpoint, a barred door – open, thank god.

He burst through and felt the space around him widen.

The central cell block. Early sunlight had just begun to penetrate the gloom, and Marco strained to see, suspicious of every shadow within the vast interior. His eyes darted to all corners, wondering from where the first corpse would charge. The dimensions were huge – an endless warehouse of cells spanning hundreds of feet before disappearing into a dark vacuum where the light finally failed. Echoes sounded from those far depths, casting back the clump of his boots on the hard tile. He stopped alongside Wu, and the two men hovered at the threshold, taking stock.

'See anything?' he asked Wu.

'As much as you.'

Outside, the muffled sound of gunfire slowed, then quit.

'Maybe the corpses ate them,' Marco suggested.

'Doubtful. More likely the Horsemen emptied the yard. They'll be coming now.'

'So which way for us?' Marco squinted, performing a fast survey of the block. Watery light filtered through steel-barred windows set high overhead. Dust drifted in the beams, and somewhere he heard wings flutter, birds roosting in the criss-cross of steel girders above. The air had a queasy stink like fertiliser – pungent, the smell of puke and manure combined. He saw no cells on the ground floor, but upward to his left and right were three floors of cells accessible by narrow walkways around the mezzanine. Here and there a skeletonised arm draped through a balcony railing. Loose bones riddled with bite marks littered the tile ahead. Ten feet from Marco were the discarded remains of a prison guard – table scraps from a feeding frenzy. The poor bastard's torso had been twisted from his legs; his spine extended a full twelve inches from where his upper body ended, so that he looked like a gruesome human lollipop.

Marco remembered the video Osbourne had shown. Was this the same mezzanine? The same guard he'd seen devoured on film? Maybe, maybe not; each block was probably a carbon copy of the next. But if so, then Roger would have vaulted – Marco scanned the walkways – over *that* railing, and landed right . . . about . . . *there.*

He dropped his gaze to the floor, almost wishing Roger had just broken his neck from the fall. An easier death. No escape to the lab, no secret email, no need for this bullshit.

The sudden loud growl of a quad engine snapped him back to reality.

'They're inside,' Wu said. His voice echoed deep in the mezzanine . . . and as it returned, it brought back another sound.

Moans.

And then the slow shuffle of feet.

Sweat rolled down Marco's cheek in a cold bead. At the distant end the shadows shifted, and, as he watched in horror, the darkness materialised into arms and legs and phantom white faces – emerging in droves from the black regions of the prison, like some monstrous army on a night march. Hundreds that Marco could see.

And hundreds more that he couldn't.

'Shit, Wu. You just rang the dinner bell.' Behind him, he heard the quad gnashing through the entry hallway. 'Come on, next floor for us!'

He busted past Wu to a bending metal staircase on the right and charged to the first walkway, half-formed thoughts bouncing in his brain with each step . . .

Horsemen can't drive up, stairs too narrow

Corpses in the cells, watch out

Oh god

. . . and, as he ran, he planned. In the satellite photo, the infirmary had been on the opposite side of this block. So . . . the upper walkway would lead there, or near to it, taking them to the proper turn-off. He was sure of that. Well, sort of sure.

Okay, maybe not that sure.

At the top of the stairs he paused to pull his handgun. He checked the clip. Full, fifteen rounds. Back in the guard tower he'd snatched the first weapon handy – couldn't find the damn shotgun – and shoved it in his holster as Horseman bullets bombarded the platform. Looking more closely now, he recognised it as an M9, a semi-automatic handgun he'd often scavenged from dead soldier carcasses. But this one was different. A thin rod was mounted on the trigger guard, just under the barrel. A switch protruded from the side.

He flicked it.

A red pinprick of light danced on the concrete floor several feet away. He swung the pistol, and the light followed – now a bright dot on the wall adjacent to the walkway, now on the mezzanine tiles below, leaping wherever he aimed.

A laser sight.

'Sweet,' he said at the exact moment the two Horsemen quads erupted into the mezzanine below. The soldiers jetted beneath the grated walkway, not yet perceiving the corpses waiting in the dark. Reflexively Marco planted the red dot on the lead driver's helmet. It was the Horseman in the leather motorcycle jacket; Marco's finger tensed on the trigger as he swivelled to follow the moving target. He licked his dry lips.

Do it, he urged, *don't think* . . .

He didn't get the chance.

From behind his right shoulder flashed an object, circular and metal, a spinning projectile like a flying saucer. A curved blade – Wu's round knife. It sailed in a taut line to the single quad and buried into the driver's neck with a meaty *thwack*. Both Marco and the soldier gasped in unison. With a clipped cry the Horseman toppled from his vehicle, arms flailing, and slid on his back at full momentum across the tiles, straight to the feet of the dead convicts.

The mob sucked him in like a vast mouth and, once inside, the meat-eating teeth went to work, chewing and skinning him alive.

The mayhem continued even as the man's death-screams multiplied a hundred times in echoes. The driverless quad veered left and then right and then overturned, almost knocking out the second quad carrying Big Skull; at the last moment, the second driver swerved and braked, stopping twenty feet short of the corpses themselves. Roaring, Big Skull aimed the Browning into the crowd, then decided better; instead he stirred a circle in the air with his finger, and the Horseman driver reversed the quad, gassing away just as the corpses charged.

They passed once more below the walkway, retreating; Big Skull glared up at Marco. The commander's eyes burned bright even through the shadows – a hateful gaze promising pain and suffering – and then the surviving quad roared up the side corridor.

Gone, leaving a *fuck-you* of smoke and bad-smelling diesel exhaust.

'The block is a continuous loop,' Wu noted, coming up beside Marco. 'They'll try a counter-clockwise path. Hoping for fewer corpses.'

Marco exhaled. 'Nice throw. Sorry you lost your cool knife.'

'That's why I always bring two.' Wu waggled his remaining blade in the air, then jogged ahead down the grated walk. The cells were ominous square caves, the doors all locked in the open position. 'Keep moving. It's a clear lane—'

Without warning, two arms knifed through the bars beside Wu. From inside the cell, a dead prisoner snared Wu by the shirt and reeled him, struggling and kicking, against the cage.

Aw, crap . . .

Startled, Marco dashed to the cell. The corpse hissed at him through the bars, a skinny male, naked with purple lesions across its scalp and a single yellowed rib stabbing out its belly like an elephant tusk. It gripped Wu in a desperate chokehold, its forehead dug against the bars, teeth snapping but unable to reach Wu and bite.

Marco centred the M9's red dot between the bloodshot eyeballs and fired.

The gun bucked, not too hard – not as much punch as his Glock – and a hole opened in the dead man's skull. Brains ejected from the back. Its eyes crossed, and it sagged, arms still draped around Wu, before releasing and flopping to the cell floor.

Wu straightened his shirt. His breath exited hard, antagonised. 'Careful with your new toy, Doctor. You could have shot me . . .'

He stiffened as the red dot swept past his chest. '*Doctor!*'

'Sorry,' Marco said, aiming down the walkway. 'Look.'

The row of cells had awoken – a shitload of corpses creeping from the doorways. The ghoulish criminals packed the walk, twenty, thirty dead men shuffling towards him single-file. Marco set the laser on a corpse in front, an Asian male with both ears missing.

Then it got worse – strangled moans sounding up the stairs.

The dead were ascending from the first floor.

Not so bad, right? Marco thought, the sarcasm bitter-tasting. The pistol palpitated in his grip. *Hundreds of corpses, closing in from both ends. Like a trash compactor with teeth.*

And fourteen bullets in the M9.

'Maybe,' he said to Wu, 'we should've hitched a ride with the bad guys.'

II.2

With lacklustre hope, Marco considered the balcony rail. *Could jump like Roger*, he thought. Then frowned. *And land on a hundred corpses below.*

Yeah. Next idea. Quick . . .

On the walkway the dead had advanced, just five cells

ahead. A grim line slithering at him like a snake with multiple faces, shrivelled, scaly, inhuman.

To his left was the gloomy cell, a shadowy box with two rumpled beds and a metal toilet. No sanctuary there – just a sure spot to get trapped and die.

Except . . .

The beds.

Now we're talking. Encouraged, he planted the red laser sight on the lead corpse and punched its face in with a bullet. Slop spurted sideways through the holes where its ears were missing, a nearly comical effect; without waiting for it to fall, Marco pinched the trigger again, bagging the next corpse in line, too. He kept firing. The red dot made it easy, inappropriately fun, like a carnival game – bam, bam, bam, until he'd splashed the walkway with another six kills. *Enough*, he thought and forced himself to stop.

That'll buy a few more seconds.

'C'mon!' he hollered to Wu and ducked into the cell. The stench inside ambushed him, like spoiled meat marinating in piss, and sure enough he noted the toilet overflowing with a sloppy red chum, and he gagged, eyes flooding hot.

'You ever . . .' He coughed and had to stop and spit. Working fast, he threw back a ratty blanket on the bed and almost puked again; the mattress was a thick squirming mound of cockroaches, shells shiny and wet as they wriggled. Repulsed, he grabbed the mattress by its stitched edges. 'Ever play football?' he asked Wu.

From the cell door, Wu watched him as if he were mad. 'Doctor—'

'Me neither,' Marco said, and yanked the mattress from the rusted bedsprings.

Roaches pelted his face, hit the concrete floor, scuttled under the bed frame. In his fingers the fabric was damp, soaked with roach shit – padded thin, not much wider than a bedroll, but it would work. 'I wasn't tough enough,' he squawked, battling another wave of sickness. 'Tried when I was ten, lasted only two practices. Cried at both.'

He thrust the mattress at Wu. Surprised, Wu accepted it in his hands. Marco wheeled back to the next bed, seized the second mattress for himself. Outside on the walkway, the corpses had tottered into view, nearing the door.

'Time for blocking drills,' Marco announced.

He flashed Wu an uncertain smile – and then, before he could begin to question his own sanity, shoved past the sergeant and out the cell.

On the walkway he carried the mattress before him like a full-body shield. To his right the corpses from the staircase had reached the top. With a silly high-pitched whoop, as if he really were a ten-year-old boy again, he charged left instead, towards the walkway convicts, his shoulder squared against the mattress. Four steps, five, and *fwump*, his lungs expelled air like paper bags popping as he rammed the first corpse – never seeing the dead man, registering only the smack of a body against the other side of the mattress. Pain drove deep into his shoulder.

Shit. That hurt.

He rumbled forward, remembering why he'd quit football – *just don't cry, okay?* – but the game plan worked. The corpse sprawled backwards, a sunken-chested male, and Marco steamrolled over it, high-stepping – another football drill he'd sucked at – to avoid the hands swiping crazily at his ankles. He'd barely recovered from the first hit when the second came, the next corpse in line, this time a glancing blow that spun the corpse into the walkway rail. As Marco passed, the rotting convict lunged at his unprotected neck . . .

. . . just as Wu blasted forward with his mattress and knocked the corpse on its ass.

Marco arched an eyebrow. 'Good hit. You just made varsity.'

The bedding wobbled in his grip as a corpse struck the other side; he heard a hiss of fabric ripping and realised the dead man had bitten the mattress.

He tightened his hold. *Don't drop it, or you're fucked.*

'*Go!*' he shouted.

He stormed forward, his weight centred low, pumping his legs as if he were pushing a car, and – *fwump* – bulldozed through the mattress-eating corpse, and then – *fwump* – the next corpse, and then the next, and the next, as dead convicts bounced and banged off the rail, unable to get at the tasty meat behind the padded shield. Following behind him, Wu dealt the finishing blows, bowling the dazed corpses flat. Marco hurdled over a wild tangle of dead arms and legs.

'Almost there,' he panted, half to Wu, half to himself.

Five cells to go, and the walkway would end. They could take the stairs down.

Three cells . . . two . . .

He pancaked the final corpse, a victory cry in his throat . . .

. . . his celebration fizzling as from the final cell lumbered the biggest goddamn corpse he'd ever seen. Four hundred pounds, wide as the goddamn walkway. Its head was a mountain of rolled fat, its chin covered with a thick, blood-dripping beard.

That's not a beard, Marco realised, recoiling with disgust even as he charged madly ahead. A dead rat hung from the mouth, gripped between the corpse's teeth . . .

He barrelled into the giant. For an agonising instant his ribcage compacted like a fist, painfully tight around his lungs, and the mattress springs coiled under him – Wu barrelled against his back, and he was pinned for half a moment between the two mattresses like an absurd sandwich, ready for eating – and then the fat corpse wobbled and toppled under him. Marco and Wu rolled across the blubbery mound, falling with it, tumbling to the free side of the walkway. The men hit the grating hard and came to a stop, sprawled atop their mattresses, gasping on the floor beside the obese male. It struggled to rise, the dead rat flopping on its chin.

Behind it, in the direction they'd just run, the walkway was choked full again as the corpses from the stairwell proceeded endlessly upward from the shadows.

Wu scrambled to his feet, gripping his shoulder. 'Now what, Coach?'

'Find the stairs down,' Marco said. 'C'mon, this way.'

They left the mattresses and ran, heading away from the dead. The walkway stretched another hundred feet, all clear; the cells had emptied, and the men reached the opposite end within seconds. The top of the next staircase beckoned downward.

'See?' Marco panted. 'Easy.'

On the walkway, the corpses advanced, but he and Wu now had a clear escape route. They skipped down the stairs, well ahead of the crowd, and emerged on the ground floor at the far end of the cell block. The mezzanine was quiet. The original multitude of hungry convicts had exited, stalking the Horseman quad down the distant halls. The path here was safe. For now.

Wasting no time, the men trotted down the empty corridor. From behind, Marco heard the dead grumbling down the staircase in slow pursuit. *Stay quick,* he thought. *They won't catch up. Just don't attract others.* Despite his caution, his boots tramped conspicuously on the tiles, and Wu's laboured breathing added an unwelcome backbeat.

Around the corner they discovered a trail of long-dried blood and smeared brown entrails. It led them fifty yards down the hall, then ended in a shredded guard's uniform.

No body in the clothes, not even bones.

Somehow that was even creepier.

Finally, beyond that, a dark corridor broke away from the main block and ventured right. A metal plate screwed to the wall read:

← BLOCK A
← BLOCK B
INFIRMARY BLOCK →

Pointing down the perpendicular hall.

'We're here?' Marco said. He heard the doubt in his voice. As if he'd meant to say, *Is it too late to go back?*

Just then he frowned, conscious of a familiar sound penetrating his thoughts. Growing louder. An engine . . .

'They found us,' he said simply.

Screeching like a speared pig, the Horseman quad skidded around the corner at the distant end of Cell Block B. It swerved, nearly sideswiping the wall, then immediately corrected itself and peeled towards Marco and Wu with a belch of charcoal smoke.

Big Skull's chiselled face leered from the turret. *He sees me,* Marco thought.

'Run,' Wu urged, then fled into the corridor.

As Marco followed, he glimpsed the dead army flooding the cell block, hot behind the quad. One huge party – on its way to the infirmary.

He sprinted, scared as shit, down the connecting corridor. The passage was a long straight hall tethering the cell blocks to the medical ward – a windowless, unlit hall, and he felt like a mouse being swallowed down the throat of a black serpent. Wu's shadow flitted ten feet in front, and Marco chased after it, off balance and bumbling, praying he wouldn't bump into some dead thing hiding in the dark.

And then he saw something worse.

Oh shit.

His sweat turned to ice water on his skin.

Oh shit shit shit shit.

Steel bars blocked the corridor – a security checkpoint, the cage door shut. Wu lunged to the door first, grabbed hold and grappled the thick bars.

Then dropped his arms and cried out in frustration.

Locked.

Marco's face drained. Slowly he turned and gazed back up the one-way corridor. A hundred yards out, the Horseman quad had turned down the entrance, rumbling through the dark, an ominous silhouette growing larger by the moment. And behind it . . .

. . . the dead followed.

Resurrected convicts jammed the lone exit, the only escape. An impenetrable mass of putrid, pus-smelling, blood-starved cadavers staggered down the corridor behind the quad, as if the Horsemen were leading a Halloween parade. Marco almost laughed – then almost vomited. Big Skull had just committed suicide but didn't realise it yet.

And he's taking us with him.

Marco sagged against the unbreakable door; the cold bars dug into his spine.

Dead end.

11.3

Pointless, was all Marco could think. Pointless, to survive all the bullshit – the past three days, the past four years – to travel so far, and fight so hard, and then die here in a rank corridor in a prison four hundred miles from home, having accomplished absolutely fucking nothing. No Roger. No Danielle. Shit, he might as well've been torn apart on Day

One of the Resurrection and spared himself the trouble. Because *of course* this was going to end badly; he'd known so from the start. Jesus Christ, how had he ever convinced himself otherwise?

Images flashed across synapses in his panicked head. Himself in his attic in Arizona, the week of the Evacuation. Hiding from Evac Squads that combed his neighbourhood, his ears squished under his palms to repel their urgent pounding on the front door. He'd huddled in the dark, alone, waxed with sweat and dried blood and fear. He would find Danielle, he told himself. He would stay and find her. Somewhere outside on the street, a man screamed, long and excruciating. He pressed his palms harder to his ears until his lobes hurt. Behind his skin he heard his terrified heartbeat, like a separate voice arguing. *But you're no hero, Henry . . .*

Shut up, he'd battled back. *I'll find her. Shut up!*

Now, here in the prison, seconds from his death, he felt his mind drifting, his consciousness detaching from his physical brain and his skull and his bones and his muscle, already departing towards the godless nothing he knew waited for him on the other side of life – abandoning his body so that he wouldn't be aware of the pain, the teeth in his skin, the sizzle of death-ridden air on his hot organs as the corpses dissected him like a rat . . .

Or, if he was lucky, Big Skull would shoot him dead first.

Pointless.

The Horseman quad had travelled half the corridor, accelerating. Big Skull had seen the barred door. The commander swore an unrecognisable curse and slammed his fist on the turret siding. Behind him the onslaught of corpses hungered forward and forward . . .

Next to Marco, Wu squared his feet and extended his knife towards the enemy. His face was grim, his skin clammy. 'I think,' he said without emotion, 'this will end soon.'

Marco flexed his hand on the textured M9 grip. Couldn't remember how many rounds he had left. Five, six? Didn't matter. Wasn't enough. Not nearly enough.

He shut his eyes and vowed not to open them again. No matter what.

He didn't need to witness his own disembowelment.

But just then a raucous buzzing startled him, ugly and loud.

ZRRRRRRRRRRRR.

His eyes snapped open. In the ceiling above, a red domed light had flickered on, and . . .

It can't be

. . . under his spine he felt the door budge an inch.

'Holy shit . . .' he breathed.

'It's open,' Wu confirmed, his face reflecting red from the bulb. Sweat beads glowed on his forehead like dollops of molten lead.

Marco didn't hesitate, didn't question, didn't care. He pounced at the bars and heaved, and with the security buzzer still cawing harshly overhead, a sound more glorious than any church hymn he'd ever heard, the door shuddered open sideways. A two-foot passage to salvation. He chucked himself through, Wu tumbling right behind.

Once through to the other side, Wu snorted a breathless '*Shut it!*' and flung his weight at the door with his good arm. Out in the corridor the Horseman quad had arrived. The vehicle swerved to a rude stop ten feet away as Big Skull bellowed, and he and his driver dismounted, charging furiously on foot, desperate to reach the half-open door . . .

. . . as Marco seized the bars in his torn hands, added his muscle to Wu's, and dragged. With a rusted groan the door herked and jerked on its rollers and then banged back into the iron frame, just as Big Skull grabbed hold with thick hairy fingers . . .

. . . and the buzzer silenced, and the red dome cut its light. The door tumblers fell with a decisive *KA-CHUNK*, and the bolts fastened, and the door was sealed again.

Dizzied, huffing, Marco gawked through the bars. Big Skull glared back at him, less than a foot away, yet infinitely separated by this decision of fate – one man condemned, one man reprieved. Up close the commander's eyes seethed like hot tar, black and scalding; his scabbed lips twisted in a hateful sneer. He was ready for his punishment.

The Horseman driver wasn't as resolute. He screamed in terror and flailed at the bars, but the door was set solid. He was young, big-eared with soft pimpled cheeks and wispy facial hair, wearing drab olive fatigues that hung too loosely on his slight chest. He was just a teenager, somebody's kid who would never reach twenty; his eyes whitened with this crazed realisation, and he pulled his handgun, contemplated it for an instant, waffling, wondering how best to use it – shoot the corpses, or Marco, or himself? And then he gasped and whirled and broke back towards the quad, seeking the firepower of the Browning, but too late . . .

Pointless

. . . the corpses crashed atop him, tackled him full force against the bars, gnashing and chewing, and he screeched, a hundred decibels of agony spiking Marco's eardrums like bloody nails, and Marco faltered away, four, five, ten steps in horror as the dead convicts shredded the youth. A wart-faced corpse chomped onto the soldier's big ear and ripped it free; the ear crunched between the cadaver's teeth like a gory Dorito, trailing tendrils of cartilage and meat, and the boy gurgled as he vomited yellow-brown bile and blood . . .

. . . and beside the dying teen was Big Skull, pinned to the bars by the horde, his arms spread wide to his left and right as if he were being crucified. The dead mouths cut into his shoulders, his biceps, his forearms, his fingers, and still his eyes drilled into Marco, defiant, refusing to cry out; the man's entire body spasmed as though an electric current ran through him, and on his bare temples veins raged like crooked lightning bolts, and his teeth bit hard on his lip, spurting blood, severing the bottom lip clean off. He spit it through the bars at Marco.

And then the dead finished him.

Shrivelled hands dug into the bony ridges on the commander's head – above his ears, under his brow, gouging his orbital sockets – and with a slow, awful, moist, sucking *craa-aaa-ck*, the big skull broke apart. The corpses dismantled the bone, peeling fragments loose like shelling a hard-boiled egg, and the brain opened, and Marco gagged as the man's face turned inside out – a red wet blob with impossibly round white eyeballs.

For a final second, the eyeballs still watched him, hated him. And then the two globes rolled back in the bloody slop that had been the man's face, and the electricity in the dancing limbs shut down. Big Skull went still. His blood puddled on the floor and seeped under the door, slinking towards Marco and Wu as the corpses devoured their kill.

Countless other dead felons battered the door, their discoloured arms reaching through the bars, swiping at the air. Begging for meat.

Marco jumped when Wu nudged his elbow.

'We'd better move,' Wu said. 'In case that door buzzes open again.'

'But . . . how?'

'I don't know, Doctor. Let's go.'

'This side has power.' Marco frowned, remembering what he'd observed the night before, gazing across the prison grounds. 'Last night. I saw it glowing.'

He turned to find Wu already hustling down the corridor. He followed gladly, eager to escape the nauseating stew of sound here at the barred door – the slurping mouths, the squishing flesh. Crisp snaps like tart juicy apples. High-pitched cries as corpses fought over gruesome handfuls. And worst of all, a deep contented murmur – *mmmph, mmmph* – the sound of diners enjoying their food. Delicious, wonderful food.

That's all we are to them, Marco thought. *Food. Not human.*

Overcome with horror, he fled.

11.4

Fifty feet he ran, to where the hall opened into a small ante-chamber – what looked like a reception area of sorts. The interior was brighter here; the breakfast-hour sun had climbed above a skylight in the vaulted ceiling and sliced open a white rectangle on the otherwise dark floor. A chest-high counter extended to Marco's right, breaking the room in two; the surface was bare but splotched with crimson handprints.

Wu leaned over the counter and tensed. Then relaxed.

On the floor, the headless carcass of a guard sprawled next to a toppled swivel chair. Spent shotgun shells dotted the tiles. No sign of the shotgun.

'Well, we know *he* didn't buzz us in,' Marco said.

A low hum called his attention to a shelf behind the counter. Poking his head over, he saw a bank of security monitors, streaming multiple videos like a miniature film festival. Black and white and fuzzy, eight of them. He recognised the yard from two angles – the abandoned military truck butting the brick wall on one screen, and corpses meandering through the torn fence on the second. Next to that was the ground floor of Cell Block B, now empty and eerie, and the upper balcony strewn with corpses Marco had dropped with the M9; and there was the obese corpse, still helpless on its back, its short fat limbs paddling the air.

On the nearest monitor he saw the locked security checkpoint. The corpses hadn't subsided. They continued their assault on the door with malevolent gusto; dead faces leered through the bars, their rag-tag bodies packed so tight that they seemed more like a solid mass than individuals. One demon-beast with a thousand heads.

Marco turned to Wu. 'We put on a good show for the camera. Action-packed.'

'One's missing.'

'What?'

'A monitor,' Wu noted. 'Look.'

He was right. The bottom row of monitors included an empty slot and a hole in the countertop where wire had once been fed.

'Interesting,' Marco agreed. 'Somebody borrowed it.'

In the corner ceiling, a mounted security camera studied his reaction with a silent black eye. A tiny red light blinked on the side. Behind that lens were tentacles of wire, Marco imagined, spooling away through the mouldering walls, deeper and deeper into the infirmary – a mechanical gatekeeper presenting two new arrivals to the secret host.

Suddenly self-conscious, Marco slit his eyes tighter, as if with proper focus he could see backwards through the lens. His pulse bobbed in time to the blinking red bulb.

'We're here,' he muttered. 'We're coming up.'

At the end of the reception area another barred door stood open, beckoning them into a smooth and featureless hallway with jarring acoustics; Marco cleared his throat, and the hall thundered. The air was rank. Jutted against the right wall was an empty hospital gurney, the padding soiled with a disturbing stain that could have been blood or bacteria-coloured shit. As the men neared, a rat burst from under the gurney wheels, squealing, and scampered a zigzag course to the far end of the hall. It disappeared around the corner with a flick of the tail like a raised middle finger, as if the rat were telling them, *Fuck you*.

The men followed. The hall concluded at an intersection forking left and right. Marco swept both directions with the M9. Quiet, not even the rat. Only rows of . . . *cells*, he realised, but different from those in the blocks. These cells weren't like cages – these had metal doors, with small portholes at eye level for observing imprisoned patients.

The doors were all shut and, Marco sincerely hoped, locked.

'Which way?' Wu wondered.

Marco shrugged. 'The rat went left. Mean anything?'

Wu shot him a look. 'My uncle would have said that rats are good luck.'

'Gamble our lives on Chinese superstition? Hell, why not. Left it is.'

They steered into the musty corridor. The space was silent, the overhead lights off. *Conserving juice*, Marco guessed. A bad intuition had begun coagulating in his gut; he felt it pressing against his lungs as he breathed. Cautiously he peered into the observation hole on the first door. Dark, but his eyes sorted through the shadows. Empty. No prisoner. Just a rumpled, half-reclined hospital bed and a forlorn IV stand positioned in the corner like a coat rack. On the floor an upturned metal food tray. He tried the door.

Locked.

The next two cells were likewise uninhabited but, as Marco crossed the third, the atmosphere corrupted, now pure evil and black; he recognised the mind-bending stench of gangrene, a god-awful horror he would never forget from his tenure at Cedars-Sinai. Like having hot egg-beaters shoved up your nose, scrambling your fucking brain. *Christ*, he thought, sputtering. The air clung to his skin. He cupped a hand over his nose.

On the door, the square window was crawling with flies, and from within the cell he heard something stir . . . a slithery, jangling sound, like pennies clinking into a coin jar.

He glanced at Wu. The sergeant's lips were pinched tight; muscles flexed at the base of his jaw, as if he were fighting back vomit.

Carefully Marco brushed the flies from the hatch and lowered his eyes to the unlit opening. The stench intensified, and he had to turn his head to suck a quick breath.

'Oh shit . . .'

A corpse reclined on the hospital bed in the cell, naked, its skin cracked like bark. It was male, no doubt, but where its genitals had hung was a hollowed-out cave. Its atrophied arms and legs were handcuffed to the bed rails, too tight; the hands and feet had ballooned to enormous proportions, like shiny black pumpkins, pooled with blood. Flies buzzed its lips, and it lapped at them with a waterless tongue, catching none. It grunted, and the handcuffs chimed on its limbs – the metallic noise Marco had detected earlier.

An IV pole stood over the bed like an attending nurse. On the hook dangled a polyvinyl bag, fat with greasy brown liquid; a tube extended from the bottom and disappeared beneath a bloodstained bandage on the corpse's bald head.

'What is it?' Wu asked, concerned.

'See for yourself.' Marco stepped aside, and Wu took his place.

A cursory inspection was all Wu needed. 'A patient?' he wondered, stepping away. 'Put in restraints, then forgotten when the prison was overrun.'

Marco shook his head. 'I've never seen a patient with an IV to their head. Not like that.'

'So what then?'

Swallowing hard, Marco ignored the question and

ventured further up the hall. Inside him the coagulated anxiety continued to expand, spilling between organs, occupying every crevice it could find. The hideous stink in the hallway thickened; he had the image of himself tunnelling through it, an invisible mud of bacteria and pus and spoiled, maggoty meat. He heard movement – *jangle jangle* – in more cells, but he didn't look inside. No need for that.

He already knew. He understood.

His eyes watered – from the stench, he tried to tell himself. *You're okay. Keep going.* He passed three more cells. Up ahead the corridor bent left again.

He inhaled a fortifying breath and turned the corner.

More cells, occupying another hundred feet of gloom. Dark sealed doors.

Except the final door, the cell farthest down at the end of the hall. Open. Yellow light flickered from the doorway, dancing on the floor.

Here we go, Marco thought. His hand throbbed, and he became aware that he was squeezing the M9 so sternly his fingers had cramped. His heart boomed somewhere outside his chest; somehow it had escaped and was now galloping loose in the corridor.

'Be ready,' Wu whispered.

'I'm trying,' Marco murmured. He edged forward, his boot-steps too loud – but then again, it didn't matter. He wasn't fooling anyone.

With Wu behind him, he plodded down the corridor, solemn and pensive.

Dead man walking. Isn't that what the guards said in prison movies, whenever they escorted a man to the execution chamber? Marco almost laughed. Too many dead men walking around here. And wasn't there always a priest, reading the Bible out loud, so serious?

Yea, though I walk through the valley of death . . .

He reached the brink, the open doorway, and took his final breath.

Stepped into the light.

He expected the voice that greeted him.

'Hello, Henry.'

Marco managed a wan smile.

'Hello, Roger.'

GOODBYE STORIES

12.1

Roger Ballard. Not dead. Not resurrected.

Roger Ballard – *alive*.

He sat propped on the edge of a neatly made prison bed, hands on his knees, looking dapper in a starched white collared shirt and blue tie, no more vexed to encounter Marco here and now, estranged by five years of hell, than if the two men had met yesterday for lunch. His chestnut hair had grown long, combed back as usual but draping to his shoulders. He looked old, far older than his actual forty years. His face was coarse and greatly malnourished; his flesh clung to his skull like shrink wrap, and he had knobbed cheeks and two grim sinkholes for eyes.

The sight of Roger walloped Marco like a sucker punch; for the second time in two days, he recalled his last morning at Cedars-Sinai before leaving for Arizona with Danielle. On his farewell walk to the parking garage, he'd passed Roger's office, vowing to avert his eyes . . . but instead he'd glanced inside, and there had been Roger at his desk, staring at the door as if somehow knowing that Marco would appear at that precise moment. *Goodbye, Henry*, Ballard had offered, and Marco had snubbed him, kept walking – sick to his stomach, wondering if Roger might follow and glad that he didn't. The image had been lodged in Marco's brain for half a decade – Roger, forlorn in his glum little office – and now, in this dumbfounding instant, Roger Ballard, the same man yet unnervingly different, had leaped across time, transported to a glum prison cell instead, gazing expectantly again at Marco in his doorway.

With a twiggy finger he tapped his thin glasses higher onto his nose, then stood.

'I'm glad you received my email, Henry,' he said. 'That was quite some time ago, wasn't it? I wasn't certain you'd come.'

The remark caught Marco unprepared – shit, not that he was prepared for *anything* Roger could say – and he gawked, his mouth a stupid circle, grappling for words. His mind spun like a roulette wheel, and he felt himself hanging on the frantic skip and bounce of the imagined silver ball, clueless where it would drop, which slot, which emotion: anger, or relief, or sadness or hatred or maybe even terror.

The wheel slowed. The ball fell.

Landing on bewilderment.

'Roger,' he croaked. 'Roger, everybody thinks you're *dead*.'

Ballard's crooked upper lip – the middle groove permanently off-centred like a sneer – twitched. 'No, no,' he said. 'I've been working. I've made great progress, in fact.'

He gestured around himself, vaguely presenting the room. In the corner a steel lab table had been dragged in, a clumsy furnishing in the small cell. Notebooks stacked the surface, the pages thick and warped with moisture. A red candle burned beside them.

'Roger,' Marco persisted. 'Listen to me—'

'I've been working, I said,' Ballard broke in, annoyed. 'I'll show you.' With an awkward gimp in his stride, he crossed to the table. Marco lowered his gaze and winced. Ballard's left foot was bent sideways – obscene, his ankle nearly dragging the floor as he walked. The bone had been broken and then healed into a deformity.

From the jump, Marco knew without asking. *Off the walkway.*

'You're the army,' Ballard observed, for the first time acknowledging Wu. The sergeant hovered behind Marco, his eyes darting between the two doctors.

'Yes.' Wu glanced warningly at Marco. His forearm muscle tensed, and the knife in his hand stirred as if he were expecting trouble. 'Sergeant Ken Wu.'

'You brought the army, Henry?'

'He tagged along.'

'Does Osbourne know?'

Marco hesitated, registering the sudden apprehension on Ballard's face. 'Yes . . .' he allowed cautiously. Despite himself, he felt oddly afraid to upset Roger.

But Ballard simply pinched his lips tight for a moment, and then sighed. 'Well. Perhaps I was foolish to hope otherwise. I'm still glad you came, Henry. If you're here, everything will be quite fine. However, those other men at the checkpoint – they were not with you?'

'No.'

Ballard nodded, satisfied. He huffed the candle flame dead, then plucked the top notebook from the water-damaged pile and, hobbling, brushed between Marco and Wu into the corridor. He carried with him a whiff of surgical soap, pleasant and jasmine-scented, as he passed. And then it was gone, and the air blackened again.

Ballard spoke. 'I really have made progress, Henry, you'll see. I'll show you . . .'

Trailing off, he navigated left, vanishing around the next bend in the hallway. Marco blinked twice, three times. His head fizzed with a sort of drunken, unsteady vertigo, and irrationally he wondered if he'd hallucinated the entire meeting with Ballard.

One look at Wu's cold green eyes sobered him.

'What do we do now?' Marco asked.

'We follow him,' Wu declared. 'But carefully.'

Around the corner Ballard was still bobbing ahead on his bum foot. Quickly the men caught up, and Marco had to stifle an urge to grab Roger by his bony little shoulder – spin him and ask just what the *fuck* was going on. Instead he fell in step behind his former associate, already dreading wherever this bizarre hike was leading.

Typical Roger, he groused. *Too deep in his own head to realise we think he's fucking nuts. And I had years to get used to this bullshit. God knows what Wu is thinking right now.*

Probably thinks I'm crazy, too.

Halfway along the corridor Ballard spoke, a subdued, almost confidential hush. 'I've thought a great deal about you, Henry. About what happened.' He fell quiet for three or four strides. And then he asked, 'How is Danielle?'

Marco stiffened. Said nothing. *Goddamn it, Roger.*

Ballard's head tilted, and he seemed to hear the unspoken answer. 'Oh,' he said, a single sad note, and pushed his glasses higher again on his nose. A darkness seemed to descend over him, the shadows in the prison corridor fusing with his skin.

'No offence, Roger, but let's change the subject. Why are you still *here*?'

'Here? Well. Because I had to finish.'

As Marco waited for Roger to elaborate, Wu paced himself a step closer behind the two doctors. 'Finish?' he pressed. 'Do you mean the vaccine?'

Ballard shook his head, clicked his tongue. 'You see, Henry? That's the military. Impatient, always pushing. Complaining. "Go faster," Osbourne would say, all the blasted time. That man, he had his own agenda, very much so. Not to be trusted. It's politics to him, not science. You do realise, Sergeant Wu, that it took four hundred years to solve smallpox?'

Wu and Marco exchanged questioning looks. Marco spoke first, drawing Ballard's searing expression away from poor Wu. 'Roger, in your email you said—'

'Quiet now, Henry,' Ballard hushed. 'Too much talking in the halls disturbs the patients. It's better to let them rest.'

'Roger—'

'Henry, *please*. In the lab.'

The corridor crossed another hundred feet of cells, then met another hallway and continued through; at the intersection, Marco was surprised to see the same brown-stained gurney they'd passed on their way into the infirmary, and the same reception area far off to the right. He'd been distracted by the rat, hadn't noticed these secondary corridors branching off. The infirmary was a goddamn maze, he observed now – a good place to get lost.

Past the intersection were open examination rooms. Marco took quick stock as he passed, braced for more bloody horrors like the corpse in the medical cell. But the rooms here were clean, strikingly so; the counters gleamed dust-free, and the floors had all been recently mopped. However trashed the infirmary had been during the outbreak, Roger had done a tidy job rebuilding here. Ballard proceeded past each room without comment. A hundred feet ahead, Marco saw another intersection waiting, but the men had travelled only three-quarters of the distance down the hall when Ballard ducked through a wide-arched doorway to his right.

They'd entered a blood lab. A white laminate counter ran the entire perimeter, and all along it were microscopes hunkered like little black vultures over meals of Petri dishes. Mounted to the near wall was a rack of phials darkened with some nauseating, mustard-coloured fluid. The room smelled like Clorox, sterile and sharp. On the counter nearest Marco rested a bulky box – a centrifuge for spinning blood – where a haematology analyser had been activated, gibbering small green numbers as it diced plasma and counted reticulocytes. A stainless-steel medical refrigerator hummed against the back wall. The fridge's glass doors were clouded with frost.

And in the middle of the lab – an unsettling centrepiece – was a full-sized operating table, spotless and polished and thankfully unoccupied. The bed had been modified, fitted with restraints; ominous buckled straps dangled from the side.

From the corner of the room, a flickering motion caught Marco's eye. There on the far end was the ninth video monitor – the unit that had been missing from the guard's desk. It sat squarely on the counter where Ballard had rigged it, looking like a chaotic octopus of black and yellow cords and an electrical box with a white toggle switch in the metal-plated centre. The screen split into nine tiny frames; all the scenes from the main console played at once.

'I like to watch while I work,' Ballard explained simply.

All right, enough of this shit, Marco decided. He was done playing polite.

'Roger. *Listen* to me, for Christ's sake. It's been four goddamn years since anybody heard from you – do you get that? You were *bit.* Your message said you were dying. We came to . . . to see if you'd survived,' he said, lying. He slipped Wu a self-conscious glance.

Ballard nodded. 'Yes,' he said distractedly and scanned the digits on the haematology analyser, his lips pursed. 'Communications have been down for quite a while now. The facility went offline soon after I emailed you, Henry, and I wasn't able to write again or call out. Those soldiers left without me. But I made the best of it, Henry. I had everything I needed.'

'Yes, but . . .' Marco faltered. 'But how did you even *survive*? I saw a video of you that day, Roger. You *were* bitten, weren't you?'

Ballard raised a wiry eyebrow. 'Yes, that's correct.' Behind his bookish glasses, his eyes glinted. Amused. Deep in the room, the refrigerator clicked and murmured.

Marco cleared his throat, uncomfortable. 'So . . . your blood, everything you said about your DNA, the new antibodies . . . it actually worked? It destroyed the infection?'

'No, Henry,' Ballard said. 'Not exactly.' His voice climbed, and Marco heard the restrained excitement he remembered from early morning conversations at Cedars-Sinai – Marco arriving with a bagel in his mouth and a Styrofoam coffee cup in his grasp, barely able to remove his coat before Ballard pounced on him to discuss some new strand of research.

'But that's what I wanted to show you,' Ballard continued. 'The progress.'

He extended his left arm and awkwardly unbuttoned the sleeve with his free hand. Then folded back the cuff, and rolled the sleeve up . . .

. . . all the way to his elbow . . .

. . . and rotated his arm in the light.

Marco heard himself gasp.

Ballard's entire forearm was rotted purple and thick, warted with grey-green splotches of gangrenous tissue; engorged veins slithered like black snakes just below the skin's surface. Midway up, a half-circle of scar tissue glistened wetly, like a shocking red crescent moon.

The arm reeked, a disgusting chemical smell like formaldehyde.

'You see?' Ballard said, and now the excitement in his voice was obvious – an insane child showing off a favourite toy. 'I *am* infected. I'm carrying the Resurrection.'

12.2

Marco stared, both repulsed and fascinated at once. And then a buried thought exploded like a landmine in his head, an abrupt panic that he'd been tricked – *oh god, Roger is a corpse, a talking goddamn corpse* – and now Ballard would lunge, rip a chunk from his throat . . .

But instead Ballard extended his infected arm, beaming. 'You see, Henry? I contained the impact. Necrotic tissue, yes, but a limited radius, extending up the arm and partially across my torso. And this was just the Beta compound of the antibodies – my leukocytes had not fully adapted, remember. The current formula would have prevented this completely.'

Marco goggled, catching his breath. The M9 in his hand was a comforting weight, ready if necessary to take Roger down with a bullet through the bridge of those wire-frame eyeglasses. Except Roger seemed harmless; he gazed back at Marco benignly, expectantly, like a dog anticipating praise for a trick well done – oblivious to the fact that it just shit the rug.

Wary, Marco relaxed his fingers on the M9 and consulted Wu with an uncertain look. The sergeant's bloodied knuckles flexed on his knife.

'That damage is from the corpse bite?' Wu clarified. His tone was curt.

'Yes, of course. What else would it be?'

'The Resurrection is in you now?'

'Yes,' Ballard said, sounding peeved. 'I already said so.'

Marco swallowed. His saliva tasted thick and gritty – too much dirt in his gums from getting his ass beat to the ground for two days straight. He longed for his toothbrush and some baking powder. 'But Roger,' he rasped. 'How did you stop it from killing you? Your email said your blood – the vaccine – wasn't ready. You said you would die.'

'Oh, I almost did, yes, almost.' Ballard shuddered, remembering. 'Extreme fever, shaking, muscle rigidity. Uncontrollable nausea. I was bedridden for days. My whole body burned. And, good Lord, how that bite itched, Henry. That was nearly the worst part. The itch.'

'But . . . ?'

Ballard brightened. 'But those symptoms passed. As I predicted, the antibodies did not prevent the Resurrection – but surprisingly they did deflect the fatal blow. I'm infected, but I'm not a walking corpse. And, as it turns out, I was correct about the Resurrection.'

Marco studied him, curious. 'How do you mean?'

'About its nature. About how to fight it. You see, everyone else has misunderstood. The Resurrection is not a virus.' Ballard twinkled. 'Prion, Henry. The Resurrection is a prion.'

Prion? The word rolled around in Marco's mind. He frowned.

Prions . . .

For a moment he felt himself stepping outside the body of Henry Marco, professional corpse-killer, wretched with blood and sweat and mud-caked clothes; for a moment he was just regular old Henry Marco again, neurologist, contemplating a diagnosis. Testing what fitted, what didn't. He nodded once, slowly, then again. *Of course . . .*

'A TSE,' he pronounced.

Ballard nodded eagerly in unison. 'Exactly.'

'And . . . protease-resistant?'

'Yes, unfortunately,' Ballard admitted, looking somewhat crestfallen. 'With a remarkably fast incubation period. Astoundingly fast, really, unprecedented. I spent an entire month administering enzymes to break the sample down, but none—'

'*Doctors.*' Wu's steel voice hammered down on both Ballard and Marco together. The sergeant eyed them admonishingly. 'Please include *me* in the discussion. You said the Resurrection was . . . a . . . ?'

Ballard darkened – annoyed, Marco knew, by the burden

of elementary explanations. Patient relationships were never Roger's strong point.

'Prion,' Marco offered, not wanting to agitate Roger any further. 'Short for "proteinaceous infectious particle". Basically a malformed protein structure, not a virus. Sounds harmless, but if it gets inside you, really bad things happen. See, your brain and your central nervous system have normal proteins called P-R-P. The prion attacks the P-R-P in your body and mutates them – folds the protein in half, kinda like a taco, into the bad prion shape. Then the mutation keeps going, a chain reaction until your whole brain is converted into a big prion mess.'

Wu listened, his jaw set hard. Analysing every word, Marco was sure.

Ballard parted his lips to speak, but Marco cut him off. 'So the Resurrection is a new kind of TSE – a transmissible spongiform encephalopathy.'

'Which means?' Wu asked.

'A brain disease. A nasty one. All the known TSEs are one hundred per cent fatal. Like kuru . . .' he said thoughtfully. 'The disease kuru originated in Papua New Guinea. Some of the native tribes practise ritual cannibalism there.'

Wu raised an eyebrow. 'In the South Pacific.'

Ballard nodded excitedly, unable to remain silent. 'The Japanese prisoner, he was the carrier, Henry. I checked them all, but his blood sample had the infected isoform.'

'Japanese,' Wu noted. 'The terrorist organisation Aum Shinrikyo. One of its officers was incarcerated here.'

Marco nodded slowly. South Pacific. It was starting to make sense.

'So basically,' he said, 'A bunch of insane bad guys fucked with the kuru prion, and bioengineered a TSE a thousand times worse. Prions convert the nervous system, then kill the rest and take over. Walking corpses, Christ, they're just prions with arms and legs. Requiring fresh protein – as in, raw meat – to repopulate the system.'

Wu studied the dead complexion of Ballard's arm, as if searching for a message scrawled in the black veins. 'Is there a cure?'

Ballard bristled and rolled his sleeve back over his forearm. 'There is no cure,' he said, sounding defensive. 'Not yet.' He sniffed moodily and buttoned his cuff.

'So, what then?' Marco asked. He, too, had grown impatient. 'What about the antibodies, the DNA vaccination? You said there's a current formula that works. That anybody exposed to the Resurrection wouldn't be infected at all. None of . . . *that*.' He gestured to Ballard's arm.

Ballard adjusted his glasses. 'Correct,' he answered. He addressed his reply to Marco, noticeably snubbing Wu. 'A true vaccine. It was difficult, Henry. I travelled many wrong paths, trying to bond the prion with another immunogen. Months developing modified protease—'

'Enzymes that break down proteins,' Marco translated to Wu.

Ballard ignored the interruption, speaking over him. '—but that proved fruitless. Then I looked at the P-R-P itself, and that's where I began to visualise the answer . . . *chemical chaperones*. You see? The right antibody produced by the DNA could stabilise the microscopic pockets in P-R-P. Much like caulk filling cracks in cement, to make them stronger . . .'

Jesus Christ, Marco thought. He felt suddenly woozy. He pinched his eyes shut with his chilled fingertips; the pressure was momentarily soothing, a dazzle of light on his retinas.

Is this for real?

Yes, he answered. *Yes, it is. Roger is really here. Really alive. Explaining to me how he's gonna save the world.*

When he couldn't even save Hannah.

The thought incensed him, a fiery blast of anger up through his oesophagus, and the floor seemed to tilt underfoot. Ballard's voice enveloped him like a fume, swirling, intoxicating. He knew he should sober up and pay attention, listen devoutly as Roger orated like some mystic medicine man around the tribal fire – *oh, Great Spirit of the Resurrection, reveal to us the secrets of your all-powerful vaccine—*

And then his head shifted, and he stopped, startled by a thought so unexpected it seemed to originate outside himself. *The science doesn't matter.* Let Ballard drone on. Let him pin the Resurrection down and cut it open, define its parts, watch the cogs grind under a microscope to determine how it functioned. The truth was, you could dig and dig – ask *how this*, and *how that*, and *how how how* – but you'd never hit bottom. Science only took you so far. After that, there was always a gap you couldn't cross; the last answer was always out of reach.

'*That's your problem, babe,*' Danielle had accused him. '*You need to know how everything works. Can't anything be magic?*'

Yes, he agreed at last. Magic. It was *all* magic – mind-boggling, impossible. *A dead man resurrects. A newborn baby takes its first breath. They're the same. Life flowing from some hidden source. A fountain switched on by a godlike hand. We call it biology, but it's a miracle . . . and we only pretend to explain.*

He swallowed uncomfortably. *Or can Roger explain miracles, too?*

The last thought unnerved him, and he trembled, teetering at the brink of some horrible chasm. He was abruptly certain that to know whatever Roger knew would destroy him – hurtle him into the same abyss his old friend had already fallen.

'. . . stop them from folding when the prion attacks,' Ballard's voice drifted on. 'And I created it, Henry, gave birth to it from my own blood. I worked non-stop the year after the military left. Ninety-three injection cycles, millions upon millions of cell divisions, and then it existed. A nucleotide capable of the required immuno-response . . .'

As Marco half-listened, images popped into his head; somewhere deep in his brain a slide projector had whirred to life, and his mind clicked from one disturbing snapshot to another, showing him a story he hated to watch, yet couldn't shut off. *Click.* Roger at the guard's desk, his hair pasted with blood and sweat, sealing himself into the infirmary as corpses overran Sarsgard. *Click.* Roger experimenting on the infected prisoners here in the hospital ward – drilling holes into poor bastards handcuffed to gurneys, scooping out meaty brain samples, running IV drips of god-knows-what into their stalled veins.

Ballard's voice drifted to him. '. . . which confirmed that the vaccine worked in rats. I was fortunate in that regard, having an infestation of rats to use for trials. But did you know, Henry, that the Resurrection only kills rodents, that it doesn't bring them back? And so the question remained whether the formula would perform as effectively on humans . . .'

Click. A corpse mauling Roger's arm during the escape attempt.

Click. Roger in freefall from the balcony.

Click. Roger hobbling to his lab, ankle shattered, skin festering. Hiding here, pecking out one final email to Marco as he waited for death.

Click. Roger – alone in this hellhole, working, eating, shitting, slicing corpses, cackling to himself at night in his godforsaken cell. Four years. *Click, click, click.*

'. . . success. A fully working vaccine,' Ballard concluded and wiped his forehead. In Marco's mind, the slideshow ended, and he resumed his grip on the lab. Roger was here, breathing hard – cheeks red, his brow greased with exertion. He glowed with some sort of sick energy, a glee that crossed beyond sanity and delved into the perverse, as if he had absorbed the prison's madness and his skin now radiated the aura of rapists and murderers.

He's crazy, Marco concluded. The verdict saddened him. *Batshit fucking crazy.*

'Roger,' he asked uncertainly, 'Does Osbourne know any of this?'

Ballard sniffed. 'None of it. I warned you about that man, Henry. His only concern was himself, not helping others.' He glared defiantly toward the hallway as though Osbourne might momentarily walk through the door. 'And so I kept my research hidden. I had to be careful until I knew. Osbourne demanded reports, but I scrubbed those clean, took out the useful bits, just to be safe. But then the rescue team left without me. Without my research.'

'They thought you were dead.'

'Yes,' Ballard conceded. 'Understandable. So I carried on without them.'

In the middle of the room, Wu stood scrutinising the operating table. Marco wondered if he, too, were imagining the atrocities Roger must have performed here. The sergeant tugged firmly on one of the restraint straps and let it drop. The buckle swung like a pendulum, clocking seconds as Wu turned and looked squarely at Ballard.

'Show me the vaccine,' Wu said. His green eyes were hard like jewels.

The buckle swung forward, then back.

Counting down to zero.

12.3

Breathing coolly through his nostrils, Wu awaited an answer from this mad American doctor, the once-great Roger Ballard. With his stare he marked the precise spot on Ballard's neck – a centimetre from the larynx, under which the jugular hid – where he would plunge his *lujiaodao* knife if Ballard refused to present the vaccine.

The plan had not changed, despite the remarkable discovery that Ballard was alive; Wu had come for the man's blood, and he intended to collect it. Briefly he'd considered abducting the doctor, presenting him to Beijing for interrogation, perhaps even forced servitude in an MSS research lab. But Ballard was obviously a radical – unhinged, subversive to authority. Surely he would refuse to aid China, even if his crumbling mind had anything left to offer. And, Wu realised, the two-hundred-mile trek to the Mexican border would be far too perilous with a hostage in tow, especially without his Droid. Alerting MSS for pick-up was still a dilemma.

I'd be lucky to survive, he judged, *against corpses* and *a crazy man the entire way.*

The truth was, he did not need Roger Ballard. What he had here was *better.* Not just the DNA, but the vaccine *itself.* The answer to the Resurrection, a formula for Chinese chemists to study and reproduce. And so he would execute the doctor, then escape with DNA samples and the vaccine like treasures from a buried temple. Beijing would laud him as a hero.

Except . . . what if the doctor didn't show him? Wu surveyed the small glass phials on the wall rack, filled with chunky slops in various shades of brown and yellow. Four rows, six containers each. Did one contain the vaccine?

Killing Ballard without the answer would be inconvenient.

'Can you show us, Roger?' Marco's voice broke into Wu's thoughts.

Wu twitched. He'd almost forgotten the other task remaining.

Kill Henry Marco.

The realisation caused him a sudden, surprising anxiety. He flashed Marco a quick sideways appraisal. His fellow survivor. His unwitting partner. Marco had saved his life, not just once, but several times. In Salton, in the prison yard, on the cell-block walkway. Would Wu have succeeded this far without Marco, even as haphazard and untrained as the man's methods were?

Of course, Wu asserted, offended at the thought. *I would not have failed.*

But within him a humble whisper disagreed.

No. You needed him.

His mind drifting, he remembered Marco at the cemetery the previous morning. The two men had sat shoulder-to-shoulder in the chapel, sharing respects for the dead; the grief in the American's heart had briefly touched his own. Wu had tried to ease the man's suffering.

But I will kill him now, Wu reaffirmed. *I will take the vaccine and kill him.*

An unexpected memory leaped across his thoughts. His first mission so long ago. Tenzin Dawa, the monk who had protested the railway, dying at Wu's feet. The shaved head, the wizened face, eyelids fluttering as blood cascaded from the wrinkled slit throat. The orange robe dyed a deep bottomless crimson. Wu's red-stained hands had shaken for hours afterward; he had not wanted to snuff out that life. But China had needed him. The railway had been built.

Now, China needed him again.

Killing Marco, he thought, *will be like killing for the first time. Difficult. But I will do it. Like Cat Catching Mice. The cat does not pity its prey.*

But first, he needed the vaccine.

'We're waiting, Doctor Ballard,' he said politely and readied his knife.

12.4

Ballard frowned; Marco sensed his reluctance. But the truth was, Roger had been waiting years to show off – to *anyone*, even someone he perceived as an army idiot like Wu. On the table the swinging belt strap lost its momentum and went still, and Ballard nodded. Ruled by pride, he turned to the wall-rack and extracted a rubber-corked glass phial from the bottom row.

He raised the container as if prepared to give a toast. Inside, a sludge resembling brown yogurt quivered as he issued it a provocative jiggle.

'The vaccine,' he said importantly, hovering just above a whisper.

Wu's eyes locked on the phial. 'You're certain, Doctor? That it works?'

'Oh, yes, very. I've tested it many times, on myself, with no additional increase of the Resurrection prion in my system.'

Marco baulked. 'On yourself? But – what do you mean, tested? Many times?'

Ballard's face clouded.

'You injected yourself with the Resurrection?' Marco tried.

'No, Henry.'

Marco persisted. 'Were you bitten again?'

Ballard said nothing. He turned and slid the phial back into the rack.

'Tell us, Doctor,' Wu warned. Marco felt his heartbeat

picking up speed. Somehow he knew – just *knew* – Roger's answer would disturb him.

'I consumed infected meat,' Ballard said. 'Corpses.'

For several excruciating seconds, no man spoke.

Marco broke first. His lungs expelled a rush of horrified air. 'Oh, *shit*.'

Wu's lip curled with obvious disgust. 'You ate the dead . . . ?'

Ballard glowered. 'To survive, yes, Sergeant Wu. The prison food locker was stocked for a year. Once it emptied, I required a new supply. Rats were an option, but small, you see – not much sustenance. A single corpse can last weeks.'

Marco shuddered, bile in the bottom of his throat, his head a gallery of yet more unwelcome pictures. Ballard butchering corpses in their cells. Carving the putrid sloppy meat from bones. Gnawing strips of tough grey skin like animal jerky.

'Roger,' he sputtered. 'Those were people . . . '

Ballard regarded him quizzically. 'Of course, Henry.'

Same old Roger, Marco thought. His anger flared again. People had never really been human, not to Roger. More like specimens. And now a daily food source.

You crazy self-centred asshole.

Ballard seemed to read his thoughts. 'I had no choice, Henry. It made sense. And it provided added confidence of the vaccine's efficacy. Consuming the prions should have overloaded my system, but there was no negative effect at all.'

'Did it ever occur to you,' Marco demanded, 'to just *leave*?'

Ballard cocked his head, puzzled. 'Leave?'

'The prison. Take your fucking vaccine and go. Get out of here.'

The malformed curvature of Ballard's upper lip tremored,

exaggerating the sneer. He contemplated Marco with disapproval. 'Of course not,' he sniped. 'I can't just leave my work. I told you I'd made progress, Henry. But the bigger problem remains.'

'The bigger problem? Don't tell me you mean a cure.'

Ballard levelled a serious look at Marco. 'The cure is one challenge, yes. With enough time I'll isolate a method to reverse the prion transformation. But even so, there is a bigger problem awaiting. I'm surprised you don't see it, Henry.'

'Yeah? What is it, the fact that you're a fucking lunatic—'

Marco's shoulders leaped in alarm as a crash sounded from the end of the room, a resounding rattle of glass from the medical refrigerator. He spun, the M9 pointed. Something had banged the wide double doors. *From the inside.*

The glass was fogged, impossible to see through – but the shape that was pressed against the condensation drove a cold spike down Marco's spine.

A bare footprint. The outline of a heel, and a pad, and five splayed toes.

'Roger . . .' Marco started, abruptly queasy.

Ballard stopped him. 'You should understand, Henry. You of all people.'

'Roger, what the *fuck* is in the fridge?'

'You already know.'

'I don't,' Marco insisted. But he was beginning to dread that he did . . .

Please no. Please tell me it's not what I think.

Please don't show me.

But Ballard had already crossed the room, fishing in his pocket. He pulled a key and twisted it into the lock on the glass door. Then he turned to Marco, his face subdued now, a melancholy smile replacing the manic grin of minutes ago.

'I'm sorry, Henry. I hope you do know how sorry I've been.' He licked his lips like a nervous tic; his eyes swept the floor. 'For my mistake. With Hannah.'

'Roger,' Marco urged. His face burned. 'Don't.'

Ballard tapped a round thermometer implanted in the glass. 'Ten degrees Celsius. Every twelve hours I alternate to twelve degrees, then back down.'

With both hands he yanked open the refrigerator.

'Hypothermia therapy.'

Hunched on the floor inside was a blue-skinned corpse, a middle-aged male with a veiny nose and eyes fogged white like the glass. Its arms were bound in a straitjacket, knees tucked to its chest. A pale grape-coloured tongue hung frozen from its open mouth, as if they'd caught it licking a popsicle. The corpse groaned and rolled its head with a slow, drowsy motion. The jaw sluggishly closed, opened, closed again. Marco realised it was biting at Ballard, but too drugged by the cold to strike with any amount of speed.

Ballard stepped back and inhaled a deep, dramatic breath, waving his open hand below his nostrils as though shovelling in air. 'The problem is oxygen, Henry,' he continued. 'Even if we could destroy the prions with a cure, how can we expect the brain to recover? After such extended asphyxia? Consider the challenge. Months, years, with no breath, no oxygen. Patients would suffer unthinkable brain damage. Extreme, debilitating cerebral palsy.'

The M9 trembled in Marco's grip, the only extension of his body able to move. 'So you're cooling them,' he clarified. 'To limit the damage.' He spoke without emotion, thankful for the numbness. If he allowed himself to feel anything, it would break him apart, like a machine pushed too hard. Bolts exploding everywhere.

'Just like you tried with Hannah,' he added. He glanced

sideways to Wu; even the sergeant seemed uneasy, his blood-streaked brow furrowed at the refrigerated corpse.

Ballard's unbalanced eyes pleaded with Marco. 'I can save them, Henry.'

I can save Hannah. That broken promise, uttered six years in the past – echoing now, clear and sharp, a fresh salty cut of the scalpel. Marco grimaced.

'No, Roger,' he said. 'You can't. That's impossible. They're gone.'

For the span of a second, a panicked expression seized Ballard; his eyes rounded, then just as quickly recovered. He gathered his haggard face into a weak smile.

'So you see,' he said with forced cheer, ignoring Marco's reprimand, 'I must continue the research. Until a viable treatment is discovered.' As if for emphasis he swatted the refrigerator doors shut, resealing the corpse into its chilled catacomb. The effort seemed to drain Ballard. He gripped the door handles and pressed his forehead against the glass. His spectacles tapped the frosty surface with a feeble *clink*.

'The truth is, I think about leaving,' he admitted, sounding far beyond tired. 'But I can't, Henry. You understand. You, of all people. That's why I'm glad you came. That's why I wrote to you, to show you how sorry I am. I had to stay here, you see, to atone for Hannah . . . '

His entire body sagged. 'You see, Henry? This is *my* prison.'

And then he laughed – a soft wheeze at first, barely audible. Then louder, harder, and his frail shoulders convulsed; he guffawed once and then fell silent, with his head bowed against the refrigerator like a man in prayer.

This is my prison.

Marco's head swam. The fact was, Roger was right. *I do understand.*

A prison. That's exactly how it felt – a windowless hell, escape-proof, a dungeon door slamming on both him and Danielle the day Hannah died. And on Roger, too – Marco had never recognized it until now, but yes, Roger, too. And none of them had ever found a way out. His chin trembled, and tears clawed at his eyes. Let them. He was tired of resisting.

He cried.

He remembered the days, the weeks, the two years after losing Hannah. Countless dark hours in bed, long after lights out, banging against the bars in his mind. Pleading for mercy – for the midnight reprieve that never came, from a governor who didn't care. It had been the solitude that hurt most. Danielle a foot away on the uncomfortable mattress, her back to him; and yet he'd always somehow known when her eyes were stuck open, sleepless, memorising the wall. She was the prisoner in the adjacent cell, punished the same but lodged apart – because he never knew what to say, or what to ask, or when to touch her, or when *not* to touch her, because his skin was too cruel a reminder of what they'd already shared and lost.

And then always came the dull horror of waking – the morning roll call, answering to a reality that never changed, never would. Another day served.

Yes. A fucking prison, exactly right. A miserable cage.

No sunlight. No Hannah.

I have to get out. Those had been Danielle's words, written in thin purple ink from a ballpoint pen. On a square of dainty flowered stationery.

The vision sickened him instantly; his stomach dropped from a great height, and he gasped, pressed his hand to his ribs as if he could push back the nausea.

You let him do it, Henry. Her voice now, loud in his ears. *You let him!*

He had to, Delle. Her asphyxia was severe – she never would have . . .

Goddamn it, Henry! You're avoiding. You're always avoiding.

I'm not, I'm not, I swear I'm not . . .

His mouth opened, a gag reflex. He realised it was time. Time to prove, once and for all, to her, to himself, that he wasn't avoiding. Time to remember.

To confront the past. The highs, the lows.

The roller coaster, he thought, and closed his eyes in terror, and with a wet, pathetic whimper he vomited, hot and brown, onto the cold tile floor.

I have to get out.

The light blurred, distorted by tears as Marco retched and choked for air; it was a disorienting underwater sensation, like drowning. Around him the room pirouetted, his mind caught in a whirlpool, and time, too, was a liquid, flowing backward . . .

12.5

. . . And Marco was in his Audi, squealing through a red light in downtown Phoenix four summers in the past, his eyes wild, each heartbeat a dynamite blast of terror. In the rear-view mirror the street was jammed with – *dead, how can they be dead? shit shit shit* – the monsters, a massive relentless tsunami of teeth and blood, smashing store windows, turning cars, burying the city. He'd been at the hospital since dawn. The day had begun with all the pacings of a normal day, but by eleven o'clock had convened into an emergency conference with the entire neurology staff as the ER swelled with new arrivals, more and more, pasty men and women and kids, oozing a sweat that stank like sour milk, and their worried families, cramming the waiting room, the halls, every last corner. No place to put them all.

Redirect to Good Samaritan. Maryvale. Kindred. But *all* the hospitals were overwhelmed. Across the city, the state. Reports from California, too. Nobody understood how fucked they were – not yet – but the fear was there, that sense of a tremendous crack zigzagging up the dam, irreversible, portending doom.

And then it had burst.

On the main stretch of Central Avenue, Marco gunned the gas, keeping up with the panicked traffic – cars and trucks speeding block to block, desperate to gain ground on the dead menace behind them. A man in a business jacket dashed from an alley, running blindly into the street, and Marco cried out as, ahead, a silver car blasted through the man, chucking him airborne; his flailing body, a pinstriped blur, sailed free over Marco's Audi and smashed broken onto the street behind. A swerving brown UPS truck crushed the body flat as Marco passed the alley where the businessman had emerged. More of the monsters spilled out, swarming the stalled UPS truck. The dead piled through the truck's open door, engulfing the screaming driver.

Marco forced his eyes ahead. *Don't crash. Do . . . not . . . crash.*

A police car blasted past him, going in the opposite direction, its siren shrieking. With grim certainty Marco knew the officer wouldn't survive the day.

Guns don't work.

The Audi was sickly sweet with the scent of blood, Marco's shirt soaked red. *Tommy.* The hospital security guard, back at Cedars-Sinai. A dead nurse had bitten deep into Tommy's throat as he'd fired into her ribs – emptied the clip, and *still* she wouldn't die. Marco had coiled a phone cord around her neck and dragged her off, then helped Tommy to the parking garage. He'd leaned Tommy against the Audi as he dug for his keys; at the end of the row, the garage entrance had darkened with shadows, and the concrete walls echoed with ghostly cries as the dead charged in from the street, and when Marco looked again, Tommy was a corpse, too . . .

The art museum zipped past on the left, eviscerated bodies face down on the marble steps. *Oh god oh god dammit*, he thought, cranking the wheel; the Audi skidded onto the entrance ramp for I-10, and seconds later he was barrelling east on the interstate towards the Gold Canyon. The highway traffic was light; he guessed he was riding the edge of a deadly shockwave rolling outward from downtown. The surrounding suburbs hadn't been hit. Yet. *Stay fast, stay ahead*, he thought. Ahead, just long enough to get home to Danielle.

He'd tried calling from his office – twice in the morning and once again twenty minutes ago, a final frantic attempt to reach her; the phone rang and rang and rang, the receiver slick in his hand, and he'd forced himself to stay on the line, let it ring even as he heard screams and panicked footsteps in the hallway, coming closer, but he couldn't hang up, he had to warn her, and just as he decided the next ring would drive him absolutely fucking insane, Tommy the security guard and the cannibal nurse had exploded through his doorway, grappling and screeching, and he'd tried to rescue Tommy.

Danielle, please, he thought in the car now. *Please be safe.*

If only he had a cell phone.

Ha. That's funny. I'll tell Danielle when I get home, she'll laugh, we'll both laugh, just please, Delle, be safe . . . be safe be safe be safe.

'*Fuck!*' he roared, the frustration scrubbing his throat raw.

On the dashboard the speedometer rocketed high above a hundred, Marco's foot an infinite weight on the pedal, and the Audi darted in and out of lanes, splitting gaps between slower cars. The Superstition Mountains towered in the distance, looking hazy and unreal – the throne of some mythological king, the god of a doomed dreamscape – and if ever Marco wanted to wake from a nightmare, the time was right fucking now.

And then he was exiting the highway, hurtling into the Gold Canyon, his neighbourhood, his street. At the base of his driveway the iron gate took an eternity to open; he mashed the button on his remote ten times like rapid fire before finally flooring the gas. The Audi bounded through the still-opening gate, snapping the side-view mirror off with a shrill plastic *crack*. The tyres scrabbled up the cobblestone; his nostrils bristled with the smell of burnt oil.

He jounced to a stop in the circular turnaround.

Danielle's car wasn't there.

He blinked at the empty kerb where she normally parked, as if he could possibly be mistaken, as if by some trick of light her car was there and he'd simply missed it at first glance. But no, the car was gone. A hundred harmless reasons could explain it – and yet his stomach plunged like a rock to the bottom of a cold lake.

Oh god . . .

And then he was running towards the front door with no recollection of having left the Audi, except his keychain was in his hand, the house key jangling in a panic.

He burst into the foyer. '*Delle!*'

His voice rang against the plaster walls, ricocheted to the high ceiling.

No answer.

He called again up the stairwell and then with a head-rush ducked into the living room, braced for the sight of her mangled body on the hardwood floor. Nothing. No broken windows, no puddles of blood. The furniture was neat and even, facing the front door for undistorted chi flow; Danielle had hired a feng shui consultant their first month in the house. He trampled through the room, a stampede of negative emotion, hollering her name.

'*Delle!*'

In the hall mirror, he glimpsed himself – terror-eyed, his face and neck smeared with Tommy's bloody handprints, his shirt red and wet like a butcher's apron. Frightened of his own image, he turned into the kitchen. Empty. The back door shut, the glass intact. Clean dishes stacked on a dish towel beside the stainless steel sink. The counter . . .

The counter.

A blue square of paper lay on the island countertop, perfectly centred atop the mosaic chips of orange and sienna and brown tiles. A note.

He snatched it up.

Henry, it said, in Danielle's soft hand. The ink delicate and purple.

I have to get out.

He frowned and re-read it, knowing even before he continued what those words meant, what this note was about to tell him; she must have written it this morning, when the world was still normal – and his impulse was to crumple it, fling it to the kitchen floor before it destroyed him, before it ripped him apart, killed him more hideously than any dead cannibal ever could . . .

His hands shook uncontrollably. The paper rustled. He read the note:

Henry,
I have to get out. I love you – I do – but it's too much, and I can't stay. I know you'll say we're fine, but we're not. I can hear your voice, even while I'm writing this, telling me 'Give it time. Time will make it better.' But that's you

avoiding. You're always avoiding, Henry. And I love you, but I hate you when you avoid. It's not fair to me, and it's not fair to Hannah.

You say give it time. How much time until she comes back to us? Never of course. And even now, as you read this, I know you're avoiding. Did it annoy you when I mentioned her? You didn't like that, I'm sure. You never want to talk about her. But I need to.

I can't be like you. I tried here, I promise you I tried so so much. The problem is, I love you with all my heart, but it feels like I love her even more, and
I have to choose her now because you won't allow her to exist here with us. You never understood. I feel like I died with her, Henry. That probably annoys you, too. But she was a <u>part</u> of me. Why couldn't I ever make you understand that?

I have to leave. I don't know if it will be forever, but right now I have to get out. I'm sorry. We tried, I know we each did our best, but we weren't strong enough.

I don't want you to worry. I'm at Trish's if you

There was more, but he stopped reading. *Trish.* Her sister.

With a cry he crammed the note into his pocket and pounced at the phone, punched numbers frantically as if he were disabling a bomb.

Two rings . . . three . . .

Benjamin's voice answered, shaken and half whispering. 'Hello?'

'Ben! Is Danielle there?'

'Henry? Jesus Christ! Are you seeing this shit—'

'*Danielle!*' Marco yelled, losing control. 'Is she with you there?'

'What? No . . . no, it's just us. Trish says are you—'

The phone crashed to the orange tiled floor. Marco was

already running, down the hall, into the foyer, out through the door, diving into the Audi. The tyres howled as he stomped the gas, and the car shot across the cobblestones. Back into the dying world.

He sped west along the Superstition Freeway, towards Scottsdale. The madness had spread, he could see that much; below the highway, legions of dead men and women marched the streets like a parade out of hell, wicked grins on their greyish faces. They lumbered on stiff legs, knees unbending. *Rigor mortis*, he judged. The facial muscles and limbs were contracting violently. Maybe they'd just fall down, not get up . . . ?

Keep wishing. Nothing's that easy.

He glued his attention to the highway, desperate for the sight of Danielle's blue Honda ahead. Twice he saw her . . . *wrong,* not her, goddamn it, just some similar-looking car, some other driver speeding away to die their own unique death.

He ditched the highway in Scottsdale, blazing past dead pedestrians, more and more on every goddamn corner; Phoenix had spilled over, or maybe new waves were breaking out spontaneously everywhere. As he shot down a side street, he encountered a savage commotion outside his right window – a man on a bicycle had been tackled by a pack of the monsters. The doomed man lay pinned to the ground, still seated on his bike, still frantically pedalling as the dead tore at him, ripped his shirt and his skin to moist, rubbery bits.

Marco's foot touched the brake pedal. Then returned to the gas. Nothing he could do. His face itched madly with sweat and crusted blood. *Nothing . . . stay focused . . .*

Six miles from Trish's house, he whitened.

Danielle's car.

He hit the brakes hard, and the tyres locked, and the Audi slid to a stop. In his mind he instinctively understood that what happened now – these next crucial seconds – would haunt him again a thousand times in his nightmares, and deep inside he felt his subconscious buck in pain. He emerged dazed to the street and stumbled towards the Honda, in a trance, the asphalt sucking at his feet like mud – all this, too, burned forever into his muscle memory. His ears buzzed, as if his fear were audible.

No

Her car sat crashed halfway up the kerb, the hood crumpled around a splintered telegraph pole, that goddamn stupid licence plate YIN•YANG . . .

No no no

Bloody brown handprints on the open doors, the engine still hissing . . .

No no no fuck fuck fuck

He peered into the trashed driver's seat. Soaked with guts, torn loops of intestine, half a bitten liver. The floor mats submerged in blood an inch deep. But no Danielle.

Delle . . .

A trail of red footprints exited the car, crossed the sidewalk and into the scrub.

Into the barren desert.

She'd left him.

12.6

In the prison lab Marco coughed and sputtered, his mouth sour with the acid aftertaste of vomit; at last he reeled in a full satisfying breath, and time kick-started forward again. His vision had dimmed, gone grey in the previous seconds, and suddenly colour came flooding back, and the room reanimated with agonising clarity. There was Wu, standing rigidly beside the operating table, his left arm wrapped in brown-red bandages, his green eyes darting between Marco and the vaccine in its place on the wall rack – as if he were debating two choices, weighing each carefully in the hidden rooms of his mind.

And there was Ballard, still slumped against the medical fridge. Whispering to himself in that unnerving half-voice of his, the mumbled secret language that Marco remembered from his last days at the hospital. Roger Ballard – the most intelligent human Marco had ever met, reduced to this gibbering, mad, pathetic figure.

I'm sorry, Roger.

The thought flipped over in Marco's mind like a card in a magic trick, surprising, impossible. But there it was, undeniable. *I'm sorry. I'm sorry this happened.*

To me, to you. To Hannah. To Danielle. To all of us.

Four lives linked – a chain reaction triggered by the same catalyst, a single spark igniting four infernos. Hannah's birth asphyxia had been the horrible weight thrust upon them all. They were like pack animals, each of them – overloaded, overburdened – and, although they'd fought bravely, they'd each finally collapsed in the end, their eyes bugging and tongues out, into the dry dust. Hannah was the first to fall. Then Marco and Danielle.

And now Roger. They'd all done what they could – and failed.

Seeing Roger now, so broken and miserable, suddenly devastated Marco. He felt the chambers of his heart flood with empathy, his love for Hannah and Danielle billowing outwards like a flame doused with gasoline, reaching further and further until it encompassed Ballard, too. He loved Roger, loved him for suffering, for self-destructing, for mourning Hannah in this fucked-up hell to which he'd damned himself. *A funhouse mirror version of me.* The words Marco had once used to describe Roger, and it was true. Roger *was* an extension of him – warped sadder, crazier, more obsessed with the need to know *why* this had gone wrong.

He could forgive Roger for that.

'Roger,' Marco said hoarsely. 'Roger, we have to get out of here.'

Ballard offered no response. From inside the fridge, the chilled corpse kicked again at the door; Ballard patted the glass like a parent pacifying a child.

Marco threw Wu a glance, then frowned. The sergeant seemed different somehow. His face looked . . . *sharper* now, his cheekbones more defined, his jaw rigid. The temperature in his eyes had dropped – cold again like the first morning in Maricopa.

Unsettled, Marco turned his attention back to Ballard. 'Roger.'

Ballard ignored him.

Marco approached gently until he stood beside his old friend. He spoke with a calm assurance. 'Roger. You did great here.'

Ballard's muttering halted in mid-vocal, and he seemed to emerge from some deep basement of himself, unsteady, blinking into the light. He removed his glasses and, rubbing the lens with his tie, met Marco's gaze, his sunken eyes slightly out of focus. 'Oxygen, Henry,' he said weakly. 'The problem is oxy—'

'I know, Roger. You'll figure it out, but not here. We have to *go*.' Nervous, Marco checked the flickering video monitor; the hallway into the infirmary was still a wild riot of corpses, body upon body jammed against the barred door. His spirits lowered. No easy exit. 'Is there another way?' he prompted Ballard.

'Henry.' Ballard's crooked lip twitched. 'Have you forgiven me?'

Marco tensed, stunned, afraid of his own answer. And then his cheeks warmed.

'Yes,' he said. The word rode from him on a beautiful chariot of air – a breath he suddenly felt he'd been holding for minutes, for months, for years.

Ballard's taut face softened. He nodded, relieved, and returned his glasses to the hump of his nose. 'I'm glad,' he remarked. 'Progress, yes, Henry?'

Marco cleared his throat. 'Progress.'

The men regarded one another, appeased.

'So,' Marco said. 'Are you coming, Roger?'

Ballard's eyes closed, and he inhaled deeply and long, and Marco could almost see inside his mind, a reverie of blue skies and green grass, the open country. Life outside the torture chamber he'd built for himself. And then Roger snapped awake.

'Yes,' he concluded. 'I'll come with you. I will. If you don't mind waiting here, you and the sergeant, I'll gather my notes, and the vaccine of course—'

SWACK.

A silver blur struck from Marco's right, so fast he had no time to react, no time to intercept or deflect its trajectory. He could only flinch as Ballard's throat split apart, two rubbery pink flaps, top and bottom. For a befuddled instant the wound grinned horribly like a mutant mouth, and then Ballard gurgled and clutched his neck, a grisly red waterfall cascading over his thin fingers. Marco gawked, stunned, terror rising as he absorbed what had just happened.

No . . .

Ballard's eyes rolled in the bony sockets, and his lips puckered, and he looked like a dying fish, mouth opening and closing with soft popping sounds. He tried to speak – to impart to Marco some last word of science perhaps, some final discovery seen through the lens of his death – but instead all he did was burp a pink sticky bubble, and his pupils contracted, and he flopped to the floor, his jugular pumping, his body a twitching island in a spreading sea of red.

Fuck no!

Marco couldn't move – still not ready, too shocked to react, his legs ignoring the screams from his brain – and then all at once every muscle worked, and he crashed backwards, overwhelmed; he struck the edge of the operating table and bounced, his boots slipping. He threw out his arms to catch himself, but not quick enough; with a surprised cry he landed on his ass, and the M9 skittered and spun free across the tiles.

It can't be . . .

Several feet away, Wu stood over Ballard's fallen body. In his hand the crescent knife gleamed wetly with a ridge of crimson. Marco gaped, astonished, as a red drop gathered and plopped like a gruesome tear to the white floor.

'Wu,' he panted. 'No . . .'

Wu regarded him gravely, then bent and retrieved the M9 near his foot.

'I'm sorry, Doctor,' he said, sounding almost genuine. He holstered his knife and reached into his vest. His left hand emerged with the rubber-corked phial that Ballard had replaced on the rack. The vaccine. Wu held it aloft. 'I have what I came for.'

What you came for? Marco paled, nauseous again. And then he understood.

Of course . . . I'm a fucking idiot.

He'd been too caught up in his own shit to see this coming, when all along it should have been obvious. Fuck, Wu had even *warned* him on the train – the *vaccine* was the prize, the checkmate in this match between nations. Roger Ballard? Just a plastic, faceless game piece.

And so am I, Marco realised, more angered than afraid.

A lump hardened in his stomach. 'You didn't have to kill him.'

Wu stared, unblinking. 'Killing is what I do, Doctor. I told you that.'

'He could have kept going – found the cure.'

Wu scoffed. 'Cure? He was insane. His mind was disintegrating – you saw it yourself. We have our own great scientists in China. The vaccine will be all they need.'

The air in the lab deadened. The after-silence of Wu's words stretched a second, two seconds, perhaps longer.

And then one word came echoing back to Marco. *China.*

His brow furrowed.

China . . .

Reading Marco's face, Wu responded with a nod, barely perceptible. The slightest acknowledgement of a secret both men could finally share.

'Fuck,' Marco spat, hit hard by sudden, total comprehension. And then panic smacked him, too, and he pawed crazily at the tiles, palms slipping, and scrambled to his knees . . .

. . . as the red laser dot of the M9 centred on his chest and hung there, quavering like a tiny round heart. He froze, dumbfounded, and beheld Wu helplessly. In the sergeant's hand, the cold black eye of the gun barrel leered back at him.

'Stay down,' Wu said.

'You're not American.'

'No,' Wu agreed. 'Then again, Doctor, neither are you. As you may recall, your country disowned you.'

'Bullshit,' Marco snapped. 'So you're a goddamn *spy*?'

Wu said nothing.

'All those computer break-ins,' Marco said. 'China, I assume. And what now? You want me to switch sides as a "fuck-you" to Osbourne?'

Wu shook his head. 'Hardly, Doctor,' he disagreed, speaking between thin stretched lips. 'It's far too late to trade teams. Besides which, I don't need your help any more.'

He paused reflectively. 'You were useful, but I must . . .' He trailed off, and the barrel of the M9 edged forward as if to complete the thought.

'This whole time,' Marco said, understanding. 'Your plan was to kill me.'

'Yes,' Wu said. A curt affirmation, perfunctory.

'The RRU team that Osbourne sent. Did you kill them?'

'Yes.'

'Jesus Christ . . . I *knew* you were a prick, that first day. Should've listened to my gut.'

Wu darkened. 'Enough conversation, Doctor. It's time—'

He jerked, distracted by a noise behind him. Ballard wasn't dead yet. Roger had hoisted himself to his feet and was now bent against the counter, crippled, dragging his broken body towards the door – a feeble escape attempt, Marco thought. Smeared blood tracked Ballard's progress along the stainless steel counter. His hobbled foot scraped the tiles; a soft gurgling emitted from his slashed throat as he exerted himself.

He reached the corner where the counter turned, and with a fresh injection of horror Marco realised what Roger was *really* after.

The electrical box on top of the monitor. The white toggle switch.

Holy Christ.

It's the goddamn security buzzer.

The same epiphany struck Wu at the same moment. His eyes widened, and he wheeled with the M9, the red dot pouncing onto Roger's spine . . .

. . . and as the gun fired, and a hole exploded in the back of Roger's shirt, and the fabric jetted blood . . .

. . . and as Marco heard himself scream, *'No Roger!'* . . .

. . . Ballard's outstretched palm slammed the electrical box and held on, strangling the switch with every last volt of power his muscles could generate. Far off in the halls, at the security checkpoint leading into the infirmary, the buzzer roared to life.

ZRRRRRRRRRRRRRRRRRRRRR.

The sound resonated through every cold bone in Marco's body, rattled his legs and arms and plucked his ribs. At the security console Ballard convulsed with a final yowl of pain and crashed to the floor, utterly, unmistakably dead, but Marco was beyond worrying about Roger now, because on the security monitor there was a *serious fucking problem*, a nightmare projecting straight from his subconscious to the black and white screen, really happening.

The corpses had the security door open and were raging through the checkpoint by the hundreds. An endless river of dead, blood-crazed convicts, flooding the infirmary.

Even now, he heard their wails reverberating up the hall.

They were coming for him.

Incredulous, he met eyes once more with Wu.

The sergeant – not a sergeant, not Army Intelligence, but a no-good son-of-a-bitch *spy* – met him with a peeved expression. 'Foolish,' he muttered, and Marco sensed that perhaps Wu was referring to himself. Sweat dripped from the man's matted black hair.

'Wu,' Marco urged. The cries of the dead grew louder. 'We've gotta get out.'

Wu laughed once – a strange sound, both amused and anguished. 'Oh, I will, Doctor.' He aimed the pistol again at Marco. His finger twitched on the trigger.

'You won't,' he said.

12.7

On Marco's chest the red laser dot seemed to swell, big and round in his perception like a basketball, and his pectoral muscles clenched, anticipating the hot pain to come – the searing implosion of his sternum, the bullet shredding his heart to hamburger meat. Desperate, his eyes counted off steps on the floor, the distance to Wu. Eight feet, at least – too far for a clumsy leap, a last-ditch grab for the gun. He'd be shot dead halfway.

Wu dominated the centre of the lab, imposing, cut with muscle; the blood-soaked bandages around his bulging left bicep made him look stronger, somehow more invincible. The M9 was locked in his grip, certain, intent on killing. His mouth and eyes had been wiped empty, a hundred miles removed from the sympathy he'd exhibited in the chapel in Hemet.

We were almost . . . friends then, Marco floundered.

But now there was nothing, nothing between them except a mechanical stare. The betrayal should have angered Marco – enraged him, made him insane with the desire to bash Wu's skull, pound that back-stabbing brain to jelly. And yet at the same time, it was all so . . . *logical,* he knew. Impersonal, inoffensive. Just Wu doing what he'd been trained to do.

I'm dead, Marco thought. The idea floated to him, oddly calm, almost acceptable – as if death were a choice he could never make for himself, but maybe, just maybe after so much misery, he was glad somebody was making it for him . . .

Bullshit, he scolded himself. His head cleared. Christ, he'd almost given up just now, but *fuck that, fuck you Wu, I thought we were a team . . . and fuck Osbourne and fuck you God . . .*

'Do not go gentle into that good night' and all that shit, you can kill me but I don't have to accept this, I don't have to pretend it's all right . . .

. . . and *there* was the anger he'd been needing so badly, belated but welcome . . .

Fuck Danielle, too, I'm sorry, I'm sorry Delle but fuck you, too, I needed you . . .

. . . setting him on fire, tears like burning gasoline on his cheeks and chin.

'You warned me, Wu,' he said, his mouth dry. A bitter smile locked itself to his lips. 'You're nothing but a killer, right? Now go ahead and *prove it.*'

Wu wavered. Barely, only for an instant, marked by the quickest tremor at the corner of his mouth and a sad flicker in his eyes. He blinked – his finger eased on the trigger, the barrel swayed – and then he blinked again, and his eyes were cold once more like emeralds.

'*Zhongguo,*' he half-whispered, like a ghost. 'For China.'

The gun steadied, and Marco braced for the explosion, still in disbelief; his eyes locked on Wu with intense, penetrating finality – as if with one last glance he might see *inside* the man, decipher him, know the *real* Wu before the pistol flashed and all light went black . . .

Wu's finger held; the moment stretched, agonising and breathless.

And then the gun lowered. The red dot touched the floor.

Wu shook his head, slow and deliberate.

'No,' he said. 'I will not.'

Eight feet away, Marco waited in stunned silence. He held to his spot, anchored – afraid to move, to breathe, to speak a word.

It's a trick. A trick – a fucking mean bullshit trick.

Wu turned his face, avoiding Marco. 'I have what I need, Doctor. Beijing is wrong. Your death adds nothing.' His voice sounded strained. 'The vaccine is mine. But you can go. Please.'

From the main corridor echoed a freakish wail, corpses herding past the check-in desk. Hesitantly Marco risked a word. 'Go . . . ?'

'Home,' Wu said. He lifted his head and nodded, his chin resolute. His gaze joined with Marco's; his eyes had softened, placid now like green stained glass, like the chapel windows in Hemet, and in that instant Marco believed him. Wu stood straight.

'China owes— *I* owe you this,' he confirmed and nodded again, agreeing with himself, unaware that a stiff-limbed shadow had risen from the floor behind him, arms reaching . . .

Marco's eyes widened in horror.

'*Wu!*' he cried out . . .

. . . just as Roger Ballard's resurrected corpse sprang at Wu's back, its face crazed and splotched white; its teeth crunched on Wu's neck and thrashed wildly, and Marco watched, helpless, as the sternomastoid muscle tore free amidst a geyser of blood . . .

. . . and sound exploded everywhere at once, deafening, as Wu let loose a needling scream and fired the M9 wildly; the wayward bullet blasted a glass phial to shards on the rack behind Marco as the lab rocked with the gunshot and the excruciating ear-ringing aftershock. Marco heard himself yelling, too, shocked by his own senses, shocked to still be alive . . .

. . . seeing Wu topple backwards, Ballard's blood-soaked corpse riding him down to the floor, gnashing and growling. The vaccine phial clattered from Wu's left hand and rolled spinning below the operating table. The sergeant bellowed in pain, his arm pinned under him uselessly as the corpse bit again, carved a glistening, mouth-sized crater just under his chin.

'*Goddamn it!*' Wu roared, thrashing his arm free.

And then came the second thunder-blast as Wu jammed the M9 up under Ballard's crooked lip and pulled the trigger. Ballard's head erupted like fireworks, a crimson starburst of blood and brain. Fragments of stale-coloured teeth spun across the tiles towards Marco. Instinctively he jerked his feet away, knees to chest, sickened.

Ballard's body dumped atop Wu, their blood merging into a thick batter.

Roger Ballard had been returned.

'*Goddamn it!*' Wu screamed again. Red spittle sparked from his mouth. He shoved Ballard off and struggled to a sitting position, clutching his torn neck, but the wound was too large; the blood emptied fast, streaming through his fingers, dribbling down his forearm to his elbow. He bit hard on his lip, his chest heaving.

Marco scrambled up and backed away, speechless as he bumped once more against the operating table and edged around it. His mind fumbled.

Roger resurrected.

The vaccine didn't work – or maybe . . . maybe Roger . . .

And then he understood. The vaccine *did* work, but it wasn't a cure; even Roger had said so. The vaccine would protect those who hadn't yet been infected. But Roger had taken it too late, too long after he'd been bitten, long after the disease had converted his flesh; the Resurrection had been *inside* him, in his blood this entire goddamn time – dormant, waiting patiently, unable to overwhelm the living tissue as long as he'd been alive.

But once he was dead, it had grabbed control. Taken what it wanted . . .

The glass phials clinked under Marco's spine as he backed against the wall. He met eyes with Wu across the lab. The sergeant's legs spasmed – wet sloshing sounds in the puddled blood. On both hands his fingers had contorted into wretched claws, the muscles seizing. The M9 lay uselessly where he'd dropped it by his right knee. His cheeks were an ashen white, the colour of driftwood, and he looked small now, puppet-like, propped against the counter with his arms limp at his sides. Already his bite wounds had coloured a diseased-looking purple, the skin brittle like charred paper around the edges. He smiled knowingly at Marco.

'Careless,' he said, inflecting the word with bitter self-judgement.

Tortured cries rocked the hallway outside the lab – very close.

'Angry hornets,' Wu observed. His voice shook.

On the monitor the dead had stormed the infirmary, overflowing the video screens, a thousand rotting cannibals mobbing the halls. Fifty feet from the lab, maybe less. Terrified, Marco glanced to the doorway – knowing it would fill in seconds with shambling bodies. Putrid faces, and meat-ripping hands, and merciless, biting jaws.

He took a single step towards Wu, then stopped. Impossible. He'd never get them both out alive. *Wu's bitten, good as dead* . . . But maybe the vaccine could help? *Shit!*

The corpses were ten feet from the door.

'Doctor.' Wu's voice caught him. Steadied him. Marco turned to the fallen man.

'It's time,' Wu advised, 'to run like hell.'

The verdict came like a blessing, calm and kind and sure. In an instant all doubt had disappeared; both men understood. Marco nodded, grateful. 'I'm sorry,' he muttered, and with a grim sense of surrender, he bolted towards the doorway – and just then an urgent thought cried out from what remained of his rational mind, and he switched direction, lunging to his right. He reached below the operating table and snatched out the glass phial.

The vaccine.

C'mon, hurry, asshole.

He stuffed the flask into his side pocket, and then, touching his hand to the floor like a sprinter at the starting line of a race, he scooped up a pea-sized chunk of Roger Ballard's spongy, blown-out brain. Shoved that, too, into his pocket.

Proof.

Roger didn't have a wedding ring – *bring back the jewellery, and nobody disputes you did the job* – but bet your ass, Osbourne was getting his goddamn DNA sample.

The dead groans in the hallway reverberated just out of sight. Shadows flickered on the wall. Time was up. The corpses were here.

'Run,' Wu urged, sputtering blood.

In obedience Marco broke for the door. A one-eyed convict popped through the frame, snapping and grabbing; Marco slung himself feet-first, sliding under the corpse's arms. An icy thumb brushed his cheek as he bounced on his ass into the hall. *Shit!* Corpses in jumpsuits jammed the corridor, surrounding him. He skidded to the opposite wall, cradling his head with his arms, deflecting kicks from their bloodstained boots. Against the wall he crumpled and coughed. Bursting into the hall had surprised the dead men – the only reason he wasn't already dead himself – but the confusion was evaporating fast. In two seconds they'd mob, a flock of freakish orange birds plucking him like a worm from the ground.

He had to move.

With a frantic kick he twisted to his right, away from the maddened corpses stumbling up the hall, and, as he rolled, his eyes darted into the lab for one last topsy-turvy glimpse. Roger's body lay broken and ugly on the floor, and against the cabinets slumped Wu, dazed and weak, watching Marco's clumsy acrobatics with a bemused grin like a child at a circus.

Their eyes met a final time, and Marco pulsed with guilt, and he wished for whatever insane reason that he'd bidden Wu a proper farewell, thanked him, as crazy as that seemed, *thanked* him for the company on this bullshit ride . . .

. . . and then he tumbled past the door, and Wu was gone.

Marco struggled to his feet, slipping and sliding, his boots wet with thickening blood; he regained his balance ten feet ahead of the oncoming corpses. The massive riot surged in his direction, goaded by the moving target, fresh meat to chase and consume. But he also noted grimly that the dead mob had split off into the lab as well, a march of empty-eyed corpses jostling through the door, swamping the room where Wu lay fallen.

Good-bye, Wu.

Marco ran, panting, his ribs throbbing, his skin hot with every kind of pain. He stumbled and cracked his shoulder against a dry whiteboard on the wall, smearing lines of black scribbled calculations, and then shoved himself back to the middle of the hall and continued running.

His legs grew heavier with each step. In his head he counted seconds, all sound blotted from his consciousness, like the expectant silence after a grenade pin is pulled.

And then it detonated – a high, hideous scream exploding from the lab, blasting down the hallway after him, a shock-wave impossible to outrun.

Goodbye, Wu, he thought again.

He staggered onwards, exhausted, a thousand corpses close behind.

He had no idea where he was going.

But he hoped – prayed – this hall wasn't another dead end.

12.8

His life spilling from him, Wu watched Henry Marco go. The American dived recklessly into the dead mob, barely avoiding the onslaught, and then vanished down the hall to either live or die elsewhere in the prison. *He'll live*, Wu decided. *He is strong.*

Strong survival instincts. The brief had been right.

As the lab entrance darkened with corpses, like an execution squad coming to collect him, Wu laughed aloud. The sudden warm impulse surprised him – he hadn't laughed in months, perhaps years – and he marvelled, wondering what this meant now, this unlikely good humour conquering his fear. And then he understood.

Bao Zhi . . .

His uncle.

Bao Zhi, who had always made Wu roll with laughter as a boy. Bao Zhi, the master of silly jokes and cherished bedtime stories told by firelight, was *here* – here but invisible, a spirit holding Wu's hand to comfort him.

Yes. Bao Zhi. Wu felt the iron muscles in his arms relax. His vision blurred; a chill swept his skin as blood fled his wounded neck like heat from a chimney. His body was descending, dropping, cooling to room temperature.

Dead convicts shuffled through the door, two and three at a time, shoulders bumping. A Hispanic male led the mob, its face half skinned, its mouth broken open. A single gold tooth gleamed in a pit of black gums and brown stumps.

Pain boiled from every pore in Wu's skin, and he forced himself to embrace it – to make it part of himself, because the pain was all he had now, and if he owned it, he would not fear it. Pain. He was going to die. He bit his lip to steel himself, and that hurt, too.

'*Shūshu*,' he groaned.

Uncle.

'*Qǐng liú zài wǒ shēnbiān.*'

Please stay with me.

He looked up. Above was a sky of grotesque faces, blood-starved corpses bending over him. His head swam. The view of his impending death dizzied him. Like gazing up at skyscrapers on a city street. *Like Beijing*, he thought, remembering the first time he'd ever visited as a nineteen-year-old soldier. It had been the summer after the Yangtze floods, to accept his new position with the MSS; he'd lived his boyhood two thousand kilometres west, cavorting amidst green forests and glistening bamboo and awe-inspiring mountains, and yet until that first day in Beijing he'd had no idea how *beautiful* his country could be. Cement and glass and steel arranged masterfully by human hand, stacked a hundred metres high – a promise of the greatness and growth and prosperity awaiting all China. The future would be proud for his brothers and sisters, a salvation from hard labour and filth-riddled villages. And *he*, young Kheng Wu, would help build the noble new China, add himself like a brick to the foundation, obey his orders . . .

Here in the lab, a dozen corpses had crowded around him like guests at a dinner table. Dry fingertips brushed his face, dabbed his tears. The touch was light, a brief misleading caress – and then the ripping began. He gasped once as jagged fingernails carved ditches into his flesh, spiked into his ears, his nostrils, his eye sockets, crammed his mouth and split his cheeks. The universe exploded, a bright, excruciating, bloody orange, forcing his eyes deep into his skull. Blinded, he bucked, overloaded, lost in the pain. He felt mouths on his skin . . .

Shūshu!

. . . and teeth, teeth everywhere, opening him to the world; he convulsed as a frigid blast rocked his gut, cold air, a savage tug that ended with a snap. He felt momentarily buoyant, his weight escaping him in wet sloppy bursts; he had the sensation of being unravelled like a spool of meaty rope. And then a new weight fell atop him, a fresh shuddering agony as a hundred hands crushed him down; his tongue splashed with something sweet, and blood flooded his throat.

He heard his body scream – loud, long, an awful earthly sound.

But he was done with the earth.

Done with Beijing.

Done being the killer.

He squeezed his right hand into a fist, tighter, tighter, until at last he felt Bao Zhi gripping back. And then it was time. Time to leave this place, peacefully and humbly and with respect. Time to join his uncle. Return to his village in Qinghai. Take his place in the realm of the dead . . . walk alongside the living, alongside his beloved sisters and brothers.

He missed them. He would be happy there, serving and protecting. Guarding over them, the way ancestral spirits do.

A smile spread across the wet mangled pulp of his face.

This was not failure.

China needs me, he thought. *My family needs me.*

And with a fanfare of blood and entrails, Kheng Wu went to them.

12.9

Right. No – left! The corridor divided, forcing Marco to choose. He cut to his left, ditching the corpses that stalked thirty feet behind him; he raced through another long hall of occupied cells – strangled moans emanated from behind the metal doors – and he gulped the toxic air as he went; panicking, disoriented by the mazelike bends and identical hallways disappearing into the gloom, he felt like Theseus stumbling dazed through the labyrinth of Crete, hunted by the deadly Minotaur – *left? no, straight*, knowing that a single wrong turn would kill him, and as infuriated cries echoed behind him and ahead, from locations impossible to pinpoint, he prayed he wouldn't accidentally double back, turn the next corner and crash right smack into the frenzied dead convicts – *left, definitely left* – and just then a rat bolted under his feet, and he hurdled it like some mad Olympian; at the next corner he careered out of control, wild, body-slamming the wall, but his adrenalin was pumping too high to feel anything like pain, so without even a flinch he stiff-armed himself back on course and sprinted – small details beginning to look familiar now, and with growing confidence he suspected he'd been this way before, recognising a constellation of bullet holes in the wall, an oblong bloodstain on the tile – and then suddenly, at the end of the corridor, a hundred feet *ahead* somehow, he saw the dead, ragged and grey and mindless, charging at him . . . his stomach shrank, but he didn't stop, didn't slow, he had it figured out now, and he ran straight at them like a crazed soldier charging across the battlefield, headlong towards a terrible death.

Thirty feet, twenty feet, ten . . .

Three steps from their groping arms, a hallway opened to his right, and with a holler he planted his left foot and leaped sideways to escape . . .

. . . and whooped victoriously as he saw he'd been correct. He'd stumbled his way back to the central corridor; there was the same gurney he'd passed earlier, like a sign posted to steer him out of this fucking maze. The hall ahead was unobstructed; the dead legion from the main block had emptied into the infirmary and turned towards the lab, a thousand corpses snaking through twists and turns behind him, as though he were leading a monstrous conga line at a bad wedding.

He heard the corpses collapse around the corner, still hot on his trail, and his nose bristled as if they'd pushed a cloud of rancid air ahead of them. He took off again, this time elated, laughing, certain he would survive – incredibly, impossibly, he would *survive* this mind-numbing fucked-up morning – and each twenty yards he ran, another sight bolstered him: the admissions desk, the infirmary entrance . . .

. . . The steel-barred security checkpoint. He slipped across a slick surface of frothy blood embellished with shapeless chunks of meat – legs and a ribcage and a half-chewed heart, and Big Skull's skinned head lying in the corner, mouth open.

And beyond that, the abandoned quad, sideways in the corridor.

Jackpot.

Thank you, Marco thought, clutching his ribs as if another breath would kill him. Giddy, he almost hopped onto the vehicle – then caught himself, feeling his mind settle to rational speed, the logic returning. He turned and grabbed the barred door, then yanked it so hard his elbows popped. The door crashed shut and locked, just in time.

The dead onslaught hurled itself against the bars, clambering and shoving and squishing the corpses in front. Eyeballs squirted loose as the crowd pushed from the back; chests cracked and oozed black blood. A starved corpse with a big chin grabbed at him through the bars; as the pressure grew enormous, its arms sliced off and slapped to the floor at Marco's feet. Marco stepped back, warily eyeballing the damp cinderblock walls. *God, don't let the door crumble loose.* It held solid. The dead screamed and raged.

'Sorry,' he addressed the crowd. 'You have to stay.'

He mounted the quad and turned the ignition key, and as the handles rumbled in his sore grip and the motor throbbed like an indestructible heart, Marco shared the sudden rush of power in his own muscles, as if he, too, were wired into the engine.

Ahead of him the hallway was quiet, empty, long.

Hope it stays that way.

He noticed the ghostly horse skull tied to the hood. Its long head pointed the way home.

'Giddy up,' he commanded, then gunned the throttle.

The quad bounded forward, whipping a tail of exhaust behind it. And then he was out. Out to the cell blocks, also eerie and silent . . . then out to the prison yard, past the crashed military truck . . . then out to the grounds, the sun high in the sky, the late morning air fantastic and fresh on his cheeks as he weaved easily between the few scattered corpses still roaming the property.

Two minutes later he'd exited through the bombed-out hole in the concrete wall, and there he'd traded the quad for one of the remaining abandoned MTVRs; five minutes afterwards he was barrelling east in the truck along Route 247 back to Arizona, back to base, back to whatever might remain of reality for him there. He studied himself in the mirror – eyes bleary and bloodshot, pink with tears that came and went in unpredictable spurts – as behind him Sarsgard Prison shrivelled in the rear-view mirror, shrinking and shrinking and then finally vanishing altogether, sucking Roger and Wu with it into the void.

Gone.

His hands draped the steering wheel. His eyes fell sadly on the loose platinum band sitting askew on his ring finger.

He felt more alone than he had in a long time.

Danielle was gone, too.

But I'm alive, he thought, and there came the tears again, a wet running salt he could taste on his lips. *After all this, all this bullshit, still alive.*

Fuck it. Fuck prison.

I've been paroled.

RETURN

13.1

Arizona. Home, just past dawn. He'd driven all night, a grim voyage across the Redlands Highway in the MTVR, four hundred miles of nothingness to numb his mind. The front door creaked as he let himself in, and all that greeted him was the ache that accompanied these lonely arrivals home; no warm welcome, no gratifying sense of being missed. The house was indifferent to whether he lived or died. He thought of the stray dogs in Hemet, those pathetic and ownerless animals, and he wondered if maybe – just maybe – the time had come to conquer his fear and find a good dog for himself. *Might be nice to have a friend.*

Upstairs, his office had a dreamlike quality, familiar yet strange, as if somewhere along the sixteen-hour drive he'd fallen asleep and was now only fantasising his homecoming. Except, he knew, it had to be real. His body hurt too much; he could never dream a pain this complete, this sharp – hot blue flames burning in a dozen bloody fire pits in his skin, purple embers smouldering beneath bruises on his arms and legs and stomach. He was a living lab specimen of cuts, scrapes, blisters, bumps and contusions.

He collapsed into his chair and turned on the computer.

He didn't give a shit about checking the barricade. Or the trap.

Trap's empty. She's not coming back.

With a sour smile, he dialled Benjamin.

The phone rang eighteen times. Finally the line clicked, and a grainy video materialised on the screen. A face. Owen Osbourne.

Marco wasn't surprised. 'Hi, honey, I'm home.'

If possible, Osbourne appeared uglier than he had four days ago, as if he truly were morphing from human to fish – the eyes seemed spaced a fraction wider, his piranha face colder. His wet white hair was slicked back like mucus on his head, suggesting he'd just stepped from the shower. His black pupils glistened. Eager.

'Welcome back, Doctor Marco. We've been waiting.'

'Yeah, sorry to keep you. Where's Ben?'

'Did you locate Ballard?'

'Where's Ben?' Marco insisted. He called out. '*Ben!* You there?'

'I'm here, man,' Ben's voice assured him from off screen. He sounded like hell – hoarse, tired. So it had been a rough few days for Ben, too. 'It's cool.'

'Okay,' Marco said, relaxing. 'Glad to hear you, buddy.'

'Same here,' Ben began, 'I was starting to freak—'

'*Doctor*,' Osbourne snapped, cutting Benjamin short. The director had momentarily lost his composure; a white strand of hair had fallen forward onto his rounded forehead. He brushed it back, then cleared his throat and resettled in his chair. 'Please. The sooner we settle matters, the sooner you and Mr Ostroff can catch up. As for myself, I only want to know one thing . . .'

He ran his tongue hungrily along his top row of bleached teeth. 'Ballard?'

Fuck you, Marco wanted to answer. He stared wordlessly at Osbourne, letting the silence speak for him, and then at last relented.

'Dead,' he reported. 'Returned. And yes, I brought back

a nice little sample of DNA as a souvenir – not that you asked me for it. Turns out, your RRU team had orders to collect Roger's blood. You only sent me to kill an old friend without informing me why.'

Osbourne's mouth twitched at the corners. He nodded, looking as if he'd just swallowed a bite of delicious filet mignon. Savouring the after-flavour.

'The DNA,' he said. 'Very good news.'

'Good and bad,' Marco continued. 'Because guess who's also dead? Every single one of your RRU soldiers. In fact, they never even showed – but someone else did. A nice guy from the Chinese CIA or some bullshit like that, and oh, by the way, he tried to kill *me*, too.'

'I see,' Osbourne remarked, unblinking. 'Not entirely surprising – I was aware of external interest in our mission. We *had* wondered why the RRU didn't report at the designated time-point. If you hadn't returned by sundown today, we planned to dispatch a back-up unit.'

'Wow, thanks. I would've been long dead by then.'

'Exactly,' said Osbourne bluntly. 'While you were alive, there was no reason to commit additional resources. It would have been necessary only if you were dead.'

Marco bristled. 'You're a great leader. Your men must love you.'

'Doctor, please, don't turn this personal. You and I, we each had objectives. I'm pleased that you accomplished yours. Your country is pleased,' the director cooed. Once again Marco felt like a child receiving insincere praise from an adult. A pat on the head.

Uncle Owen. Wu's disdainful moniker for Osbourne.

'So,' Marco said. 'Are you going to tell me finally what this was all about?'

Osbourne lifted an eyebrow, pretending not to understand. 'About?'

'Why? Why did you need Roger's DNA?' He knew the answer, of course. But Osbourne *owed* him the same truth, goddamn it. Osbourne, the grand master in this New Republican chess match, the man scouring the board from above and toppling pawns like Wu and Marco.

Osbourne answered him with stone eyes. 'I'm afraid that's classified, Doctor Marco,' he said, and crossed his legs politely, effeminately, at the knees.

'You have what you need, in other words,' Marco translated. 'So there's nothing else I need to know.'

'Well said.'

Marco inhaled, cooling his anger before it reddened his cheeks. 'All right, fine,' he breathed. 'I figured you'd say that. The thing is, though . . . I already know more than you think.'

A shadow flickered across Osbourne's face.

Marco chewed his lip. Should he tell Osbourne everything? That Roger had been alive? Alive, still working, still unravelling the Resurrection?

How great, Marco thought, *it would be to see Osbourne squirm.*

To see the regret in the director's eyes as he realised that Roger's murder was a *loss*; that Roger might have contributed so much more to the world if he'd survived.

To see Osbourne feel one-tenth of the grief in Marco's own chest.

You smug fucking asshole. Roger's death should be mourned.

'There's one more thing to show you,' Marco said. He dug into his vest pocket – cringing as his fingers brushed the clammy chunk of Roger's brain – and pulled the glass phial he'd grabbed from the prison lab. He waved it teasingly for the camera. 'This.'

Osbourne blinked, and his gaze narrowed just perceptibly; the man's piranha face hungered towards the computer, and

Marco felt a flutter in his stomach, a nervous anticipation, like a fisherman watching a trout circle the hook before it bites.

And, sure enough, Osbourne snapped at the bait. 'What is it?' he asked, cool and even, but just below the surface Marco sensed a torrid undercurrent of alarm. The director uncrossed his legs and edged forward in his chair. 'The DNA?'

Marco leaned back, prolonging Osbourne's discomfort.

'Better,' he said. 'A vaccine. A working vaccine.'

Osbourne's face was unchanged. But his eyes – his eyes detonated with something like lust, a nearly electric discharge of desire. It burned intently and then extinguished, and Osbourne breathed out through flexed nostrils. The microphone emitted a sustained hiss.

'You found that with Ballard?' Osbourne asked, attempting nonchalance, and yet he sounded strained, as if an invisible hand had grabbed him by the throat. His rigid jaw worked side to side, teeth silently grinding. He wanted the phial, Marco knew. Badly.

'Yes,' Marco answered. 'With Ballard. And, according to his private notes, it's the real deal. Apparently Roger didn't share everything he knew with you.' A twist of the truth – Marco still wasn't sure how Osbourne would react if he learned Roger had been alive.

Pissed that I didn't save him? Hold me to blame?

Why take that chance?

Osbourne glowered. His brow creased, suspicious; the skin bunched on his forehead, creating rubbery wrinkles in his bad facelift. 'What proof did Ballard have that it works?'

'Roger Ballard was a *genius*. I know you're quite well aware of that. I also know you're aware how close Roger was to succeeding.' He paused to give Osbourne a chance to comment – to admit to the email that Roger had sent. Osbourne said nothing. *Bastard,* Marco thought and then concluded simply, 'If Roger said the vaccine works, I believe him.'

A light blush had soaked into Osbourne's cheeks; his cold-blooded circulation had evidently begun to heat up. He licked his lips. 'I need you to bring that sample to me, Doctor Marco,' he said. The statement was matter-of-fact – a foregone conclusion.

Marco set the phial on his desk, beyond camera range; Osbourne's eyes twitched, narrowing as the container disappeared. Marco sat forward again; absently he pinched his earlobe and studied the man on the cross side of the transmission, two thousand miles away in Benjamin's Pennsylvania studio. Osbourne countered his gaze. The piranha. The predator.

How much of this is your fault? Marco wondered. *The Resurrection, the outbreak? How much did you know* before *it happened? How much did you initiate . . . ?*

He recalled Roger's warning. *Osbourne is not to be trusted.*

Unsettled, he probed the black space of Osbourne's pupils. Nothing there to connect with as a fellow man. Nothing but a vacuum. It was the same look he'd seen in Wu's eyes – right near the end as Wu had aimed the gun, prepared to pull the trigger . . .

Osbourne will kill me, Marco thought. *The moment I hand over the vaccine, he'll kill me. Can't have me running around the Safe States, telling stories.*

'I won't bring it,' Marco said.

Osbourne darkened.

'I'll leave it here, and you can come get it,' Marco continued. 'Send someone. Another RRU team, the entire US army, I don't care. People need this – the Safe States need vaccinations – so I *do* want you to have it. But I'm not bringing it.'

'I'd rather you did, Doctor,' Osbourne admonished. 'It would be a great service.'

'No, thank you,' Marco insisted. 'You'll get what you want – but not from me. I'll be staying here in the Evacuated States. That was our agreement, right? I can stay and finish.'

The director stewed, glowering, emitting waves of discontent. A burst of noise – *tap tap tap* – peppered the microphone, and Marco realised it was Osbourne drumming his fingers on the desk. Uncomfortable seconds passed. At last Osbourne cleared his throat with a growl and sighed. 'I see. You wish to stay and locate your dead wife.'

The summation roiled like acid in Marco's gut. 'Yes,' he said.

'You're a faithful husband, Doctor. You love her that much?'

'Yes.' He forced his voice to sound strong.

'Very well, then.' Osbourne settled back again in his chair and clasped his hands together. A malicious humour crept onto his face, and he leered at Marco; the tips of his eyeteeth protruded from his curled upper lip.

'In that case,' Osbourne said, 'allow me to say – and I'll repeat your own words back to you, Doctor . . .'

He smiled broadly now. 'There's one more thing to show you.'

He waved a spidery finger, and a blue-uniformed soldier appeared from the depths of the room. The soldier reached and took control of the computer mouse, and Marco heard a barrage of terse clicks like a ratchet tightening a clamp on his heart.

Some nasty surprise was coming his way, no doubt. He remembered the video of the prison riot – Roger's apparent death – that Osbourne had sprung on their first call.

Osbourne seemed to read his mind. 'I warned you once, Doctor Marco. I always come to class prepared. In this case, another video that might interest you. Of particular interest is the fact that it was *taken just last week.*'

His emphasis made Marco shudder without knowing why.

The screen blackened, erasing Osbourne in mid-chuckle, and an instant later an image exploded onto the screen, like a new universe created in a millionth of a second. At first Marco didn't understand – and then suddenly he did, and the air superheated, and the oxygen caught fire in his lungs, and he choked. His breath stopped. His heart stopped. His nerves short-circuited. Beneath him the leather chair squawked and pitched . . .

Bright sunlight, a living room with a giant picture window

Oh god

vibrant green leaves in the yard

God

and a blue sofa below the window, and a woman sitting

God oh god

with soft, auburn, lavender-scented hair tucked behind her ears, each delicate lobe with three jade piercings too small for the camera to see.

Marco reeled – confounded, unable to make sense of himself – sucked into a mad wormhole stretching across space and time. He was aware of his hands, white-knuckled and creased with dry blood, clenched tight upon the chair arms and yet utterly beyond his control. His head had detached, a thousand miles away.

'Delle,' he croaked.

She smiled sadly at him. 'Henry.'

13.2

He jumped as she spoke his name, and he almost responded – the word '*How*' balanced on his lips before he pulled it back, remembering that the video was pre-recorded and uncertain what he would have asked anyway. Danielle, sitting there on the sofa, was nothing but the echo of Danielle at 7.48 a.m. 23/09/18, according to white digits ticking in the corner of the screen. His breath came in short gulps, his pulse bounding. Under the desk his feet trembled, a patter upon the hardwood as though his boots were begging him to run.

'Henry,' she said again. She swallowed and grimaced, his name hurting her throat, and then hesitated, seeming reluctant to continue. Her eyes darted off camera. A mumbled unseen voice encouraged her, and with a rush of hatred Marco recognised the patronising inflections.

Osbourne.

You fucking bastard. You found her. You went to her, and didn't tell me until now.

His stomach boiling, he refocused on Danielle. She'd begun to speak.

'Oh god, Henry, I . . . I don't even know what to say,' she stuttered. Her voice was throttled high like a whine, and her cheeks were ruddy and damp, the look she had whenever she was on the verge of crying. She appeared exhausted, beaten emotionally, aged ten years in the span of four. Her pixie dust had worn off, the magic gone. This wasn't the Danielle he'd met in Tech Town, not even the Danielle who'd struggled so hard to love him here in Arizona. The spell had been broken. This was Danielle *now* – real, not some idealised memory; just a sad, frightened woman banished from the fairy glen, her dreams shattered.

His heart plummeted.

'I thought you were dead,' she said, battling to stay composed. 'I swear, Henry, I thought that – or I would have told you to . . . to get out of there, to come here, the Safe States. I didn't know until this morning, I swear. These . . . men, these soldiers came, they wanted me to make this message for you. They told me about you, what you're doing, you and Ben. I thought you were both . . . Why weren't you on the Survivor Register? I had you declared dead . . .'

Her words dissolved into tears. Marco sickened. Ben had never bothered to register them. What was the point? Everyone they knew was dead. Trish was dead. Danielle was . . .

Shit, Danielle was *alive*.

Another quiet encouragement sounded from Osbourne off camera. Danielle steadied herself, breathing deep from her belly, and then resumed.

'They told me . . . what you thought, about me, I mean. Oh, Henry. I'm sorry. I'm so, so sorry you thought that. I never meant . . .'

More deep yoga-breaths, the way she'd once taught him.

'I know you found the Honda, empty,' she said. 'Oh god, that day. Henry, it wasn't me. I got away. Janis, you remember her, *she* was driving me to Trish's. I was too upset about leav— about going to Trish's. I was a mess, I couldn't think, and Janis said she would come take me. And then everything was crazy . . . there were monsters chasing us, and she crashed, and these dead people opened her door and grabbed her, and I got out my door and ran . . .'

Her face crumpled, and she again broke into sobs. *Delle*. He wanted to reach through the screen and comfort her, tuck her hair back behind her ear where it had fallen loose. He had to restrain his hand. Instead he wiped his own face with his sleeve.

A soldier in tinted sunglasses stepped into the video frame, a black HK416 slung on his back. He presented Danielle with a box of tissues and disappeared once more. The gesture was absurd, unreal, like some ridiculous comedy skit. Danielle dried her face, her nose. Ten or twenty seconds passed, occupied by her quiet huffing.

'I hid,' she finally said, 'in the bushes. I was too scared to move, even though Trish's house was just a few miles, but there were dead people everywhere, killing other people. It was so, so *awful* . . . but the funny part is, I almost thought, "This isn't happening." Like I was in a movie, that's all – some bad horror movie, the kind I always swore I'd never do, except now I was acting in one and somehow I'd forgotten this was all pretend.'

She laughed once, mirthlessly, and rubbed her nose. 'A few hours later I saw an army truck, an evacuation team. They picked me up. I told them to find you, Henry. I promise I told them. They looked, they went to the house, but you weren't there, or I guess you were and you didn't answer. You thought I was . . . one of those dead people? This man says you stayed to find me. Oh, god, I wish you hadn't done that, Henry.'

She stared into her lap. Reflecting.

I wish you hadn't done that.

He slumped in his chair, miserable, wishing the same – wishing for *everything* to be different. He pressed his eyes shut, and when he opened them again, his gaze met hers. She was intent, imploring. 'Henry, *please* listen now. I'm sorry. I'm sorry I left – but you understand, don't you? I had to. I promise I had to. I had to move on. And I think there's *meaning* that it happened when it did, on that day. I've thought about it so many times . . . how I was dead in my life, dead and buried with Hannah. And then the Resurrection came, and it was like all the death and sorrow I'd been holding onto was unleashed into the universe – not just me, *my* sorrow, but people's everywhere – and nobody knows why, and it was horrible, horrible. But the Resurrection brought me here, to the Safe States. And I know it sounds selfish, but I'm glad. I'm glad, because after all that, I'm not dead like I was before. I'm *alive* here . . .'

She cupped her hands to her mouth, perhaps surprised at her own candour.

And for the first time he noticed the ring on her left hand. A wedding band. Gold with small crisp diamonds laid horizontally across the cusp – not platinum, not Cartier, not the ring he'd slid onto her slender finger eight years ago.

A pit opened in his stomach, and he felt himself slide to the bottom.

Gradually he became aware that she was again speaking. '. . . remarried, Henry. You don't know him. I met him here, after it all calmed down . . .'

Married. Delle married someone else.

So soon.

He grimaced, scouring the depths of himself for outrage – for anger, for the gut-busting pain inflicted by betrayal. It should have been there, all of it. But it wasn't.

He found nothing.

Four years, he thought. *That's not so soon.*

Shit, you know better than anybody how long four years can be.

When you can barely survive a single day at a time.

'Henry,' she said, and his attention drifted back to her. 'This is my life now. Here. It had to be this way – couldn't you feel it, the universe telling us? It told me to move on. It's telling you, too. Move on, babe—' she slipped, wincing at the old pet name, then caught herself and continued. 'Move on. You can't stay there. You don't need to. Get out and come to the Safe States. Find your happiness.'

I'll never be happy. Her words that day by Hannah's grave.

Perhaps the same memory stirred within her now. 'You were right, Henry. It's what Hannah's spirit wanted for us. To start our lives again.'

Start again, he thought. *Start again, just like Joan Roark.*

Start over without Danielle. Go east, take Osbourne at his word, bring the vaccine. Join civilisation. Cash in that big bank account Ben's been saving for you, and buy a wonderful fucking house and live there, happy but not real happy . . .

And wait for this whole fucking mess to happen again.

'And please, Henry, please please, forgive yourself. It wasn't our fault . . .'

'Are you happy, Delle?' he wondered aloud, not caring if Osbourne heard him on the microphone. He rubbed his knuckles across his chin and studied her.

Yes, he answered himself. *She's happy enough.*

Her mouth opened, but she seemed empty, all the words released. She shook her head, a tender gesture. 'Take care of yourself, Henry—'

And then blackness crashed down on her in mid-sentence. The video stopped, and she vanished, jerked abruptly from him for the second and final time in his life, and in that flash of nothingness he could almost see her departing him like a cloud of breath on a freezing day – as if he were a boy again, watching his own essence twist and dissolve into the atmosphere, irretrievable, gone forever – and then, just as suddenly, time returned to collect him, and he was once again a forty-two-year-old man hunched over his desk in his lonesome home in death-ridden, dirt-coated Arizona.

'Bye, Delle,' he said.

The universe answered him with silence.

13.3

Back again on the screen was Osbourne's ugly, smirking complexion.

'No need to see more, Doctor. You understand,' he said. 'Your wife – beg pardon, your *ex*-wife – is here, alive. Meaning your personal mission in the Evacuated States is no longer relevant. Quite pointless, in fact.'

The director propped his elbows on the desk and laced his fingers together.

'I'm happy for you, of course,' he purred, lousy with insincerity. 'Such a horrible burden removed. Which brings us back to the subject at hand. In light of these revelations . . . seeing you have no reason to hold your current location . . . you *will* bring me that vaccine, won't you, Doctor? Our original deal still stands. Amnesty.'

'You knew about her,' Marco said, and in his tired voice he heard neither surprise nor indignation. It was just a statement. 'That she was alive. You knew all along. I'd bet a damn dollar you had that video in your back pocket on the first call, in case you needed it then. Except you didn't need it. I took the fucking job – stupid me.'

Even his curses sounded flat, like airless tyres.

He had nothing left.

Osbourne served him a look of bemusement, perhaps even approval. The skin around his eyes flexed. 'Of course I knew, Doctor Marco. Knowing is my job. I could tell you the shoe size of every terrorist in the Middle East, if you asked. Locating your missing wife took me less than a morning. I didn't even miss lunch.'

Fuck you, Marco thought, but it didn't really matter what Osbourne knew, either now or then, and Marco's mind was already floating back towards Danielle, to the fresh memory of her on the sofa, flowers in the giant vase, green trees in the window. Full of life. *I'm alive here*, she'd said. Danielle was not dead. But his marriage . . .

His marriage had been dead a long, long time.

Crumbled, decayed, wriggling with worms.

And at last he understood – understood that these past four years had been a goddamn trick he'd played on himself. A ploy to keep his marriage alive, breathing artificially, jump-starting the heart because it couldn't beat on its own. The constant search, returning and returning to the same damn places – the obsessive reliving of each happy memory he could recover from those hundred billion brain cells in his head . . .

Tech Town . . .

Nights in LA . . .

Lake Hemet . . .

And a thousand others, all dead, dead, dead, sealed off forever into the past.

And *he'd* been the force reanimating Danielle, again and again and again. Because he couldn't accept that her love had run out. That it was done.

You're avoiding, Henry. You're always avoiding.

He'd pulled it from the grave, over and over. His own personal Resurrection.

'Doctor Marco.' Osbourne flagged him back to the present.

Marco stared wearily at the director. So what now? In Osbourne's famished expression he saw the Safe States waiting for him, eager to swallow him back into organised society – gnash him between the teeth of the New Republican government and all the rules and politics and relationships with people and stupid television shows and even the simplest of mundane things like trips to Shop Rite to buy milk – a society that would digest him, break him into smaller and smaller bits until he was nothing. Alive, but nothing.

At least the corpses here killed you first.

He shuddered.

He wasn't ready. Not for that.

Before Danielle, he'd always been alone, adrift. No friends, no socialising, not even a goddamn cell phone. And then he'd met her. Danielle. His link to life.

But now . . .

He surprised himself with a chuckle.

'Hang on,' he told Osbourne. He held up one finger. 'Gimme a second.'

Bending, he tugged open the bottommost drawer on his desk and thumbed past the hanging files stuffed with rubber-banded manila folders. From the back he dug out a fresh folder and a clean Ziploc sandwich bag. Just as he was about to kick the drawer shut with his boot, his eye snagged on the first folder in the stack.

Flynn, Thomas.

His next job – the missing logger, the contract Ben had booked for January.

Ruminating, he left the drawer open and turned back to his desk. He sensed Osbourne watching him with impatience, a smouldering in the man's coal-black pupils, but Marco didn't care; he moved methodically, at his own pace. From his pocket he scooped the spongy blob of Roger's brain and shovelled it into the Ziploc.

'Is that—' Osbourne began.

'Not yet,' Marco said. He shuffled the phial containing the vaccine into the plastic bag, a tight fit but good enough. With three loops of a red oversized rubber band, he wrapped the Ziploc into the folder and then, opening the top desk drawer, found a black Sharpie marker and labelled the folder *Ballard, Roger.*

He lifted the folder up for Osbourne to see.

'Everything you need,' he explained. 'The vaccine. And for extra credit on my report card, a genuine authentic Roger Ballard tissue sample. I'm leaving these right here in a folder on my desk. Tell your pick-up boys they can't miss it. Also, they can help themselves to anything they find in the kitchen. Won't be much, though.'

Osbourne pressed both hands flat on the desk, furious. Marco imagined a sound effect of splintering wood. Gratified, he smiled to himself. *Here we go. Now he's pissed.*

'Doctor,' Osbourne growled. 'You've tested me enough. Consider this your final warning. Cooperate – *immediately* – or the offer for Safe State amnesty and all accompanying privileges is rescinded. Permanently, I assure you.'

Marco pushed back his chair and rose. 'I'll lock the front door – don't want corpses getting inside, wrecking up the place. Feel free to shoot the lock.'

'*Doctor Marco.*'

'Marco,' Ben said, off camera, then edging just into frame behind Osbourne. 'C'mon, man, don't be stubborn. This is your chance.'

'Exactly,' Marco said. 'My chance.'

With a giddy thrill he watched Osbourne seethe. A plump vein zigzagged on the man's cosmetically tightened forehead, and thin tendons bulged along his neck, stiff and rigid like bamboo stalks rising from the white-collared shirt. Marco laid the folder on the desk and angled the camera to centre the rubber-banded bundle in the frame.

For your viewing pleasure, asshole.

'I'll leave this on while I take care of some things,' he said. 'Enjoy.'

He'd crossed the room halfway when Osbourne called him one last time.

'Doctor.' Casual – as if in the span of five footsteps all had been forgiven.

Marco hesitated, turned. 'Yes?'

'I will respect your decision,' Osbourne declared, then lowered his chin. 'Due to the fact that we may require more from one another in the future. As you can imagine, there is still much work to be done in securing a new and safer America. Perhaps more contracts – "returns" to be made, as you say, in the interests of national security. However . . .' and here his tone darkened again, instantly ominous, 'your refusal to accommodate me has been noted.'

The implied threat lingered in the stale air for several seconds.

'Fuck you,' Marco said. 'I don't want your jobs.'

He strode from the room. Osbourne's cruel laugh clawed at his back.

'*You will, Doctor*,' Osbourne called. '*You will*.'

13.4

Three hours later the truck was packed with clothes, firearms, camping gear, suitcases, maps, MREs, all the Tang and canned goods from the pantry – enough for a week's drive, he estimated, and then he'd need to scrounge for more – plus books, his favourite pillow from the bed upstairs, and the computer. He'd unplugged Osbourne in mid-sentence. *Be rational, Doctor, and consider*, Osbourne had urged, and then *click*, that was all, and as the hard drive powered down, a white pixel of light blazed once in the blackness and then disappeared like the final star extinguishing at time's end.

In a cardboard box on the truck's passenger seat floor were all the folders from past jobs, all the rings and necklaces and bracelets and wristwatches he'd collected over the years. He would return them someday, but not soon. On top sat the folder for Thomas Flynn, stuffed with dog-eared sheets of notes, photos, transcripts of his interviews two months ago with Gary Flynn – Tom's grief-stricken father. Nice guy.

Returning Flynn will be good, Marco reasoned. *Keep me busy*.

Back on the desk in his office lay Roger's file, exactly where he'd left it, waiting for pick-up. Without doubt

Osbourne would dispatch another goon squad to come collect the prize – probably the orders had already been given, the team scrambling.

Maybe I'm paranoid, Marco thought. *Maybe they're nice, and I could just hand over the vaccine, and we'd all have a beer and laugh and tell jokes about Uncle Owen.*

Right. Or maybe they'll just blast a bullet in my head.

Hell no, he wasn't taking that chance. No need to stay in the Gold Canyon, not any more. Danielle wasn't coming back. She'd moved on.

His eyes misted. *My turn now.*

One good thing about the Evacuated States – there were plenty of places to conceal yourself. Houses, office buildings, hotels, shopping malls, even a cave someplace in the goddamn mountains. Osbourne could send a hundred search teams and never find him.

And the Horsemen – what about them? Was there still an army lurking out West, eager to hunt him down, extract revenge for what he'd done to Big Skull and the others?

Marco sighed. *Yes, Henry,* he thought. *Better lay low for a while.*

But just remember. The trouble with hiding spots.

You think you're safe . . . until you're not.

He flexed his hands on the steering wheel. His left ring finger looked bizarre – the golden tan broken in half by a white stripe of skin, wrinkled and pathetic.

Back in the office, a second folder lay on the desk beside Roger's. A fresh new file. *Marco, Henry* scrawled on the tab, and inside, in a Ziploc, his wedding ring.

He wasn't sure why he'd done that, but somehow it made him feel better. It felt . . . more official, he supposed. Done and over with.

He wondered if the goon squad would take his ring back to Osbourne.

At the bottom of the driveway he nosed the truck through the gate and peered one last time into the rear-view mirror. He'd never return to this house again. He silently wished it goodbye and thanked it for the years. Seeing it there, dark and sealed and vacant, he felt a door inside himself seal and lock as well. In the sky, black specks of vultures had begun to gather like an oncoming storm – somewhere nearby, he guessed, corpses were on the move – and so he cleared his throat and turned left out of the driveway.

North, he thought. *North might be nice.*

Hell, he even knew a great vacation cabin on a lake in Montana.

Ten or eleven corpses greeted him outside on the street – he glimpsed a ponytailed male in a Starbucks apron, and an older female burnt black and crisp, and a white-eyed postal carrier with blue uniformed shorts and what looked like a crowbar lodged in its ribcage – throwing their rotten arms wide, cheering awful noises through torn-out throats, like a going-away party organised in his honour. In the sturdy truck, he wasn't afraid. He bumped through the crowd, ignoring the grunts and desperate *clunk-cla-clunk* of hands slapping the doors. The truck jostled as it turned, catching the kerb, and then straightened, and he goosed the gas and left them.

The truth was, he'd grown accustomed to this. The corpses, the suffering. This existence he'd claimed for himself, here in the shade between living and dying. Just Henry Marco and the corpses and all the useless memories rattling around in all their confused heads. His, too.

Along Route 60 he rolled his window down and watched the crusted landscape chug past – the scrub, the ocotillo, the crumbling planks of old wood fences, and now and then a corroded dirt-caked radio tower. Yes, the Arizona desert was an endless brown. And yet, everywhere, the brown was tinged with green – vegetation adapting to the environment.

Out here, brown was alive. Prospering.

He thought of a guided nature hike he'd taken five years ago, he and Danielle, through a preserve near Tucson the summer they'd moved. Trudging along a dirt trail between thirsty cactus and arid rocks, the biologist had stopped the group and knelt beside a dead brown clump of vegetation – what looked like a shrivelled-up fern the size of a baseball. *Rose of Jericho*, the biologist said. *Also called the Resurrection Plant.*

'Resurrection Plant,' Marco half laughed now. 'Hilarious.'

It's not dead, the biologist had explained. *It can't store water, so it turns brown in a drought and withers up to conserve moisture. Then it goes dormant, no metabolic function until the next rainfall. Could be years like this. You'd swear it's dead* – he'd poked the stiff tangle to prove his point – *but it's doing fine. A little rain and it turns green again. Opens up nice, and keeps growing until the next dry spell, then repeats the cycle.*

Like me, Marco realised as the truck rumbled north. He wasn't a zombie – not yet, anyway – but he wasn't quite alive, either. *Dormant.*

Brown and green. Yin and yang. Two halves of the whole.

And who knew? Perhaps Wu had been right. Danielle, too. Perhaps Hannah *was* here alongside him – a beautiful amazing spirit, escorting him, nudging the wheel in his hands towards the correct road. And perhaps, if he tried, if he kept straddling this murky line between death and life, and if he believed at last what he'd never believed before, then he'd be granted what he so desperately wanted. The power to perceive her. Hear her. See her again.

He inhaled a long hopeful breath, alert for any sign of her presence.

Nothing. Only the musty scent of the truck's vinyl seats, the mildewed canvas.

A thin smile hardened his lips.

He just needed a little more time.

EPILOGUE

'*Your man failed.*'

The words crackled rudely from the speaker phone, a small black box of insult on Director Zhang Hao's desk. The head of MSS scowled. He scooped a wrinkled walnut from a bowl on his side table and squeezed. The shell resisted.

'You disrespect us. And you displease me,' he admonished the speaker phone. His English was ragged at times, a source of some embarrassment for him in these international matters, but effective nonetheless. 'Kheng Wu was our most elite operative. He died honourably to serve his homeland. Our objective, and yours, would not have been possible without his excellent actions. China is *proud*.'

'His "honourable death" was a great inconvenience to me,' the American voice grumbled. 'If he'd lived to deliver his payload, you'd have the vaccine in your hands as we speak. Instead I put myself at greater risk. And I've risked quite enough already.'

Zhang bristled but ignored the complaint. 'Where is the vaccine now?'

'Being retrieved. Due to your man's demise, there will be an unfortunate delay,' the American explained, not bothering to hide his annoyance. 'Certainly you understand. Additional precautions must now be taken to hide this discreet transaction of ours. But I assure you, Director Zhang – China will have the vaccine as its own.'

The walnut cracked in Zhang's strong hand. 'When?' he demanded.

'Soon,' Owen Osbourne promised. 'And I expect you to honour our deal.'

ACKNOWLEDGEMENTS

Thank you dearly to all who made this adventure possible:

My father, who taught me to work hard and do it right;

My mother, who taught me the possibilities found in books;

Both my parents, who stayed beside me through twists and turns;

My sister and all my family, who've been great cheerleaders;

My wife Krissy, who gives the world's best pep talks and is my true soulmate;

My girl Maggie, whom I love more than I can say aloud, so I'm writing it here;

Francine T., who granted me this opportunity and then guided me to make the most of it;

Jason B., Penny I. and everyone else at Hodder & Stoughton who added their talents;

Everyone who joined the hunt at TheReturnMan.com;

Zombie Ed of *The Zombie Times*, who put me in the right place at the right time;

Everyone who sent me encouraging words that were so deeply appreciated;

Noah L., who politely corrected my gun errors and voiced his support;

Jordan G. for contributing your mad skills;

Sherry H., Julie O., Ashley C., Justin W., Paul B., Jamal L.,

Ben S., Boe P., Kari M., and Nancy J., who have been great friends to the book;

George Romero, who gave us the subgenre;

Richard Matheson, who led the way.

And finally, thanks to Jörg Tatzelt, Stanley B. Prusiner and William J. Welch, whose research into prion diseases – (1996) 'Chemical Chaperones Interfere with the Formation of Scrapie Prion Protein', *The EMBO Journal*, 15, 23: 6363–73 – provided the inspiration for Roger Ballard's vaccine in *The Return Man*. Their study may someday save us all from a prion-triggered zombie apocalypse.

extras

meet the author

V. M. Zito resides in Connecticut, USA with his wife and daughter. When not writing, he spends his weekdays working as Creative Director at a New England ad agency and his weekends running on forested trails. THE RETURN MAN is his first novel.

an interview with

V. M. Zito

What made you want to write *The Return Man*?

I've been a zombie fan since I was twelve, gobbling up every zombie movie or book I could find. But around five years ago I started to feel like it was all mostly the same story, told over and over with interchangeable characters – or, sometimes, it was too different, too far astray from the 'classic zombies' I loved. I wished somebody would write a cool book that felt new but still adhered to the Romero zombie mythos. Then I thought, hell, why can't that somebody be me?

If you've ever seen the (non-zombie) movie, *Apollo 13*, you'll remember the scene where Ed Harris dumps a bunch of random junk on the table in front of NASA scientists and says, 'Build something that will save the astronauts.' Writing *The Return Man* was a little like that. I knew the parts that I felt had to be in the book, the elements of a traditional zombie tale: dead and mindless zombies, a crumbled society, a brave survivor, a military presence, and of course the mandatory disembowelment of the bad guy. The challenge was, how could I arrange them into a fresh story that I'd want to read as a zombie fan myself? Soon I was day-dreaming scenarios. In May 2008, I put the first words to paper.

Where did you get the idea for the novel?

Many zombie movies touch upon the fact that the dead 'monsters' were once human. I extrapolated this logic a bit further. If they were human, they'd had families. And what if the families were still alive? Wouldn't it be horrible to know that your dead wife or child was out there in the world somewhere as a zombie?

From there it all seemed to snap together. The main character would be a professional corpse killer, operating out of love and mercy rather than a 'zombie extermination squad' mentality. Although the zombie apocalypse had arrived, there would need to be a large number of grieving survivors as well – and so I split the United States into two zones, one for the dead and one for the living. *Dawn of the Dead* had long ago hinted that zombies might gravitate to 'places that were important to them,' so I decided to explore that further – the idea of using insight into the living person to find their zombie.

What draws you to zombies in particular?

Zombies are scary because they de-humanize us in every way. They violate the most ancient hallowed rule of society – an agreement by our ancestors not to eat each other, thus allowing civilisation to function – and they strip us down to our most basic, animalistic fears, like the fear of being devoured. When a zombie kills you, you're nothing but a piece of meat. At the same time, if you become a zombie, you're nothing but a piece of meat. Being the killer is arguably worse than being the victim. And yet, for all that intellectual mumbo-jumbo and theological implications, zombies are my favorite monster now for probably the same reason as when I was twelve: I can't imagine a death more mind-bogglingly bad than being surrounded and pulled apart by hungry dead people.

Do you prefer fast zombies or slow zombies?

Slow zombies give me the creepy, dreadful sensation of seeing my death lumber toward me, one tortuous step at a time. Slow zombies are what I consider real horror, a black, incomprehensible revulsion in your stomach, fearsome and fascinating at the same time; fast zombies are terror, adrenaline-fueled fear that whips your heart into a frenzy and ignites your 'fight or flight' instincts. From a horror aspect, I prefer the slow Romero zombies, but I'll be honest – I like my survival odds better against them, too. Fast zombies would kick my ass.

Who, or what else, influences your writing?

In terms of how I write and what I write about, a ton of great writers have influenced me (and still do) – Ray Bradbury, Richard Matheson, Paul Auster, Jack Ketchum, David Morrell, Bentley Little, John Banville, John Gardner, Shirley Jackson, to name a few. Another inevitable influence seems to be my personal uncertainty about religion. Questions about a god who does or does not exist seem to creep into many of my stories, whether I'd originally intended to go there or not.

Characterwise, are you more similar to Marco or Wu?

I'm probably more like Marco – introverted, cynical and agnostic, more trusting of empiricism and science but hopeful for a higher power. Except I'm not good at witty retorts. I never say anything clever when arguing with my wife.

What was it that inspired you to choose the settings of California and Arizona?

My wife and I honeymooned in Arizona, and it just stuck in my head as a unique location – beautiful in its spartan way, carved in rock, shaded every kind of brown. It was so alien compared to New England, where I live, where you're surrounded by trees and green grass everywhere you turn. When I was ready to choose the setting for *The Return Man*, my mind just gravitated to Arizona as the perfect backdrop for a zombie apocalypse – superficially dead and barren, yet teeming with life that has adapted to the environment. It also represented Marco's state of mind, echoing his removal from civilised society, far far away from the Safe States. In that regard, I began to envision Marco's spiritual progress as measurable by compass directions – any motion to the east, toward the Safe States, was positive, while motion to the west was a regression. To achieve his goals, Marco had to travel physically away from the Safe Sates to confront his past failures. In a good hero myth, the hero achieves his salvation at the moment he seems farthest from it, and for that reason, *The Return Man's* culminating events take place in California, as far west as possible.

How much research did you have to do, when writing the novel?

Filling in the details of the Arizona environment – the flora, the fauna, the geography and eccentricites of the desert – was a key focus. Also big was the 'scientific' basis for the Resurrection; I didn't want to rely on the common 'virus or bacteria' explanation, so I did a lot of digging around to learn about proteins called prions. And, of course, I also learned about Sunset Limited dining cars, deerhorn knives, prison layouts, Chinese history, how to drive a locomotive, how to treat birth asphyxia, and how a gas pump works. And I learned about the Resurrection Plant. It's a real thing. Google it if you don't believe me!

Do you have any particular habits or a strict routine when writing?

My writing routine during *The Return Man* was strict: Every night after dinner and homework with my daughter, I'd run out for a large Dunkin Donuts coffee with milk and two sugars, then head upstairs to my office and write for 2 to 3 hours. The coffee was an absolute necessity. In fact, I might ask my accountant if all my DuDo's receipts are tax-deductible. Besides that, I'd listen to 'creative energy' music on iTunes – nice soothing instrumentals to keep my vibe positive.

What advice would you give to aspiring writers?

Read good books, and think, 'That's what I need to do.' Read bad books, and say, 'Hell, I can do better than *that*.' Practice a lot. Expect some failures, but remember that failure is a required step on the path to success – in a two-hour movie, the hero doesn't succeed until the last 10 minutes. And finally, don't worry about getting published. Just focus on writing something that makes you proud.

Will we see Marco again in the future? Are you planning any more books?

There are still millions of survivors in the Safe States who need Marco to return their zombified loved ones, so whether it's in a second novel or some episodic format like television or graphic novels, I think it would be pretty cool to follow more of Marco's adventures, contract by contract. And I do have ideas!

And…if there was an outbreak of The Resurrection, what would you do?

My household is very prepared. Each morning I run a twenty-minute zombie escape drill with my wife and 10-year-old daughter. At night I clean and arrange the guns while my wife monitors the police scanner for any reports of an outbreak. I keep the car running in the driveway all night long, ready to go. Meanwhile, my daughter works hard in the basement, digging a vast underground tunnel system that will eventually connect to a remote cabin in Vermont. She is making progress, although the late hours are beginning to affect her grades at school.

introducing

If you enjoyed
THE RETURN MAN,
look out for

FEED

Book 1 of The Newsflesh Trilogy

by Mira Grant

"Alive or dead, the truth won't rest. My name is Georgia Mason, and I am begging you. Rise up while you can."

The year was 2014. We had cured cancer. We had beat the common cold. But in doing so we created something new, something terrible that no one could stop. The infection spread, virus blocks taking over bodies and minds with one, unstoppable command: FEED.

NOW, twenty years after the Rising, Georgia and Shaun Mason are on the trail of the biggest story of their lives-the dark conspiracy behind the infected. The truth will out, even if it kills them.

Our story opens where countless stories have ended in the last twenty-six years: with an idiot—in this case, my brother Shaun—deciding it would be a good idea to go out and poke a zombie with a stick to see what happens. As if we didn't already know what happens when you mess with a zombie: The zombie turns around and bites you, and you become the thing you poked. This isn't a surprise. It hasn't been a surprise for more than twenty years, and if you want to get technical, it wasn't a surprise *then*.

When the infected first appeared—heralded by screams that the dead were rising and judgment day was at hand—they behaved just like the horror movies had been telling us for decades that they would behave. The only surprise was that this time, it was really happening.

There was no warning before the outbreaks began. One day, things were normal; the next, people who were supposedly dead were getting up and attacking anything that came into range. This was upsetting for everyone involved, except for the infected, who were past being upset about that sort of thing. The initial shock was followed by running and screaming, which eventually devolved into more infection and attacking, that being the way of things. So what do we have now, in this enlightened age twenty-six years after the Rising? We have idiots prodding zombies with sticks, which brings us full circle to my brother and why he probably won't live a long and fulfilling life.

"Hey, George, check this out!" he shouted, giving the zombie another poke in the chest with his hockey stick. The zombie gave a low moan, swiping at him ineffectually. It had obviously been in a state of full viral amplification for some time and didn't have the strength or physical dexterity left to knock the stick out of Shaun's hands. I'll give Shaun this much: He knows not to bother the fresh ones at close range. "We're playing patty-cake!"

"Stop antagonizing the locals and get back on the bike," I said, glaring from behind my sunglasses. His current buddy might be sick enough to be nearing its second, final death, but that didn't mean there wasn't a healthier pack roaming the area. Santa Cruz is zombie territory. You don't go there unless you're suicidal, stupid, or both. There are times when even I can't guess which of those options applies to Shaun.

"Can't talk right now! I'm busy making friends with the locals!"

"Shaun Phillip Mason, you get back on this bike *right now*, or I swear to God, I am going to drive away and leave you here."

Shaun looked around, eyes bright with sudden interest as he planted the end of his hockey stick at the center of the zombie's chest to keep it at a safe distance. "Really? You'd do that for me? Because 'My Sister Abandoned Me in Zombie Country Without a Vehicle' would make a great article."

"A posthumous one, maybe," I snapped. "Get back on the goddamn *bike*!"

"In a minute!" he said, laughing, and turned back toward his moaning friend.

In retrospect, that's when everything started going wrong.

The pack had probably been stalking us since before we hit the city limits, gathering reinforcements from all over the county as they approached. Packs of infected get smarter and more dangerous the larger they become. Groups of four or less are barely a threat unless they can corner you, but a pack of twenty or more stands a good chance of breaching any barrier the uninfected try to put up. You get enough of the infected together and they'll start displaying pack hunting techniques; they'll start using actual tactics. It's like the virus that's taken them over starts to reason when it gets enough hosts in the same place. It's scary as hell, and it's just about the worst nightmare of anyone who regularly goes into zombie territory—getting cornered by a large group that knows the land better than you do.

These zombies knew the land better than we did, and even the most malnourished and virus-ridden pack knows how to lay an ambush. A low moan echoed from all sides, and then they were shambling into the open, some moving with the slow lurch of the long infected, others moving at something close to a run. The runners led the pack, cutting off three of the remaining methods of escape before there was time to do more than stare. I looked at them and shuddered.

Fresh infected—really fresh ones—still look almost like the people that they used to be. Their faces show emotion, and they move with a jerkiness that could just mean they slept wrong the night before. It's harder to kill something that still looks like a person, and worst of all, the bastards are fast. The only thing more dangerous than a fresh zombie is a pack of them, and I counted at least eighteen before I realized that it didn't matter, and stopped bothering.

I grabbed my helmet and shoved it on without fastening the strap. If the bike went down, dying because my helmet didn't stay on would be one of the better options. I'd reanimate, but at least I wouldn't be aware of it. "Shaun!"

Shaun whipped around, staring at the emerging zombies. "Whoa."

Unfortunately for Shaun, the addition of that many zombies had turned his buddy from a stupid solo into part of a thinking mob. The zombie grabbed the hockey stick as soon as Shaun's attention was focused elsewhere, yanking it out of his hands. Shaun staggered forward and the zombie latched onto his cardigan, withered fingers locking down with deceptive strength. It hissed. I screamed, images of my inevitable future as an only child filling my mind.

"Shaun!" One bite and things would get a lot worse. There's not much worse than being cornered by a pack of zombies in downtown Santa Cruz. Losing Shaun would qualify.

The fact that my brother convinced me to take a dirt bike into zombie territory doesn't make me an idiot. I was wearing full off-road body armor, including a leather jacket with steel armor joints attached at the elbows and shoulders, a Kevlar vest, motorcycling pants with hip and knee protectors, and calf-high riding boots. It's bulky as hell, and I don't care, because once you factor in my gloves, my throat's the only target I present in the field.

Shaun, on the other hand, is a moron and had gone zombie baiting in nothing more defensive than a cardigan, a Kevlar vest, and cargo pants. He won't even wear goggles—he says they "spoil the effect." Unprotected mucous membranes can spoil a hell of a lot more than that, but I practically have to blackmail him to get him into the Kevlar. Goggles are a nonstarter.

There's one advantage to wearing a sweater in the field, no matter how idiotic I think it is: wool tears. Shaun ripped himself free and turned, running for the motorcycle with great speed, which is really the only effective weapon we have against the infected. Not even the fresh ones can keep up with an uninfected human over a short sprint. We have speed, and we have bullets. Everything else about this fight is in their favor.

"Shit, George, we've got company!" There was a perverse mixture of horror and delight in his tone. "Look at 'em all!"

"I'm *looking*! Now get on!"

I kicked us free as soon as he had his leg over the back of the bike and his arm around my waist. The bike leapt forward, tires bouncing and shuddering across the broken ground as I steered us into a wide curve. We needed to get out of there, or all the protective gear in the world wouldn't do us a damn bit of good. I might live if the zombies caught up with us, but my brother would be dragged into the mob. I gunned the throttle, praying that God had time to preserve the life of the clinically suicidal.

We hit the last open route out of the square at twenty miles an hour, still gathering speed. Whooping, Shaun locked one arm around my waist and twisted to face the zombies, waving and blowing kisses in their direction. If it were possible to enrage a mob of the infected, he'd have managed it. As it was, they just moaned and kept following, arms extended toward the promise of fresh meat.

The road was pitted from years of weather damage without maintenance. I fought to keep control as we bounced from pothole to pothole. *"Hold on, you idiot!"*

"I'm holding on!" Shaun called back, seeming happy as a clam and oblivious to the fact that people who don't follow proper safety procedures around zombies—like not winding up around zombies in the first place—tend to wind up in the obituaries.

"Hold on with both arms!" The moaning was only coming from three sides now, but it didn't mean anything; a pack this size was almost certainly smart enough to establish an ambush. I could be driving straight to the site of greatest concentration. They'd moan in the end, once we were right on top of them. No zombie can resist a good moan when dinner's at hand. The fact that I could hear them over the engine meant that there were too many, too close. If we were lucky, it wasn't already too late to get away.

Of course, if we were lucky, we wouldn't be getting chased by an army of zombies through the quarantine area that used to be downtown Santa Cruz. We'd be somewhere safer, like Bikini Atoll just before the bomb testing kicked off. Once you decide to ignore the hazard rating and the signs saying *Danger: Infection,* you're on your own.

Shaun grudgingly slid his other arm around my waist and linked his hands at the pit of my stomach, shouting, "Spoilsport," as he settled.

I snorted and hit the gas again, aiming for a nearby hill. When you're being chased by zombies, hills are either your best friends or your burial ground. The slope slows them down, which is great, unless you hit the peak and find out that you're surrounded, with nowhere left to run to.

Idiot or not, Shaun knows the rules about zombies and hills. He's not as dumb as he pretends to be, and he knows more about surviving zombie encounters than I do. His grip on my waist tightened, and for the first time, there was actual concern in his voice as he shouted, "George? What do you think you're doing?"

"Hold, on," I said. Then we were rolling up the hill,

bringing more zombies stumbling out of their hiding places behind trash cans and in the spaces between the once-elegant beachfront houses that were now settling into a state of neglected decay.

Most of California was reclaimed after the Rising, but no one has ever managed to take back Santa Cruz. The geographical isolation that once made the town so desirable as a vacation spot pretty much damned it when the virus hit. Kellis-Amberlee may be unique in the way it interacts with the human body, but it behaves just like every other communicable disease known to man in at least one way: Put it on a school campus and it spreads like wildfire. U.C. Santa Cruz was a perfect breeding ground, and once all those perky co-eds became the shuffling infected, it was all over but the evacuation notices.

"Georgia, this is a hill!" he said with increasing urgency as the locals lunged toward the speeding bike. He was using my proper name; that was how I could tell he was worried. I'm only "Georgia" when he's unhappy.

"I got that." I hunched over to decrease wind resistance a few more precious degrees. Shaun mimicked the motion automatically, hunching down behind me.

"Why are we going *up* a hill?" he demanded. There was no way he'd be able to hear my answer over the combined roaring of the engine and the wind, but that's my brother, always willing to question that which won't talk back.

"Ever wonder how the Wright brothers felt?" I asked. The crest of the hill was in view. From the way the street vanished on the other side, it was probably a pretty steep drop. The moaning was coming from all sides now, so distorted by the wind that I had no real idea what we were driving into. Maybe it was a trap; maybe it wasn't. Either way, it was too late to find another path. We were committed, and for once, Shaun was the one sweating.

"Georgia!"

"Hold on!" Ten yards. The zombies kept closing, single-minded in their pursuit of what might be the first fresh meat some had seen in years. From the looks of most of them, the zombie problem in Santa Cruz was decaying faster than it was rebuilding itself. Sure, there were plenty of fresh ones—there are always fresh ones because there are always idiots who wander into quarantined zones, either willingly or by mistake, and the average hitchhiker doesn't get lucky where zombies are concerned—but we'll take the city back in another three generations. Just not today.

Five yards.

Zombies hunt by moving toward the sound of other zombies hunting. It's recursive, and that meant our friends at the base of the hill started for the peak when they heard the commotion. I was hoping so many of the locals had been cutting us off at ground level that they wouldn't have many bodies left to mount an offensive on the hill's far side. We weren't supposed to make it that far, after all; the only thing keeping us alive was the fact that we had a motorcycle and the zombies didn't.

I glimpsed the mob waiting for us as we reached the top. They were standing no more than three deep. Fifteen feet would see us clear.

Liftoff.

It's amazing what you can use for a ramp, given the right motivation. Someone's collapsed fence was blocking half the road, jutting up at an angle, and I hit it at about fifty miles an hour. The handlebars shuddered in my hands like the horns of a mechanical bull, and the shocks weren't doing much better. I didn't even have to check the road in front of us because the moaning started as soon as we came into view. They'd blocked our exit fairly well while Shaun played with his little friend, and mindless plague carriers or not, they had a better grasp of the local geography than we did. We still had one advantage: Zombies aren't good at predicting suicide charges. And if there's a better term for driving up the side of a hill at fifty miles an hour with the goal of actually achieving flight when you run out of "up," I don't think I want to hear it.

The front wheel rose smoothly and the back followed, sending us into the air with a jerk that looked effortless and was actually scarier than hell. I was screaming. Shaun was whooping with gleeful understanding. And then everything was in the hands of gravity, which has never had much love for the terminally stupid. We hung in the air for a heart-stopping moment, still shooting forward. At least I was fairly sure the impact would kill us.

The laws of physics and the hours of work I've put into constructing and maintaining my bike combined to let the universe, for once, show mercy. We soared over the zombies, coming down on one of the few remaining stretches of smooth road with a bone-bruising jerk that nearly ripped the handlebars out of my grip. The front wheel went light on impact, trying to rise up, and I screamed, half terrified, half furious with Shaun for getting us into this situation in the first place. The handlebars shuddered harder, almost wrenching my arms out of their sockets before I hit the gas and forced the wheel back down. I'd pay for this in the morning, and not just with the repair bills.

Not that it mattered. We were on level ground, we were upright, and there was no moaning ahead. I hit the gas harder as we sped toward the outskirts of town, with Shaun whooping and cheering behind me like a big suicidal freak.

"Asshole," I muttered, and drove on.

News is news and spin is spin, and when you introduce the second to the first, what you have isn't news anymore. Hey, presto, you've created opinion.

Don't get me wrong, opinion is powerful. Being able to be presented with differing opinions on the same issue is one of the glories of a free media, and it should make people stop and think. But a lot of people don't *want* to. They don't want to admit that whatever line being touted by their idol of the moment might not be unbiased and without ulterior motive. We've got people who claim Kellis-Amberlee was a plot by the Jews, the gays, the Middle East, even a branch of the Aryan Nation trying to achieve racial purity by killing the rest of us. Whoever orchestrated the creation and release of the virus masked their involvement with a conspiracy of Machiavellian proportions, and now they and their followers are sitting it out, peacefully immunized, waiting for the end of the world.

Pardon the expression, but I can smell the bullshit from here. Conspiracy? Cover up? I'm sure there are groups out there crazy enough to think killing thirty-two percent of the world's population in a single summer is a good idea—and remember, that's a conservative estimate, since we've never gotten accurate death tolls out of Africa, Asia, or parts of South America—but are any of them nuts enough to do it by turning what used to be Grandma loose to chew on people at random? Zombies don't respect conspiracy. Conspiracy is for the living.

This piece is opinion. Take it as you will. But get your opinions the hell away from my news.

—From *Images May Disturb You*,
the blog of Georgia Mason, September 3, 2039

Zombies are pretty harmless as long as you treat them with respect. Some people say you should pity the zombie, empathize with the zombie, but I think they? Are likely to *become* the zombie, if you get my meaning. Don't feel sorry for the zombie. The zombie's not going to feel sorry for you when he starts gnawing on your head. Sorry, dude, but not even my sister gets to know me that well.

If you want to deal with zombies, stay away from the teeth, don't let them scratch you, keep your hair short, and don't wear loose clothes. It's that simple. Making it more complicated would be boring, and who wants that? We have what basically amounts to walking corpses, dude.

Don't suck all the fun out of it.

—From *Hail to the King*,
the blog of Shaun Mason, January 2, 2039